The Seaside Cocktail Campervan

CAROLINE ROBERTS

One More Chapter an imprint of
HarperCollins*Publishers* Ltd
1 London Bridge Street
London SE1 9GF

www.harpercollins.co.uk

HarperCollins*Publishers*
1st Floor, Watermarque Building, Ringsend Road
Dublin 4, Ireland

This paperback edition 2022

1
First published by One More Chapter 2021

A catalogue copy of this book
is available from the British Library.

ISBN: 978-0-00-848348-7

Set in Birka by Palimpsest Book Production Ltd, Falkirk Stirlingshire

Printed and bound in UK using 100% Renewable Electricity by
CPI Group (UK) Ltd, Croydon CR0 4YY

The Seaside Cocktail Campervan

Caroline Roberts lives in the wonderful Northumberland countryside with her husband and credits the sandy beaches, castles and rolling hills around her as inspiration for her writing. Caroline is the Kindle bestselling author of the 'Pudding Pantry' and 'Cosy Teashop' series. She enjoys writing about relationships; stories of love, loss and family, which explore how beautiful and sometimes complex love can be. A slice of cake, glass of bubbly and a cup of tea would make her day – preferably served with friends!

If you'd like to find out more about Caroline, visit her on Facebook, Twitter and Instagram – she'd love to hear from

f /CarolineRobertsAuthor
🐦 @_caroroberts
📷 @carolinerobertsauthor

Also by Caroline Roberts

The Desperate Wife
The Cosy Teashop in the Castle
The Cosy Christmas Teashop
My Summer of Magic Moments
The Cosy Christmas Chocolate Shop
The Cosy Seaside Chocolate Shop
Rachel's Pudding Pantry
Christmas at Rachel's Pudding Pantry
Summer at Rachel's Pudding Pantry

For hugs, celebrations and new beginnings

You are cordially invited for cocktails and celebrations
For the 21st Birthday Party
of
Harriet Carter-Cresswell
Saturday, 8th May, 6 p.m.
at
Eastburgh Hall, Northumberland
RSVP Abigail Carter-Cresswell by Friday 16th April prompt

Chapter 1

Jack was prepped and ready to pour. A hundred polished prosecco glasses stood glinting in the soft early-May sunlight, lined up in perfect rows on wooden trestle tables which he had just finished setting out, working with the butler. Oh yes, there was a real-life butler. Jack grinned as he thought about it; every function was different. He certainly got to go to all sorts of swish places and meet all kinds of people with this job.

When he'd turned his pride-and-joy vintage campervan off the narrow lane earlier, his jaw had dropped at the event's stunning location. He'd arrived at the Birthday Girl's country home, and *what* a home it was: weathered cream stone walls, three storeys high, set a mile inland from the golden sands and estuary of Budle Bay. The view from Jack's designated parking spot – just off the gravel driveway on the front lawn of this impressive pad – was glorious, stretching across rolling green farmland to the inky blue-grey sea. All framed by a fading gold-tinted azure sky.

Jack liked to dress the part for every occasion. So, he had his tux and bow-tie combo for weddings and formal events, shorts and Ts for any festivals or fêtes, and he was sporting his smart-casual, celebration-party look for the 21st Birthday booking this evening. He wore beige chinos and a crisp white shirt, teamed with a pressed black apron with his *Jack's Cocktail Campervan* logo, stylishly swirled in grey lettering on the front.

He'd started up this mobile bar business four years ago. It was a bit of a risk putting his last wedge of savings into buying the characterful but rather rusty VW campervan – 'Ruby', as he'd named her. Over the following three months, he'd spent every weekend and many an evening doing her up, courtesy of a bank loan, with his own blood, sweat and tears, via many a YouTube 'How To' video, plus a bit of professional help on the engine and electrical side of things. It had felt like plunging in at the deep end when he finally handed in his notice at the bistro where he was working as the manager, having worked his way up from waiter.

Ruby was a glorious vintage red, and whenever Jack hit the driver's seat and headed off on the open road, he just wanted to sing out 'Ruby, Ruby, Ruby!' so damned loud, in the style of the Kaiser Chiefs' anthem. He had never looked back, even with the inevitable ups and downs of running his own business, and was proud of his venture, building it slowly but surely. He loved the freedom of being his own boss, and enjoyed the buzz of working a function, whilst making his clients' wishes come true.

Abigail, Birthday Girl's mother and the party organiser, suddenly came dashing down the grand stone steps of the hall, clucking away to herself about some pizza van she'd booked being late, all the while scouring the driveway as if she might be able to will it into view. She approached Jack, spouting a last-minute list of details and demands, whilst delivering a peaches-and-cream-coloured floral display for the drinks table. Jeez, that thing looked hideous, like some floral throwback from a 1970s wedding, but Jack kept schtum. He knew better than to upset the paying clients. *And hey ho, what do I know about flowers,* he mused? It was *absolutely hideous,* though.

Abigail's voice cut in over the early-evening birdsong: 'Now then, young man, do you have plenty of ice for the evening? There're spare bags, if need be, in the chest freezer in the larder room. You may enter the house via the side door,' she added pointedly.

Basically, as one of the staff, make sure you don't go in by the front door, was what Jack grasped.

Abigail was on a roll. 'Oh, and those pretty little violas, the ones you had at the tasting to decorate the Raspberry Fizz drinks, do you have those as promised?'

'Yes, I have the flowers here, Abigail. I'm just waiting for the guests to arrive before I pour out the chilled prosecco, and then I'll use them to garnish the cocktails, as agreed.'

Jack was thankful that his parents had a good-sized, well-stocked garden – his mum's pride and joy – and they were happy for him to help himself to the various herbs, foliage and flowers he needed to support his cocktail venture, making it that little bit more unique.

'Good ... that's good. They did look so pretty at the tasting.' Abigail paused, taking in the table-top display, pushing it a couple of centimetres to one side, and then giving an approving nod. Then she was off again, 'Oh, and can you ensure that Harriet's younger brother, Hugo, takes no more than one drink, as he's only sixteen?'

Oh yes, Jack had spotted him earlier – a tall, lanky youth of the blond floppy fringe variety, bit of a dickhead from what Jack had seen, to be honest, bossing around the butler and doing very little of any use himself.

'And that Grandma Judith, who I introduced you to, is served an elderflower fizz rather than a gin or prosecco cock-tail, as she's on medication? We don't want her having a funny turn or such like.'

Jack gave a smile, responding politely, 'Of course, that's no problem, Abigail.' *I am here to serve, smile and make sure that everyone has a good time,* he thought wryly. *And hopefully that no-one ends up in Abigail's bad books or A&E.*

Abigail tutted, then gave a heavy sigh. Jack feared he'd done something wrong for a moment, casting his mind quickly over all the arrangements, until the middle-aged woman commented tersely that the other caterer was terribly late. '*Typical*,' she muttered, studying her wristwatch dramatically, 'She'll be arriving at the same time as the guests, which is no good. No good at all.'

'Is there anything I can help with?' Jack offered.

'Well, not unless you can conjure up a hundred slices of cooked pizza in the next hour or so.'

'Right-o! Sorry Abigail, that's not quite in my powers.' He put on his most charming smile, guaranteed to soften the hardest of hearts. 'But I'll make sure everyone gets a glass of something gorgeous to start their evening off well. And I'm sure the pizza company will get here any minute.' Jack was trying his best to keep things positive. There was often a glitch or two at these occasions, and he'd learnt you just have to keep everyone calm and carry on. Half the time, the guests were often blissfully unaware of any issues, anyhow – especially a drink or two down the line.

'Thank you, Jake.'

Jake? He didn't bother correcting her. Abigail evidently had enough on her plate as it was.

'Well, thank heavens I've booked my usual caterer to provide a finger buffet in the dining room. It's just typical, Harriet persuaded me to try something new for the younger ones, and look what happens ...'

After the organisational ear-bashing, Jack stood and watched Abigail's rather large, pale-pink rear (she was clothed in a dress that unfortunately far too closely matched her skin tone) march back up to the house; all three beautiful stone-built storeys of it. It was the sort of place you might imagine spending a country weekend away in, with a bottle or two of Bollinger champagne and croquet on the lawn. (Not that Jack had ever had much chance to do that kind of thing.) The grounds were vast, with rolling lawns cut as smoothly as a bowling green for today's event, along with shrub borders that were bold and beautiful with purple hydrangeas and pastel-shaded azaleas.

There was a moment of calm as chilled music and chatter drifted down from the house, and Jack double-checked that he had everything perfectly ready. There were just ten minutes to go until 6 p.m., when the first guests were due to arrive. It had been a beautiful blue-sky day so far and it looked like it was going to be a gorgeous night for a party. Summer had definitely started early this year in Northumberland.

Jack's attention was drawn to the intriguing space opposite him which had been marked out with plastic cones, and wondered briefly what had happened to the other caterer. He wouldn't want to be in their shoes, having to face the wrath of an already stressed-out Abigail, when they finally got here.

His thoughts drifted as he waited for the first arrivals. The house, the gardens, the family gathering ... it pulled him back to the past. There was a tug, deep inside, as he remembered. This was all a darned sight different to his own – extremely low-key – 21st Birthday celebrations, held reluctantly at his family home in Alnwick, eight years ago now. A 1930s stone-built semi-detached property with a decent-sized garden. It was a great place to have been brought up in, full of warmth and love. Yeah, it was a good place for a party, with its big family kitchen, a few friends and family gathered around ... or it always used to be.

But he hadn't been bothered about having a party to mark his 'coming of age'. It was his parents who'd persuaded him that he should in the end, that they all had to try to carry on, but Jack really didn't have the heart for it. Just wanted to get it over with; after all, nothing would ever feel the same again after what had happened.

Jack found that his hands were trembling slightly as he pulled himself back to the present and started re-polishing a glass, intent on finding something to do. He shook his head; enough of those dark thoughts.

It was then he spotted a black Jeep, towing what looked like a horsebox rather erratically up the gravel driveway, having turned in from the lane. Blimey, was someone bringing a white steed or something for Birthday Girl to start her party off with? Honestly, you never knew what was planned at these events sometimes. He could write a book on it all!

As the vehicle approached, he spotted a dark-haired young woman at the wheel, with a teenage girl sat beside her. The driver looked tense, her brow creased in concentration, as she began to slow on the approach to the house. It suddenly made sense as he read the writing on the horsebox's side: *All Fired Up – Wood-fired Pizza just like Papa used to make!*

Pizza woman rather deftly reverse-parked the trailer, then leapt out, her conker-coloured hair bouncing around her shoulders.

'Bloody hell, this place is hard to find,' she huffed, sounding stressed, partly talking to herself and partly to Jack as he stepped forwards, catching her attention. 'My SatNav took me right off course. I've been trailing about these tiny country lanes for the best part of an hour. I did try to ring and let someone know, but there's hardly any phone signal out here, and when I finally got through, it bloody well cut off. And there was no-one about to ask directions, not until the last five minutes, anyhow. Argh, we are *sooo* late.'

The woman, who appeared to be a similar age to Jack, was dressed in blue jeans and a red polo shirt. She quickly swept her glossy dark hair away from her face and tied it up with some kind of scrunchy thing. 'Are any of the guests here yet?' she asked a little frantically, as she began to unfasten the bolts on the back of the horsebox.

'Nope, not quite yet,' Jack answered. 'Though you are cutting it a bit fine.'

She shot him a sharp look. 'Don't you think I know that?'

Oops, that probably wasn't the most helpful thing to state under the circumstances, Jack realised.

'Right, well, no time to waste. The pizza oven takes an hour to heat up, as it is. I'll get that lit straight away. Come on then, Tamsin,' she called out to the younger girl. 'We need to get set up as quickly as possible, and I'll need to find Harriet and her mother to apologise for being so late.'

He watched for a few more seconds as the woman levered down the metal ramp-style door, and then pulled a large oven and its stand from the back of the trailer, soon loading logs into its igloo-shaped dome.

'Uh, can I give you a hand at all? Help you get set up ...?' Jack ventured, but she didn't seem to have heard. Pizza Lady was inside the trailer now, opening up a wooden, grey-painted hatch. Jack was just about to repeat his offer of help, when he spotted a couple of taxis turning in at the estate entrance. The first guests were here, and the party was about to begin. He'd better get back to Ruby for his bar duties.

At that moment, the birthday girl, Harriet, appeared at the top of the old stone steps in a pink floaty frock that looked like something out of a fairytale, or very possibly *Vogue*.

'Mummy, they're here,' she called out, looking happily flustered.

Abigail came to join her daughter with a fixed, anxious beam of a welcome smile in place, as the first guests spilled out of the vehicles. 'Oh, and so are the pizza company, at last. Thank heavens for small mercies,' she added tersely.

A group of young women gathered in a highly perfumed and colourful display of high heels and fancy dresses, and the celebrations began with a flurry of air kisses, laughter, greetings, gift bags, and a chorus of 'Happy birthday, darling!'

Okay, Rubes, let's get this party started. The Cocktail Campervan is ready to rock and roll.

Jack sprang into action, mixing his first dozen Raspberry Bellinis: an inch of raspberry liqueur topped with chilled sparkling prosecco, placing a viola flower on each. He also poured out fragrant G&Ts using the local Northumberland Hepple Gin, as well as non-alcoholic elderflower fizzes, finishing them off with a garnish of delicate white elderflower blossom, revelling as usual in his attention to detail. The welcome drinks looked delightfully inviting, all lined up on the wooden tables.

Jack had placed tea lights in pretty green glass holders on the tables too, which would later give a soft glow through the evening. And, he even had to admit he was weirdly starting to get used to Abigail's floral peaches-and-cream backdrop. In a haze of flouncy chiffon and silk dresses it didn't look quite so out of place, after all.

The evening was beautifully balmy and Jack was feeling pretty warm already. He undid a button on his white shirt, revealing a small V of lightly-tanned chest. With more cars now arriving and the gathering growing, he'd need to keep his cool, as he was going to be pretty hectic serving everyone by the looks of it.

The first group of Harriet's friends were soon gathered around a rather splendid-looking Ruby. Her deep-red paint-work was gleaming and Jack's bar was all set out with an array of glasses and garnishes: lemons, limes and oranges on a tiered stand, vivid green mint and basil leaves bunched in cut-glass jugs, plus stainless-steel metal cocktail shakers. There was an eye-catching blackboard within a quirky light-bulb frame inside the raised campervan roof, handwritten by Jack earlier and listing the welcome drinks plus some cocktail classics for later: Mojito, Pimm's, a Cosmopolitan, Sea Breeze, a Morpeth Mule and one of his all-time cocktail favourites, Espresso Martini.

'Good evening, ladies. I'm your barman, Jack. Please help yourselves. There are Raspberry Bellinis or Gin and Tonics to start. And a gorgeous elderflower fizz for those who might prefer something non-alcoholic.' He gave his trademark grin.

A group of female guests dived in and were soon chatting away stood beside the campervan, teetering on high heels that were sinking into the grass and the gravel driveway. Several pairs of false eyelashes were already batting in Jack's direction. He played along with the flirting, ready to respond with some fun banter, but he was nothing but professional on nights like these. Work was work. Always. He knew where to draw the line.

Another group of young women arrived, giggling and chat-tering as they approached.

'Oh my, look at that cute cocktail bar. Hang on, I need to

take a photo. That is so cool ... and all in a campervan too.'

'Now then ladies, you are all looking rather gorgeous this evening, I must say. What would you like? I've some Raspberry Fizz cocktails ready for you to help yourselves to, or I can offer you *the* perfect Gin and Tonic to get this party started.' And he was off, launching into his barman repartee.

'Hey, Em, look, these are so pretty.' One of the girls was picking up a pink Bellini flute.

'Gorgeous, aren't they.'

'The staff aren't looking so bad either,' chuckled another of the young women in the group.

'Hmm, have to agree with you on that,' one of her friends purred, loud enough for Jack to hear, whilst darting him a foxy look.

Jack just shook his head, giving a friendly grin. He was used to the chit-chat, and carried on pouring prosecco into glasses with a steady hand.

An attractive blonde placed glossy lips against her flute. 'Oh my, the taste. Sophie, come and have a sip of this, it's divine.'

'What are you on, the raspberry one?'

'Yeah.'

'Cocktails will be served throughout the night, ladies. And if you have any personal favourites, I can make up whatever you like. My bar is well stocked.'

'Oooh, I bet it is.' The blonde's tone was flirty as she flashed him a cheeky smile.

Okay, so he did play up to the flirtiness a tad, but that was it, a charming front. Keeping the customers entertained and happy was all part of the job, and once the welcome drinks were over and it became a pay bar (as it would later this evening), it was his chance to make some extra money, which would help keep Ruby and this business venture going. A smile and a bit of banter kept the punters happy, and the money rolling in.

Cars began to park up along the edges of the driveway and more taxis arrived. The partygoers stood sipping their welcome drinks, talking and laughing. Birthday Girl, Harriet, was soon on her second Raspberry Bellini, and younger brother Hugo had already darted in whilst Jack was busy, pilfering a G&T, which he had more or less downed in one. Jack gave him an 'I see you' sign, along with a stern shake of the head, whilst making a mental note to keep a close eye on him – if he kept downing alcohol like that, Hugo would no doubt end up on the floor, and Abigail would be laying down the law to Jack.

Grandma Judith was up next, steadying herself on the arm of another elderly relative. 'Oh, these look good, Faye.' Her pale wrinkled hand was drifting towards a Raspberry Bellini, bless her. Jack remembered his instructions however, and though part of him felt she should be able to have a cheeky tipple if she wanted, he really didn't want to be responsible for a 'funny turn' or worse on his watch, so he moved in respectfully.

'Now this one is the bees-knees, ladies. Why don't you give it a try?' He lifted up two of the elderflower fizzes. 'Summer in a glass. Let me know what you think.'

They took them with a smile. 'Thank you, young man. That's very kind.'

'Hmm, nice, very refreshing dear,' the other lady commented.

Grandma was on it like a car bonnet, however: 'Not very strong though!'

Jack suppressed a grin, and deftly switched the focus of their conversation. 'Love the outfits, ladies. The pastel shades suit you both. Very smart indeed.'

'Thank you,' Grandma smiled. 'And yes, *this* is very nice indeed, too.' She raised her glass.

Jack gave a wink. 'Cheers to you both, and have a lovely evening.'

'Oh, we will do.' They linked arms once again, their aged eyes a-sparkle. They certainly looked like they were going to make the most of it.

As they wandered off, he smiled as he heard one of them say, 'What a lovely young man.'

The other answering, 'Yes, our young Harriet would do well finding someone like that ... Hard-working and polite. Instead of that waste-of-space Cameron chappie that she seems to have set her sights on.' Their chatter drifted off into the evening air as they strolled away, no doubt looking to find a comfy seat and hopefully a knee-blanket to ward off any evening chill out in the gardens.

In a rare quiet moment a little later, the party in full swing, Jack looked across the driveway to his catering companion. Rich cheese and tomato aromas were drifting across from the Pizza Horsebox, and he felt his tummy rumble; perhaps he should have had a bite to eat himself before setting off. His gaze fell on the dark-haired young woman who was busy slicing wedges of pizza at the countertop. There was something about her that gave him pause. Had they met somewhere before? He didn't think so, he'd surely have remembered those striking dark eyes and that bounce of glossy dark hair, now up in its bun, but hmm, she did seem familiar. He felt a tweak of emotion in his chest. He wasn't quite sure what it was, but it felt significant somehow.

Chapter 2

*W*hat is he staring at?

The guy at the mobile bar opposite was looking fixedly her way. Surely, he should be getting on with serving, or in fact *flirting*, with his customers like he had been. Oh yes, Lucy had heard all the noisy giggling going on over there. It was lovely to see and hear everyone enjoying themselves, all dressed up in their fabulous outfits, but honestly, that particular group of girls were like bees round a honeypot. A free cocktail and a cute barman were evidently an instant draw. Lucy reluctantly had to concede that he did have the looks to go with the chat, what with his sun-kissed blond hair, lightly-tanned skin and beaming smile, but boy did he know it. She glanced over. Come to think of it, there was something kind of familiar about him ... Ah, perhaps it was just the cheesy TV-style persona, you saw it everywhere on those American shows these days.

Lucy got back to work, hand-stretching the dough balls as she made up more pizza bases, ready to bake. She was trying to train up newly-recruited assistant Tamsin, who was seventeen, and unfortunately was already proving to be slightly sullen. She'd shown her several times how to spread the pizzas with her homemade tomato sauce, made to Papa's special recipe with real Italian San Marzano tomatoes, garlic and basil, but the girl still slopped on the mixture half-heartedly. Another problem to deal with; Lucy hadn't realised how hard it would be to find the right staff. The teenage girl, who'd responded to her advert in the local press just two weeks ago, had worked as a waitress, and seemed fine when she'd met her for a casual interview. They were still getting to know each other, and of course she'd need to give her a chance.

Lucy *so* needed this event to go well. She was trying desperately hard to get her new business established and get her name out there. It was only her third booking, and it was bloody typical that she'd got lost in the lanes getting here. Once again, she groaned inwardly that she'd arrived so late. The bloody barman didn't have to make a point of rubbing it in though, did he? '*You're cutting it a bit fine though.*' The cocky prat.

All Fired Up had taken up all of Lucy's time and energy lately. It was a huge change in direction for her, after her life had been somewhat flipped upside down and she'd decided to leave the steady job at the accountancy firm where she worked. It was a risk, but it was the chance to finally do something she was passionate about. Several months of research led to trying to find the right horsebox at a good price and getting it kitted out (at a small fortune).

Bringing it home to her seaside cottage for the first time after its conversion, she couldn't resist opening up the new hatch, stringing it with bunting, and placing a pot of bright-yellow primulas on the counter-top. She'd then popped the cork on a mini bottle of prosecco, with an excited Daisy, her cute dachshund, scampering at her feet, whilst she gazed at her horsebox happily. 'Papa's Pizzas' came to mind – she knew that her beloved grandfather would be so proud of her. But this venture was much more than that, it was about *her* as well as paying homage to him. She felt all fired up for her new life, these new beginnings ... 'All Fired Up' – that was it! Perfect.

The next day, she'd painted the horsebox a pretty soft-chalky grey, putting the finishing touches to this quaint and quirky mobile pizza van. There was so much at stake, not least the chance to finally try and achieve her dream.

Back to the here and now, the oven was up to temperature, thank goodness, and she and Tamsin soon managed to serve out the first pizzas, phew! A few partygoers drifted their way, grabbing just-cooked slices and murmuring their 'Mmms' and 'Aahs' of appreciation.

In a bid to get back onside with tonight's clients, Lucy had tracked down an unfortunately sour-faced Abigail a little earlier, apologising for their delay and explaining the SatNav failure. She really didn't want to get off on the wrong footing, especially not when she was trying so hard to build her name and reputation, or she'd be getting her clients 'all fired up' for the all the wrong reasons. Oh well, she'd just need to crack on now and make the most delicious pizzas and homemade garlic breads for their party this evening, then perhaps Harriet, her mother, and the 21st Birthday guests might instead remember her and her pizzas for all the right reasons.

More guests were arriving by the minute, so she'd better get a move on with her next round of toppings – goat's cheese and red pepper with rocket and balsamic glaze, and BBQ chicken with red onion and a drizzle of smoky sauce. Lucy stood beside Tamsin, rhythmically chopping mushrooms and onions, to the beat of party music that drifted from the beautiful, grand house. When Lucy had gone in earlier to find Abigail and Harriet to make her apologies, she'd stood wide-eyed in the mansion-like space. A grand, polished, dark-wooden staircase curved down to a black-and-white tiled entrance hall. There were huge vases filled with beautiful fresh flowers, and above there was even a sparkling crystal chandelier. It had reminded her of Downton Abbey. Hah, the whole of Lucy's quaint but tiny cottage would probably fit inside the lobby area.

Thinking of home suddenly reminded Lucy of her little dog Daisy, a gorgeous black-and-tan smooth dachshund who was settled in her pet bed in the back of Lucy's truck – well out of the way of the food zone. The vehicle's windows were open and the dog had a bowl of water beside her, but she'd need to remember to let her out for a breath of air and a toilet break at some point. Lucy liked to take Daisy with her whenever she could, rather than leave her pining at home in the little seaside cottage that they shared. She'd found her at the local animal rescue centre ten months before. Her owners hadn't been able to cope with her 'bad' habits: eating huge chunks off of the wooden skirting boards whilst they were out at work being one of her regular misdemeanours, and barking constantly.

The beautiful brown-eyed dog had looked up at Lucy from her kennel, and she knew there and then that Daisy just needed some love, a little TLC – Lucy knew that feeling well enough too. They had bonded instantly, and though Daisy could still be a diva at times, she was the best companion ever, and had helped Lucy through some emotionally tough times.

The evening rolled on in a hot and hectic whirl of topping pizzas, cooking pizzas, and serving pizzas. At times, Lucy felt very like the Muppet chef. There were some special requests, including a young man asking for Lucy to create a heart-shape from the pepperoni slices, to surprise his girlfriend, which was rather sweet of him and made Lucy smile. So, there was still some romance in the world, she mused – shame it had upped and buggered off rather spectacularly from her own life over eighteen months ago. She put that thought neatly aside.

It was nearing nine o'clock. They'd managed to serve everyone in the queue that had formed, and there seemed to be a bit of a lull. There was a genial buzz amongst the groups standing chatting outside, some guests drifted in and out from the house where there was music and dancing and laughter. 'Umm, I'm just going to take a quick break, if that's alright, Tamsin? Keep making up more bases, but just take orders for now. No need to touch the oven at all,' she confirmed, 'and keep an eye out that no-one else is going anywhere near it. Let anyone that might want pizza know we'll be ready to serve again in about ten, fifteen minutes. Okay?'

'Yeah, no problem,' the young girl answered, reaching for her phone to no doubt pass the time.

As Lucy stepped down from the trailer, she couldn't help but notice that the sandy-haired campervan guy across the way was making a big show, shaking a metal cocktail canister vigorously with his chest all puffed out. Crikey, did he think he was Tom Cruise or something? Like in that old film *Cocktail* she'd seen on Netflix a while back? She wasn't quite sure why, but his manner irked her.

The barman then dramatically poured a frothy deep-brown liquid into two martini glasses with a flourish, garnishing them with a floating coffee bean. 'Voila, madam. Your espresso martinis,' she heard him gush.

'Ooh, they look amazing. Thank you,' replied the auburn-haired woman at the van's hatch, likely fluttering her eyelashes.

'The very same colour as your beautiful deep-brown eyes.' Lucy was sure he'd slipped into a French accent then. Hah, he was as North-East as the rest of them here, with his Geordie-style lilt she'd heard earlier.

Cheesy or what.

She left the corny bar show behind and went for a brief toilet stop before letting Diva Daisy out for her own. The little dog was eager to get out of the truck and into her arms. Lucy stroked her soft short fur; it always felt soothing.

'Hey, what a good girl you've been there, haven't you. Shall we go for a little walk?' Those dark eyes looked up at her lovingly, Daisy happy as always to be reunited with her owner. 'Come on, then.'

Lucy clipped her lead onto her navy velvet collar and set

her down on the ground. Daisy gave an excited bark. They could take a few minutes' stroll in a quiet part of the gardens, Lucy decided; let her sniff the borders, and do what she needed.

The sun had gone down in a soft smoulder of peachy-greys, the garden now bathed in a magical half-light. The fairy lights Lucy had strung across the hatch of her vintage horsebox twinkled merrily. She had to admit, the mobile pizzeria looked really pretty, and she felt herself glow with pride. She'd give it her best shot, whatever it took. The party was in full swing, the sounds of laughter and the beat of the music getting louder now as the celebrations ramped up, drifting from the open windows of the big house.

Daisy was too busy taking in all the people and the hubbub around her to settle. She sniffed and scratched at a border or two, Lucy pulling her away before her digging got too obvious and left its mark, but unusually she didn't seem to need a wee. Oh well, she'd had her chance. Lucy had better head back to the horsebox, give her hands a thorough wash, and get on with her pizza making, before her absence and the lack of fresh pizzas were noted by Abigail and the guests.

She and Daisy had to pass Mr Cocky Cocktail Man on the way back. Although she did have to admit his ruby-red VW, *Jack's Cocktail Campervan* as the sign read, did look pretty impressive. And she supposed she may as well be friendly and say hello. After all, they might well be working at the same events together in the future.

He had just finished creating a gorgeous-looking lemony drink in a tall glass, which he passed to a rather glamorous forty-something lady, who thanked him with a beam of a smile and walked off.

'Now that looks good,' Lucy commented.

'A Tom Collins. A lemon, gin and soda classic,' the bartender replied with a smile.

'Sounds good, too.'

'Oh, I'd have made you one, but you're the pizza lady, right? You'll be driving later, won't you? And they do tend to be quite strong.'

'Yup, you got it. So, no cocktails for me tonight,' she responded. He was staring at her ... a little too intently. She suddenly felt uncomfortable. 'Right, well anyway, I'd better get back to my pizza station and back to work, I suppose ... Ah, I'm Lucy, by the way.'

'Hi Lucy, I'm Jack. But that's probably no surprise.' He glanced down at the logo on his apron front, his eyes then crinkling with a smile as he extended a hand in greeting. She took it and felt its warmth, his firm grip. He flashed her a white-toothed grin. 'Lovely to meet you.' Was that a wink he'd just given her?

'Hello, Jack,' she replied, her voice a little clipped. Yep, he was a right charmer, just as she had thought.

It was then that Lucy looked down and realised what had been going on whilst they were chatting. Worryingly, the wooden corner of his A-frame chalkboard was looking decidedly ragged, *chewed* in fact. It then fell over with a clatter as Daisy nudged up against it, and then decided her call of nature was due, proceeding to walk and then pee all over the writing, smearing the lettering of the Classic Mojito and obliterating the Strawberry one and its little hand-drawn pictures alto-gether.

Oh god, Daisy no, what have you done!

Jack looked down just as the little dog was triumphantly moving off, kicking up the grassy dirt around her, spattering the board with that too.

'Uh, did your dog just do what I think it did?' The guy was gobsmacked, his smile frozen, and ... he looked decidedly angry. 'Jeez, look at my bloody sign. I spent ages writing that out. What the hell is it doing here anyway? I can't imagine pizza-making and dogs go very well together!'

His sharp tone got Lucy's back up, and even though Daisy had been rather naughty, it was just an unfortunate accident. '*She* is Daisy, and she's been safely out of the way 'til now. It's not the end of the bloody world. I'll go and get some water and get the, er ... wee off a bit.' She wasn't sure how she was going to disguise the gnawed edges, mind. 'Or I'll buy you a new one, if need be,' she added, a little more conciliatory.

'But my sign. Look, it's bloody well ruined now. I haven't got time to write it all out again. It was a work of art that, took me ages.' He sounded well and truly miffed.

The sign did indeed have lovely swirly writing on – well, about half of it that was left readable now – with hand-drawn pictures of strawberries, limes and mint leaves, but honestly, this guy was making a mountain out of a molehill.

'It'll stink of dog pee now too,' he continued gruffly. 'Here, get it off, quick, before the girls go and ruin their dresses on it.' He passed her a pint glass of water.

Lucy swiftly drenched the sign, which did now look a sorry

mess. She propped the board back up, uttered a further apology as she handed the empty glass back, and headed off to put Daisy back in the truck, out of sight and mischief, for a while. Oops.

'Daisy, I cannot believe you just did that,' Lucy shook her head as she walked away, feeling rather mortified, yet suppressing a small smile too. Back at her truck, she lifted the cheeky little dachshund back into her secure place, popping a dog biscuit in with her to keep her happy. Diva Daisy just looked at her owner with those cute brown eyes. 'I'll see you later, Miss Mischief.' The dog slumped down with a small sigh, resigned to her fate, and ready for another snooze after that little adventure.

Lucy stole a quick glance over at Jack and saw him shaking his head at his sorry little sign. I bet he didn't bank on *that* being on the menu, she thought with a chuckle. Who's Mr Cocky now then?

Chapter 3

Lucy was back at her little cottage after midnight, having dropped Tamsin off en route. She was enjoying a much-needed cup of tea and a snack of buttered toast, perched on a stool in the cosy galley kitchen with Daisy at her feet. The room was rustic, yet comforting, with thick, stone, white-washed walls and a low ceiling, and two small square-paned windows that looked out upon the little back courtyard area. All was still and dark outside now.

She'd done it – she'd made it through her third event. Abigail and Harriet had made a point of coming over to thank her at the end of the evening, impressed with how many of the guests were talking about her delicious pizzas, and Harriet was even going to post some pics of the gorgeous horsebox and give All Fired Up a mention on her Instagram. It sounded very much like they'd forgiven her for her late arrival. Phew!

Even her new assistant, Tamsin, had worked pretty hard in the end and had helped it all to come together; though Lucy did wonder if the young girl would want to stick with it. She'd kept firing off messages on her phone throughout the evening, and furrowing her brow when she thought Lucy wasn't watching.

Crikey, all this was so new and different from her accountancy work at the office in Morpeth. *I can't believe you've just upped and packed it all in on a whim!* Her dad's strong words rang in her ears. His reluctance to see her give up a regular monthly salary and a steady job in the accounts department of Edwin Grant's was well known. For years, he had persuaded her to commit to that stable kind of a life, saying that was the sensible and well-paid thing to do work-wise. But Lucy had become sick of the same old, four-walled number crunching.

And when Lucy had broken the news to her family that she was going to give up the accounting job, saying she was buying a vintage – aka slightly decrepit – horsebox to turn into her very own pizza business, well, her dad hadn't been happy at all.

Mum, Sofia, who'd lived on her own for many years now, since Dad needed 'more space' (space enough to find a new partner six months later), had been more supportive; happy at least that Lucy was trying to do something entrepreneurial, and in her beloved Papa's memory. She'd seen how Lucy had been struggling in her relationship and career, how unhappy her daughter had been, and recognised the need for Lucy to get out and change things in her life.

And Lucy truly believed the pizza venture was something she could enjoy doing and be proud of, albeit with sore feet and a sweat on – my, that oven was damned hot to be standing beside – and soon, hopefully, it would turn a profit and be something she could make a living from too. It *had* to be.

Lucy had three further events booked in so far, and she'd been looking into market stall slots in the local towns as well. Word would spread, she was working on her website and the All Fired Up Facebook and Instagram pages. She'd get some pictures of tonight's party out on her feed first thing in the morning. Maybe, fingers crossed, with hard work and determination, she really *could* make a success of this business, and turn her life round, after all.

For some reason, her mind drifted to the campervan guy then. She wondered what had made him go into his mobile bar business and how he'd got established? He seemed to have a pretty slick venture going there, albeit his showman manner was damned cheesy. Hah, he might be cute – she'd seen Tamsin giving him the eye too – but he was downright cocky. And he'd been a right grump when Daisy had had her peeing accident on his chalkboard. Lucy was feeling a bit riled just thinking about it again. Daisy hadn't done it on purpose or anything, after all. Anyhow, why was she even dwelling on it, or him? Yet, somehow, she felt a little uneasy, like she'd been caught off her guard. Hah, it was probably Cocky Cocktail Man's attitude, that sense of arrogance about him that had got to her.

Her eye snagged on a photo that sat on the mantelpiece above the old stone hearth; she'd only kept the picture because Mum and Nonna were in it too ... and there they were, her and Liam, her ex. Bloody hell, another one – alongside her dad – who'd kept down her dreams with his insistence on maintaining the regular job, the steady income.

Liam had been arrogant enough to think that she'd never find out he had another girlfriend in the wings, or that if she did, it might *not* spell the end of their four-year relationship.

It did.

Lucy hugged her mug and gazed out of the little window beside her. All was dark out there but for the glowing crescent of a waxing moon.

And despite her worries, it seemed to hold the hope of things to come.

At that moment, Jack was driving back along the winding coastal roads to his lodgings in a village just outside of Alnwick. Usually, the late-night drive home along country roads soothed him; a chance to wind down after the evening's bar-work buzz. But that bloody pizza girl crossed his mind again. Hah, turning up late, so unprofessional, and then her stupid dog wrecking his sign like that. What was she thinking, taking a dog along to a food event, anyhow?

A weird rhyme started to form in his head as he drove:

There was a young woman made pizza,
With a dog that was long and a diva.
She seemed kind of mean
With a look of Ice Queen …

He repeated it out loud, trying to think of a good rhyme to complete the last line. He navigated a tight bend in the lane, headlights flashing up hawthorn hedgerows.

What the hell was he doing anyhow, making up daft poems about some annoying woman he'd just met, and her dog? Had he been a bit harsh on her, though? She seemed pretty new to the catering scene ... and the dog, well, it was just a dog doing its thing ... He'd let rip in the heat of the moment, he realised. Now, he wasn't quite sure how he felt about it all.

Ping! That was it:

And the barman was left with a fever.

He laughed at himself, bloody idiot, making up limericks in the middle of the night. It passed the journey, he supposed. He thought he might even jot it down when he got back. Saying it over once more to see if it worked, he wondered if it really was worthy of putting to paper?

He'd not written any poetry in a while now. It used it be his thing, he remembered ... not daft stuff like this, but finding the words, needing to spill out his hurts. He'd used it a bit like a therapy, when he couldn't talk to anyone else. When his soul was in the sorest of places.

Jack fixed once again on the road ahead. Just him and Ruby, the hum of her engine and the rhythm of the night drive; the adrenaline of the evening gradually starting to dissipate. The sky above was an inky black, with an arc of a new moon that just caught his gaze.

Chapter 4

It was a bright morning, and Lucy woke early with the light filtering through her bedroom curtains. She reached out to find Daisy there in her favourite spot, curled up by Lucy's side on top of the double duvet.

'Morning, Daisy Doo.'

Daisy gave a contented doggie sigh.

'I think we'll go and have a walk on the beach first thing.'

Daisy snuffled and buried herself a little deeper into the covers as if to hide, which made Lucy laugh out loud.

'Hah, maybe after some tea and toast then.'

Ten minutes later, and Lucy was sat on a stool in her kitchen – Daisy was still snoozing upstairs – munching wholemeal toast with peanut butter, with a big polka-dot mug of tea beside her. A message buzzed on her mobile phone.

So, how did it go last night? Are you all pizza'd out? X

It was from her friend, Becky. Lucy smiled. It was great that her close pal was so interested in her new venture, that she supported her in this. In fact, she had done so with all the twists and turns of Lucy's life these past few years. When the bombshell hit that Liam was having an affair behind her back, when she'd thrown him out of their lovely new house, when Lucy had had to find a new place to live all alone, Becky had appeared with hugs, chat, cake and a cuppa, sometimes prosecco and pizza, sensing exactly when and what was needed.

Yeah, it went off really well, thanks. X

She didn't think she'd mention the delayed arrival, or ... her mind drifted to the antics with Daisy and the Cocktail Campervan guy.

Thinking of popping around this aft for a coffee and a catch-up? You about? Becky asked.

Yes, why don't we meet at Driftwood? Lucy typed.

It was their favourite little coffee shop, right here in Lucy's village, with a cosy sea view, that did the most amazing cakes and traybakes.

2 p.m.? was fired back without hesitation.

Perfect.

See you later then. Xx

Finishing her toast, Lucy then nipped upstairs to shower and dress, choosing a striped Breton top and jeans for her Sunday beach stroll. Adding a swipe of mascara and a smudge of pink lipstick to finish her casual look, she headed towards the bed to shift a still reluctant Diva Daisy downstairs ready for her morning walk.

The tide was out this morning, and the beach was a crescent of golden sand, backed by marram grass dunes. A line of twisted, shiny brown kelp marked the high tide. Towards the shoreline, the sands had shifted into smooth pale-brown ridges with little pools. Frothy-topped waves rolled in. Sea and sky met on a horizon that was azure, with puffs of fair-day white clouds up above.

Taking in the salty sea air plus an array of other scents, Dachshund Daisy gingerly stepped over the seaweed to reach the flat sands of the bay. She wasn't a huge lover of water but enjoyed her treks on the beach with her owner, meeting many four-legged friends on their way and barking merrily in greeting as she went. Size didn't matter to her – she was as happy meeting a Labrador as a terrier. They'd do a quick spin around her, a greeting sniff or two, and then she'd be off again, her nose pointed in the air, her short legs trotting along. Then she'd watch them haughtily, especially those crazy spaniel types and the border collies, whizzing off after balls and sticks like loonies, when all you had to do was walk and sit nicely now and again to receive a pat on the head and a tasty biscuit.

Lucy sighed, taking in the fresh air and the rhythmic sounds of the sea. It was lovely to live so near to the coast. She was pleased that she'd gone with her heart and bid for the old stone cottage at Embleton; though very small, it was within walking distance of the beach. It didn't quite have a sea view. Well, not unless you were on tiptoes and craning your neck out of the double bedroom window to catch a tiny glimpse of ultramarine below the skyline. But it was hers, it was home. With a small mortgage to her name and half the furniture from her house with Liam, she'd set off on a brave and slightly wobbly new path.

It wasn't where she'd expected to be at the age of thirty-one.

Newly single, a proud owner of a dachshund and a tiny cottage by the sea, no longer working at the accountancy office she'd started in after her A-levels, but CEO (hah!) of the All Fired Up horsebox pizza-catering company. Crikey, life took you off in all sorts of weird and wonderful directions at times. It was a journey, hers a pretty bumpy one of late.

But she had her friends, her family: brother Olly who lived in Alnwick with girlfriend Alice and their gorgeous toddler, Freddie; her mum who was still at the family home in Rothbury; lovely Nonna nearby, and her dad living not too far away in Whitley Bay with his new partner – another explosive twist in the family tale that had happened many years ago now.

Thoughts of a partner and family of her own that she'd once harboured were now very much on hold. To be honest, she wasn't sure if she could put herself through all that relationship heartache and stress again. Romance was definitely overrated. Life moved on, your dreams shifted, some of them shattered and you had to let go of them, but then new goals and opportunities came to light.

'Morning, Luce.' Cathy from the village store was walking nearby on the beach with her beagle, Max, who was now eagerly greeting Daisy in a twist of leads and tails.

'Oh, hi.' Lucy snapped out of her reverie and offered a warm smile.

'Getting out early, before the crowds descend,' Cathy grinned.

'Yes, it's wonderful here when it's quiet like this.' Lucy took in the expanse of golden sandy bay.

'Mind you, can't complain, as long as they come and spend a few of their pennies at my shop.'

'Hah, yes, of course.'

'Lovely day,' Cathy added, as she moved on.

'Yeah, it's beautiful.'

And it *was*, the glow of the sun was warm on her cheeks, the sea view – a glorious wash of greys, golds, blues and white – was just stunning, and walking this bay that she could now call home was so calming. Despite the heartbreaks and hurts of the past two years, and the fears that her new business might yet struggle to get going, she felt a sense of hope. That life could and would get better.

Onwards and upwards, Lucy, she told herself. Onwards and upwards.

Behind the counter of the Driftwood Café, owner Louise was cutting into a rich velvety chocolate cake and then plating a slice of citrussy lemon drizzle loaf. Lucy and her friend, Becky, were happily chatting away, sat at a pretty white-chalk-painted table, with mugs of swirly-cream-topped hot chocolate in front of them. (Okay, so it was nearly summer but some things were worth having all year long!) The cakes had their names on them – it was most definitely treat-time, and why not?

The tea room was decorated with driftwood-framed coastal prints, and various arts and crafts for sale, including cute wooden puffins and seabirds carved and painted locally. There were even little rows of tiny colourful beach huts. Lucy had bought several gorgeous bits and bobs from here to cheer up her nearby cottage over the past few months.

'So, tell me more about last night?' Becky was curious. 'What was the big country pad like?'

'It was an amazing house. Huge garden, massive driveway. And inside ... well, it was pretty much a mansion. You could get lost looking for the loos. In fact, I did!' She grinned, pausing to take a sip of her creamy drink. 'And yeah, it went off pretty well ... overall. Only, I do have to confess I was bloody well late getting there. That was embarrassing, and not the best of starts.'

'Oh no, were the organisers okay about that?'

'Um, no, not at first, the mother gave me a bit of a dressing down when I got there, but I just got stuck in, made the best pizzas I could, and thank heavens they seemed really happy by the end.'

'Well, that's good. So, what was the new girl like? How did that work out?'

'Tamsin, yeah, ah, I'm not sure. She was okay. She got going in the end and we both worked bloody hard, we had to, making and serving sixty pizzas in all. It was like a bloomin' production line, and I'd only just enough ingredients. It was really full on, and I don't know ... I got the impression that it was harder work than she'd imagined. We'll see how it pans out ... if she wants to come back, that is.'

Lucy really wasn't sure which way that would swing. She couldn't afford to pay her much above the minimum wage whilst she was finding her feet and trying to balance the books, and the girl might be able to earn more doing her waitress work. Oh well, time would tell. One more little hurdle to leap.

She then remembered the incident with Daisy's bar-side pee stop. She couldn't help but smile to herself, thinking back to how it had rolled out like a comedy sketch, and the subsequent tirade from the cocky barman.

'What's up? You've gone off in a little daze there.'

'Oh, just thinking about this Cocktail Campervan that was there, and the barman getting shirty with me.'

'What on earth for?' Becky raised her eyebrows.

'Hmm, let's just say Daisy had a bit of a moment. I was just giving her a bit of air, and well ... she proceeded to pee all over his blackboard sign! She even managed to wash off two of the listed cocktails.'

The girls started giggling then, Lucy picturing Jack's reddened face.

'OMG. Hah, good old Daisy.'

Daisy was in fact snug at home right now, settled in her cosy kitchen crate. Dogs weren't allowed inside the café; though sometimes Lucy enjoyed a cup of coffee outside at one of the little street-side tables with the dachshund at her feet, both of them watching the world go by.

'Anyhow, the big question is, do you think you've made the right decision jacking in the day job, or is it too soon to tell?'

Lucy paused, weighing everything up, before answering. 'Hmm, I am enjoying it. Being able to do something I love is brilliant, and I especially love that I'm using Papa's recipe, so that side of it's fine. But that oven is roasting, I'm sure I'm going to burn my bloody eyebrows off one of these days. Honestly, the heat it gives out!'

'Instant eyebrow waxing,' Becky added with a laugh.

'Hah, more like eyebrow elimination. But yeah, it's good being my own boss,' Lucy continued, 'but that also has its issues, like it's *all* on you. And, I could do with being a bit busier. Getting some regular bookings. I've not made that much money as yet,' she admitted.

Lucy was feeling the pressure, she knew she had to make this work out. She'd paid out on hygiene courses, all the equipment from the (very expensive) oven down to the wooden platters to serve the pizza on. The main set-up costs had now been met, but after having to put a reasonable deposit down on her cottage too, there wasn't a lot left of her savings now.

'Well honey, when life gives you lemons ...' Becky started, bringing her back to the here and now.

'Make lemon cake!' the café owner chipped in, popping Lucy's lemon drizzle down on the table with a flourish. The two girls grinned at her.

'Or *pizza*,' Becky added with a beam. 'I'm with you all the way, Luce.' Her friend reached to touch her hand.

'Oh, are you talking about your new venture, Lucy? How's it going, my love?'

'Yeah, pretty good. Three events done, and I've survived in one piece so far. It's just a big learning curve, I suppose.'

'Of course, it will be. It's a big step, running your own business. Well, if you ever need any advice you can always ask me,' Louise added. 'I've faced many a challenge here over the years.'

'Aw, thank you.'

'Oh, and if you want a bit of time out, ladies, don't forget the Driftwood Book Club. Last Thursday of the month, 7 p.m.

All are welcome. We've got a great little group going on here. Book chat, cake and coffee. Just let me know if you fancy popping along, and I'll tell you which book we're reading.'

'Sounds good. Just my kind of thing,' Lucy replied.

When she wasn't working, Lucy could often be found with her nose in a book. It was one of her favourite things to do. How lovely for them both to be invited to be part of the village group, and for Louise's offer of help and advice with her new venture. And the icing on the top was that she also happened to make some of the best cakes in the world. Lucy looked down at her wedge of lemon drizzle with a smile.

With friends like these on board, it made her challenges seem a little lighter.

Later that afternoon, the weather took a bad turn. Lucy and Daisy watched little plops and streams fall like teardrops down the small window panes of the cottage. Lucy switched the living-room lights on to give a cosy glow and took up her latest book.

She was just getting to a new chapter, all settled on the sofa, when the cast-iron knocker on the front door clop-clopped, and Daisy gave a protective bark. Who on earth might that be? Lucy wasn't expecting any visitors today. She headed out to the front door.

A tall, lanky twenty-seven-year-old was stood on the step, his dark wavy hair dripping rain into his eyes. 'Hey, sis.'

'Olly! Quick, come on in. This is a nice surprise. I wasn't expecting you today ...' She glanced over his shoulder, no sign of his partner Alice or Freddie, their toddler. 'On your own?'

'Aye, I've escaped for a half-hour.' He gave a mischievous grin. 'I *have* been putting up shelves in the little man's room all afternoon, mind. Then I was sent out to get some bits and bobs at the supermarket for supper; thought I'd drive the extra few miles and have a quick catch-up. I'll be back at work tomorrow and it'll be all go again for sure.'

Olly was an electrician, working for a local company.

'Fancy a coffee?'

He put a thumbs up. 'Never known to refuse. Unless there's a bottle of beer handy, of course.'

'*That* kind of a day, hey? But sorry, no beer.' Lucy smiled.

She got on well with her younger brother. Yeah, they'd had the odd minor tiff as kids, but there was none of that dreadful sibling rivalry between them. They'd been a team, and even though he was four years younger than her, she thought of their childhood fondly. They had fun together: beach days playing rounders, huddled in towels after a chilly dip in the North Sea, practising their basketball skills at the net in the back garden, and noisy games of Twister, Connect Four, and Mousetrap on wet days at home. She'd always felt a bit protective of him too, especially with the fallout between Mum and Dad happening whilst she and Olly were still living at home. Though teenagers, it was still tough to deal with. And, she absolutely adored his new family unit. Cheeky little Freddie was the spitting image of him as a little boy.

'Get on okay at your pizza gig last night?' Olly asked.

He had helped install the electrics to the horsebox, all in his own time and for free, bless him, so he had an added interest in her new venture.

'Yep, went off pretty well overall, I think.'

'As long as the customers were happy and you got paid, that's all that matters.'

'Yeah.' She hoped the balance payment from Abigail would show up in her account tomorrow. It was much needed.

They headed into the kitchen and Lucy clicked the kettle on, spooning instant coffee into mugs.

'I just wish Dad would be a bit more positive about it all, though.'

'Yeah well, that's Dad for you. He'll just be worried it's a bit of a risk, and after everything ... He just doesn't want to see you get hurt, Lulu,' Olly added.

The word *again* hanging in the air between them.

'Yeah, I suppose,' she conceded with a sigh. A lump formed in her throat as tears began welling in her eyes. She batted them back down, turning away for a brief moment. She wasn't one to be wearing her heart on her sleeve, even with the own brother. But break-up life after Liam's bomb of an affair had been so damned tough.

'Luce, you okay?'

'Yeah, fine. Just, ah, kettle steam ... getting in my eyes.'

He nodded, knowing very well she was putting on a front.

'Okay, well, you'll just have to show Dad that you can make it work.'

'Hah, no pressure then!'

'If anyone can do it, you can, sis.'

'Thanks, Ol.'

They sat for a while drinking coffee and chatting about their everyday lives – including little Freddie's latest antics,

Olly producing a video clip on his phone of her nephew grinning away whilst being sprayed by the garden hose, fully clothed, which had the two of them in stitches. With a busy day ahead, and shopping in the car, it wasn't long before Olly had to go, but his words stayed in Lucy's mind.

Could she really do it? Could she make Papa's pizzas work, or was her mobile catering idea just pie in the sky?

It's party time!

Geoff and Hannah Allan

are delighted to invite you to join them in their

Silver Wedding Celebrations

At Foxton Farm, Old Holburn

Saturday 22nd May

Supper, drinks and live music with the Border
Busketeers

8 'til late!

Chapter 5

A couple of weeks later, Jack was steering Ruby into a field beside a country farmhouse – 'the paddock' apparently – for a Silver Wedding bash. He'd headed inland, passing through gently rolling hills dotted with grazing sheep and cattle, and stretches of moorland with patches of zingy-yellow gorse bushes, to find the quaint stone-built house. The old farm nestled alongside a couple of old red-tiled barns which had been decorated with festive silver-grey bunting for the occasion.

After a soggy spell, the weather had thankfully dried out at last. So at least Ruby shouldn't get stuck in the mud, Jack mused, as he parked up on the lush grass. Oh yes, that had happened all too often before! As a couple of other catering vans arrived, one of them being *Bob's Gourmet Burger* van, a regular on the Northumbrian mobile catering scene, Jack pondered that there'd been no sign of the pizza horsebox at any of his bookings over the past two weeks. Of course, it was unlikely they'd get booked for the same events all the time, he told himself sagely. After all, it was only occasionally that he worked alongside Bob, or the bubbly forty-something Carrie who was now pulling up in her polka-dot themed

Classy Cupcakes touring caravan. But although a large part of him was relieved, another part of Jack had wondered if he might catch up with the dark-haired girl again – Lucy, that was her name. Goodness knows why. Jack remembered her being particularly frosty when they'd met and then there was her little pesky dog peeing all over his sign. But the thought that they might never cross paths again ... Well, it left Jack feeling strangely unsettled.

These mental diversions weren't getting him anywhere. His focus needed to be on tonight's event and getting his bar ready to roll for the first arrivals. He had a trayful of Silver Martinis to rustle up, and sharpish. They'd pour out a beautiful shade of pale-silver – perfect for the Silver Wedding event. After lifting the lid on Ruby and switching on his globe lights, he set out two cocktail shakers, retrieved the gin, vermouth and orange bitters he needed first, and went about finding his jar of maraschino cherries.

Just as he was setting out his counter display with a row of classic V-shaped martini glasses and a colourful array of fruits and garnishes, Jack happened to look up, spotting a Jeep towing a grey wood-panelled horsebox coming through the five-bar gate. His stomach gave an unexpected flip as he recognised the mass of wavy dark hair and the rather serious-looking face of the driver, who was negotiating the narrow gap. So, they *were* to meet again.

Jack smoothed down his hair distractedly, and was ready to give a small wave, just as the daughter of the Anniversary Couple appeared beside Ruby to check over a few last-minute arrangements. By the time she'd gone, he'd missed his moment and Lucy had already parked up and was head down, setting up her pizza van.

Both the Cocktail Campervan and All Fired Up had a busy start to the evening, with a constant stream of hungry and thirsty guests arriving. There was a buzz of chatter and laughter as family and friends huddled happily outside, some sitting at a medley of tables and chairs borrowed for the event, and a local folk band started up with a jaunty tune from the shelter of a tipi-style tent. Though it wasn't his usual taste in music – his favourite bands being The Arctic Monkeys and The Kaiser Chiefs, even if it meant he was a little stuck in his fun and free teenage years – Jack couldn't help tapping his toes along as he worked.

It was a dry evening but the silver-grey cloud was thickening, making it feel warm and sultry. As dusk began to fall, slowly the lights from the catering venues began to show up like festive fireflies; Ruby's big fat stage bulbs, along with the horsebox's trails of delicate white fairy lights, and Carrie's cakes had strings of pink and blue bulbs, even Bob had a lit-up burger sign on the top of his van roof! Enticing smells of burgers and baking, and warm cheesy-tomato pizzas, filled the air.

Jack glanced over to the horsebox. Pizza girl looked to be working flat out tonight, not having stopped as yet. Despite himself, Jack had taken a few quick looks in that direction in the past hour, seeing her stationed at her oven cooking post. Her cheeks were endearingly rosy, and every now and again she'd pop a strand of errant hair back in its work-mode bun and give a little flustered huff. A constant queue gathered at her homely-presented hatch with its Italian flags and twinkly lights. However cold she'd appeared towards him at the last event, there was something intriguing about her too. Maybe as things quietened down a bit, he might go across and have a quick chat with her, perhaps be a bit more welcoming, have a heart to heart from one business owner to another. Setting up your own venture was hard, but Jack had a fair bit of experience now, having built up his mobile bar business over the past four years. He knew the local catering scene – what events were worthwhile and which to avoid. Okay, so he and Pizza Girl hadn't got off to the best of starts, but if they were going to be at the same events they'd better learn to rub along.

As dusk began to fall, with smouldering peachy hues and sultry grey clouds darkening above, the music from the tipi began to beat louder, voices were raised, laughter rang out and along with the warm, slightly static evening air there was a sense of vibrancy, of charging electricity. Jack was busy mixing and shaking, chatting and charming. The guests were having a good time, though some perhaps a little *too* good; with the hosts happy to pay for everything at the bar tonight, a group of younger males were taking advantage and having their fill. Hmm, he'd have to keep a little eye on them. The rowdy group were now jostling around the makeshift dance-floor that was just inside the tipi, pretending to do *Riverdance* moves. In particular, one thick-set chap was getting carried away and knocking into a few of the couples already dancing. It looked very much like the lads were taking the piss out of the folk band. Jack shook his head, but was then soon distracted by the next bar order.

A tall chap in a smart navy suit leaned against Ruby's polished-chrome counter top. 'Hi, do you have a cold bottled lager? And a glass of prosecco or something for the girlfriend.'

'Of course, I've an Italian lager, or can I recommend something more local? The brewery at Wylam do a great lager-beer, perfect for a warm summer's evening.' Jack loved to support the local Northumberland breweries and distilleries.

'Ah, go on then, I'll give it a try.'

'And for your lovely lady, why not pump up your prosecco to a sparkling wine cocktail? Passion fruit, raspberry?' Jack gave a persuasive smile.

'Sounds the biz. Better go with a passion fruit, then.' Tall guy grinned.

About to prep the cocktail, Jack handed over a very welcome chilled beer to the chap.

'Thanks, mate. Great party. I'm Mark, by the way. It's my mum and dad's anniversary.'

'Jack, and good to meet you. I hope your parents are having a wonderful evening.'

'Yeah, they certainly are. They're the ones still dancing away in the tent. Twenty-five years on and still going strong.'

'Brilliant. Good for them.' He felt genuinely happy that some couples could make it that far.

Jack glanced across at the tipi, whilst reaching for the passion fruit syrup. The rowdy lads were still giving it large on the dancefloor. Jeez. Jack hoped to goodness things didn't get messy.

Prosecco poured, and a sprinkle of passion fruit seeds and a garnish of orange zest later, Jack handed over the cocktail creation. 'There you go, my passion fruit fizz. Hope the good lady enjoys it.'

'Wow, cheers, mate. Well, I think I'll definitely have earned brownie points for this one.' Mark headed off, grinning broadly, with his bottle and the fantastic flute glass to hand.

It had been pretty hectic, but Lucy was enjoying the buzz of the evening. They'd been on the go for three and a half hours and some of the toppings were beginning to run out, but she had plenty of pizza bases, cheese and sauce left. She and Tamsin were rubbing along better tonight, and getting used to how each other worked. A system evolved between them as Lucy stretched the dough, Tamsin spread the tomato sauce, and either or both of them topped, depending on how big the queue was.

It was lovely when the Anniversary Couple had wandered over earlier, hand in hand, to order themselves a pizza.

'Oh, now then, what flavour shall we have, Geoff?' Stood beneath a string of twinkling lights under the characterful horsebox's open hatch, his wife, Hannah, addressed him fondly, suddenly waxing nostalgic, 'Oh, do you remember that night, down on the quayside all those years ago, when you got down on one knee?'

'I do indeed, my love,' he answered wryly, yet with a smile that had served him well over all the years. 'I remember it well, as my knees were killing me and I was quaking inside.'

She batted his arm gently, before continuing. 'You must have known I'd say yes. I'd been hinting for long enough ...' Hannah gave a wistful smile. 'And then you took me for that Italian meal. And we shared ...'

'A ham and pineapple pizza,' they both chanted, grinning.

'I think I was on a budget at the time,' Geoff chuckled.

'Well, that's got to be it, then.'

'Ham and pineapple please, lass.'

Lucy smiled at their lovely memories, yet felt a twist of pain deep inside too, that her own love life had been such a bloody disaster. But that didn't mean she couldn't make sure this couple had the best party ever, and suddenly remembering the romantic lad from her last booking, she made the toppings into a heart shape for them.

Five minutes later, the couple were absolutely delighted when, after tending to it at the wood-fire oven, Lucy served the anniversary pizza to them.

'Oh, look Geoff. How special! Thank you so much, Lucy.'

Aw, and they'd even remembered her name, how sweet!

'What a fabulous evening. Everything has just been perfect, and it's so wonderful to see all our friends and family here enjoying themselves.' Hannah was joyful.

Lucy was thrilled to be a part of that occasion, and over the moon that her new business could make people so happy. 'I'm so pleased for you.'

'Enjoy the rest of your night, and your pizza!' Tamsin added. Lucy soon spotted them sharing slices of her pizza beside the tipi's 'dancefloor'. Still happy and smiling together after twenty-five years. She sighed, she supposed marriage must work for some people, but for her ... well, with asshole Liam's affair, it had felt like she'd had a lucky escape.

Not long after that, a group of lads came roaming across.

A slight sway to their gait telling of a few too many welcome martinis and beers.

'Spicy pepperoni for me,' one of them said with a slight slur, leaning heavily and rather sweatily against the counter.

Oh blimey, Lucy realised, it was that thick-set rugby-shirted lad and his mates from before. They'd been a bit leery with Tamsin, and she'd had to intervene and send them on their merry way. She'd then seen them getting a bit boisterous over on the dance area. 'And a ham and mushroom,' one of his mates added gruffly.

There was no 'please' from either of them.

'Sorry lads, I'm now down to either margherita or chicken with peppers,' Lucy stepped up to explain, having just used up the last of the ham.

'You're kidding me. What kind of a catering joint are you?'

'It's late,' Lucy kept her cool. 'You should have ordered earlier when we had all the other options available, including your pepperoni and ham and mushroom.' *Instead of leching over the staff,* she thought to herself.

Hearing raised voices, Jack looked up, on alert, across the way.

'Well, that's no bloody good ...' Rugby Shirt swayed a bit and then, leering at Lucy across the counter top, brushed a sweaty hand over her forearm, tightening his grip as he staggered a little.

'Whoa ... that's enough,' Lucy's voice was firm, yet calm. She didn't want to cause a scene here, but if he gripped any harder, she was afraid he might end up bruising her.

Chapter 6

Jack had seen enough. Those blokes were *so* out of line – it was the same idiots he'd seen mucking about on the dance-floor. Okay, so he and Pizza Girl hadn't exactly hit it off so far, but no-one should have to put up with that kind of loutish behaviour. He couldn't help but feel protective of her all of a sudden. Something flipped inside him. He dashed out from his campervan and marched over, shouting, 'That's enough lads. Step back. Leave the woman alone.'

The big one in the rugby shirt – the one who looked like a bull – didn't budge. He was about twice the width of Jack and a good few inches taller; quite some size indeed, as Jack himself was fairly tall at just over six foot.

'We're only after a couple of pizzas,' one of the group answered gruffly.

'And *a pizza* the action,' Rugby Shirt added, staring at Lucy lecherously as he gave an arrogant chuckle.

'I said that's enough,' Jack's tone was firm.

'It's alright, Jack. I can handle this,' Lucy interrupted.

The air crackled with tension.

Sometimes it was best not to inflame a situation, Lucy

knew that. She didn't want a row to upset the party that had been going so well. The lads were just a bit tipsy. They'd wander off soon enough, fill themselves with beer and pizza – if they gave her a chance to cook it – and no doubt would be scarpering off somewhere else within the next half-hour or so.

'Move away right now and leave the lady alone,' Jack warned.

Rugby Shirt didn't budge position, though he had let go of Lucy's arm.

His mates were laughing.

Jack stood his ground. He was boiling inside. How dare they spoil what had been such a great night? How dare they intimidate Lucy?

And then the punch flew.

Not Jack's, though his arm was twitching.

Bosh, the blow landed right on his brow-bone. Jack felt the crunch. It made him feel sick as he staggered back a step or two.

Lucy gasped.

Tamsin instinctively took a step back, then called out angrily, 'Hey you, dickhead, stop!'

Lucy leapt down out of the horsebox, ready to intervene if need be.

Jack's own fist was balled. He nearly, *nearly*, punched back – but he was working, he reminded himself, he had his business and its reputation to keep. The last thing he needed was to be found fighting with the guests. But the bloody tree trunk of a twat was standing opposite him, now shaking his hopefully sore hand. Jack hoped the ignorant tosspot had broken a few bones in there, at least. Time stood still for a moment, the two men breathing heavily and staring each other down. Then, Jack had to let him walk away.

'Alright, sod off you lot, you're not worth it! And *this* guy,' he snarled, pointing to Rugby Shirt lad, 'get him home. *Now.*'

Jack stood there breathing heavily, his nose throbbing, his fist still itching, and him undecided about whether his pride had been badly wounded or saved.

'Gosh, are you alright?'

Lucy took a step forward, her face creased with concern, to find Jack stumbling a little. She had heard the thwack as that idiot's knuckles had hit the barman's brow-bone. Ooh, there was a split now showing, pooling with blood, above the lad's left eye.

'Here, sit down.'

There was a table and two chairs set out by her pizza stand, and she ushered Jack onto a seat. A small crowd had gathered to see the action.

'Okay folks,' Lucy called out, 'the show's over, you can get back to your partying again. Help yourself to pizza, but you might just have to wait a little while for a cocktail. I think the bar guy needs a short break.'

Lucy hated the way the one-way fight had suddenly become a spectator sport. She abhorred any kind of violence or aggression. She also hoped the Anniversary Couple wouldn't get alerted to the trouble. The guests thankfully began to disperse, amidst a murmur of chatter.

'Hold fire,' she turned to Jack. 'Just stay right there, I've a First Aid kit in the truck.'

She returned a minute later, kneeling beside Jack as she opened up her box of bandages, plasters and more. She found some antiseptic wipes, and dabbed at the wound.

'Ouch.'

'Sorry, best to clean it up first.' It looked sore. 'Hah, who'd have thought that running out of ham and mushrooms could lead to a black eye,' she said with a small laugh, trying to take the guy's mind off it.

'Huh, glad you can see the funny side,' Jack remarked, wincing as he quirked his painful eyebrow. 'The bloody tosspot,' he continued, still worked up about the drunken idiot.

'Yeah, he was a bit of a dickhead. But I am quite capable of looking after myself, you know,' she added snippily. 'I don't need saving, I'd have handled it fine ... probably better than you did, in fact.' Her tone was sharp, but then she gave him a wry smile.

'Yeah, well ...' Jack sighed.

Jeez, the Ice Queen wasn't even grateful for his valiant efforts! And she could be a bit bloody lighter with her touch. She was whacking on some kind of dressing now.

'Can you keep still a moment?' her tone was impatient, and she was shaking her head at him.

Jack suddenly realised just how close Lucy was. And, damn, she did smell rather good, an intoxicating mix of fresh-baked pizza and perfume. Perhaps it was just the blow to his head making her seem alluring.

'Thanks, I'll be fine now. Cheers, Lucy.' He went to stand up, still feeling slightly giddy. At least he was bandaged up and wouldn't be dripping blood into the cocktails. He brushed himself down, thanked Lucy once more, and headed back – still feeling slightly wounded – over to his campervan bar, where a few partygoers were loitering, ready for another drink.

'Bloody Mary anyone?' he blurted out comically.

The group waiting at his bar couldn't help but laugh.

Across the way, the pizza oven was cooling down whilst Lucy and Tamsin cleared the decks. Lucy's feet, even in trainers, were throbbing. It was her fifth pizza gig, and probably the hardest so far, she hadn't quite realised what the effects of standing on your feet for five hours solid would be. She was glad she'd left Daisy with her mum this evening. It had been a long and rather dramatic night.

She glanced over at Jack the cocktail guy, still bemused as to why he had stepped in all gung-ho like that. At least he seemed to be okay; he was working away again, serving some of the dwindling guests with a couple of beers. They caught each other's eye, just for a second, and she couldn't help but give a brief smile – daft idiot that he was, bet his head would be sore in the morning.

'Are we nearly done here?' Tamsin asked, sounding shattered and slightly grumpy.

'Yeah, no worries. I'll get you back now. You did a good job tonight, thank you. Even amidst all the drama.'

'Those stupid lads ...'

Lucy wasn't quite sure if her assistant was including Jack

in that too. 'Yeah, what a bunch of schoolboys, eh?' she added.

'Arseholes,' Tamsin cut to the chase.

Lucy had to give a wry grin. 'Right, let's get out of here and get home.'

Jack was still riled up about those bloody idiots as he was driving home, grumbling out loud to Ruby. It was very rare for something like that to happen; since he'd owned the Cocktail Campervan, he could count on one hand any drunken issues they'd encountered, and none of them had ended in violence. Most of the events were great, with the guests just out to celebrate and enjoy themselves. In fact, he'd never been punched whilst working at a bar *anywhere*. And he'd done bar shifts in all kinds of places around the world, having taken on casual work to fund his travels. That was when he'd fallen in love with the bar-side banter, making friends, the mixology – picking up tips and cocktail recipes along the way. It was just the best feeling to serve the perfect cocktail, with a sea view and a smile; whether it was Barbados or Beadnell.

He still wasn't sure why he'd gone and got himself involved this evening; he usually steered clear of all that loutish behaviour. It was the girl, Ice Queen Lucy, there was just something about her. It had got to him, and he wasn't quite sure why. Why had he felt so protective of her? She hadn't exactly seemed too impressed with him trying to help. This girl was definitely a bit of a cool cucumber. If she were a cocktail it would have to be a Frozen Margarita, all crushed ice, tequila and sharp lime.

He gave a groan, and pulled over briefly to turn on some music on his phone, something easy listening. Anything would do. He just needed to get his sore head into a better place.

Fifteen minutes later, he was pulling Ruby up on the driveway. All the lights were out in the small semi-detached house he currently called home; his mate Matt, who he lodged with, no doubt having gone off to bed hours ago. Jack crept in, not putting on any of the downstairs lights, trying hard not to disturb his pal.

Time for bed, time to sleep, if his throbbing head would allow that.

Time to put a certain Pizza Girl out of his mind.

Chapter 7

'Morning!' Matt called, strolling in through the kitchen door in his sweat-stained running gear. Tall, broad, with shaggy mid-brown hair, he had recently qualified as a vet. Matt gulped down a glass of water, and then popped two slices of brown into the toaster. He turned to face Jack and then frowned, taking in the bruising.

'Good night, was it?' he asked ironically, and waited for his friend to answer. 'A bit of a shiner you've got there, mate.'

Jack's brow was throbbing even more than last night; perhaps he ought to take a couple of ibuprofens. He managed a slow, sore nod.

'I thought you were meant to be *serving* the guests, not fighting with them.'

'Yeah, well ...'

'Toast?' Matt gave a smile, offering toast as a gesture of goodwill, guessing the time for quizzing his pal was perhaps not right now.

'Cheers, yeah, chuck me in a slice ...' Jack sipped some of his coffee. 'Umm, well I was just stepping in to help a friend ...' The word slipped out. She was hardly a *friend* really; they'd only recently met. But somehow, even though they hadn't quite hit it off, he still felt some kind of warmth towards her. *Hit it off*, hah, even sore-headed as he was, he had to give a wry smile at that.

Lucy, he'd been thinking about her again this morning. Okay, and in the middle of the night, in fact. Her thoughtful dark-brown eyes. That long sweep of glossy chestnut hair. At the end of the evening, once she'd packed everything up – oh yes, the image had stuck in his mind – she'd pulled at that bun thing her hair was twirled up in, and let it all tumble down. And she'd come across, just before leaving. 'Night, Jack. You feeling okay now?' she'd asked, cautiously.

'Yeah,' he'd managed to answer, suddenly feeling awkward. 'Yeah fine, thanks for helping out, uh, and see you around.'

'Well, watch that eyebrow. And no more getting into any scrapes, hey.' She'd shaken her head gently as she smiled.

She looked so much prettier when she smiled. Yet, he'd suddenly felt very much like a schoolboy who'd been told off.

'Hah, no. Scout's honour.' *Why on earth had he come out with that?* He hadn't even been a boy scout. That was his brother's domain. Jack'd been too busy playing rugby and flirting with girls as a youth. Jack had stood, watching her open her truck door. 'So ... umm, when's your next booking?' he'd blurted out.

But she was already sat in her vehicle, slamming the door to a close, with the younger girl sat beside her; she hadn't heard. Laughter rang out from a group stood nearby, along with the rhythmic beat of dance music. The folk band had left a while back and a makeshift disco had been set up. The last few guests and family members still lingered.

Slowly, the pizza horsebox trundled off into the night.

And, he hadn't even thought to ask Lucy for her phone number or anything. Blimey, he must be losing his touch. That blow to his head had a lot to answer for.

'Alright, mate?' Matt was stood there, passing him a plate of buttered toast, bringing him back to the here and now.

'Ah, yeah, sorry. Thanks.' Jack took the toast, suddenly realising how hungry he was as he bit into a warm, buttery slice. This morning's stream of thoughts, and the flashbacks to last night had left him feeling perturbed. 'Good run?'

'Yep, the usual 10K. Done and dusted now.'

'What've you got on today then?'

'Catching up with Jess for a few hours later.' Jess was Matt's steady girlfriend of a year now. She was a nice enough girl, but blimey, at times they were like an old married couple. Netflix nights in with a glass of wine, and slippers on. Jack often felt like the spare wheel in the house at those times, and made himself scarce by heading up to his room or taking a drive out in Ruby, off along the coast or up in the hills. 'Bit of five-a-side footie this aft too,' Matt continued.

'And you? Any plans?' Matt sat down opposite him, with a stack of thickly spread Marmite toast. That guy could eat for England.

'Nothing particularly exciting. Said I'd visit the parents this morning.'

The day loomed. He had felt a bit adrift of late. Couldn't put his finger on it. The business was going pretty well. He had some good mates, but he didn't feel he was at the same point as them. Several were in long-term relationships, settling down, getting married, and that really wasn't in Jack's line of sight right now. He was turning thirty next year, still young, and no way did he want to feel tied down. Right now, the Cocktail Campervan was his main focus, but he had to admit, there were only so many hours you could buff Ruby's red paint. Yeah, he'd give her a good tidy up and a polish after last night's shift, get all those glasses put through the dishwasher; he liked to know she was back in good order. Then, this afternoon, he might think of setting off on a hike, or doing a run himself.

Jack finished his toast and drained the dregs of his much-needed coffee, feeling slightly better. Yep, he'd better get a shower, get dressed, and make his way to his parents' house. The house that still felt far too empty.

Chapter 8

An hour later, Ruby pulled to a halt on the block-paved driveway of a red-brick, semi-detached house in the market town of Alnwick. Stepping out from the driving seat, Jack left on his Ray-Ban sunglasses. Well, it was a bright morning, after all.

'Hey, Mum, Dad.' He knocked, calling out, as he entered the front door. It felt natural to stroll in, as it had been his home too until four years ago; it was where he had grown up.

'Oh hello, Jack, darling.' His trim fifty-something mum, Denise, greeted him in the hallway with a warm smile and a hug.

'Hello, son.' Dad, Simon, gave him a firm yet friendly pat on the back, before finishing with a half-hug. His father's salt-and-pepper hair was greying rapidly, with ... Jack suddenly noticed, weird little tufts starting to sprout from his ears and nostrils. Blimey, he'd have to get him one of those trimmer things as a birthday gift, he mused. Middle age was creeping up on them both with stealth. Though Mum's bobbed hair, once the same sandy-blonde shade as Jack's, was now high-lighted to a paler blonde (her regular hairdresser visits keeping any signs of grey at bay), the lines on her face were beginning to show. She looked tired, bless her.

Jack was still wearing his sunglasses. It would look odd keeping them on in the house, he realised. Time to bite the bullet and take them off.

'I'll put the kettle on, shall I?' Denise called cheerily as she headed off down the hall.

'Yeah, that'd be good. Thanks, Mum.'

Tea was very much a key ceremony in the Anderson household. Jack followed his parents into the kitchen, which had been the family's hub since they'd moved in when he was a little boy. It was like the beating heart of the house and had witnessed good times and bad, laughter and tears.

His mum began to fill the kettle at the sink. 'So, how did last night g—?' Her mouth dropped open as she half-turned, taking in the purple-green of her son's bruised and cut eyebrow, the water suddenly leaking out over the top of the kettle's rim. 'Good lord. Oh … Jack.' Her voice was concerned and also tainted with disappointment. 'What on earth has happened to you? I thought you'd put those troublesome days behind you?'

Simon looked up then too, his eyes widening. 'I thought you were working last night, son? What the hell's gone on?'

Jack raised his eyebrows at their tone. *Ah*, even that gesture was uncomfortable. Honestly, they were confronting him as though he was fifteen, not a grown man. Yes, he'd had a couple of troubled years, but he'd been angry and hurt back then, feeling at odds with the world. He'd changed a lot since then. He'd grown up.

'I was,' Jack countered calmly. 'Something blew up out of nothing.'

'Like it always did ... Oh, Jack,' Denise's tone was downcast; like he'd let them down again.

'But fighting? Really son? You're almost thirty now.' Dad shook his head.

'I wasn't fighting. I was trying to defuse the situation, if you must know. And then, I just happened to be in the wrong place when the punch flew.'

'Hmm, okay. Well, are you alright?' Mum's tone softened, realising she'd been quick to assume that he'd drifted back to his old ways. But he'd had such a troubled time a few years back. Coming home late. Getting into scrapes. And she still remembered that dreadful occasion when a policeman – who also happened to be a family friend – had turned up at their door, letting them know that Jack had been cautioned after being found fighting in the street. It hadn't been taken any further, thankfully, but goodness, they had been so worried.

'Bit sore, but yeah, I'll survive,' Jack answered, feeling that familiar sense of falling short in their eyes.

Denise poured boiling water into the teapot. 'I do worry about this new business of yours, at times, Jack.'

New? He'd been running his Cocktail Campervan for four years now.

'The sort of people you'll be mixing with ... drinking and all that,' she continued.

'Mum ... it's a *bar*,' Jack was trying to keep the frustration out of his voice. 'I'm bound to be mixing with people who drink, that's the whole idea.'

'Exactly.' His mum clearly wasn't going to be won over with sarcasm.

'Look, most of the people I deal with are just having a nice time. I'm there to provide a unique and fun bar service for parties and celebrations. Last night there were plenty of older family members there, even good old Grandma. It was a Silver Wedding party, not some rave. A family anniversary celebration, not some drunken mob event.'

'Yes, but you can always get that element. Why else were you getting punched in the face?' Dad joined in now.

Why indeed? He didn't have an answer to that one, unfortunately.

Jack still felt their disappointment, like a cloud hanging over him. He hadn't taken their preferred route: the four years he was supposed to have knuckled down at uni, taking a law degree before landing that sensible, well-paid job. He'd only managed a year before dropping out to see the world, taking some time out, and landing some bar work abroad. Eighteen months later, coming back home to work as a waiter, soon working his way up to manager, at a busy bar and bistro in the town. Then, of course, he'd branched out on his own, buying and converting Ruby, and starting the Cocktail Campervan.

'I like my job, Mum. It's a good little business.' The campervan bar gave him freedom and flexibility. He was working for himself, he enjoyed it. Every penny he earned was his, and he was doing pretty damned well. He'd managed to save a tidy sum. Okay, so it had its issues, of course. No business was problem- or stress-free. But he worked through all of those issues as they came up – they were challenges, that was all. He could choose his events and working days; giving him time to go and do the things he loved – cycling, running, hiking. He loved the outdoors life. And this was an outdoors job. How many of his mates could work just three or four days a week, make enough money to comfortably get by plus save a bit, *and* get to enjoy all that free time too?

'It just doesn't seem the kind of job to settle down with, though.' Denise's brow was still creased as she passed him a mug of steaming tea.

Here we go. Mum was still hoping he'd find the perfect partner, settle down, and have the 2.4 children or whatever the going rate was nowadays. There'd be time for all that ... at some point ... some distant point.

'I like it. It's doing well, and I'm making decent money.'

'Well, that's good.' Dad, at least, was now shifting towards some positive support.

Simon generally preferred to sit in the middle ground on the home front. He focussed his energy on his role as deputy headteacher at the local secondary school; that took up enough of his attention, he didn't need to start arguing on the domestic front too. Most of the time, he was easy-going and genial. Well, until the stuffing had been knocked out of him eleven years ago ... out of them all. That was the only time Jack had ever seen his father cry.

Life could be cut short; they had learned that the hard way. It shouldn't be spent wasting away in some 'sensible' job, not if you hated the thought of getting up to do it every day. Jack was sure about that. The lawyer thing, it had always been *their* dream for him, not his. He had realised that as soon as he'd started the course, but he'd tried to stick with it, at first.

It was Daniel who was the clever one. Daniel who loved studying, and was all set to become the medic. As young boys, they had always been very different, although Jack had always looked up to him. Jack was more entrepreneurial; selling sweets and cans of fizzy drink from his school bag at break times, boosting his pocket money each week. Daniel was the studious one. It was always going to be hard trying to walk in his shoes; they had always seemed just that little bit too big.

Daniel, his big brother, who he still missed like crazy.

Who had left a huge Daniel-shaped hole in all of their lives.

The conversation rolled on to other things. The three of them took their tea with squares of homemade flapjack outside into the garden; a space that Denise tended so well. Borders of purple irises stood tall in a swathe by the pond, red and yellow tulips bunched boldly beneath neatly-pruned shrubs, and there was a scattering of delicate pastel-shaded aquilegia. The grass was kept short and cut into orderly stripes by Simon.

The garden was one area of their lives that Denise and Simon felt they could control. Though neat, it was abundant and colourful, and spoke of a warmth and love that they hadn't totally lost, in spite of everything, thankfully. It was a place of solace.

Sat at the wrought-iron table with his parents, Jack soaked up the late-morning sunshine for a while. He wished they could understand his career choices; how the campervan was a way of life as well as a job, how it suited him. But they were old school, traditional, set in their views and expectations. He did love them, of course, but there was always this nagging feeling that he'd let them down somehow.

Jack rubbed his eyes and winced at the throbbing pain from the punch. After last night, getting in the thick of the drama once again, maybe he had ...

Chapter 9

A copy of Jane Austen's *Pride and Prejudice* was tucked under Lucy's arm as she headed into the balmy summer evening. She hadn't read the book since her school days, when she'd found it a bit dry, to be honest, her teenage self wondering what the fuss was all about. But now, aged thirty, and three quarters of the way through, she was seeing it in a whole new light. The characters seemed to jump off the page this time; both Mr Darcy and Lizzie, for their faults, and their fun. It had made Lucy smile on many occasions as she read through the pages this week, perched on a chair in her back garden whilst catching a few rays of sunshine, or curled on the sofa of an evening with Daisy tucked beside her.

She was making her way past the little row of stone cottages, on her way to her first Book Club evening at the Driftwood Café. How lovely that she'd been invited to join in; she was feeling very much a part of this little coastal community now, and was looking forward to making some more new friends. She was delighted to be asked, thinking that it might make her pick up books that she'd not have otherwise chosen, with the chance to rediscover authors too. Becky, who'd also been invited, had texted to say she was going to be a few minutes late with work commitments running over, but would meet her there.

Peering through the café window, Lucy could see a small group had already gathered around one of the large circular tables. As Lucy stepped inside the door, with its bell giving a welcome tinkle, she couldn't help but spot the freshly baked goodies set in a mouth-watering display at the centre of the table. Louise was busy behind the counter brewing a large pot of coffee and another of tea. Books and cakes together, bliss.

'Hello,' Lucy called out, slightly nervously. She was sure they'd all be friendly in the Book Club, but it was always a little nerve-wracking being the new one on the scene.

'Oh, hi,' Louise gave a warm smile as she saw who it was. 'Everyone, have you met Lucy, our new village resident? She lives at Cove Cottage just along the road.'

A chorus of 'Hi's and 'Hello's rang out, with Cathy from the village shop following up with, 'Hello, Lucy. We have met before, of course. Welcome to Book Club ... or should I say Cake Club.' She gave a wink and a small chuckle. 'Louise always looks after us *very* well.'

'*Too* well, my waistband is always groaning after Book Club,' chirped a lady, who looked to be in her sixties, with a broad grin.

'No-one's forcing you to eat them, Glynis!' Louise called out.

'I know. But just look at them, how could anyone resist?'

Lucy smiled too, 'Hi, everyone. Thank you so much for inviting me along. I love reading, can't get enough of it really, so I'm really looking forward to this.'

'So,' Louise said, as she approached the table bearing a large tray with a colourful assortment of mugs, a cafetière and a navy polka-dot teapot, 'this is Glynis. She lives in the nearby hamlet of Dunstan. You know Cathy, of course, from the shop, and Abby, I take it, who helps out as our lovely waitress here?'

'Yes. Hi. Yeah, we know each other.'

'Good, good. And then these two trouble-makers are Sarah and Helen.' The pair of forty-somethings, one blonde and one dark, gave a welcoming smile. Lucy had seen them around the village and on the beach, often walking together with their dogs.

'Hi, there. And don't listen to a word she says, there's no trouble about us at all. And well … if there is, then Louise has taught us everything we know.' They were obviously all good friends.

'Ah yes, we've said hello before, when I've been out with Daisy, my dachshund, but I didn't know your names,' Lucy confessed.

'Yes, of course. The sausage-dog lady. I knew I recognised your face. Lovely to see you here,' answered blonde Sarah.

'Oh, and sometimes we have Paul along too, lovely chap, but he's off to some folk concert tonight. Well then, my lovely, take a seat, don't be shy,' encouraged Louise. 'Oh, and don't worry, no-one's too – how can I put it? – *academic* about the Book Club. It's more of a chit-chat about how you feel about a book. What you got – or didn't get – from it, that kind of thing.'

'Yeah, the book chat normally lasts about a half-hour and then we have a good old chin-wag, to be honest,' said Cathy. 'Something in the book usually starts up a topic of conversation and well ... off we roll.'

'And we read all sorts. From the classics to crime to Jilly Cooper,' added Helen.

'Sounds great.'

'But first ...' Louise started.

'And most importantly ...' Cathy added with a broad grin.

'Cake!' the others shouted out.

'Pass them around ladies, and do help yourselves.'

At that very moment the bell jingled above the door, announcing Becky's arrival.

'Good timing,' laughed Lucy. 'We were just about to get stuck into the cake. Everybody, this is my friend, Becky.'

'Hi all! Thanks for having me here, especially as I'm not strictly a villager,' Becky said with a wink.

'Oh, everyone's welcome. It's always nice to see some new faces.' Louise was evidently as generous with her friendship as she was with her cakes. And the introductions were made around the table once more for Becky's benefit, as the tea and coffee were poured.

Little tea plates were set out ready by each seat, and Becky and Lucy took up the last two chairs. The plate of baked goodies was passed around. Which to choose? The fluffy-looking cream sponge, marshmallow-loaded Rocky Roads, or some kind of rich-gooey brownie. Lucy's eyes lit up and her tummy rumbled, even though she'd just had a supper of scrambled eggs on toast.

Outside, it would soon begin to cool, with the sun now dipping in the sky, but the café was cosy, and it wasn't just the radiators at work, there was such a homely feel there too. Where Lucy had previously lived with Liam – a large housing estate on the edge of Morpeth – well, it was a little soulless, with everyone busy to-ing and fro-ing to work, getting on with their daily lives. She and Liam had slotted into that same suburban lifestyle, existing in their bubble of two. But it was only lately she'd realised how empty that had been.

Here, in this little coastal village other forces were at work; people seemed to have a little more time for each other, to care about each other, in fact. It felt good. It felt like she was becoming a part of the community.

Between mouthfuls of delicious Victoria sponge and chocolate traybakes, they chatted about this month's read, *Pride and Prejudice*.

'Oh, I loved it,' Glynis started, 'Jane Austen has been a favourite of mine for many years now. Her books feel like old friends. Her characterisation is amazing ... and all the twists and turns between Darcy and Elizabeth, it's just delightfully written.'

'It's not my usual read,' added Abby, 'and it took me ages to get into the language of the book ... it's a bit old-fashioned and wordy, but yeah, I quite enjoyed it. The romance between Darcy and Elizabeth, that slow build, all the apprehension and misunderstandings ... yep, in the end, I quite liked it.'

Helen, the dark-haired forty-something, snuffled. 'I'm not

sure I'm with you two on that. All that pent-up romance, and for what? Elizabeth, she should have bloody well run while she could. Trusted her first instincts about the Darcy bloke. Bloody romance books. All happy-ever-afters. Well, it doesn't always end up that way.'

'Yes, but oh, I do like a good romance and a happy ending,' Louise chipped in. 'Heaven knows we need it. Real life's hard enough at times. Surely books can be a bit of an escape.'

'Yeah, but we don't need to have it rubbed in our faces about Mr Bloody Right. It just sets us up for a fall.' Helen grimaced, then took a sip of tea.

There were nods of empathy from around the room.

'Hmm, I can see both sides,' Lucy contributed, without going anywhere near mentioning her own failed and messy relationship. 'I know life's not like that, but I actually don't mind a little romance in a book. I can just switch off for a while, and pretend that life, that love, can work out.'

Becky gave a supportive smile, knowing exactly where her friend was coming from. 'There's no harm in that, is there. Books can be all sorts of things: an escape, uplifting, challenging, downright scary ...'

'Hmm, a little hope can't be a bad thing,' Glynis added thoughtfully.

Oh yes, and didn't Lucy know that. Real life wasn't quite like her favourite romantic reads, but she loved her escape-time curled up with them. And the books she chose, they weren't all soppy and rose-tinted. No, they were relationship stories, looking at love and life and that rollercoaster we are all on, but she had to admit she liked the stories that held a little hope too. You should never give up on that little ray of hope.

'And a good sex scene,' added Cathy with a cheeky grin. 'Not that you'd find much of that in a Jane Austen novel.'

'No, it's all pent-up and prim and proper,' Abby chipped in.

'But you do get where she's coming from with that. Remember when this book was written, it was of its time. Though also *timeless* in some ways. Yes, there's so much unspoken, unsaid, but you can also read it all between the lines. That was her genius.' Glynis was a staunch supporter.

'Hah, well, I'd much rather a crime book at the moment,' Helen added wryly. 'Preferably one where the husband ends up under the patio.' She gave a grin, as the group burst into laughter.

'Hah, don't mind Helen, it's no secret that she's going through a messy divorce.' Louise gave the two newbies the nod, as Helen rolled her eyes dramatically.

'Oh, I'm sorry to hear that Helen, that must be tough,' Lucy responded kindly.

'Ah, no worries, I'm surviving, and better he left when he did than end up under the patio!' she added with a chuckle.

And the conversation turned to their lives and relationships, their families, the latest episode of the police TV series *Line of Duty*, and this week's Driftwood bakes to look forward to, including a summery Lemon and Strawberry Fresh Cream Sponge.

All too soon, it was time to go home. It had been wonderful, chatting about books and life, meeting some of the locals, and making new friends. Lucy was definitely intending coming back again. The group set off home with full tummies, warmed hearts, and the next Book Club read agreed: *One Day* by David Nicholls. They were to stick with a little romance for now.

'Well, that was a good evening, wasn't it?' chirped Lucy on her way back down the street with Becky at her side.

'Yeah, they seem a really nice group. A good mix.'

'Yeah, and the cakes, wow ...'

'Worth going along just for that!' Becky grinned.

'Hah, I know. Isn't Louise lovely, too.'

'Yep, really warm and friendly. Village life is really working for you, isn't it, Luce?'

'Yeah, it is.' Lucy gave a happy sigh.

'No sign of any hunky single men around?' Becky raised an eyebrow.

'Hah, no, 'fraid not. Most of the blokes I've seen who live here are at least over sixty. But that's fine by me, I've had enough of all that. I'll stick to Mr Darcy and my books, thank you very much.'

Weirdly, the campervan guy, Jack, popped into her head right then. He was nothing like Mr Darcy, except maybe full of pride, and arrogant as a peacock.

They were now approaching Lucy's cottage, where Becky had left her car.

'Want to pop in for a quick cuppa or a cheeky glass of wine before you go?'

'Yeah. Go on then. Just a small one, mind. Work day tomorrow.'

'Of course.'

After such a nice evening, Lucy hadn't wanted it quite to end. Though her cottage was lovely, it was just her and Daisy, after all. And some nights could seem rather long.

Daisy was delighted to see the pair of them. The little dog was soon out of her crate, barking happily and wagging her tail at their ankles.

Sat down a few minutes later, in the cosy front room, with a glass of chilled white to hand, Becky asked how the pizza venture was going.

'Yeah, it's coming along slowly but surely. I'm finding my feet. One booking at a time.'

'So, are there other catering outlets at these bookings? Is there, like, a catering scene?'

'Hah, yeah, a bit.' Should she say something about the cocktail guy, and that weird fight starting up out of nowhere? Or would Becky just read more into it? 'A few local businesses seem to turn up quite consistently. There's a coffee place, a posh burger van, and ... there's this cocktail bar in a cute VW campervan.'

'Sounds our kind of thing. Cocktails and a campervan.'

'Yeah. And the guy there, well, we've chatted a little.'

Her friend's eyebrows arched with interest. 'And?'

'What? No, nothing like that. He's a right cocky thing, really. Anyway, at the last event, he waded right in when a few blokes had had a few too many pints and only ended up getting himself punched. Right in the face.' Lucy didn't add that it was over an incident at *her* pizzeria.

'Ouch.'

'Yeah. Trying to be the big guy, I think. Although I suppose I felt a bit sorry for him. He was left with a proper shiner.'

'Crikey.'

'That's just a one-off though. It's the only trouble I've seen at all. Most of the bookings and the guests have been lovely.'

'Well, that's good. Didn't think serving pizzas was a dangerous occupation.'

'Hah no, me neither. I just hope I can build the business soon, and make this all work out.' Lucy could feel her old fears resurfacing, blurring into the joy of the evening.

'Have faith my friend, have faith. Onwards and upwards.'

'Yes.' *With a few bumps along the way,* Lucy conceded.

And with that they clinked glasses.

Chapter 10

Jack had spent the whole morning disinfecting, scrubbing, buffing; getting Ruby ship-shape for their next event. He liked to know that his campervan companion was clean to the point of sparkling. And now he found himself with the afternoon free. The coast was calling.

He decided to take a jog along the dunes and the cliff path between Beadnell and Craster. A gorgeously scenic stretch of six miles each way. A twelve-mile run didn't faze him; he'd done half marathons, including the Great North Run, many a time, raising money in memory of his brother. Running came easily to him; that sense of pace and freedom.

Dressed in shorts and a sports T, with his favourite (to the point of being worn down) running shoes on, he set off from the beach-side car park at a steady jog. The view as he hit the bay was stunning: a panorama of sea, sky and sand, in a palette of blues, greys, and golds. There were dog walkers aplenty, and young children toddling down to the shoreline to find shells, filling their colourful castle-shaped buckets with salty water and seaside treasures, their parents close behind. He didn't mind kids, they were fine, he just never imagined having one of his own ... not for a long time yet.

Fresh air pumped through his body. He felt energised and his limbs felt strong as he strode out over the sands. Onwards, rhythmic, along the two-mile beach then up the dune bank, over a wooden footbridge, and up and along the short grassy banks of a low cliff. A further sweeping bay and then the ruins of Dunstanburgh Castle rose on the skyline ahead, ragged where they had crumbled and tumbled over time, yet still managing to appear grand. What battles and stories had those ruins to tell? Jogging on with the sea crashing softly against low rocks now, the village of Craster came into sight.

Jack stopped for a harbourside coffee at the small village, with its cluster of stone cottages. Felt the sun warm on his salt-sweaty skin, enjoyed the rich earthy taste of the coffee, the kick of caffeine. He soon set back off, away from the tourists who were gathered like noisy herring gulls at the little port. The sun was warm, the breeze gentle. In less than two hours he was back at the start, guzzling a much-needed bottle of water. Shower facilities were non-existent in Ruby's converted interior, so a dip in the sea was the next best thing. He tore off his sweaty T-shirt, and jogged back down to the shore, dashing in. The rush of the salt water welcomingly cool and refreshing, invigorating. The North Sea always being on the chilly side. He swam out confidently, enjoying a spell rolled on his back, bobbing over the swell of the deeper waters, watching the beach and its dwellers who looked small and cartoon-like from a distance.

The wind was warm and dried most of the salty water off

of his skin as he walked back up the bay. He finished off by towel drying back at his campervan. Jack felt a pang of hunger then, and grabbed a tasty bacon sandwich and a Diet Coke from the Beach Shack kiosk at the car park. Beadnell was busy today, a Friday in late May; it was a popular spot with tourists and locals alike. So, Jack thought he'd head on to somewhere quieter for the evening.

There were several spots he knew of, at the end of no-through-road seaside lanes, where you could park up, walk the dunes, find an isolated spot and do a bit of unofficial wild camping. His two-man tent (he'd only ever used it for one), his camping stove, a snack and a couple of beers were all he needed at those times. Where all you had to do was take in the peaceful wash of amazing colours in a fading sea and sky – pale blues, infused with pinks, orange, gold and greys, that deepened by the second. Matt was used to Jack and Ruby disappearing for a day or two, so his housemate wouldn't be concerned if he didn't come home tonight.

He took to the road, heading north along the coast, to a hidden stretch of shoreline, well away from the main tourist spots. Sun, sand, sea and ... solitude.

Afternoon rolled into evening and Jack enjoyed a simple supper of Frankfurter sausages from a can – warmed on the little gas stove he kept handy in Ruby – served in soft bread rolls with some fried onions and ketchup. Nothing gourmet but damned tasty, followed by a couple of apples for good measure. He didn't like to exist merely on junk food. He sat on an old tartan rug with his back against a large driftwood log, and opened his second can of beer which gave a fizzy hiss. Real ale, thirst-quenching, still cold from his cool bag – bliss.

The sea was a gentle swell this evening, rolling in with a low, reassuring rumble. The sky now softening to a dusky deep navy. A couple of stars glowed way up high, intriguingly. What was out there? He thought of Daniel. Was he all gone? Jack wasn't religious, he thought that that was that, a life extinguished ... and yet, now and again, there was a sense of his brother's spirit. Maybe it was just *within him*, his memories, his love for his brother, that made him feel that way.

His mind drifted. Daniel had had a serious girlfriend for a couple of years at uni: Emily. Jack had met her back at home in Alnwick on a couple of occasions. Dan had been proud to introduce her to his folks, who of course made her feel very welcome. They'd all thought that an engagement might have been on the cards.

Afterwards, she and Jack had kept in touch for a while – united by grief – just the odd message, but even that had drifted these latter years. It all just seemed too hard, too pointless. Jack wondered now if she was with someone else. Of course, she would be by now, it was over eleven years ago. Did she find someone new, get married? Did they have kids? It was weird, seemed so unfair, to think that someone else was now living his brother's life.

He needed an outlet for these intense emotions.

Under a sky full of stars, and by the light of his iPhone, Jack took up a pen and began to write.

Chapter 11

Lucy was delighted to hear she'd managed to secure a weekly position for All Fired Up at the Alnwick market. The market was held every Thursday on the quaint cobbled square of this historic Northumbrian town, with its old stone buildings and local shops, not far from its imposing castle and the famous and rather magical Alnwick Gardens. Lucy had been nervous when pitching for this slot, trying to be her most charming when talking to the organiser on the telephone, and making sure to tell him all about the fresh local ingredients she sourced for her toppings. A regular slot was a good step forward in building her business!

The first event quickly swung around and Lucy was there bright and early and all set up, ready for the market's eight-thirty start. The clock tower of the town hall showed that it wasn't yet nine, and already it was brilliant how many customers had called by for a slice of 'breakfast' pizza! A bit of a brainwave she'd had when she realised the market would start so early. Her crispy bacon, Northumbrian sausage and mushroom pizzas were going down a storm – the word, as well as the aroma, soon spreading around the stallholders who seemed to be the first in line.

She'd even had the forethought to bring a kettle, milk and some eco-friendly takeaway cups to make good-quality instant coffee and tea to serve alongside her food – ever the entrepreneur. Lucy really hoped this event would become the bread and butter of her new business venture.

'Have you got a wedge of that there breakfast pizza, lass?' A burly-looking, grey-bearded chap in a red lumberjack shirt and jeans, approached with a warm smile. 'Never tried anything like it before, but Alf on the veg stall says it went down a treat, so I'll give it a go.'

'Of course. And can I get you anything to go with it? I'm doing coffees and teas too.'

'Aye, go on then, I'll have a coffee – white, two sugars. Mind, don't let Maggie see what you're up to – she's the hot-drinks van – you don't want to be putting her nose out of joint.'

'Oh, I hadn't meant to tread on anybody's toes ...' Lucy floundered. Crikey, market politics were creeping in already, and she'd only been open for an hour. She hadn't even considered that might come into play.

'Hey, only teasing, kiddo.'

Kiddo? She was over thirty.

'Look, each to their own,' he continued with a wink. 'She does all that fancy bore-ista stuff. I'm not really into all that.' He chuckled. 'I'm sure she'll have plenty of customers still wanting her fancy-pants stuff.'

'Well, I hope so.' Lucy began to feel uneasy. She didn't want to be upsetting anybody so early on in her new pitch.

'Ah, it'll be fine. I shouldn't have said nowt. I'm Derek, by the way. The plant-stall man.' He gestured towards a tented stand full of nursery plants and garden tools. He then offered his hand in greeting, which Lucy shook. It was rough and a little bit calloused; the weathered palm of a real hands-on gardener.

'Ah, well nice to meet you, Derek. I'm Lucy.' She served him an extra-large slice of the pizza. 'And if you're still peckish around lunchtime, or later on, I'll have lots more flavours on offer then too ... a classic margherita, local chorizo with peppers, BBQ chicken, and a char-grilled veg.'

'Now don't tempt me, young lady, my waistline won't thank you for it, even if my tastebuds will.' He gave a broad grin that crinkled around his eyes, and then set off back to his stall.

Lucy glanced over at Maggie's coffee van and ventured a friendly smile. The dark-haired woman there gave her a very cool look back – or was she just being paranoid?

And then, she spotted someone turning around from the coffee stand. A familiar face, the way he stood. Oh crikey, yes, it was the Cocktail Campervan guy. He was dressed casually in jeans and a black T-shirt, his dark-blond hair a little tousled. He looked up and seemed to clock her straight away, pausing for a second, before coming over.

'Hey, hello you. It's Pizza Girl.'

'Lucy,' she answered, setting him straight on her name. *Has he forgotten?*

'Hello, Cocktail Guy.' She could play him at his own game. 'Are you working here or something?'

'Nope.' He shook his head. 'I actually think 9 a.m.'s a bit of an early start for cocktails, don't you?' He sounded a little sarcastic as he gave a wry smile.

'Okay, well yes, I suppose ...' she said with a blush.

'So no, I don't do the markets generally, only the occasional food festival or if there's a special evening market event on.'

'Ah, okay, yeah, that makes sense.' She suddenly remembered the last event they were both working at and looked a little closer at his brow. It seemed to have pretty much healed, with just the hint of a scratch left. 'Umm, how's the eye been?'

Jack suddenly looked a little awkward, the bravado knocked out of him. 'Ah, yeah, bit sore for a few days, but right as rain now. All fixed ... Not my usual approach, you know, getting involved like that. Anyway, enough about that. How's it all been going for you then? The new business?' He seemed keen to move the conversation on.

'Yeah, pretty good. I'm starting to find my feet ... building some trade. I was really pleased to get this slot.'

'Right ... well that's good.'

There was a pause. Jack sounded like he was struggling for things to say, which wasn't at all like the lad she'd watched at the bar, the one with the gift of the gab.

'Well then, I suppose I'd better crack on,' Lucy gave them both the chance to get out of this awkward moment.

'Yeah, of course. Umm, well, if you ever need any advice, or info ... business-wise, I mean, feel free to ask.'

It was kind of him to offer, but right now Lucy felt she needed to find her own way.

Pizzas were very different to cocktails, after all. She wanted to put her own stamp on her business. Do things the way Papa might have done, if he were still here today. And maybe she didn't want to admit that she was finding this new venture difficult to a virtual stranger. 'Okay, thanks. Well, I'd better get more of this dough rolled out.'

'Ah, no worries,' he responded. 'And well, I know it can be hard setting up your own business. There are pitfalls, but there are lots of plusses too. Anyway, you can always find my Facebook page, and message me or something.'

'Yeah, sure. Thanks.'

Jack looked up, trying to fathom her. He had to admit she didn't seem that interested in taking him up on the offer of help. But hey, she was working and probably just wanted to crack on with her pizza making. A chap was now loitering at Jack's shoulder, trying to read the toppings list. He shifted slightly to one side, yet something kept him anchored by Lucy's stand.

He'd only come here to pick up some lemons, limes, strawberries and oranges for his garnishes. The market's fruit and veg stall was really good value. He hadn't expected to run into the Pizza Girl. And he certainly hadn't expected to feel ... what was it exactly? Kind of awkward in her company. This was new territory. He didn't usually have problems chatting with women. The lines just rolled off his tongue. He felt an odd tug inside, and he wasn't even sure why.

'Right well, I suppose I'd better let you get on.' He turned to go and then paused, adding, 'Good to see you.'

'You too,' was her brief answer.

Aha, still Miss Cool. But she did then give him a glimmer

of a smile, and what a lovely thing that was. Hah, she needed to practise using it more often.

'Bye then.' Jack headed off with one last glance over his shoulder, his step strangely feeling a little lighter.

*What could be better than family, friends, a fairground,
fabulous food and fizz?!*

*Come and live life to the fullest and join our
Big Fairground Get-Together!*

Friday 11th June from 7.30 p.m.

Glenhaven Lodge

RSVP Frank and Linda

Chapter 12

Jack was driving through country lanes with the camper van's windows rolled down, the early-evening breeze rushing in over him as he sang loudly to the Kaiser Chiefs: of course, a bit of rousing 'Ruby'. In the roadside fields, the odd cow and sheep looked up from their grazing, bemused by the blast of noise. Reaching the hamlet of the booking address, he slowed, checking out his directions. Soon, he was turning in through two large stone gateposts. A beech-tree lined avenue led up to an impressive country house. Set in the beautiful rolling foothills of the Cheviots, this country pad was the venue for tonight's celebration.

The latest e-mail had advised him to head for the stable courtyard area to the right of the main house, where a member of staff would meet him. He glanced at his watch. It was just before 6:30 p.m., and the party was due to start at 7:30. Perfect, he'd given himself plenty of time; he generally liked to have an hour or so to get set up.

As he made his way along the gravel driveway, he noticed several fair rides were already there, including a gorgeous-looking Victorian-style merry-go-round, the kind with wooden horses on gold-painted poles, as well as a Hoopla stall, and a Strong Man basher-style thing. Ah, now it made sense, the request to have at least two cocktails with a 'fairground' flavour. He had tried out a few concoctions this week on Matt and his girlfriend, and had settled on a Candyfloss Cocktail (vodka with cranberry and lime, topped with a pretty dollop of pale-pink candyfloss) and a Toffee Apple Martini. Hah, with the theme of 'all the fun of the fair', this was pretty damned cool, he had to admit. He loved all the party ideas he got to be a part of, pushing himself creatively.

He spotted a stone archway off to the right and headed that way. As he drove into the courtyard, he spotted Bob's burger van already parked up, and then ... his heart gave a skip of a beat as he recognised a familiar-looking horsebox and the logo of All Fired Up. So, Lucy was here.

He hadn't heard anything more since they'd met by chance at the market just over a week ago. She hadn't taken him up on his offer of advice at all. And he'd thought better of messaging her, conceding that his entrepreneurial insights would have to wait for another day. She'd been on his mind however, popping up uninvited now and again, catching him unawares whilst he was out running or when pottering about with Ruby. A fleeting glimpse of that flowing dark-brown hair, the curve of her smile, would creep up on him. *Strange.*

A chap in a yellow high-viz vest was pointing to a particular space, pulling him back to the here and now. He was in fact indicating the space right next to All Fired Up. And, there she was, Lucy, lifting the side hatch to her horsebox, popping a tin bucket of napkin-wrapped cutlery onto the counter, next to an extremely large wooden pepper grinder. He felt a glimmer of anticipation. And, hah, if that little mutt of a sausage dog was in tow, he'd have to damn well watch out for his signs too. This should make things a little more interesting this evening, anyhow.

He leapt down from Ruby with a spring in his step. 'Hey,' he called out. 'So we're neighbours for the evening.'

'Oh, hello,' Lucy looked up with a clipped smile. 'Yep, looks like it.'

'Have to watch out for my signs then,' Jack quipped.

'Hah, well Daisy's not here tonight, so they should all be fine,' Lucy's lips tightened as she responded, remembering that embarrassing occasion all too well. She'd left the dachshund with her brother tonight. Toddler Freddie had been having great fun with her in the garden, and didn't want the little dog to go. With Lucy working all evening, that seemed to suit them all.

Jack hadn't really intended winding her up, so he persevered: 'Only kidding. So, everything okay? How did the market day go?'

'Yeah, pretty good thanks. It's all a bit of a learning curve just now, but yes, it's going alright. And you?'

'Yeah, good thanks, been busy. All go with three events in three days. Not complaining, mind you. It's bringing in the money, and that's what it's all about.'

'Absolutely.' Lucy paused, thinking how frustratingly slowly bookings were coming in for her. Other than the market, this was the first event booking in a fortnight. If things stayed like this, she knew she couldn't afford to carry on this way. Her dad would be proven right and she'd be back looking for office-work. Back within four walls and pinned behind a desk. 'Was it always as busy for you?' she asked, unable to hide the slight frown that crossed her brow.

Jack cast his mind back to his early days with Ruby – a half-empty diary and a half-empty bank account. 'No, not at all. It just built up, kind of organically, I suppose. Getting the word out there. Social media and suchlike. Going to events ... getting seen, building a reputation. Oh, and I had flyers out on the bar counter, still do actually. That's always a good thing to do.'

'Hmm, that sounds a great idea.' *Why the hell hadn't she thought of that?* Sometimes it felt like she still had so much to learn. Running this business certainly wasn't just about making tasty pizzas.

'Right, well I'd better be getting Ruby set up,' Jack said with a flash of a smile.

'Ruby?'

'Yeah, my campervan. She's called Ruby. Ruby red and all that.'

'Hah, yes. That's cute.' Despite herself, Lucy smiled, finding she couldn't help but warm to this guy. Okay, so he might be a bit cocky, a bit of a showman bartender. But maybe she should accept a bit of advice here and there from someone who knew the ropes.

Tamsin then appeared, having waltzed off in search of a can of something sugary and fizzy. On the way there, she'd confessed to having been at an 'awesome' party the night before and was still evidently feeling the effects. Lucy wondered with concern how hard-working she might be tonight.

'Well, anyway, if there's anything you need this evening, just shout,' Jack offered cheerily, as he headed back to set up his Cocktail Campervan bar.

'Thanks.' And well, maybe she'd take him up on his offer of help after all.

Wow, it was all go. There must have been a couple of hundred people at the event. After welcome cocktails, organised and paid for by the host, Frank, Jack was doing a 'free' bar for the night (the tab again to be picked up by the generous Frank) which was proving to be full-on and lucrative. The guests were certainly enjoying their drinks, with the fairground-themed ones especially going down a storm.

Jack noticed that Lucy had queues at her food counter for much of the evening too. In between mixing and serving his drinks, he'd glimpsed her stood at the wood-fired oven, working away with her pizza paddle, and sometimes chatting away with her customers whilst slicing and handing over the deliciously-topped bases. Mmm, another waft of hot baked dough, cheese and tomato, came his way. He'd been tantalised by the aromas drifting across to his bar all evening. They were far too tempting; he'd have to try one of her pizzas himself if he got the chance later on. He'd grabbed a quick sandwich for supper earlier and his tummy was now protesting and feeling rather empty. He'd heard several passers-by commenting on how good they were, and he couldn't help but feel pleased for Lucy and her fledgling business.

Halfway through the evening, at around nine-thirty, Frank appeared, taking the time to chat with each of the stallholders in turn.

'Good evening, so this is the famous Cocktail Campervan. I have to say, she looks rather wonderful.'

'She is, thank you. I converted her myself, well mostly,' Jack responded proudly.

'You've done a cracking job. A seventies classic?'

'She is indeed, a 1971 VW Westfalia, chianti red.'

'Hah, yes, I spotted the left-hand drive. Used to own one myself back in the day. A '74 T2, baby blue. Ah, those were the days, trips to the coast, lazy afternoons by the sea, surfing ...' Frank's blue-grey eyes glazed with nostalgia.

'Sounds cool. They all have their own characters, don't they. Well, what an amazing party you've organised here. Love the fairground theme.'

'Thanks. It's been wonderful getting everybody together.'

Jack smiled; Frank seemed such a nice guy. 'So, what can I get for you? Glass of champagne, a cold beer, cocktail, mocktail? Whatever you fancy, and this one's on the house.'

'Well, thank you. A nice cold bottle of beer would go down a treat. I should probably be having a fresh juice,' he winked, 'but our Linda's not around just now ...'

'So, what're the celebrations for?' Jack asked. He was curious as no-one had mentioned a birthday or anniversary event.

'Well then, I wanted to get all my friends and family together ... to celebrate the fact that I'm now cancer-free. A bloody miracle and all credit to the NHS. It's been a tough couple of years, so I figured we needed a bloody big party and a whole heap of fun. Hence having the fairground here, too.'

'Oh, wow. Well, good for you. What a brilliant idea.'

'Yes, it made me realise that life is too short. My money was sat wasting away in the bank, with my body at that time wasting away around me. Well, I feel like I've got a second chance. I gave a chunk to charity and I'm going to live life to the full from now on, and I intend to enjoy every damn moment. And, if you've got your wits about you, young man, I suggest you do the same. What is it you young people say? YOLO, or something?'

Jack felt a lump rise in his throat. 'That's the one, You Only Live Once. Well, congratulations on your all-clear. Have a wonderful night, all of you.'

'Grandad, Gran-dad, come on ...' A young girl, about ten years old, dashed over, grabbing Frank's hand. 'Mummy's waiting for you on the Merry-Go-Round!'

'Of course, darling. On my way. Wouldn't miss it for the world.' He turned to Jack, 'I'll fetch that beer later. Have a good night.'

'You too.'

Jack watched him go; he felt warmed with emotion, yet a little bit raw around the edges too. Life ... it seemed to balance on a pinhead at times.

Ruby's bar was buzzing throughout the evening, and Lucy had to admit it looked great. The deep glossy red of the campervan's paintwork was set against its chrome countertop, which pulled down, hatch-like, to one side. Jack had it set out with a three-tiered stand of colourful garnishes, gorgeous cut glasses, a metal ice bucket filled enticingly with chilled sparkling wine bottles, and the jazzy backdrop of the light bulb-lit blackboard menu behind him in the raised white roof section. And as she stole a quick glance whilst cooking, there was Jack himself, spinning his most charming banter to a crowd of young ladies, all the while performing his sleight-of-hand mixology. It was indeed like watching a show, and although he still appeared a little cocky, he clearly loved what he did.

The odd snatch of conversation filtered Lucy's way, and she found herself listening in: 'So ladies, do you have a favourite drink in mind? Or, would you like me to take a guess at your likes and then create your ideal personal cocktails?'

Three rather pretty twenty-somethings were gazing up at him with awed smiles.

'Ooh, yes, choose us something!' one of them said.

'So, what do you think I'd like?' Lady No. 2 purred.

'For you, something a little exotic, with a hint of *juicy* pineapple and a swirl of *creamy* coconut, perhaps?' Blimey, he was sounding like a male version of Nigella Lawson. Making cocktails suddenly sounded *sooo* sexy. Of course, it was far too over the top for Lucy's liking. Pretty damned cheesy, to be honest, but still she listened in, with a hint of a smile across her lips, as she loaded another pizza base with toppings.

'Oh my, that sounds delicious,' No. 2 answered.

'So, I'm talking piña colada but not just any old piña colada. Oh no, a Jack's Cocktail Campervan Special Colada with an extra hint of lime and my secret ingredient.'

'Oooh, what's that?'

'I'd love to tell you, but it's top secret. You'd have to kill me first.' He gave a wink.

'Hah, okay yeah, go ahead. I'll take one of those. It sounds divine.'

He started prepping, slicing and pouring, and was soon shaking his cocktail mixer dramatically.

'And for you,' a minute or so later, he turned his attention back to the first girl. 'I saw how much you loved the candy-floss cocktail earlier, so I'll make you another, but a different flavour this time. Watch and learn, it's going to be a flossy little Sex on the Beach.'

Lucy was stood beside Tamsin, the pair of them slicing red onions at this point, when she suddenly felt the tip of the knife graze her thumb. Oops, she looked down quickly – thank god it hadn't pierced the skin. Right, enough of watching that guy's cocktail shenanigans, she'd better concentrate on her own catering. Time to load these next two pizzas into the oven. She too had customers waiting.

'These'll just be a few minutes cooking. So, here's your ticket and I'll call out the number as soon as they're ready. Don't stray too far.' Lucy gave a friendly smile as she spoke to the next people in the queue.

'Thanks, darling.'

The two lads she'd been serving headed off towards the Campervan bar. Her eyes couldn't help but follow them. Just before she was about to turn away, Jack caught her eye. 'You okay? All going fine there?' he mouthed.

'Yeah, thanks,' she replied with a nod.

Jack gave her a thumbs up, and then a middle-aged couple approached her counter, talking with Tamsin and obscuring Lucy's view. She and Jack cracked on again, getting lost in their work for a while. It was proving to be a hectic and thankfully profitable night.

Lucy found herself relaxing into her role this evening, not feeling quite so nervous about getting things wrong, even though it was full-on. The partygoers were a genial bunch, of all ages. It seemed to be a huge family and friends' event. And the fairground theme had given the party an extra fun dimension. Smells of hotdogs, burgers, candyfloss and toffee apples were tantalisingly filling the air from the other stalls; bringing back memories of years gone by. Pulling her back to nights spent at The Hoppings down in Newcastle-upon-Tyne, when the fair was in town. Nights filled with excitement, treats, whizzy rides and flashing lights. The twopenny-pusher machines that she and her brother, Olly, could happily spend hours on. And Dad winning a soft toy monkey for her – after many attempts – on the Hoopla. She'd named him Mr H. 'H' for Hoopla. In fact, she still had him, sat on a shelf in her bedroom at the cottage. Nights when they were still a family unit, many years ago now, when Mum and Dad were still together. Lucy felt a pang of nostalgia.

Chapter 13

Midnight came around in a whirl, the sky was dark yet comforting, cloaking them all with a magical star-lit background, the perfect foil to the flashing fairground lights and music. Jack watched as Frank picked up two of his grand-children simultaneously, giving them a joyful whizz in his arms. Family, happy moments, the simple things in life, that's what mattered. He let out a slow breath, refocussed. It would soon be time to start clearing up and packing away. Jack completed an order for two mojitos and, with the partygoers now few and far between, he felt drawn to head across to see Lucy.

'Hi.'

'Hey there.'

'Wow, that was a busy old night, wasn't it?'

'Yeah, you can say that again. We've been run off our feet. Thank goodness I had Tamsin here to help.' The young girl looked up, hardly able to suppress a yawn, and went back to scrolling through her phone.

'Luckily,' Lucy continued, 'I'd brought plenty of bases and toppings. Thought I'd gone a bit overboard, to be honest, but

I'm glad I did now. I've just got a couple of margherita pizzas left and that's it.'

'That's great. Talking of which, could I buy one? I'm absolutely famished,' Jack said, rubbing his empty stomach.

'Of course, here. Have one on the house. I've already cooked them, as I needed to let the oven cool down. They'd only go to waste otherwise.'

'Ah, that's brilliant. I appreciate that. Cheers.'

Lucy popped a pizza into a box for him. *Could the ice queen finally be thawing?*

Jack took a big bite, unable to wait any longer. 'Delicious, thank you. So, is there a real Papa?' He gestured to the logo and the strapline on the side of the horsebox:

All Fired Up. Wood-fired Pizza just like Papa used to make!

'Yes, there is,' Lucy paused, looking a little distant. 'My grandpa. He was Italian. My mum called him Papa, and it kind of stuck for the whole family.'

'Oh, so you're part-Italian. Now *that* explains those gorgeous dark-brown eyes.'

Lucy felt herself blush for a moment. What was it with this Jack and his cheesy one-liners? Of course, it was the kind of charming spiel he came out with all the time.

'I am indeed. Papa came over from Italy as a child. His family had a restaurant in Newcastle. Many years ago; it's all gone now ... He fell head over heels with Nonna, my grandma, who was a proper Geordie. Hah, they used to love telling the story of how they first met.' Lucy's eyes were bright as she remembered the tale.

'Go on then, you'll have to tell me now,' Jack urged. This

Papa sounded a real character. 'Hang on, can I fetch you a drink? It's gone quiet here now. I think we can get away with a break before packing up. A glass of prosecco, or a soft drink, maybe?' He recognised that they'd both be driving. He kept in some alcohol-free lagers, which he himself enjoyed now and again at the end of a busy night.

'Something non-alcohol, yeah, that'd be good,' answered Lucy.

'Anything for you?' he turned to include a rather sullen-looking Tamsin in the offer.

'Oh, now you're asking,' the young girl perked up. 'I've been working like some kind of slave all night. So yeah, I'd love a cocktail. Something strong and sassy.'

The young girl was now batting her eyelids at Jack, and had evidently recovered from her hangover, Lucy mused.

'Right-o,' Jack said, somewhat taken back, 'I'll fix you both a surprise and then you can tell me that story, Luce. Two tics.'

He whizzed back to the campervan, and with a stir and a shake, some mint, strawberries and crushed ice, soon reappeared with two cocktails in hand. 'Virgin Mojito for you, Lucy. All the taste, and none of the alcohol. And,' he turned to Tamsin, 'a Strawberry Mojito for you – sassy strawberry, with plenty of kick.'

Lucy took a sip. 'Wow, this is great. Thank you. I love the sharpness of the lime and the mint, so refreshing.'

'Lush,' was all Tamsin said, after taking a huge slurp. She flashed Jack a grin, made a token gesture of wiping over the counter, then went back to her phone scrolling.

'So, Papa's story?' The party was winding down, there was

no-one waiting at Ruby, so Jack took up one of the little chairs beside the horsebox trailer.

Lucy finished wiping down the surfaces and then leaned out of the hatch, with her mocktail in hand, ready to tell the tale.

'Okay, so, how my grandparents met ... Well, my grandma – or Nonna as we call her – Nancy, she came into Papa's family's restaurant down near the quayside in Newcastle for dinner one day, with her then boyfriend. Papa was working and happened to be their waiter. Some item had been missed from their order, and the boyfriend guy was really rude and offensive about it. Papa took an instant dislike to him, but the lady with him seemed lovely, trying her best to calm the situation.'

Jack nodded, enjoying the story.

'And, Papa was taken in by this lady's beautiful blue eyes and her dark hair.'

Jack instinctively looked up into Lucy's eyes – dark brown, not blue – but very distinctive; and her hair, yes ... those glossy dark waves he'd noted the first time he ever saw her.

'He wondered what on earth a nice young woman like her was doing with such a chap,' Lucy continued. 'Well, that was it. After they'd left, Papa was determined to find out who she was, and at least to talk to her. He realised he might only get one chance, might never see her again after tonight. He suddenly spotted an umbrella that had been left hanging around by the main entrance. He knew it wasn't hers, of course he did. But he grabbed it anyway.

'The two of them, Nonna and the boyfriend, were away

up the street, walking some distance apart, obviously having taken umbrage with each other. "Excuse me, madam," he called out as he chased after them. "I think you must have left your umbrella."

'She looked confused, about to say it wasn't hers, and then saw his broad smile and vigorous nodding. "Oh yes ... right, thank you," she said. He approached, close enough to whisper, "If you'd like to come out on a proper date, I'd really love to be the one to take you." He then handed over the umbrella along with one of the restaurant's business cards. "My name is Antonio."

'"Well, thank you, Antonio," she said.

'The week after that he always said was the longest of his life, until the day a phone call came, his mother shouting across the restaurant floor: "Antonio, someone is asking for you ..." And well, the rest is history.'

'That's a nice story.'

'It is, isn't it. I never got tired of Papa telling it.'

Lucy climbed out of the horsebox and took a seat next to Jack; her feet were killing her, it was a relief to take the weight off them and just relax for a moment.

'And what about the pizzas? The link with your business?' Jack asked, not quite wanting the story to end.

'Oh yes, they were the best pizzas in town at the time. Everyone said so. A recipe handed down from his family in Sorrento. But when the recession hit in the 80s, it got harder to make ends meet. Papa's father had some problems with loans, and sadly the restaurant had to close. When Papa was in his late thirties, he got a job as a bus driver. He was still doing that in his fifties, when I came along, his first grand-child, but he was always nostalgic about those days in the restaurant. He wanted to recreate that for us when we were young. Hah, I was the only kid at school whose grandparents had a wood-fired pizza oven in their back garden. We used to love it, me and my brother. Loading up our own pizzas, with homemade tomato sauce, on the thinnest, most delicious bases you can imagine ...'

'That must have been cool. He sounds a real character.'

'Yeah, he was,' Lucy's tone softened, surprised to find herself opening up so much to this guy.

Jack was smiling softly too, happy just to listen and sensing there was more to this story.

Lucy took a slow breath. 'He died several years ago ... he was in his late sixties. It was so sudden, an aneurysm. We never got the chance to say goodbye.' Her eyes had misted. She missed him so much.

'Oh, I'm sorry, Lucy ...' Jack's own past came hurtling in. He knew that feeling too well. Never saying goodbye. Not knowing that the last time was *the* last time you'd ever see that person.

Lucy looked up, seeing a shadow cross his face. Suddenly recognising that they might share that same deep shard of grief, but not daring to ask.

Jack was suddenly very quiet.

'You okay, Jack?'

'Yeah, yeah, fine. Good pizza.' He switched tack, keen to cut that conversation short. Today wasn't the day to go there. He didn't want to pick at that particular scab right now, just wanted to enjoy the last of the evening. And perhaps, make the most of getting to know this intriguing Pizza Girl, who'd finally opened up a bit.

'Come on,' Jack found himself grasping her hand, which was warm, reassuring. He remembered Frank's words from earlier about living life to the full. 'I don't think the Merry-Go-Round's packed up quite yet. Do you think he might let us have a go for a couple of bottles of beer and that last pizza you've got?'

'Worth a try,' Lucy said with a shy grin. She couldn't help but get caught up with Jack's enthusiasm, his energy. 'Tamsin, would you mind just keeping an eye on everything here ... just for five minutes?'

The girl gave a bit of a huff, followed by a 'S'pose so.'

'I used to love the Merry-Go-Round as a kid,' Lucy admitted. 'It was my absolute favourite when the fair came to town. My friends all liked the fast rides, the ones that whizzed you round making you feel sick, like the Waltzers and Twister, but this ...' The Merry-Go-Round came into view as they dashed across the yard. 'This just used to make me smile.'

Jack wasn't sure why, but he suddenly wanted to be able to make Lucy smile. 'Wait a sec, and I'll see if they'll let us on.' The chap in charge was already taking down some of the lights, and like all those who'd worked hard all night, was evidently ready to pack up and get away home. Jack darted over. A short conversation ensued, with a shrug from the fellow, then some nodding and a thumbs up.

'We're on! Choose your horse,' Jack called out with a grin.

Lucy glanced around her, then headed for a dark-grey horse with a carved flowing white mane, and a red-painted saddle. She climbed on with a giggle, taking hold of the gold-sprayed handlebars by the horse's wooden cheeks. Jack took up the horse just inside of hers.

The chap walked to the centre of the ride, and pressed a button. Old-fashioned music started up and that long-missed slow swirl began. White lights glowed above them, and the elegant wooden horses began to rise and fall on their gold-twisted stems.

Jack watched as Lucy's smile broadened, until it lit up her whole face. She looked so much prettier when she smiled. In fact, tonight she seemed very different from the stressed-out girl he'd met just a few weeks ago.

Lucy looked across at him. 'Thank you,' she mouthed. Then she closed her eyes, enjoying the rhythm of the fairground ride, the music, the steady swirl.

Jack in turn, found himself enjoying watching her. It was like seeing a glimpse of the young girl she must have once been. A happier, carefree, less troubled Lucy, than he'd witnessed so far. Then, he looked beyond her, catching sight of the night sky; clear and crisp, the stars out in force. And for a second or two, Jack too was transported to a happier place and time. As the ride revolved, for a few precious moments, the worries of the world seemed to fade away for them both.

But as all special moments do, it had to end. The horses slowed and the ride came to a soothing halt.

'That was lovely, thank you,' Lucy said to Jack.

'Well, we need to go and get our payment sorted. I've bartered two beers and your last pizza for that.'

'Hah, no worries. I'll go fetch the pizza. It was well worth it.' It had been so nice just to chill out and do something fun, however brief.

'Absolutely.'

It was worth it just to see that smile too, thought Jack. And, as they headed off the ride, taking the three steps back down to where their feet met the ground, he instinctively placed his palm on the small of her back to help guide her.

Something had shifted between them. The Ice Queen had melted a little.

Chapter 14

The following evening, Lucy had arranged to meet friends, Becky and Katie, in the village pub. A girlie night was very much in order – what with setting up the new business, she hadn't had much time, or money, lately to get out and about much socially.

Saturday night, 8 p.m., and The Oyster Catcher was buzzing. There was going to be a live band on later and locals and tourists alike were jostling for seats. As a couple got up from a corner keg table, Becky seized her chance and moved in speedily to bag the three stools there, just as Lucy came back from the bar balancing two G&Ts and her large glass of rosé.

'There you go, girls. Great manoeuvre there, Becks.' Lucy placed the glasses down on the circular wooden table top.

'Perfect. Cheers!' Katie grinned, her wavy blonde hair bouncing around her shoulders.

'Yes, cheers. Well, this is nice. I must say it's good to be on the other side of the serving counter for a change.'

'Oh yes, how's it all going?' Katie asked, keen to catch up on all the goss.

'Yeah, pretty good, I'm getting there. I've taken a few more event bookings, and the Alnwick market was a good day last week and I now have a regular slot, so it's all building, slowly but surely.'

'Well, I think it's bloody brilliant. You taking the plunge, creating your own business,' said Katie, who spent three days a week working at a children's nursery, as well as looking after her own little girl the rest of the time.

'Thanks. It's still a bit scary. The money side is a bit hit-and-miss just now. I really can't afford to fail.'

'You won't, hun. I've seen your grit and determination in action. You'll make it work.' Becky was onside, as always. 'Anyway, tell me more about this mystery cocktail-bar guy?'

'Oh, what's this, Luce?' Katie's eyes lit up.

Blimey, Becky was on it like a car bonnet. They had chatted on the phone this morning, when the Merry-Go-Round ride was still fresh in Lucy's mind; but she'd only mentioned Jack briefly.

'Oh ... don't get excited, you lot. It's just someone I've bumped into a couple of times at these events. He's often booked in at the same things. He's a bit cocky, actually.' She tried to act casual, but remembered chatting about Papa at the end of the evening ... the showy barman persona had mysteriously disappeared at that point. The Merry-Go-Round ... and the warmth of his hand resting gently on the small of her back ... Hmm, why on earth was she remembering that right now?

'And?' Katie probed, barely containing her grin.

Lucy had to smile too, raising her dark eyebrows, 'What do you mean, "*and*" ...?'

'Lucy Brown, I've been your friend for over fifteen years,' Becky declared. They'd met at high school when Becky's family had moved into her childhood home town of Rothbury, bonding over a love of chocolate brownies and Justin Timberlake. 'Your voice changes when you mention him.'

'Don't be so daft.'

'It does, I'm telling you.'

'*So?*' Lucy said, exasperatedly.

'Ooh, this sounds intriguing,' Katie joined in. 'So, what's he like then, this cocktail guy? Looks, personality?'

'Oh, for goodness' sake! Is this an official interview?'

'Yep, and we need answers,' Becky pushed on.

'Ah, okay, dark-blond hair, blue-grey eyes. Medium height.'

'So, good-looking then?' Katie was fishing.

Yes, he was, Lucy supposed. But she knew better than to admit to that. 'Look, he's just helped with a bit of advice on the catering scene. We hardly know each other really. And like I say, he can be a bit cocky.' Lucy tried to keep it matter-of-fact.

'Oh, but you've forgot to mention to Katie that he stepped in and took a punch for you ...' Becky said with a laugh, clearly revelling in dangling that juicy fact.

'What? How have I missed all this goss?'

Lucy rolled her eyes, 'It was nothing ... just some drunken lad mouthing off at a party, who happened to be at my pizza stand at the time.'

'And then Campervan Guy charged in to the rescue,' Becky added with a cheeky grin.

'"Just friends" then, is it, Luce? Are you sure?' Katie was smiling.

'Absolutely. Look you two, I'm allowed to talk to a guy without it meaning I'm thinking about a bloody relationship. I had enough of all that shite with Liam, remember.'

'So, are you swearing off men for life?' Becky said, tongue-in-cheek.

'Oh Luce, you'll be turning into a shrivelled-up prune, and end up keeping a load of cats ...' Katie chipped in.

'Or an army of sausage dogs,' Becky took up, with a daft grin on her face.

'Arrgh, enough, you two! I'm just not looking for a relation-ship right now, that's all.'

'Yeah, but a *fling* might work. Get back in the saddle and have some fun, girl!' Becky added. It was all good-humoured banter.

'Stop!' Lucy raised a hand dramatically, and then took a large sip of wine. 'I'm out to enjoy myself tonight, not to face the Spanish Inquisition. So, get off my case, you two.'

'Okay, soz, Luce.'

'Fair enough, hun. We only want you to be happy.' Becky rested a caring hand on her friend's shoulder.

Both Becky and Katie were now in settled relationships. Becky was now all cosied up with Darren, and living together in Alnwick, after several ups and downs in her earlier frazzled love-life, and Katie had got married to Lee three years ago and now had a gorgeous, on-the-go toddler back at home.

She too was more than ready for a chill-out tonight. 'Well then, here's to letting our hair down and dancing on the tables.' Katie raised her glass.

'Cheers to that!' Lucy smiled.

The girls chatted away, and were soon getting another round of drinks in. The band came on and were great, with a fabulous female lead doing some covers of Pink, Lady Gaga, plus some original stuff too. The girls clapped and cheered. They didn't quite get to dancing on the tables, but they talked with some local lads, and boogied in their corner of the bar next to where the band were playing. They felt happily merry on gin and wine, and they all trundled back to Lucy's cottage after closing time, still singing along to 'So What' by Pink as they linked arms.

Becky had arranged to sleep over on Lucy's sofa. The tiny cottage didn't have a spare room. Mind you, when they rolled back in, Daisy was looking very cosy on that sofa already, having been settled there for the evening. The little dog was not being moved easily, giving in only for a brief and begrudging toilet stop in the yard.

It was already past eleven and Katie had a taxi ordered for eleven thirty. With her partner, being a delivery driver, having to work early the next day, she'd be on toddler wake-up duty for her little girl, Ella – probably with a slight hangover, by the whizzy feel of her head right now. But that was tomorrow. The girls had had a thoroughly good night and were now enjoying a fabulous finale in the form of a Baileys nightcap while huddled cosily in the cottage's front room. All too soon, Katie had to leave, whisked away in one of Ron's Taxis, after kisses, hugs and a promise that they must do this more often. Life had a way of rolling on, and before they knew it, weeks could pass before they next saw each other.

It was now just the two girls left, and it wasn't long before Becky launched into one of those tipsy truthful chats.

'You really okay, hun?' Sat side by side on the sofa, she took Lucy's hand in her own. 'You just sounded, well, a bit tense in the pub ... on the relationship stuff. We were only teasing, you know.'

There was a second's pause before Lucy answered. 'Yeah, I know that. It's okay.'

Daisy was back in situ, wedged between the pair of them. A sausage-dog sandwich.

'And you don't mind it here ... on your own? After selling the house of your dreams and all that?'

'Hah, those bloody dreams were well and truly shattered when the bombshell hit about Liam. But you know what, I *really* do like it here. It might be small but it's *my* space. And I love being near the sea. Being able to go for a walk any time I like with Daisy down to the beach. And the people here in the village, well ... they've made me feel welcome already. Like at the Book Club. And ... I have cake and coffee just down the road.'

'Yeah, of course. I'm glad you're starting to make some friends here, that's good.'

Lucy paused. Though she was finding her feet in the village, there *were* things that were bothering her still. 'Oh Becks, I just hope to goodness this pizza venture works out ... only time will tell with that. And the new girl, Tamsin, is a bit of a nightmare. Truth be told, I'm not sure if she'll stick it out. She came across well at the interview, but she seems more interested in keeping up with her mates on her mobile phone than making pizzas.'

'Ah, I suppose you'll just have to see how things go. But you don't have to keep her on, not if she's no good.'

'No, I suppose not. But then what'll I do? I'd need someone else and quick.' Running the pizza van solo was nigh on impossible.

'You'll work it out, hun. Or I can help ... for a shift or two, if you need. Until you get someone new in ...'

'You'd do that?'

''Course I would.'

'Aw, thanks, that's good to know.' Lucy felt a little easier. 'And well, here in the cottage, I've learnt that maybe being on your own isn't so bad. It's better than being in a toxic relationship. Better than being fooled and strung along by a lying bastard.'

'True, Luce. And I'm always here, or near, at least. You know that.'

'Yeah, 'course I do.' Lucy let out a soft sigh. All that recent heartbreak and hurt was beginning to pass, but occasionally it could still feel raw. She stroked the silky black fur of Daisy's back. 'Thank you, Becks.'

Friends propped you up through all the shit. They were there to dance and talk and hold your hand, sticking with you through the best times and the worst times. Over the top of a very cosy dachshund, she gave her best friend a hug.

Yes, there were issues with the new business, but she was

sensible enough to realise it was never going to be all plain sailing to start with, and relationships ... well, best to stick with her friends and family. But Lucy did feel that better times were rolling in, like the waves rolling to shore, washing away the hurts of the past.

Chapter 15

'Right, Daisy, what's on for us then? A walk on the beach maybe?'

Daisy was curled up in her cosy dog bed in the kitchen, and didn't seem that excited about a walk just yet. With a hangover headache lurking over her right brow, Lucy could identify with that feeling. Becky had just left after nursing several strong coffees, and the day stretched out ahead of them. A blast of fresh air and a stretch of their legs would do them both good.

'Come on. You know it makes sense.' She was persuading herself as much as Daisy, so she reached for Daisy's lead from the hook on the back of the kitchen door, and gave it a tinkle above the dog's dark, smooth head. Daisy's head dipped lower, as if she might hide if she sank down further. Lucy had to laugh. 'Right, I'm going,' she coaxed, as she pulled on her trainers then stood up, setting off towards the door. Daisy begrudgingly moved, not wanting to be left on her own after all.

There was a fresh sea breeze, but it was a gorgeous morning in the village, with the row of stone cottages beside hers glowing golden in the sunlight. They headed for the lane that passed the golf course down to the sea. A ten-minute walk and they'd be on the sands, ready to stroll the bay. Vehicles used the grass verge to park here for the beach, and several cars were there already. Halfway down the narrow lane, she spotted a familiar-looking dark-red campervan. Oh ... she felt a little lift of excitement. *Could it be?* The magic of the Merry-Go-Round from two nights before rose in her mind again.

Of course, there were lots of campervans about, and there'd be more than one red one, for sure. But as she neared the vehicle, she spotted the distinctive logo on the side: *Jack's Cocktail Campervan.* She couldn't help but smile. Blimey, maybe Becky was right about her getting animated when she mentioned him. Was there something in that? She quashed that thought quickly.

Realistically, the chances of actually seeing him here on the beach were slim. He could be walking anywhere in the area, or playing golf or something. As they wandered past, believe it or not, Daisy took that opportunity to stop and pee up the wheel of the campervan, leaving a damp trail across the lower tyre and sprinkled around its base.

'Daisy! You naughty dog,' Lucy scolded. 'What *do* you have against Jack, hey?'

Thankfully, no-one was around to witness that. That diva dog did choose her bloody moments.

Lucy walked on, heading for the path that led from the lane end on through the dunes. She couldn't help but scan the area, just in case she might get a glimpse of Jack. She couldn't decide whether she'd want to bound over to him or simply hide. There was no sign of him on the little sandy track, nor where the marram grass gave way to the beach and the view of the bay expanded.

Lucy liked to stroll along the shoreline on the way out, close to the waves that pounded and crashed as they rolled in a froth to the shore, then she usually headed back on a trail that swept just below the dunes where the sand was softer underfoot, taking in the curve of the bay. Daisy quite enjoyed a bit of digging here and there, especially if there was an interesting scrap of picnic debris about. At one point, the little dog resurfaced with her nose covered in sand. Lucy laughed, then crouched down to brush the dachshund's face off with her hand.

'Look at you, Miss Scruffy. You'll get sand in your eyes.'

Daisy merely gave her a look, as if to say it was worth it for that morsel of scrumptious sausage roll.

Lucy was still crouching when she felt a rhythmic thud vibrating through the sands close by. Someone must be running. As she stood up, she found herself facing a very sweaty but not-unattractive-looking man. A man she knew. Jack.

'Hey, I thought it was you,' he said breathlessly, pausing beside her and jogging on the spot for a few seconds.

'Oh, hi.' Lucy's lips lifted into a smile.

'So how are things? Did you have a good night Friday?'

'Yeah ... yes, all fine,' she stuttered vaguely. *Was he referring to the Merry-Go-Round or the pizza van takings?*

'Well, it's good to see you here. Out for a walk with the peeing Devil Dog, I see.'

Daisy looked up at him haughtily, with a slight curl to her lip, which made Lucy's smile broaden. Never diss a Dachshund. 'Hey you, don't be cheeky. She's not usually a nuisance. And yes, well, I live nearby, I have a cottage in the village, so it's our usual walking spot.'

'Ah, right. I fancied a change of scene for my jog today. The sands are always a good workout.'

'O-kay.' She took in the running shorts and sweat-marked vest. He evidently had put some effort into his run. And, she had to admit, zooming in for a sneaky peek, his physique did look pretty fit in the sports gear. With bare legs and arms showing, and clingy Lycra over the rest, it revealed a lot more than his smart-casual workwear did.

'Look, do you fancy a cold drink or a coffee or something?' Jack mooted. 'I mean, I won't stay like this, but I can quickly freshen up at the van ...'

Lucy felt frozen for a moment. Part of her wanted to bolt back to the cottage, and part of her wanted to jump at the invitation. What was with her?

'Well, er, Daisy and I were about to head back to the cottage, weren't we, Diva Dog?'

Daisy looked up at her with a bemused expression, as if to say, 'That isn't the plan and you know it!'

'But, well, I suppose we could stick around for a little bit. It's such a gorgeous day, after all ...'

'Maybe I could fix us up a drink in Ruby – the camper's always well stocked – and we could take it and sit in the dunes?'

Should she agree to a drink? It was just by chance they'd

met up, and it did sound a nice idea. They'd have to rattle along at future events, for sure, so better to keep things friendly. She was also a little dehydrated from last night's pub antics. Where was the harm?

'Okay then.'

'If you fancy, I could even fix you up a cocktail? It's nearly lunchtime and I take it you'll not be driving anywhere, if you live nearby.'

'Urgh ...' The acidic dregs of last night's drinking session were still lying in her stomach, not to mention her just-cleared head. 'Maybe not alcohol,' she confessed. 'Bit of a heavy night last night ... with my girlfriends.'

'Hah, I see. Well, I do some great mocktails and juices, so no worries. Right, well, I'll just freshen up a bit first.'

And with that he whipped off his top, then his running shoes, left them in a little pile by her feet, and dashed down the sands in just his shorts. *Oh!* ... Lucy had to admit it was a very pleasant sight indeed, as she watched him dash into the shallows and then take a neat dive over the first big wave, out to the open sea. Well ... that was one way to freshen up.

She wasn't quite sure whether to watch and wait for him, or to wander slowly up the sands, back to the lane where she knew the campervan was parked up. But Jack wouldn't realise that she knew Ruby's whereabouts. So, she sat with Daisy at the base of the dunes, not far from Jack's little heap of clothing, and watched the world go by – as well as taking several glances in his direction – until Jack came sauntering back out, shaking off his wet hair on the way. Just watching him stirred something very basic in her, a need ... a desire ... that she hadn't felt for quite some time.

Bloody hell! Well, that was disconcerting and rather inconvenient.

Jack jogged back up the beach, the sun already drying his salty skin. He spotted Lucy, sat at the base of the dunes. She looked tanned and pretty in casual cropped jeans and a yellow spotty T-shirt, her dark hair loose at the back but swept behind a yellow-and-white scarf thing that looked kind of cute in a sixties sort of way. Her smile was gentle as he approached, warming him.

He gathered up his T-shirt. No point putting that sweaty thing back on. 'Okay? Ready for a cooling drink in the dunes?'

'Ah ... yeah.' She sounded slightly hesitant. 'Of course.'

'Great, I'm parched.' That run had really dehydrated him. A large glass of water and then an icy cool beer were totally in order.

They walked together, with short-legged Daisy strutting in between them.

'Nice place to live. It's a great little village,' commented Jack on their way back up the lane.

'Yeah, I've only been here a few months, but it's perfect for me. It's a pretty spot and I love my little cottage.' It really was beginning to feel like home. 'What about you? Where's home?' *Surely, he didn't base himself out of Ruby?*

'Ah, I lodge with a mate at his house in Glenton, a village near Alnwick.'

'Oh yeah, I know it. It's just inland, isn't it? Not too far.'

'Yeah, I rent a room there. And ... sometimes, well, I choose to just roam free with the campervan and my two-man tent. Not really a four-walls kind of guy.'

'Oh, I think I'd find that strange. I like my home comforts too much.'

'Nah, it's not strange at all. It's kind of grounding. Sitting out under the stars in the middle of the hills, or waking up to watch the sun rise over the sea. It's pretty amazing.'

Lucy nodded. Put that way, it did have some appeal.

'And it's not like I do it all the time. Just when the whim takes me, if I don't have work lined up for a day or two. Drive, park up, climb a mountain, swim in the sea or a lake. The world's a pretty cool kind of place.' He had an aura of boyish wonder about him as he spoke.

A family passed by with a toddler in tow, loaded up with buckets and spades, fold-up chairs and a picnic box. The little boy dropped his blue plastic spade, and Jack swept it up and caught up with him. 'Hey, little guy. Ah, excuse me ...' he called out.

'Ah, thank you!' The mother stopped, taking the toy spade from Jack. 'What do you say to the man, Archie?'

''Fank you.'

The lad and his clan trooped on. Beach days. Sunny times. Family times. It was lovely to see. Lucy was filled with a delightful warm feeling.

Jack and Lucy soon reached Ruby; her shiny red paintwork was gleaming in the sunshine.

'Right, just give me a couple of mins. I'll grab a clean T-shirt, and then I'll fix you a fabulously refreshing drink.'

'Sounds good to me.'

'Does Devil Dog need some water?'

'Hah, stop calling her that! She'll take offence. And yes, I'm sure she'd like some.'

Jack thoughtfully fetched that first, opening up the cab and climbing through to reappear with a large plastic bowl. Daisy was straight in there, lapping it up. Jack disappeared for a further minute or so, and then the side hatch opened up, so he could chat to Lucy while he prepared their drinks. He was now sporting a khaki-coloured top, with a logo saying *Seize the Day* on it.

'So, what would madam like today? Wait ... let me think. Fresh lemon and lime juices, squeezed over crushed ice, with soda water and a sprig of mint?'

'That'll do nicely.' Lucy couldn't help but grin.

'Except I don't have any ice ready, sorry. No electric hook-up out here. And I hadn't imagined I'd be making cocktails at the beach today.'

'Oh that's okay, I'll let you off this time.'

'There's a couple of cold beers in a cool bag. If you'd rather have one of those?'

'No, that's fine. The lemon-and-lime soda sounds good.'

Jack pulled two fold-up seats out of the campervan, then set about making Lucy's drink, slicing and squeezing the zingy green and yellow fruits into a tall cut-glass tumbler and pouring over soda water from a bottle. He topped it with some fresh mint leaves, left over from a function last night, and passed the glass to her, then grabbed a cold beer for himself.

'I think we need a sea view,' he suggested. 'A view from the dunes, perhaps?'

'Okay.' So, after taking a big and delicious sip from her glass – quenching her thirst – they each carried a chair and their drinks, with Daisy close at Lucy's heel. The trio walked a little way back down the lane, soon diverting into a sandy track on the dunes.

They set up their seats in a slight dip in between the marram grass mounds, sheltered from the sea breeze, yet still having the full panorama of Embleton Bay. That sweep of golden sand arced before them, metallic light glinting off the gentle summer waves of the North Sea. The cries of kittiwakes and herring gulls. The rhythmic sounds of the surf.

Why had Lucy never thought to bring a chair down with her, and set up base with a book and a cooling drink? Hmm, on pleasant days, she might well do that from now on.

'So, when did you move out here, then?' asked Jack, as they gazed out to sea. 'Such a cool spot.'

'Ah, about four, no five, months ago now.' Time was rolling on, thank heavens, putting space and distance between her and Liam and all the hurt that had gone with that.

'Where were you before that, then?'

'Ah ...' she shifted a little in her seat. 'Well, I had a house, in Morpeth, with my boyfriend. *Ex*-boyfriend.' She didn't mention the word 'fiancé'. There was no need to go into any of that.

'Right-o. Sorry, I'm not prying ... So, how's the drink?' He deftly switched the conversation, sensing her unease.

'Delicious. Really refreshing, even without ice. And at least I'm not going to get brain freeze.'

'Cool.' He took a slug of his beer from his bottle. 'So Lucy, where are your dreams taking you?'

'Ah … what do you mean?' Lucy was taken aback for a second. Who asked that kind of question of someone they hardly knew? Hmm, Jack, evidently. She didn't think Liam had *ever* asked that question of her, he'd just assumed their dreams were the same … the sensible house, quality car, dual income in good steady jobs. Hah, they hardly sounded like dreams at all, did they?

She still hadn't answered.

'Okay, well what did you want to do when you were a kid then? What was the burning ambition? What did you want to be?' Jack fired on.

Nothing had been particularly *burning*, and she had to laugh out loud as she confessed, 'Well, I certainly didn't harbour any dreams about becoming an accountant.'

'Is that what you were doing before this?' Jack quirked an eyebrow.

'It wasn't that bad … just …'

'Boring?' The eyebrow quirked higher.

'Exactly. And stifling.' She couldn't help but smile as she said it, opening up to this guy.

'Hah, well I can probably match you there. I was training to be a lawyer, many moons ago.'

'Really?' Lucy couldn't imagine that at all.

'Yep, had started uni and everything … but God, it just wasn't me. Would have sent me demented, I think. All those hefty tomes to study ... the case law, and then a life trapped in court rooms and smart stuffy offices.' He paused, taking in the beautiful azure of the sky, the rush of rolling surf. 'My parents didn't quite see it that way, mind you,' he continued. 'Especially when they'd helped support me that first year ...' He still felt bad that he'd disappointed them, but had managed to pay back most of the money over time.

'Oh, don't suppose that was cheap ... Well, my dad's still reeling from me leaving the accountancy job.'

'Ouch.'

'Yeah, it's like everyone wants what's best for you ... only maybe it isn't,' the words spilled from Lucy's mouth.

Jack was nodding thoughtfully. 'Anyway, you never said what your real dreams were?' he continued.

'Ah, well,' she smiled, thinking back. 'I did always make my dolls play restaurants. And I always pictured having my own fabulous eatery that overlooked the sea ... by a beautiful beach somewhere. Where people would love to come and eat and, well, just enjoy themselves. Hah, I think some of Papa's dreams must have rubbed off on me.' She paused. When had she stopped imagining that?

How big were their dreams, how little their lives. The words flitted hauntingly in her mind. Had she read that in a book somewhere?

'Well, you're nearly there then, aren't you?' Jack cut in.

Lucy's brow creased, not sure what he was getting at. Was he being sarcastic?

'Your pizza horsebox ... you can pull up at all these fabulous places, park up at events that are right by the sea. You're just not stuck at any one. And hey, you're already serving fantastic food. You're living the life, Luce. Well, almost ...' He was smiling earnestly.

Wow, he suddenly made her see things so differently. 'Well, if you put it that way ...' But her sensible-self reminded her, she still had a long way to go, for sure. Her business was only just finding its feet, but hey-ho. Onwards and upwards and all that.

'Just keep moving forward, Lucy. You really are getting there,' Jack flashed her a supportive grin. 'But for now, let's just kick back and enjoy the sunshine and this glorious view.'

'Yeah.' That sounded perfect – time to let her anxieties over the business drift away on the sea breeze, for a little while at least.

Daisy had snuck under Lucy's chair, making the most of the shady spot. She soon started to snore. 'Did you hear that?' Lucy asked with a smile.

'Yeah, that rumbling noise, didn't like to mention it. Thought you might have some wind issues.'

'Shut up, you. It's Daisy ... snoring.'

''Course it is. Handy having a dog to blame, isn't it?' He raised his eyebrows cheekily.

She batted a hand out at him and her chair lost its grounding in the shifting sand, lurching perilously to one side ... towards Jack. He reached out, stopping her seat from toppling over, his forearm muscles taut beside her. Then he pushed her back upright, as he burst out laughing. 'See, that dog's a bloody liability. Trouble wherever she goes.'

Lucy couldn't help but giggle.

'Well, you've soon downed that.' Jack noted her near-empty glass. 'Good job it wasn't a real cocktail. Ready for another?'

'Oh ... well, I was thirsty. But ...'

'It's fine, I'll nip back up to Ruby, no problem. I might well fetch another beer for myself. There's no rush to be anywhere particular this afternoon.'

Lucy realised she had nothing pressing on either. Maybe there was no harm in staying for one more. 'Well, okay. Yes, thanks.'

'Do you fancy a real cocktail this time? I take it you're just walking home?'

Her head was in fact feeling a lot better. One drink would be rather nice. 'Nope, not going anywhere today. So yeah, go on then.'

'Any favourites? Gin-based, vodka, or a surprise?'

'Nothing too sickly or sweet, but go on, you choose for me.'

'A summer's day beach drink. You're on. I won't be long.'

He stood up, swigging the last of his beer from his bottle. 'I'll bring some water for Devil Dog too. She's looking a bit hot under there.'

Lucy looked at Jack, her head tilted, as if she was somehow looking at him anew. Perhaps he did actually have a sweet side to him, she thought. Here, he seemed different from the bravado-filled barman she'd witnessed at the events. Softer somehow, more thoughtful. More like the quieter man she'd glimpsed as they chatted before the Merry-Go-Round ride that night. Lucy sat looking out to sea, with the breeze caressing her skin. The warmth of the sun making her feel a little sleepy. It had evidently affected Daisy who was snoozing soundly, *very soundly*, with all the snoring going on from beneath her seat. Lucy felt very thankful to be living so near to all this, this gorgeous Northumberland coastline, and ... for today's company.

Fifteen minutes later, Jack appeared with a cocktail 'glass' in hand – in fact it was a tin mug. It was icy cold with condensation as he passed it over.

'Managed to bag some ice from the village pub!' he explained, 'Brilliant!'

'Ooh, what is it?'

'Try it first – tell me what you taste.'

'O-kay.' She sniffed, it was fresh and fragrant. She took a slow and delicious sip. There was ginger and mint and a light fizz, lime. 'Wow, it's zingy and it's good. Getting ginger, lime, minty flavours.'

'Yep, you've got it. A Morpeth Mule ... my take on a Moscow Mule, with mint from my mum and dad's garden, and local Fentiman's ginger beer. Didn't make it too strong.'

It tasted strong enough to her! 'Well, it certainly has a kick as it is. That is *nice*.' She took another long sip. 'Love it. Never tried anything like that before.'

'Thought you might like it.' He looked pleased with himself.

He also had another bottle of beer for himself, and raised it up in Lucy's direction. 'Cheers! Don't worry, this one's non-alcohol. I don't drink and drive with Ruby.'

So, he wasn't totally gung-ho then. She was glad to hear he had a cautious side.

They settled down into their sea-view seats, drinks to hand.

'So, the other evening, you mentioned your Italian grandad ... do you have some exotic Italian surname then?'

'Papa, yes.' She couldn't help but smile, just saying his name. 'And no, sorry to disappoint you, it's a straightforward Brown. Lucy Brown. Papa was my mother's father, – he was a Romano. Now that *does* sound very glamorous, doesn't it.'

'Lucy Romano ... you could adopt it for your pizza venture. Gourmet Pizza by Lucy *Romano*!' He put on a daft Italian accent, rolling the words over his tongue.

'Hah, no, I think having Papa's name there is enough. Anyway, what about you?'

He quirked an eyebrow.

'Your surname?'

'Ah ... Anderson, Jack Anderson. Just kind of normal too.'

'It has a ring to it. And "Jack's Cocktail Campervan" – now, that really does have a ring to it. Good name. So, when did it all start ... and how?'

Jack paused, a distant look crossing his face as he seemed to be thinking back. 'Oh blimey, it was about four years ago now ... Needed to break out and do something different. I'd been travelling a bit, after giving up on uni, working a few bars as I went. There was this great cocktail bar on the beach in Vietnam, that kind of stuck in my mind. The bartender, Sammy, was such a cool guy. I got some great tips and experience just from watching him.' He smiled as he remembered. 'Then I came back to the UK, picked up a few casual jobs – restaurants, bars and the like – put in all sorts of hours. I suppose I was learning the ropes. I even did a mixology course;

that was great fun. Ended up as manager in the Gatehouse Bistro, in Alnwick. And over time, I came to realise that I wanted to do something for me. My own business. I went down to a festival in Leeds around that same time, and there were all sorts of these mobile food and drink businesses, but back then there was nothing much like it around here. I saw the potential.' He took a sip of lager. 'Then, I saw Ruby advertised on Sales and Wants – she was a bit of a wreck when I went to look at her, mind you. But that was it … the two things sparked off in my mind, and I knew I just had to buy her and give it a try. The rest, as they say, is history.'

'Wow, and it's worked out for you?'

'Yeah, I'm doing well financially, and more than that, I love the way of life, the freedom it gives me. I never feel tied down.'

Lucy nodded. It was a different way of working, of living, she was learning that fast. The uncertainties were always there, but it had its plus sides. Not being tied to a desk or an office or a grumpy boss was a big part of that.

The next hour rolled lazily by, as they found themselves chatting easily about all sorts. The Morpeth Mule was long gone, but the taste still lingered. Lucy glanced at her watch. Crikey, it was nearly 4 p.m.! Where had the day gone?

'Well, this has been great. Thank you, Jack. I'm so glad we bumped into each other.'

'Yeah, me too.' He gave her a broad smile.

She could see a smattering of freckles coming out across the bridge of his nose. His skin already a golden tan. His hair looked blonder than she remembered; maybe it was the summer sun streaking it. He looked a typical surfer dude, an outdoorsy kind of guy.

She realised she'd been staring. He was gazing right back at her.

'Right then,' she announced, getting up quickly and feeling the alcohol whizz a little through her veins, making her slightly heady. Lucy gave Daisy a gentle prod, stirring her from her Sunday afternoon slumber.

'Yeah, suppose I'd better get on and back up the road too.' Jack stood up, collecting up his bottle. 'Only leave footprints,' he said.

'Oh, yes, absolutely.'

They reached the campervan and Jack loaded the chairs inside, then reached to take Lucy's empty tin mug which she'd carried back up with her. Their fingertips brushed as he did so, zipping a surprise jolt of electricity through her.

'She's a real beauty,' Lucy said, quickly switching focus, to admire the gleaming exterior of the vintage campervan.

'She is indeed,' Jack beamed proudly. 'Hey, do you want to hitch a ride? Take a quick cruise along the coast?'

'Umm ...'

Lucy had to admit she was curious. Ruby, the campervan, always looked so wonderful. She'd love to try her out.

'Okay then – yeah, why not? Just a quick spin. I've probably taken up far too much of your time already.'

'Ah, it's no problem. I love showing off my best girl.' With that, he swung open the passenger door for Lucy.

She clocked that, unusually, it seemed to be on the wrong side.

'She's a left-hand drive classic. Ruby has German heritage, you know. You're not the only one with exotic roots.' He grinned, 'Jump on board!'

Ruby started up with a chug then a whirr, and they set off on the coast road, diverting inland for a countryside spin, then taking the route seawards again. Winding through the lanes, past fields of crops now tinged with gold and swaying in the light breeze, the blue of the sea glimpsed through a gap in the hedgerow every now and then.

'It's the original dashboard and everything.' Jack was proud to share his pride and joy, as Lucy took in the three circular dials in front of them. 'Mind you, that does mean there're no mod-cons ... like air conditioning,' he explained.

'Hey, no worries.'

It *was* getting a little warm in there.

'So, it's the good old-fashioned method,' he announced. 'Wind the windows down!'

Lucy giggled as she wound the traditional plastic handle. A woosh of air blasted the cab, blowing her hair wildly. Even Daisy's ears began to flap, bless her, as she sat there on Lucy's lap.

'So, let the good times roll,' Jack shouted over the rumble of wind and the chug of the engine.

And it felt like summer ... and seaside ... and fun. All the worries of the world fading away. The here and now was all that mattered.

It wasn't long before they took the turn towards the little coastal village of Newton-by-the-Sea, slowing as they reached the brow of the hill, where the view of the bay across to the ragged ruins of Dunstanburgh Castle was stunning.

'Wow, it looks amazing today,' was all Lucy could muster.

'Beautiful, isn't it.'

They both took in the view as Jack slowed, making the drive downhill at a leisurely crawl. The road ended here at a cluster of white-washed fishermen's cottages, now converted into holiday lets and cosy homes. The Ship Inn, all old stone and the heart of many a mariner's tales, nestled in one corner.

'Thanks ... for showing me Ruby ... for bringing me here,' Lucy whispered, barely able to tear her eyes away from the breath-taking scene. It was just a small trip out, not far from her cottage even, and yet it was so special. Lucy felt like she'd been set free.

'You're most welcome,' Jack grinned.

'Suppose we'll have to head back ...'

'Yep, I'll be blocking the entrance to the cottages.'

They somehow ended up singing on the way back. Jack, apologising for the lack of a radio, started by blasting out Bryan Adams' 'Summer of '69', along with the guitar noises and all. Lucy was stirred to join in halfway through; a shared love of soft rock was apparent, as they both knew the words. Hedgerows whizzed past, the wind in their hair, sun streaming through the windscreen. She couldn't remember the last time she'd felt so alive.

Back at her village ten minutes later, Jack parked up at the exact spot he'd left.

'Ah ... well, thanks for that drive, that was brilliant, and for the drinks earlier. I'll definitely be having another of those Morpeth Mules sometime.'

'Hah, my pleasure, and at our next event, don't forget to tell the guests how good those cocktails are. And ... I'll be sure to let everybody know about your amazing pizzas too. What do you call the business again, Fired Up?'

'Yep, All Fired Up.'

'Okay, well I'll drum up some extra business for you, for sure. When I get enquiries, I'll check if anyone's looking for food outlets as well as the cocktail bar.'

It felt so good to have his support. 'Thanks, Jack. I appreciate that.'

There was a moment of silence as though strangely, neither felt quite ready to go. Maybe it was because it had been such a nice afternoon, with the drive and everything ... a bit of much-needed time out. Or maybe, the Morpeth Mule had been stronger than she'd realised. Hmm, the fact she hadn't eaten since her bacon sandwich at 10 a.m. might well be a factor too.

'Right ... well, I'll just walk up the lane. There're a few chores I need to get on with back home. It's only five minutes to the cottage from here. Come on then, Daisy.' Lucy turned to go.

'Ah ... well, let me walk you back.' Jack, too, seemed reluctant to leave.

Well, Lucy could hardly say no, could she? But, despite the effects of an afternoon cocktail on a near-empty stomach and having had a lot of fun, she knew better than to do anything like ask him in. Her earlier fluttery tummy at seeing him, all male and muscular, coming out of the sea, was unwisely coming back in to play. Crikey, where *were* her thoughts taking her today? They hardly knew each other. It was all Becky's fault last night, telling her to get back in the saddle. It was putting extremely dangerous images into her mind.

Jack wasn't sure why he'd said that, about walking her back. He supposed he'd just enjoyed the afternoon, enjoyed her company. And he didn't fancy turning up at his lodgings too soon. Sundays were often Matt and Jess's together-days; he didn't particularly want to be stuck in the house with them being all lovey-dovey. Okay, so it *was* Matt's house, he appreciated that. They could do what they liked, but he didn't have to be a witness to it all.

Maybe he'd squeeze in a quick visit to his parents'; they'd like that. There'd always be the chance of some supper there too. His mum was a good home cook and he knew that he was always welcome. He was sure she still made meals for three, or four, just in case …

But for now, he was going to make the most of strolling along on a sunny day with this attractive and interesting girl. She wasn't half as cold and haughty as she liked to make out.

Daisy was trotting along between the two of them as they wandered back up the narrow road.

'Been a lovely day. Great weather,' Lucy said, a touch nervously, as they strolled, resorting to the safety of chit-chat.

'Yeah, gotta make the most of days like these. One day sun, the next rain. Good old English weather.'

'You're right about that. And in Northumberland you can get all four seasons in one day.'

'Hah, yes.'

'So, have you got any bookings coming up?' Lucy asked.

'Wednesday evening's the next, and then Friday, a birthday bash. Oh, and Saturday, there's a wedding do over Rothbury way. You?'

'Just the Thursday market in Alnwick again, then nothing else at all until a week Saturday.' Lucy felt a small punch of disappointment. 'Think I'll be living on beans on toast if this carries on too long,' she smiled as she jested, but Jack understood there was an element of fear and truth in her words too. Lucy exhaled with a small anxious sigh.

Jack reached for her hand, giving it a supportive squeeze.

Lucy slid him a sideways glance. Their hands parted swiftly again, and they were soon at the top of the little hill where the village began with the first row of cottages and The Oyster Catcher pub on the corner.

They turned along a further street, and Lucy stopped near its end. 'Right, well this is me.'

Jack found himself standing outside a pale-grey painted door set in a honey-coloured stone-built cottage, nestled end-of-row. It was small, yet quaint. It suited her.

'Right ...' he echoed, suddenly feeling a little awkward. He hadn't had any ulterior motive in walking her home, wasn't sure why the words had come out of his mouth. It wasn't like it was late at night or anything either, when she might have needed a chaperone back. 'Well, it's been a great afternoon,' he added.

'It has. Thanks again.' A sunny smile lit up her face.

So, this is it. Time to go.

'See you around then,' her tone was casual, yet she was still looking at him with those dark-brown, thoughtful eyes.

Oh, sod it! The urge to kiss her suddenly overwhelmed him.

Before he had a chance to think straight – *Might not be a good idea. Just friends. Have to work together etc. etc.* – Jack leaned across and went to place a kiss on her rather luscious lips.

It was then Daisy tugged on her lead, impatient to go in. Pulling them apart, with a jolt.

'Oh ...' was all Lucy could say as she stepped back, a bit baffled about what had just unfolded. 'Okay, Daisy, home time it is.' Fumbling for her key in her jeans pocket, she could hardly look at him. 'Uh, bye then, Jack.'

'Bye.' He watched her duck away inside. It looked like Lucy couldn't disappear quickly enough.

Hah, bloody dog! Or maybe, just maybe ... it was a timely escape for him too.

He gave a final glance at the cottage and then started to head back to Ruby. What a glorious, surprising, confusing day it had been ... And he couldn't help but hope he'd experience it all again – every emotion – very soon.

Chapter 16

Well, *what* was that all about? Had Jack Anderson really been about to kiss her? Wow, it was the first time anybody had been anywhere near her lips in almost two years. Had she wanted him to, or would she have stepped back anyhow, despite Daisy's timely intervention?

Two hours later, and Lucy was still thinking about that promise of a kiss. *Jack's* kiss. What would it have felt like? His golden-tanned smiling face filled her mind again. The straw-coloured hair, the fringe a little too long; he was undeniably handsome. Looking back at her with those intense blue-grey eyes, with their colours of slate and sky.

It had just been such a gorgeously carefree and unexpected afternoon. One of those times she knew she'd remember for a long while to come. She could feel the skin on her cheeks tight from the summer sun, no doubt slightly pink with a flurry of fresh freckles across the bridge of her nose. The taste of vodka and ginger, and salty sea air.

What if Daisy hadn't pulled them apart? Would it have been a tender brush on the lips ... or a full-blown snog of a kiss?

The ringtone on her mobile took her out of her reverie. She glanced at the caller ID: Becky. Ah, well, that brought her back down to earth.

She answered, 'Hi, Becks.'

'Hey, lovely. Fun night last night, wasn't it. How are you feeling now? I've felt rough as anything all day!'

'Hah, yeah, I'm fine. Been out and got some fresh air on the beach. Done me the world of good.' Thoughts came flooding in of Jack, making the corner of her mouth lift into a smile as she spoke. 'Actually ...' Lucy paused, unsure, 'I saw that cocktail-bar guy, there on the beach. Just by chance,' she clarified.

'Ooh, now this sounds interesting. You mean the one you don't fancy at all, but you keep on telling me about?'

'I suppose that's the one, yeah.' She was grinning as she spoke.

'*And?*'

There was another pause, while Lucy figured how to mention the near-kiss.

'Go on, tell me you've had wild sex in the sand dunes or something.'

A near-kiss at her doorstep sounded rather tame compared to that. 'No, not quite. Just, well ... we had a chat for a while, sat in the dunes ... then he walked me back, and ... I think he was about to kiss me ...'

'What do you mean, about to? He either did or he didn't!'

'Didn't,' Lucy confessed. 'Daisy yanked us apart at the crucial moment. So, I'll never find out now, will I?' She gave a mock groan.

'Hah, well that's just typical of you, Luce. And Daisy, what a naughty girl, spoiling your fun like that. Well, what are you going to do about it then?'

'What do you mean? Nothing much I can do, I suppose.'

'Of course there is. Organise another meet-up, get yourselves on a date. I can tell you like him. There's a spark there, for sure.'

'Oh, I'm not sure about that. A spur-of-the-moment kiss is one thing, but organising a date, that'll give him all the wrong signals. Nah, I'm not going down that route.' She thought of all his flirting and flattery with a host of women from behind his bar. He probably wasn't even the dating sort. She might have got it all wrong about this kiss anyhow, misread the signals. How downright embarrassing would that be?

Becky, despite her excitement, had helped her get it all back in perspective. No way was Lucy going to take it any further. It had just been a very special afternoon, nothing more, nothing less. A few stolen hours to think about, and perhaps savour on her own for now.

'Anyway, how's your head?' Lucy deflected, neatly.

'Ah, not bad. Nothing a couple of paracetamols couldn't fix. Mind you, Darren had me dragging around Homebase this afternoon, looking for paint and new shelving for the second bedroom. Normally, I'd be right up for that. That he's at last come round to the idea of decorating that room, but today of all days ...'

Lucy chuckled. Back to real life. Safer ground. No daft daydreams about bar guys and summer kisses. She'd keep all that romantic stuff for her books.

Chapter 17

Back at his lodgings, Jack was also dwelling on the day. It was a long while since he'd spent such a relaxed time with a woman. There were no strings, no expectations, just the chance to chat and chill out together as they'd started to get to know each other. He'd really enjoyed her company, and she was pretty damned gorgeous too – all dark bouncy hair and those soulful brown eyes. They'd talked easily, yes, but he instinctively knew there was so much more to this woman. She played her cards close to her chest, about her past, her feelings, who she really was. But that just made him all the more intrigued.

He still felt a bit mortified about that daft attempt at a kiss. He wondered what would have happened if that bloody Devil Dog hadn't pulled her away? The jealous little mutt. But maybe it was for the best. It might only have served to confuse matters. It wasn't like he was looking for anything more from her.

Maybe he'd get to see her again at an event in the coming weeks. He hoped her venture would soon get off the ground and thrive; she deserved that. She was ambitious; a hard worker.

Jack sighed and made his way to his laptop; no rest for the wicked. He'd jazz up his social media business pages. He'd taken a few shots of Ruby in full swing at his last event, with some close-ups of his summer-style cocktails to pop on his Insta and Facebook pages. He had some great online supporters, and loved the chat and banter there. It had also helped to get Jack's Cocktail Campervan noticed.

Later, he made a couple of calls confirming this week's bookings; a professional and friendly approach. He liked to check timings and details, giving the clients a chance to go over any last-minute requests too. He'd only once been let down – the organiser having totally forgotten about booking the event, and due to a change in circumstances hadn't asked any guests along either – and fool that he was back then, Jack had taken no deposit. He'd learnt from that mistake.

'Hi, it's Jack from the Cocktail Campervan,' he said cheerily, launching into his call for a 40th Birthday Bash. 'Is that Nikki?'

'Hello, there. Yes, yes, it is.'

'Hi, I've got a booking with you for this Friday evening, so it's just a courtesy call to double check timings and any last-minute details or requests you might have.'

'Oh, hi Jack, thanks for the call. Thank heavens *you're* still okay to come.' She sounded rather stressed on the other end of the line.

'Well yes, of course. Why, has there been a problem or something?'

'Bloody hell, yes, you could say that,' she huffed. 'I had a call earlier from the caterer who was meant to be doing the buffet. They've only gone and had a case of suspected E-coli. Got to shut the whole thing down for a couple of weeks and totally disinfect. I've been making calls frantically, trying to get a new caterer, but to no avail. Where the hell do I find someone good, who isn't already booked up, this late in the day?'

'Well then ...' This was it, Lucy's chance. Jack was sure she'd step up to the mark. 'I think I might just be able to help you there.'

'You can?' The woman sounded relieved and a little surprised.

'Yeah, I've a friend who's just set up her own pizza van – well, horsebox, in fact. It looks really great. Got that cute vintage feel. So, how does pizza sound? I mean they're amazing, top-quality, homemade, stone-baked, and delicious. I've tasted them, so I can definitely vouch for them.' He was doing his best salesman pitch.

'Umm, pizza's a start, but I really need a bit of variety. I had a full buffet booked with this catering company: starters, salads, dessert, the works.'

'Oh well, I'm sure she'd be keen. She does garlic breads ... perhaps salads would be fine. I can ask about dessert options for you, too.' He was really going out on a limb here, he knew, but Lucy had said she was desperate for more business. Even if she went and bought in some good puddings from the local cash and carry, that could work. He was thinking on his feet.

'Sounds interesting ...'

'Okay, well let me give her a ring. And then, if she's up for it, which I'm pretty certain she will be, then is it okay to pass on your number? I'll get her to call you as soon as poss. Put your mind at rest.'

'Oh Jack, you might just be a life-saver, well a party-saver anyhow. I was stressing out that I'd have to try and cater for sixty people myself. And it's meant to be a surprise. It'll be a bit of a giveaway if I'm stood cooking all bloody day!'

'No worries, I'm happy to help.'

'Thank you so much.'

'And I'll be there for 7 p.m. as planned, yeah?'

'Yes, perfect. Thanks again,' Nikki's voice had lifted with relief.

He couldn't let her down now. As he turned off the call, Jack suddenly realised that he didn't have Lucy's mobile number. Right, well he'd have to message her via her Facebook page which he'd spotted the other day, and quickly. He didn't want another catering firm stepping into the gap in the meanwhile.

He started typing:

Hi Lucy. I've a gig for you this Friday if you're interested? 40th Birthday. A pizza booking with some extras needed too. Filling in for a last-minute cancellation. Job's yours if you're up for it? Give me a call asap, Jack

He paused ... should he finish with a kiss or not? Ah, go for it:

X

He added his mobile number and pressed Send. *Done.* And now all he had to do was wait.

Chapter 18

Lucy was making sandcastles in her brother's back garden, having some hands-on fun with her two-year-old nephew in his sand-pit, when her phone buzzed.

A notification from Facebook. She clicked onto it. Oh, it was Jack, via her page. *That* Jack. She quickly read the message. Oh, it was a work thing ... and great ... there was a job coming up ... this Friday. She laughed out loud at 'some extras needed too'! Was that for cocky barman Jack the Lad or the party organiser, she mused? But, wow, a new booking, and just when she needed the business so badly. He'd come up trumps.

She swallowed the small feeling of disappointment that he hadn't been messaging to meet up again. *Stop dreaming, Lucy. Enough of that.*

'Pat it, Annie Lucy.' Little Freddie brought her back to the here and now. He'd not quite mastered the word 'Auntie', so she was Annie Lucy. Lucy turned over the castle pot, and they patted it together with little plastic spades. She was really fond of her nephew. Her own dreams of having a family sometime soon had been blown apart with the news that Liam was leaving her – well, to be fair, after his appalling behaviour, it was more like a bloody big shove out the door on her part. She lifted off the pot carefully.

'Yay, it's a good one, Freddie.'

'Yesss! I find flower ... put on it.' And off he toddled happily, towards the garden border where Daisy dog was sniffing about.

'Olly,' Lucy called out to attract her bro's attention. 'Can you come and watch Fred a mo? Got a call to make.' Her nephew was at the age where he needed constant monitoring. And well, she really couldn't afford to miss out on this booking. It was great that Jack had thought of her business. She did feel a bit anxious after the near-kiss moment, but she only needed to be polite to him, after all; no reason to have to mention it.

'No worries.' Olly headed out the back door of their modern brick semi-detached home, ready to take over.

'Be back in a minute, little man,' she called to her nephew.

'Pop the kettle on while you're in there, sis. I was just about to make us a cuppa.'

'Will do.'

Lucy felt strangely nervous typing in Jack's number. She wasn't sure if it was about the possible booking or just having to speak with him after that rather gorgeous afternoon they'd spent on Sunday.

He picked up quickly. 'Hello, it's Jack.'

'Hi, it's Lucy.'

'Oh, Lucy, hi. So, you got my message ...'

'Yeah, about a booking?'

'Yep, I'm doing a 40th Birthday party this Friday, and the

family have been let down by the catering company. Had to cancel due to a case of E-coli or something.'

'Oh crikey.'

'Anyway, Nikki, that's the woman organising the party for her husband, is desperate for someone to replace them.'

'Okay, sounds good so far. How many is it for?'

'Around sixty guests. The only thing is ... it's not just pizza she's after.'

'Oh?'

'Well, the original company were doing a full buffet, so Nikki's thinking of salads, and perhaps something else to go with the pizza ... oh, and puddings.' She could hear Jack's voice dip as though he realised this was a bit of an ask.

'*Oh.*' How could she do all that? Her brain began to whirr. Well, okay, salads, pizza garlic breads, and yes ... perhaps some antipasti with olives and charcuterie. Yes, that could work, but *puddings*? She'd never been much of a dessert maker. But oh blimey, this ... this was too damn good a chance to miss.

'You'll be well paid, I'm sure. I've already received a decent deposit on the booking. Anyway, look, I can give you her number. She'd like you to call her to chat things through, if that's okay. I just thought of you, and it seemed too good an opportunity to miss.' He echoed her thoughts.

'Yes, thanks; yes, it is ... umm, thank you, Jack.' She then punched the details into her contacts. 'Right, well, I suppose I'd better make that call then. Cheers.'

No mention was made of their afternoon together, Lucy wasn't sure if she was relieved or concerned by that – had she been over-dramatising things? And the call ended swiftly.

And so, she found herself chatting away to the hostess, Nikki, and agreeing to cater for sixty people in just three days' time; providing pizzas, sides, and a selection of puddings. *Oh my god*, it was a good booking, but bloody hell, she'd have her work cut out. She poured out the tea for her and Olly in a bit of a daze and took two mugs out to the garden bench. 'Here you go, Olly. Oh, and Freddie, wow, that looks amazing.' A big purple trumpet-like petunia flower had been placed on top of the castle they'd just made, along with a stick flagpole that Olly was busy attaching a leaf to. Daisy dog bustled up next to little Freddie who patted her head excitedly in a slightly rough manner, but the little dog was fine with that. Daisy was good with small children, and they in turn seemed to love her.

'Any luck?' Olly asked cautiously, aware that the pizza venture had been going rather slowly so far.

'Yeah, I'm glad I made the call. I've just taken a booking for *sixty* people, Ol ... for this coming Friday.'

'Oh, wow. Well done you.' Her brother gave her a big thumbs up. 'You see, it's building. I have every faith in you.'

'Yeah, I'm going to have to do some serious blagging though, I need *pudding* options and I'm no baker!' She pulled a grimace.

'Hmm, there are no pizza puddings as far as I know, sis. And I hate to remind you but your last attempt at a Victoria sponge wasn't exactly a success.' He gave a wry smile.

'I know.' She groaned. That particular cake had sunk in the middle, and looked rather sorry for itself. Mind you, she was just getting used to the oven's settings in her new cottage. 'Maybe I need to come up with some Italian-style desserts, easy ones. Oh Olly, have I just bitten off more than I can chew with this?'

'Nope, you just have to think creatively. So, who do we know makes good puddings?'

'*Nonna*,' they both chimed together.

'Nonn-a,' Freddie shouted out, copying them, as he raised and waved his little plastic spade triumphantly into the air, whilst Daisy ducked wisely out of the way.

Lucy wasted no time. Nonna lived in a sheltered accommodation flat in the little town of Rothbury, not far from Lucy's mum. Though it was a half-hour drive from her cottage, Lucy visited often, so it wasn't an unusual trip. She made sure to pop into the supermarket on the street corner on the way, picking up a bunch of carnations in bright pinks and yellows to cheer her grandmother up. The old lady wasn't as active these days, with arthritis riddling her hips and knees, and though she always had a ready smile, she no doubt must have found it hard, having to make her way in the world without Papa by her side over these past ten years. Lucy was certain those four sheltered walls could feel pretty lonely at times.

Nonna was a proper Newcastle-born Geordie through and through, but she'd been happy to take on the name of Nonna for the grandchildren, giving homage to Papa's Italian roots. It had stuck, and suited her warm and homely personality. She was always pleased to get a visitor, and her voice came through loud and clear on the intercom at the main doors. 'Come on up, pet!' she called cheerily, as Lucy pressed the buzzer to gain entry.

Lucy was greeted at the door, with Nonna's grey eyes twinkling and her beam of a smile. 'Hello, my darling girl, and how are you?'

'I'm fine thanks, Nonna. How're you doing?'

'Not so bad, not so bad. Knees a bit creaky, but other than that I've got nothing to complain about. Ready for a cuppa, pet?' She began to head a little stiffly towards the small kitchen.

'Oh, let me do it, Nonna. And I'll pop these flowers in a vase for you too.'

'Okay, my lovely. Thank you, they're beautiful. Oh, and there're some custard creams in the tin too,' she called after her granddaughter.

Nonna's kitchen was compact, the units old-fashioned but tidy, with everything in its place. On the wall was an old faded picture of Sorrento, Papa's home town overlooking the Bay of Naples. There was his large wooden pepper grinder stood on the side, a relic from his restaurant days, and a pottery spoon rest hand-painted with olives and lemons, bought on their last holiday together – a trip back down memory lane for the pair of them. Little memories of Papa and his heritage still singing out to them all.

As Lucy returned shortly afterwards with a tray of tea and biscuits, Nonna asked, 'Well then, how's the new pizza business going? Are you keeping up to Papa's standards? Come and sit down, pet, and tell me all about it.' She was always interested in her family's lives, keen to know what the young ones were up to. Obviously, she had an extra interest in this particular venture of Lucy's, with it being so close to all their hearts.

Lucy sat on an ageing, yet comfortable, green floral-patterned sofa, with Nonna propped in her high-backed chair beside her. Papa was there with them both; his dark, kind eyes looking on from his pride-of-place photo on the mantle-piece.

'Yes, of course. Only the best ingredients as always, I insist on making all my own dough ... and it has to be Papa's tomato sauce with *tons* of garlic.'

They both smiled. Papa loved to use plenty of garlic. They'd all have garlic breath for days after eating his pizzas and pastas. His 'Sunday Sauce' was the stuff of family legend. Long after he'd stopped working in the restaurant and even after a busy week on the buses, he'd still be keen to make it – with rich, tomato-garlic aromas flooding the house.

'Well then,' Lucy continued, 'the pizza horsebox has started off pretty good. I've been finding my feet these past couple of weeks and I've got a few new bookings in now.' She kept a positive spin on it, happy with her new booking, and not wanting to give Nonna anything to be concerned about.

'Oh, I'm so proud of you, pet. And it's wonderful that you're using Papa's recipe. Ah, how I wish he could be here to see this happen.' She glanced at his photo on the side with a sigh. 'Mind you, you know your Papa, he'd be wanting to pitch in and help. Butting in with how to make the best tomato sauce.'

'Hah, yes, wouldn't he, and I wouldn't have minded one bit.'

They both gave a nostalgic smile.

'In fact,' Lucy moved on to her pressing dilemma, 'it's a recipe idea that I'm after, Nonna. You've always made the best cakes. And well, I've been asked to cater for pizza and puddings at my next event ...'

'Oh, that sounds lovely.'

'Yes, but I haven't got a clue where to start with the puddings! I thought some cakes might work, and I remembered your special chocolate cake. The one you used to make for our birthday parties sometimes. Remember that one for my eleventh birthday in your garden?'

Her mind cast back to that happy day with Papa working away at the outside pizza oven he'd made, and Nonna bustling about with cakes and ice-creams in her red-checked apron.

'All my friends came over for pizza and ice cream. It was brilliant, and I could tell Papa loved doing it. Stoking up the wood-fire and feeding the oven with pizza after pizza, whilst singing away to "O Sole Mio". He used to love that song.'

Nonna's smile lifted as Lucy chatted away. 'Oh yes, I haven't made one of those cakes for a while now, pet. I think you mean the one made with chocolate sponge and a chocolate mousse topping.'

'That's it. When I was little you used to load it with chocolate sprinkles too. All my friends used to love it. Is it hard to do? And more importantly, can it be made it for a crowd?'

'Yes, of course. And it's not that tricky at all. For a bigger cake, just multiply up the ingredients, and you could use a big square tin to bake it in. The mousse is fairly straightforward, then you could just cut it into individual squares.'

'Scrummy. Do you still have the recipe?'

'Oh absolutely. That recipe is so special; it was handed down from Papa's mother.'

'Was it really? Wow, I didn't know that. That's even better. So, it's Italian-inspired too?'

'Yes, my lovely.'

'Brilliant. You don't happen to have another easy pudding tucked up your sleeve, do you?' Lucy ventured. She'd need at least one more dessert option.

'Hmm, let me have a little think, while we have our cup of tea.'

So, after a happy chat about life in Lucy's cottage, Daisy's latest antics (who was now sat at their feet, on the lookout for custard cream crumbs), and Nonna's gin club – oh yes, apparently the common room turned into a gin parlour every Thursday evening, along with a bingo session – Lucy left with two recipes to try: Nonna's chocolate extravaganza and a Clementine and Limoncello Cake. Nonna had even donated a half-full bottle of Limoncello from her sideboard for Lucy to take with her.

With a host of things to do to prepare for this unexpected booking, Lucy soon had to make her goodbyes.

'*Ciao*, Nonna.'

'*Ciao*, pet.'

They'd said this on parting ever since Lucy had been a little girl.

Lucy left after a heartfelt hug on the threshold to Nonna's flat, with a promise to return very soon with a slice or two of both cakes by way of thanks. She had a smile on her face and a lift in her heart as she waved up at Nonna's first-floor window from the little car park below, grateful to have such wonderful support in her life. *La famiglia* was everything, and today she was particularly thankful to have a keen baker for a grandmother. Her nonna.

Chapter 19

Driving down the A1 on his way to the drinks supplier, and stuck behind a tediously slow tractor, Jack found himself thinking about Lucy. He was looking forward to seeing her once again at the function at the end of the week. He was glad he'd been able to help her out and get her the gig. It was good to give someone a step up on the ladder. He'd certainly needed a few pointers when he'd started out with Ruby and his campervan cocktail bar.

He was also feeling slightly nervous. What had she really thought about him making the move to kiss her on her step? Had she enjoyed the afternoon on the beach as much as he had? Jeez, he hadn't felt like this since he was a teenager, getting giddy about some girl. What the hell was the matter with him? The traffic was busy, with a trail of lorries stuck behind that tractor up ahead. He'd better concentrate on the road, instead of daydreaming like some love-struck kid. Better to keep her out of his mind altogether, in fact.

As he neared the wholesaler's depot, he happened to pass a secondary school. He could see into the sports field where a football match was being played, by what looked like a group of older teenage lads. There was one boy with sandy-blond hair, his arm in the air as he called out for the ball ... Jack froze for a second.

Shit, one of the lads had looked *just* like his brother Daniel from the back, just for that split second ... Of course, it wasn't, would never be. Jack found his hands were trembling on the steering wheel.

And there it was again, over eleven years later, that punch-in-the-gut blow of grief. He was jolted back to the past. He remembered the excitement of the two of them going for new football boots. Jack's first-ever pair, and Daniel's second – his big brother as always having got there first in life, not that Jack minded, it was just the way it was. His eyes had lit up at the row of boots in the sports shop: blue with black stripes, a vivid yellow pair, green Nikes. The measuring, feet having grown again, now a size 4. The trying on. And of course, he went for the pair just like Daniel's. He could still picture them now – Adidas, white leather with black stripes, and bright-green laces. And he'd felt like the coolest dude in town heading out on that football pitch for junior league the next Saturday morning. By the end of the match his feet were sore and a blister had formed, but he didn't mind one bit. New boots needed breaking in, so that didn't stop him adoring them and *him*. His big brother.

When you were a younger brother, you were never on your own. You always had a constant companion ... or at least you should, Jack thought with a fresh bolt of grief.

It had happened when Daniel was just twenty, on a pitch

at uni, mid-play. If only they'd known that Daniel had been stalked by a silent, undetected killer. The fallout of that fateful day still haunted Jack. And perhaps it always would.

Jack carried on driving on autopilot, found himself at the wholesaler's depot, took the turn into the car park and pulled into a space. Still feeling overwhelmed, he listened to the engine fall silent and looked down at his lap, trying to stop the tears that were misting his eyes. Sniffing, he took out the pad and pen that he kept on Ruby's dash, mostly used for jotting down supplies he'd need to restock. He paused, and then started to write:

> *Smell of cut grass and mud, sweaty football boots.*
> *Kickabout in the back garden,*
> *You the shooter, me in goal.*
> *He shoots, he scores, yay!*
> *We were always going to be winners, me and you.*
> *But you lost the big one, Danny,*
> *You lost at life.*
> *And that day I lost everything too.*
> *Am still lost.*

He stopped with the pen hovering over the page, wiping his face as fresh tears blotted the paper.

If only he and Daniel could kick that ball around again, play some five-a-side for a local team. He took a slow, steadying breath. Had to pull himself back to the present. It was just him in a campervan in a tarmacked cash-and-carry car park. Needed to crack on, get the supplies he needed for the function. Just function himself. Keep going. Move on, move forward.

But sometimes, it damned well felt like he couldn't move at all. Floored by these aftershocks of grief. It didn't matter how long it had been. It was still, would always be, a part of him. Jack had learnt that sometimes you just needed to let that grief take hold, reach its roots down to your soul and then out towards that person you missed so much. He'd bottled it all up for long enough now.

Maybe it was time to reach out and let someone in too. Break down those walls he'd built around himself for so long.

Lucy flashed into his mind again with her glossy chocolate waves, her thoughtful eyes. Could she be that someone?

Chapter 20

Lucy was in a mist of 00 flour, having spent the last hour binding batches of pizza dough in her industrial-sized mixer, ready to prove and then feed the festive gatherers at the 40th Birthday Bash tomorrow. *To-morr-ow*, and that was coming around way too fast. The kitchen clock warning her that already it was 7 p.m.

Now mid-knead and plastered in sticky dough, she heard her mobile phone buzz into life on the side. She shifted sideways to check who was calling. 'Becky' was flashing up on the screen. Ah, she'd have to call her back in a while. By the time she'd cleaned her hands up enough to answer, it would have stopped anyhow. And these dough mountains weren't going to make themselves, no way, José. Get this job out of the way, and then she might find a chance to pour a cuppa and take five mins out. A brief chat with her friend would be a welcome distraction then.

Just ten minutes later, and the phone sprang to life once more. Lucy had just placed the huge dough ball in a tray to prove, and was about to prop it along with the others near the old-fashioned stove that kept everything toasty warm in there. A pizza production line that filled her galley kitchen. Dashing to the phone, she spotted that it was Becky again – oh, was everything alright? Or better ... was her friend maybe wanting to meet up soon for coffee and cake or something? Get tomorrow over with, and she'd be well up for that. Wiping her hands vigorously against her apron, Lucy just managed to pick up in time.

'Hel-lo.' The phone was propped under Lucy's chin as she dried her fingers some more.

'Hey-y ...' Becky sounded ... different. After all these years, the girls were so in tune, it was scary.

'You okay?' Luce asked.

'Oh, yeah ... but there's just been something on my mind, hun.' Her voice sounded troubled down the line. 'Okay, so you were all excited about this Jack, the bar guy ... and well, naturally I looked up the Cocktail Campervan thing. Being nosy, like I am.'

'Okay ...'

'Well, I found him on Facebook and Instagram, the Cocktail Campervan pages ... Lucy, I saw his picture ... I'm sure I know him.' Her friend's voice had dipped warily.

Lucy had a prickly feeling that she wasn't going to like the way this conversation was heading. 'Where are you going with this, Becks?'

'What's this guy's surname?'

'Umm ...' She thought back to their recent conversation on the beach. 'Anderson, I think. Yes, Jack Anderson.'

A beat of silence from Becky, then, 'Oh shit. That's it ... I bloody well knew it. Jack twat-faced bloody Anderson ... the guy who only went and wrecked my 21st Birthday with his two-timing antics.'

'*Honestly?* Are you sure, Becks?' Lucy felt the blood drain from her cheeks. It all began to fall horribly into place. *That* Jack.

Lucy had met him briefly back then, but it was years ago, and yeah, he'd worn his hair really short, and he and Becky had only been on a few dates – time enough for her friend to have fallen head over heels for him, mind you – and time enough for him to have been seeing someone else too. She still remembered that night, at the restaurant bar that had been booked in town, Becky waiting excitedly for her new boyfriend to turn up and meet all her family and friends ... except, he never showed. Halfway through the night, some apologetic ducking-out text from him. And then, a week later, news on the Rothbury grapevine that'd he'd been seen with some other girl at a club in Newcastle they often hit.

'Oh shit. Becks. *That* Jack.' Lucy felt a bit queasy.

'Yeah, so be careful, Luce. That guy is toxic. Really, you don't want to touch him with a bargepole.'

'Bloody hell ...' Lucy's voice drifted, she was still trying to process the news. Friday ... tomorrow ... the birthday booking he'd helped her secure ... How could they not see each other?

'Luce?'

'Bloody hell, we're both at a birthday do tomorrow. Yikes, that'll be awkward, won't it?'

'You'll be fine. Just play it cool. It's not like you're best buddies or anything, is it? And that kiss moment ... well, it was all a near-miss. Nothing actually happened, did it. Just put it down to experience.'

Lucy couldn't help but notice that Becky had well and truly changed her tune. All excited and egging her on about the near-kiss, and now playing it down like it was nothing at all. Well, her friend was only trying to protect her.

'Yeah, you're right.' She now also felt stupid that she'd even entertained any possible romantic notions about Jack. The beach day and the drive were never going to be mentioned ever again.

Thank god she hadn't let him into the cottage. Was that his technique? A fun-filled afternoon, a cocktail or two, and then charm his way in with an innocent kiss? It shouldn't have been a surprise to her, not really. He was still the same smooth-talking charmer that Becks had fallen for. It kind of made sense, all the Jack the Lad banter she'd heard him spouting at his cocktail bar. God, she might have ended up as just another notch on his bedpost. She felt so very naive. Jack might have managed to open up a little chink in her heart on that beach afternoon. But no more, that door was being well and truly closed again.

Her poor wrecked heart had been through enough this past couple of years. She vowed, there and then, that if she ever, *ever* looked to have some kind of relationship in the future, it certainly *wouldn't* be with someone like Jack Anderson.

The next morning, Lucy's fingers were stiff from once again kneading and shaping dough. She was now creating individual balls, enough for the pizza bases for this last-minute birthday event, sixty of the little knuckle-busting monsters in fact, and – truth be told – the dough was taking a real pounding after the bombshell phone call from Becky last night.

Let it all out, Lucy had thought to herself, channelling her frustration into the production line.

Yep, she just had to refocus and crack on. Next, she switched on the oven, ready for step two of the day, making two humungous chocolate-cake squares to turn into the Italian chocolate mousse party cake. This needed to be freshly baked and that meant the pressure was on. Thankfully the Clementine and Limoncello cakes were already made, as Nonna had advised that if you made them the day before they'd taste even better.

And after that, hah, all she had to do ... was prepare the cured meats and olives ready for the charcuterie boards, along with green salads and cherry tomatoes. Her To-Do list still looked rather daunting, and she was now down to *hours*, not days.

She'd raided both her mum's and Nonna's kitchen cupboards, borrowing as many nice platters and dishes as she could, along with a trestle-style table found lurking in her mum's garage. Online she'd also discovered a fabulous red-checked oilcloth to cover it with (typical Italian restaurant-style, very much like it might have been in Papa's restaurant of old), and some new olive-wood serving boards to complete the look. With her string of Italian-flag bunting and some extra fairy lights for above the counter area, she hoped the styling would prove attractive too. She really needed to impress and make her mark with this food feast. Fingers crossed.

To add to her woes, not-so-helpful Tamsin was adamant that she had an 'unmissable' party lined up for herself that evening and couldn't help at All Fired Up. There was *no way* she'd be working on some 'poxy pizza van' all night. So, Lucy had been well and truly left in the lurch, with her anxiety levels cranking up a gear.

Thankfully, and rather surprisingly, her saviour came in the form of her brother, Olly. Though Becks had offered to step in to help if push came to shove, she knew her close friend had an early start the day after the event with a family wedding to go to on the Saturday, and Lucy really didn't want to spoil that for her.

She was letting off steam about it all on the phone earlier with her brother, about to hurtle a dough ball across the room in frustration, when he'd come up trumps and offered, rather marvellously, to stand in and help her out. So, her new event was to be a real Papa's Pizzas family affair, and whilst she was still in a bit of a spin about seeing Jack after Becky's revelation, and of course anxious for it to all go off perfectly for her *and* her guests, a part of her was also looking forward to having Olly's support and company.

Cheers to 40 Years!

You are invited to

A Surprise Birthday Bash for

James's 40th

Friday 18th June evening

Cocktails, canapés and capers guaranteed!

RSVP Nikki and remember SHHH it's a surprise.

Chapter 21

'Well, this is it,' Lucy announced, as the SatNav deposited them at the gates of a large property in the rather exclusive residential area of Darras Hall, not far from Newcastle-upon-Tyne. It looked like they'd be parked up in the block-paved driveway for the evening, which was a bit of a relief, as some of the uneven ground she'd had to drive on so far for events had proven to be a bit of a challenge for the vintage horsebox.

'I'm quite looking forward to this,' confessed Olly, with a grin.

'What, a night out working your socks off with your big sis?'

'Well, it's something a bit different. My life seems to consist of electrical circuits, wiring, and potty training at the moment.'

'Hah, well yes, and I bet little Freddie's having fun with Daisy staying there tonight, at least before he toddles off to bed. Then, she's bound to find herself a cosy spot with Alice on the sofa.'

'For sure. And as for us two tonight, well, parties are usually pretty fun, aren't they?'

'You do know you're here to work ...' Lucy gave him a stern sisterly look.

'Of course, Lulu.' He slipped back to his childhood name for her. 'Anyway, it'll be good to get an insight into your new business. You never know, I might be able to get a word in with Dad on how well you're doing when we next catch up, too.'

'Ah,' she groaned, 'don't tell me he's still banging on about how stupid I've been, giving up a steady job?'

'That's about the sum of it, yeah.'

Lucy sighed, 'Having a steady job's not the be all and end all, Olly. Not when it starts to feel like a noose around your neck.'

'I know, I know. But you know Dad, he's just worried about you really.'

'Yeah, I suppose. Well, let's get this party started, hey. I'd better turn things around with All Fired Up and show him how good a decision it was.'

As the gates opened before them, no doubt by some fancy remote system, revealing a large garden and bungalow, Lucy concentrated on reversing the horsebox carefully into position on the driveway. Jack wasn't there as yet, Lucy noted – her heart rate going up a notch just thinking about how annoyed and disappointed she was at having been taken in by him – but he probably wouldn't be long. At least it'd give her a chance to get set up, get her head in the right place before having to face him. The catering was the most important thing for her this evening, anyhow, not concerning herself with that player of a barman.

She took a slow breath. 'Ah, well, here we go, Ol. We're on. Let's get All Fired Up!' Lucy turned off the engine, took a deep breath as she drummed her fingers against the steering wheel, and then stepped down out of the horsebox.

The door to the large detached bungalow opened to reveal a smiley middle-aged blonde. 'Oh, you must be Lucy. Hello. Fabulous that you're here. Thank heavens, after all that palaver earlier in the week. Thanks so much for stepping into the gap.'

'No worries, it's no problem at all. Great to have the opportunity, actually,' Lucy smiled. 'Nice to meet you, Nikki. Oh, and this is my brother, Olly, who's helping me tonight.'

Olly joined them at the doorstep, and they shook hands.

Little did the host know that he'd never done an event like this before. Lucy was determined to keep her nerve and professionalism, even if she was quaking a little inside. Olly was sensible and sociable. The pair of them just had to work hard and make sure it all went smoothly. At least Lucy was pretty certain that the food she was offering was really good, and that was the main thing.

'Super. Well, is there anything you need? Can I help you get set up at all?'

'I don't think so, we're here to make sure your guests have wonderful food and a memorable evening, so you can relax and have fun.' Lucy sounded far more confident than she felt.

'That is music to my ears, Lucy. Thank you. Can I get you a cup of coffee or something, or a cold drink?'

'Ah, well, a can of Coke would be nice, if you have that.'

'Certainly, and ...?' she gestured towards Olly.

'Oh, something like a cold beer would go down a treat.' Olly gave a cheeky, hopeful look.

'Of course, I'll go fetch them.'

'Just the one,' Lucy mouthed to her bro. 'What did I say ... don't forget you're working.'

'Hah, I'm twenty-seven, not twelve, Lucy.' He gave her a wink.

The pizza horsebox had arrived a good hour before any guests were due. The kiln-dried logs needed to be lit as soon as possible, to give the oven plenty of time to heat up. In the meanwhile, she and Olly had the antipasti platters to set out and garnish creatively, as well as a host of other practical jobs.

With Jack's arrival imminent, Lucy was pleased she'd be busy for a good while, and having Olly here would act as a deflection too. She still wasn't sure how she was feeling about that near-kiss, especially when it had been followed so soon afterwards by Becky's damning revelation.

But it wasn't long before that familiar gleam of deep-red appeared and the Volkswagen's distinctive front end turned into the driveway. Lucy's stomach gave a little uneasy flip.

Jack found himself very much looking forward to this evening, with the chance to see Lucy again. A touch of nerves hit his belly as he neared the booking address, and it was in no way to do with the function. It had been a very long time since he'd felt any of this ... what was it, a sort of gut-wrenching, falling kind of feeling? Jeez, it was as unsettling as it was exciting, to be honest. But ... he told himself, all he really wanted was to get to know Lucy some more, see how things went. Small steps ... big feelings.

He reached the gates. She was already there; the grey horsebox in position on the driveway, and he could see her setting up. He pulled in, waving a friendly 'Hello' across to her. But ... who the heck was that? Jack spotted a *guy* in the horsebox; tall, dark-haired, good-looking. He stopped in his tracks. When Lucy had had help at other functions, it had always been that surly-faced young girl. Was a friend helping out, perhaps a *boyfriend*? It was then he spotted them goofing around behind the counter, grinning away and looking far too familiar with each other. He was hit by an odd sinking feeling.

Lucy looked up, with a brief, 'Ah, hi, Jack.' And that was it. That was all she said.

The bloke with her merely gave a confident, steady smile.

Shit, was *that* why she'd pulled away from the kiss on her cottage doorstep? Because she had a boyfriend already? Maybe it wasn't Daisy's doing after all. Everything was just a tangled mess of emotions. But why hadn't she said anything? He suddenly realised just how little he knew about her.

Jack trailed back to Ruby feeling weirdly crushed. Glad for something to distract him, he concentrated on lining up his champagne flutes and cocktail glasses to perfection; presentation was everything. He loved the campervan bar to look the part, theming it individually for each event. Tonight, he'd got grey-and-white birthday bunting ready to string along the front of the counter, and two pearlised 40th birthday helium-filled balloons to tie at the far end of the van. He filled an ice bucket ready to chill bottles of champagne, then proceeded to decorate his counter with limes, oranges, lemons, passion-fruit, plus jugs of fresh mint, rosemary and basil. As well as the champagne, he had a Tom Collins 'welcome' cocktail to prepare, and plenty of Italian lagers chilling in the fridge. Yep, despite the mixed emotions about Lucy, he was able to flick the switch and become Master of Mixology for the night. Jack's Cocktail Campervan at your service.

There was a buzz of guest arrivals, champagne corks flying and flutes filling. He was soon in the swing of it all. Yet, in the midst of all the chat and cocktail creation, Jack couldn't help but steal the odd glance the way of the horsebox. The two of them over there, prepping platters of food, standing far too close for Jack's liking. The guy leaning in and whispering something in Lucy's ear which made her giggle. She seemed extremely comfortable in his company – no hint of Ice Queen about her at all. There was a close easiness in the way they were together. There was no way this guy was a mere workmate. Jack's initial excitement at seeing her again had wilted like a popped balloon.

The evening rolled on and by 9 p.m., Lucy and Olly had tidied away the grazing boards – the contents of which had been pretty much demolished – served over fifty pizzas, and *ta dah*, it was time for the cake display. This was the most nerve-wracking part of the evening for Lucy. So, could she come up trumps with dessert as well as with her savoury dishes? The proof would be in the pudding.

Lucy had discovered two antique silver trays in Nonna's

kitchen cabinet – brought all the way across from Italy with Papa's family, apparently – which her grandmother was happy for Lucy to take and keep; saying they were far better being used than gathering dust in the back of her cupboards. Lucy had carefully assembled the chocolate layers earlier in the day, cutting them into neat squares with a raspberry on each to decorate, then she had placed them onto the pretty antique trays, covering them gently with foil. She hoped to goodness they'd travelled okay in the back of her trailer – she'd driven super-carefully. Lifting one corner of the foil tentatively, Lucy gave a sigh of relief. All present and correct, bar the odd toppled raspberry, which she was able to easily pop back in place. Phew!

For the Clementine and Limoncello Cake, which was packed with zesty sunshine flavours, she sliced neat triangle wedges and now arranged them on a pretty, white, scallop-edged platter of her mum's. Nonna had recommended making some crème fraiche laced with orange zest, to dollop next to each portion. That was already prepped and ready, and was looking delightfully creamy in a white-and-blue pottery bowl, which she garnished with an extra curl or two of orange zest. She set the dish out beside the citrus cake platter so the partygoers could help themselves. Well, the cakes certainly *looked* the part as Lucy placed them out on the linen-covered trestle table. Now, for the taste test.

'Pudding is served!' she called out to the happy gathering in the garden, who were chatting away merrily, the odd peal of laughter ringing out.

Word soon spread around the guests, and Lucy quickly

had a little queue forming. She held her breath as the first spoons were lifted … and … there were plenty of 'Umm's and 'Ahh's and 'Gorgeous'es as the partygoers tucked in. Phew! She'd hopefully managed to pull that pudding palaver off. She said a silent 'thank you' to Nonna. With Papa's pizzas and Nonna's puddings, All Fired Up was turning into a food force to be reckoned with.

'Looks like you nailed it, sis.' Olly had clearly been watching the guests' reactions too.

The pair of them high-fived behind the counter top.

Who *was* that bloody guy working with Lucy? Jack still couldn't tear his eyes away from the antics at the pizza van. The two of them had been chatting away most of the night, working smoothly side-by-side, and now they were high-fiving like a match made in heaven.

Lucy's *boyfriend*. Could it be true? Jack realised he really didn't want it to be. He felt like such a fool.

But the evening moved on, the party in full swing, keeping Jack busy. And the party crowd were *certainly* enjoying their drinks – with a few high jinks involved, including a hilarious, if somewhat saucy, party game involving the guests passing around several of Jack's lemons and limes with no hands allowed, and a full-on caterwauling version of Queen's 'Bohemian Rhapsody' sung en masse in the garden.

In the lead-up to midnight, several taxis arrived and other guests began their slightly wobbly walks home. Some friends of Nikki's, who were staying on overnight, ordered a last, rather large, round of drinks for good measure. With Jack's temporary licence finishing at midnight, it was soon time to get packed up. He was exhausted from another busy event but, disconcertingly, he found he now had more time to think.

Jack had envisaged chatting with Lucy as the guests filtered home, had been looking forward to it. Not much chance of that now, he mused grumpily, not with good-looking guy in tow. Yet even now, seeing her stood beside the settling embers of the pizza oven, he told himself to just buck up, and steel himself. He'd been wanting to talk to her all night, so why didn't he just bloody well go over there ...? But why did that suddenly feel so hard?

Chapter 22

'Hi guys. How did it all go? A good evening for you, Luce? You certainly looked to be flat out.'

Lucy looked up sharply. There he was, Jack the Lad, striding over to the horsebox. Trust him to burst her balloon after the success of the evening. But she supposed she'd better be polite, he had got her this job after all, though she couldn't help but bristle on seeing him approach.

'Oh, hi,' she stuttered. 'Well yeah, we've never stopped. Pizzas, platters, cakes. It's been a good booking.' She was leaning on the horsebox's counter top, trying her best to look casual, all the while thinking: so this was the guy who had hurt her best friend so badly.

'Well, I thought you might be ready for one of these then.' He offered up the flutes of fizz. 'Prosecco and pizza, you really can't go wrong, can you?'

Hah, did he think he could smooth things over with a glass of fizz? Another classic Jack tactic, for sure. 'Oh, okay. Well thanks, Jack.' She kept her tone cool.

Jack looked a bit confused, staring sheepishly down at the prosecco glasses in his hands.

'Cheers, mate.' Olly smiled as he took both glasses from Jack, handing one across to Lucy.

'Oh Jack, this is Olly,' Lucy said casually.

He was tall and olive skinned, with dark cropped hair. *Undeniably and irksomely handsome, in fact,* Jack thought.

'Hi.' Jack forced a tight smile.

'Yeah, thought my little brother could help me out for the night.'

There was a second of silence as Jack registered her words. 'Y-your ... *brother?*'

'Yes ...'

The penny dropped with a bloody huge clang. Jack had been jealous all night of her *brother*. Now, who was the stupid idiot?

'Right, right ... Hi Olly, g-good to meet you,' Jack found himself stuttering.

'Hey, looks like you've had a busy night too, mate,' Olly commented, happy to make small talk.

'Yeah, been a great party, hasn't it? A really good atmosphere,' Jack responded, still trying to get his head around this scenario.

'Well, thanks Jack,' Lucy added, 'for putting my name out there ...'

Her smile seemed cautious, yet it still lifted him. The revelation that he'd got it wrong all night was now lifting his hopes, despite her coolness. The Ice Queen had crept back in. She seemed different from the girl he'd chatted with so easily in the dunes that day. But they were both busy working tonight, it was a different environment here altogether. Perhaps she was just trying to stay professional?

'You're welcome.' Despite his misgivings, Jack couldn't help the slow grin that spread across his face.

'Nice of that bar van guy to give us a drink there at the end,' Olly said to Lucy on the way home. 'So, have you two have met up before, then?'

Lucy felt a little uncomfortable. She gazed at the headlamp-lit road ahead before answering. 'Yeah, a couple of times. Jack is okay. Been a help to me, getting me tonight's job and all that. Though ...' She was *almost* going to mention his past misdemeanours as far as Becky was concerned, but for some reason she found herself not wanting to run him down to her brother.

Oh, why did Jack have to turn out to be such a disappointment? All that business with Becky was years ago now, she supposed. But did a leopard ever change its spots? She sighed heavily and pretended to concentrate on the road for a while.

'Ooh, it's a late night,' she then commented, after a yawn escaped her lips. The clock on her dash read 12:25 a.m. It always took a while to pack up at the end of a function; especially with needing to let the pizza oven cool down fully before setting it back inside the horsebox.

'Yeah, I hope Freddie isn't up too sharp tomorrow,' Olly said, pulling a woeful face. 'He was awake at 6:10 this morning.'

'Ouch.'

'Yeah, he certainly hasn't grasped the definition of weekends as yet.'

'Hah, he's only two! Just wait 'til he's twelve, then you'll never be able to get him out of bed. I remember what you were like!'

'Hah, yeah.'

'Yeah, you my little bro, were like a bloody bear going into hibernation. And all the moaning and groaning that went on, just to get you out of that sweaty pit of a bedroom.'

'Hey you.' He gave her a jokey, gentle prod on the arm.

They enjoyed teasing each other, as siblings often do, but their love was evident too. Through their parents splitting up, they were always a team, turning to each other when the going got tough. There'd been Olly's disappointment at flunking his A-levels, which meant his chances of going to uni had been pretty much obliterated; Lucy's devastating rocky patch with her ex; and all the other ups and downs of life they'd experienced so far. They'd always been there for each other. Tonight had been no different; when Lucy had confessed she was in a bit of a spot with young Tamsin dipping out on her already, he'd offered to help out straight away. Even though he'd been working all week beforehand and most likely fancied a cosy night home. Even his girlfriend Alice had come up trumps, offering to keep Daisy there with her for the evening. They were planning on having a 'Girls' Night' on the sofa with Netflix, Lucy had learned, once Freddie had hit the deck, that was. Daisy would have been in her element, for sure.

And the big plus in having Olly there at the function too, so soon after Becky's revelation, was that her brother had been a great foil for Jack's attentions, giving Lucy some much-needed space to think and retreat.

The whole bloody thing was just too confusing. It was late, she was tired, and all she needed to do right now was to drop her brother off and collect Daisy Doo. Then, she'd sleep on it and hopefully dream about anything or anyone but Jack Bloody Anderson.

Chapter 23

Jack woke in a crumpled bed, alone, with sunlight streaming through his window.

Remembering last night, he felt a churn of disappointment about Lucy's renewed frostiness. He'd hoped they'd have had a chance to chat, maybe mention the great afternoon they'd had at the beach last weekend. He supposed it didn't help that she'd had her brother in tow. Maybe he was overthinking it all.

Today was a new day. It was time to shake himself out of this daft Lucy-shaped reverie. Yep, he needed to check and update his Facebook and website this morning. He'd taken some great photos of his cocktails, plus some shots of the campervan in the driveway with the party in full swing last night. Nikki had said she was happy for him to use them. It would freshen up the pages and give potential customers a taste of what was on offer.

He got up. As he stood there in his boxers and stretched, he caught sight of a blue, wispy-clouded sky. It looked to be a nice day, so why not get out and on the bike too? Maybe go for a cycle ride down the coast and cut back into the hills

– a forty miler. Get a welcome blast of fresh air and exercise. Perhaps Matt might fancy tagging along? His housemate pal had mentioned having a rare day off from the veterinary surgery, with girlfriend Jess having something on with a friend. It would be good to have some company. Hmm, perhaps they might stop for a chilled draft pint in a beer garden somewhere en route. The idea was forming nicely.

Sat outside of The Horseshoe Inn, in the quaint village of Kirkholme in the foothills of the Cheviot hills, Jack's first sip of his refreshingly-cold pint of ale lived up to expectations. Twenty miles into their bike ride, the scenery was glorious with rolling hills and rugged moorland all around. The lanes were quieter out here, being away from the tourist traffic of the coast, though the cycling duo had plenty of challenging ascents. Jack's muscles were aching but in a good way. He loved the outdoors life, and the feeling of pushing himself, whether it was with exercise or his business. He was never one to rest on his laurels.

'So, how's it all been going lately? Still winning at life with the Cocktail Campervan?' Matt asked, stretching his long legs out at a pub picnic bench.

Though they lived together, it was rare for the two lads to sit and chat in any great depth. It was more casual banter, over a pizza or burger and a bottle of lager at the end of one of Matt's long shifts, or watching the occasional footie match on the TV, or perhaps a *Call of Duty* session on the X-box. That, of course, was when Jess *wasn't* about – which seemed to be increasingly rare. She was starting to become a permanent fixture. It was only a matter of time before she'd be moving in, Jack figured, and then he'd have to be on the lookout for alternative accommodation. He was pragmatic about it, as it was Matt's house after all. Such was the way of life. But he'd had a few good years staying there, since finishing his travels, and coming back Alnwick way. It had suited him. He really hadn't wanted to go back to living at his parents'. There were just too many memories there, ready to slam into him at every opportunity.

'Jack? The campervan?' Matt repeated.

'Ah, yeah, it's going good thanks,' he said, shaking off the reverie. 'I'm having a successful year so far, which is great. The bookings still keep rolling in.'

In fact, he had just been given the nod that morning about a new music festival coming to the area, which – with any luck – would provide an exciting new opportunity. A mate who he'd done some bar work with a while back was also in an up-and-coming band and he'd called to let him know there were a few catering pitches left for the inaugural Holy Island Music Fest. You did have to put down a decent deposit for your pitch, but it sounded like you could do really well with there being a captive audience, *and* you got to listen to some great music too. Jack told Matt about this new opportunity, buoying himself up as he spoke about it. He resolved to call the organisers as soon as they got back – and yes, he could call Lucy too, why not? Give her a chance to get a pitch. It'd be good to speak with her.

'Sounds like it's going brilliantly, mate.'

'Yeah, and I still enjoy it too.' Jack had found it had

become more enjoyable lately, wondering if a certain horsebox and driver might pull up at the same events this summer. Well, until last night, that was, when it had all got a bit confusing.

'Great. That's cool. I always loved the idea of it, and Ruby is a proper beaut.'

'She is that,' Jack answered proudly. Ruby was indeed his pride and joy. 'So, what about you? How's life as a vet?'

'Well, not as glamorous as yours, I bet. I spend half my life sticking a thermometer up animals' arses, getting scratched by feral cats whose owners swear they are little sweethearts, and getting stomped on by cows in a strop. But weirdly, I love it.'

'Well, I always knew you were a bit odd. But really, I'm pleased for you, mate. You were always meant to be a vet. It was your calling.'

'Yeah, something like that.'

Matt was modest, but Jack had known him from school, known all the years he'd spent studying, working so hard to achieve his goal. It was more than a career; it was a way of life. Whilst Jack was drifting across the globe taking casual work, Matt was studying hard.

'And you and Jess, looks like that's going strong?'

'It is indeed.' Matt was a man of few words, so his affirmative nod and broad smile said it all. 'Yeah, we're good.'

'What about you?'

'What *about* me?'

'Love life? Where have you been hiding all the pretty girls lately?'

'Ah ... now that would be telling,' Jack jested, feeling suddenly uncomfortable.

The truth was that there had been no overnighters for Jack in quite some time. No awkward mornings at Matt's house, making coffee and polite conversation. And the odd night he'd spent away himself, had been just that, by himself. Most of the time he was up in the hills, or down at the beach, with Ruby ... gazing up at the stars in a vast, empty sky. His sex life seemed to have disappeared, actually.

Yeah, he supposed he could go out, get himself a date, enjoy the buzz and the freedom of a casual one-night stand, like he used to do ... But he'd totally lost the inclination of late. The last few times he'd ventured there, it had all seemed pretty soulless, mechanical. He wasn't in any rush to go back to that.

'Right then, Jack me lad, let's hit the road.' Matt downed his pint as he rose from the bench. 'Next twenty to go.'

Jack joined him, setting off first, through winding stone-walled lanes, rolling green dales all around, with the breeze at their backs and the baa of moorland sheep in their ears. Soon finding themselves freewheeling down a sharp incline, Matt overtook him with a cheeky roar, 'Keep up, mate!'

Jack grinned, but then found himself feeling a little uncomfortable, as he watched the retreating back of his close friend. Matt seemed to have his life pretty much sorted, didn't he? Matt and Jess ... weren't they the ones who were moving forward, whilst he was still stuck in second gear, after all?

He suddenly pedalled harder.

Chapter 24

It was finally time for Lucy's second Book Club night. She had really enjoyed her sneaky sofa moments and late-at-night bedtime reading of *One Day* over the past couple of weeks. Losing herself in the world of Emma and Dexter, and their complicated friendship and near-miss love lives, with Daisy curled up by her side as always. Yes, Lucy found herself very much looking forward to this month's bookish Driftwood meet-up.

Later that evening, Lucy was sat at a big circular table in the café with a mug of tea and a generous wedge of coffee and walnut cake beside her. Louise introduced her to Paul who'd been missing last time – a jovial forty-something with a love of crime novels and a secret penchant for Mills and Boon, apparently. He seemed fun, and it would be great to get a male perspective on the books they were reading.

As there were still one or two of the group yet to come, Lucy started to chat with Helen who was seated next to her.

'Hey, how are you? How've the past few weeks been?' she asked kindly, remembering that this was the woman who was in the middle of a messy marriage break-up.

'Oh, so, so. Not so bad. The kids have kept me busy.' Helen sounded purposefully vague. 'Me mam's got them tonight, so it's nice to get a bit of time out.' She gave a smile.

Lucy had the feeling that she was putting a brave face on things, whilst no doubt making the most of a chance to get away from it all.

'What about you, aren't you the lady with that lovely-looking pizza horsebox? I've seen it parked up down the village. That must be a fun kind of work?'

'Yeah, it is. Hard work too mind, but yep, I get to go to all sorts of cool parties and places. No two events are ever the same.'

'Ooh, it's my cousin's birthday soon. We'll have to bear you in mind. She was wondering what to do for it. The kids'd love that too. How many people do you need for a booking?'

'Well, to make it worthwhile, umm, probably twenty or so pizzas as a minimum, but yeah, I can do small or large events.'

'Sounds good, I'll mention you to Jilly. Be nice to have something to look forward to. Something a bit different too.'

Louise stood up then, clapping her hands together. 'Right then, ladies and gents, welcome all. It looks like Cathy is running late, and Becky can't make it this week, is that right, Lucy?'

'Yeah, she'd already got something on. A meal out with her partner's parents.'

'No probs, so it's us merry band for now. So, what did you all make of the delightful *One Day*?'

'Ah, well I liked the concept of two people over twenty years,' Paul began eagerly. 'And seeing how their lives went.

Seemed to be very much wrong place and time for them both as a couple for much of the book ...'

'But weren't they great characters?' Sarah, chipped in. 'Yeah, Emma seemed pretty mature from the get-go and Dex, well, he was by no means perfect, but he was just so warm and vibrant, and okay, damned well sexy.'

'Oh, you think so? I just found him bloody annoying,' contended Helen.

'Hah, I'm with Helen. He was definitely a bit of a knob,' young Abby added. 'But it was interesting that he wasn't perfect. He was just human. He got it wrong. A lot.'

Why did Lucy's mind spring to Jack all of a sudden? Was it that happy-go-lucky, yet seemingly immature side she'd seen in him? And then all the Becky stuff ...

'Yeah,' Lucy joined in, 'he had his issues, big ones admittedly, but they were just finding their way, getting on with life, like we all have to.' She picked up her well-thumbed copy that she'd parked beside her cake.

'Well, I think Emma had always loved him from the very start, hadn't she?' added Louise.

'I think he frustrated her,' Lucy countered.

'And hurt her,' added Helen.

'Didn't she hurt him at times too? Wrong time, wrong place? Doesn't love just do that to you?' Louise ventured.

'Yes, and it was so sad when his mum died,' Abby said with a frown, helping herself to a second brownie from the stack left enticingly centre-table.

'Ah-hah, well if that bit got to you, what about the bloody ending? I thought these romances were meant to have happy endings. Caught me right unawares, that did – I was sobbing,' Cathy said, who'd just arrived, and was pulling up a seat.

'Well, I suppose it plays out more like a Greek tragedy in that way,' Phyllis contributed.

'I liked that about it, it seemed more realistic,' Helen spoke up. 'Yep, just when you finally get going, the shit hits the fan. Did nothing to lighten my mood, mind you.' They all then heard a big sniff. All of a sudden, Helen's veneer slipped, and there were tears flowing. 'Bugger it,' Helen dipped her head.

'Oh, petal. Can we do anything to help?' Louise stepped in, reaching a hand across the table, all maternal and full of concern.

Lucy felt for Helen, remembering the roller coaster of own break-up, and gave a caring smile.

'Sorry folks, been a tough week, that's all.' Helen sniffed again, fumbling in her handbag for a hankie.

Paul passed across his clean napkin. 'There you go, love.'

'Thanks. Sorry, don't know what's got into me. It's just the decree absolute came through ... and I know I wanted him out and it's all for the best, but it's all so bloody final. And the kids are missing him – they don't realise what a useless bastard he's been most of the time – and I feel like it's all my fault.' She blew her nose.

Her friend, Sarah, wound an arm around her shoulders. 'We're all here for you, Hels, you just have to say the word.'

There were nods of agreement from around the table. 'Yes, if there's anything we can do.'

'Of course.'

'I know. And thanks. It's nice just knowing that.' She dabbed at her eyes.

Helen gathered herself, and nipped to the loo, whilst Louise got in another round of tea and cake to perk them all up. More bookish chat ensued, with a thumbs-up from the group for *One Day*, then the conversation rolled on.

'So, how's the pizza business going, Lucy?' Louise asked.

'Pretty good, getting a few more bookings coming in, which is great. I could just do with some help on the bigger events though. It's too much by myself at times, I'm run ragged. And well, my first recruit looks like she's ducked out already.'

'Oh ...' Louise's eyes trailed to young Abby. 'Didn't you say you were looking for a few more hours, Abs? We don't always have quite have enough shifts to offer here, what with my sister helping out too.'

'Hmm, when would it be?' Abby's eyes lit up. 'I'm trying to save up for a skiing trip this winter. My mates are desperate to get something booked. But I'll need the gear and everything, and I've just seen the prices of the ski passes ... scary.'

Abby always came across as lovely serving in the café. This could work really well for Lucy. 'Okay, well it's mostly evenings, Fridays and Saturdays, oh and sometimes on a Saturday afternoon. It really depends what comes in.'

'Well, evenings generally aren't a problem. My shifts here end by five. And if I slotted into the Sunday shift for you here Lou, then maybe the odd Saturday ...?' The young girl raised her eyebrows, leadingly.

Louise winked. 'I might be able to work it now and again, yes. As long as you don't steal her away too much, Lucy.'

'Well, that sounds brilliant. I'll take your number, Abby, and we can have a proper chat about it all. But yes, I'd love to have you on board.' Lucy couldn't believe her luck.

After throwing around ideas for the next read, with Paul desperate for some Mills & Boon, Phyllis vying for another classic like *Room with a View*, and Helen demanding something as far away from romance as possible, they settled on *The Beekeeper of Aleppo*, a book which Lucy had heard a lot about and was more than happy to launch into. So, Book Club night ended on a high, with smiles and hugs of support for Helen, Lucy finding herself amongst a lovely and interesting group of new friends ... and hopefully with a new assistant for the pizza horsebox. Things were looking up.

The Farmer Wants a Fiftieth!

Alan's Birthday Bash

Come along for some Moo-ving and Grooving!

Pizza, Hog Roast, Cocktails and more

Saturday 26th June

8 'til late.

Down on the farm at Morwick Steads

Chapter 25

A damp and drizzly Friday in late June had thankfully turned into a sun-kissed evening as Jack began setting up Ruby's bar for a special 50th birthday celebration. His bar-with-a-view tonight looked out over gently rippling crops of still-green barley and lush grassy fields where cattle grazed languidly. Away in the far distance was a tantalising glimpse of slate-coloured sea.

Ruby's allocated space in the farmyard was next to a large stone barn which had been emptied out and converted into a quirky party venue. There were square straw-bales set out to sit on, as well as various wooden chairs and tables, with bold sunflowers and ox-eye daisies pretty as a picture in milk jugs, hessian-style birthday bunting, and a 'disco' area set up in one corner of the barn.

Requests for Jack from tonight's hosts were to stock up on plenty of real ale and prosecco, with a few quirky cocktails – including a Moo Moo (Irish Cream based) and the ever-popular Morpeth Mule. The party was going to be pretty big, with around a hundred and fifty people coming, so Jack had arrived extra early to give himself plenty of time to get organised.

The farmhouse, on the opposite side of the yard, was a fine-looking traditional Northumberland stone building. Outside its porch were bunches of colourful helium balloons with '50' on, drifting on silver strings in the breeze. Sounds of mooing and baaing from the surrounding fields accompanied the clinking of Jack's glasses as he set them out. There were also some whiffy countryside aromas, he noted, which would add an interesting, and perhaps rather too authentic, ambience to his farm-themed cocktails.

It was just over a week since the Darras Hall party, the last time Jack had seen Lucy, and now she was due to work the 50th birthday bash too. Jack felt a rising sense of anticipation. And when, just a few minutes later, he spotted the familiar grey-painted horsebox turning into the yard, he couldn't help but feel a strange, hopeful lift in his heart.

'Hi,' he called out, as Lucy stepped down out of her Jeep, looking casual but pretty in her pizza-serving uniform of blue jeans and red polo shirt with the *All Fired Up* logo. 'All okay?'

'Yeah, fine. You?' Lucy's response was polite, clipped, with Becky's revelations still very much on her mind.

'Yeah, good thanks.' In fact, he was feeling much better now that she'd arrived.

From the passenger side of the vehicle, a teenage girl then leapt out. Phew, at least the brother wasn't around. And this was a different girl from the one that Jack had seen helping before. In fact, she was actually smiling.

'This is Abby. My new partner in crime. Someone I know from the village,' Lucy said, politely introducing her new assistant. 'And this is Jack.'

'Hi, Jack. Good to meet you, and your campervan looks amazing. Love it.'

'Well, thank you. All fired up for a busy night then, ladies?' he quipped.

'Hah, we are indeed,' Abby said. 'Raring to go!'

Lucy just raised her eyebrows coolly.

And with that, the two girls turned away, and bustled into action, opening the horsebox up, and getting everything prepped. Lucy never gave him a second glance.

What was going on with Miss Ice Queen now? He'd thought they were getting on so well at the beach that afternoon, but this woman was so damned hard to fathom. He trundled back to Ruby, hiding the feelings of dejection in a cloak of barman magic – well, his Cocktail Campervan apron.

A hog roast van, called *Pig Out*, turned up soon afterwards, pulling into the space between the two of them. Jack recognised the lad from other events they'd been at. He was from the local butchers in Alnwick, and his catering venture was a side-line on the weekends. Unfortunately, the large white van now obscured part of Jack's view of All Fired Up, which was rather annoying. He had to admit he rather liked taking a sneaky peek at Lucy as she worked ... even if she was trying her hardest to ignore him.

Lucy had her work cut out tonight. This booking was for seventy-five pizzas (all, thankfully, paid for up-front), in four different flavours, to be sliced and served throughout the evening. With lacklustre Tamsin leaving her in the lurch at the last event, she was so glad she'd had her light bulb moment with Abby at the latest Book Club night. Abby was a bubbly girl, full of youth and enthusiasm, and already they were working well as a team, chatting as they wrapped and stacked napkin cutlery packs, and chopped up onions, ham, mushrooms and peppers standing side-by-side. The disco guy was doing his sound checks, and the girls found themselves humming away to Beyonce's 'All the Single Ladies'. There was definitely a bit of girl power going on behind the pizza stand. All Fired Up was gearing up for a busy and hopefully enjoyable night.

Every now and again, Lucy was aware that Jack was looking over at the horsebox whilst setting out his bar, and tried to avert her own gaze. She had to remember the red danger sign that was pointing squarely in his direction. She still had Becky's warning about him ringing in her ears, no matter how attractive he looked serving up those cocktails.

The evening was balmy, and as the oven warmed up, so did Lucy. Even in her polo short sleeves she was already getting extremely hot. But she had a job to do, and a pizza production line to crack on with. Her reputation was beginning to build. She'd had a fabulous review posted on her Facebook page from the funfair night and more glowing comments from hostess Nikki after her last-minute slot at the birthday bash. But she was very aware that there was no resting on her laurels. She needed double the event bookings to start turning around a decent enough profit to make a living for herself, as well as covering her assistant's wages.

There was no slacking, and the partygoers soon began to arrive, gathering around Jack's campervan for welcome drinks and chatting in amiable groups. Jeans, Ts and casual wear was the order of the day for this farmyard function. Everyone seemed to be in good spirits even as they got there. And, wow, someone had even turned up – well, two people actually, by the looks of it – in fancy dress, as the front and back end of a Friesian cow! Which caused much hilarity amongst the other guests, and a guessing game as to who was inside.

'Hey, Abby. That'll be fun seeing them *moo*-ving and grooving on the dancefloor later.' Lucy couldn't help but smile as she delivered the pun.

They then heard Jack call out, 'Can I interest you in a Moo Moo cocktail?' whilst sporting a cheeky grin, as the furry 'cow' waddled past en route to the party barn.

There was music and merriment, their meat feast and garlic mushroom pizzas were going down particularly well, and the two girls kept up with demand, just! Where anyone did have a short wait, the guests were more than happy to stand chatting away with a drink from Jack's campervan to hand.

There was a bit of a lull serving-wise as the dancing got going, with a traditional barn dance starting up. Many of the youngsters didn't have a clue how the steps were done but still joined in regardless, along with the cow in costume. Blimey, they'd be hot in there, Lucy mused, feeling their sweaty pain. There was much laughter, and good-natured jostling on the dancefloor. Lucy took a little time out to let Daisy, who was with her this evening, out for a quick wander on her lead and a pee stop – this time well away from Jack's campervan and signage! The dachshund sniffed the air with great interest near the hog roast van, and then again beside the cowsheds.

The music and noise didn't bother her, she was generally a confident little dog, and a few guests stopped and cooed, bending down to give her a pat and in one case a full tummy tickle, which she was very happy about. And then, when a corner of roasted pork roll got tossed her way, well, she was in doggie heaven.

Lucy popped Daisy back into her dog bed in the rear of the truck, ensuring the windows were open wide, just as she spotted the queue that was building by the horsebox.

'Sorry, Luce, I need a hand here,' Abby called out, looking decidedly hot and flustered.

Blimey, where had all those people come from? Lucy dashed back over, washed her hands and dived back in to help.

The party was in full swing. There was much giggling as a singalong started up and a conga began snaking its way around the yard. The bottom half of the cow turned up for a pizza, his top half exposed in a plain white T, his trousers hilarious black-and-white-patched furry fleece. The top half of the cow then pulled off his head and sat down opposite, placing himself beside Jack's bar with a pint.

'Bloody brilliant night, this,' the young lad at their pizza-stand commented. He had dark hair, ruffled rakishly from his costume wearing.

'Yeah, it's great here. Love the costume by the way,' Lucy heard Abby say. She was so much chattier with the customers than the surly Tamsin.

'Hah, yes, me and Josh thought we'd go for it. A bit of fun. We're Alan's nephews, thought it'd make him smile on his birthday. Bloody hot stuck inside there all night, mind.'

214

The young man ordered a meat feast with extra mushrooms. Abby loaded it up with sauce and toppings and Lucy took it on her wooden board, ready to place in the oven. She could certainly empathise with the sweltering cow in costume, having been stuck by a 400-degree oven on a balmy June night. She could hear Abby and Mr Cow Trousers talking away as he waited for his pizza to cook. They seemed to have hit it off, and Lucy couldn't help but give a smile at that.

After a star-spangled fireworks display, the rockets soaring up into the navy twilight sky with 'ooh's and 'aah's sounding from the guests as they gasped at the flashes of colour, it was all too soon time to pack up. The hosts came across to thank Lucy and Abby, saying how delicious their food had been. Lucy felt proud that her pizza venture was finally coming together, and in turn thanked Abby for her fabulous help. She had a feeling this was the first night of many more with her new partner in crime.

With the oven cooling, Lucy went to the back of her Jeep to pop in one of the now empty storage boxes. *Oh*, the boot was slightly ajar ... Had she closed it properly after taking Daisy for her brief walk earlier in the evening? *Daisy* ... Lucy felt her heart race as she peered in.

'You okay, Daisy?' She raised the tailgate fully, a horrid lump lodging in her throat as she looked in to find the dog's bed empty. She scanned the rear space again. Had the little dog just shifted into a corner or something? But no. Lucy raced around to check the back passenger seats, then the front ... nothing. *Empty. No Daisy.* Oh my god, where the hell was she? Could she have been stolen? Escaped? Had some drunken idiot opened the vehicle by accident ... or on purpose? Had she not quite shut the hatch down properly herself?

She checked it all again, calling out, 'Daisy! Come on, girl!' She might well be close by. But even with the boot open, it would be unusual for her to leave the safety and familiarity of her cosy bed.

But shit, yes, there had been the fireworks display towards the end of the celebrations. Her little dog hated fireworks. Poor Daisy, if Lucy had known about them, she would never have brought her. She'd have made other arrangements for her tonight. Where on earth was she?

'Daisy? Daisy!' Lucy's voice was tight, high-pitched with fear.

She could be hiding. She could be anywhere. It was a farm, for goodness sake. She could have been trampled by cows, attacked by pigs, marauding cockerels ... marauding party people? Lucy felt panic rise, prickly and chilling within.

'Are you alright, Luce?' It was Jack, striding across and looking concerned. 'What's Diva Daisy up to now?'

'I-I don't know. She was here before ... but she's gone.' Lucy felt the sting of tears welling up in her eyes.

'Okay, when did you last see her?'

'About an hour ago. I took her for a quick walk. She seemed fine, but ... I don't know if I left the boot open. She's vanished.'

'She'll not be far away. Don't worry, we'll find her. Let's get looking.'

Abby joined the hunt immediately too. A search party began with word spreading amongst the remaining revellers.

Ah ... not only had Lucy lost her dog, but she'd managed to put all the guests out too. Lucy cursed herself.

But there was so much dangerous stuff on a farm, places for a small dog to get stuck in ... lost in. Had she sniffed out a rabbit, got stuck in a burrow? Oh, bloody hell, why had she even brought her here? She might have been lonely back home, bored and in need of a wee, but at least she wouldn't be missing.

Right, it was no good fretting. It was time to get on and get searching. Lucy got on her hands and knees and looked under the Jeep, then all around and under the horsebox – inside the horsebox. Thank god, the little dog couldn't climb as high as the oven.

Food ... the hog roast van, that could be a place to check ... But Jack was already there and on the case. Adam, the hog roast guy, hadn't seen a dog at all. Mind you, a dachshund on a mission could very well slink purposefully by, unnoticed.

To add to the mix, heavy drops of rain starting plopping down. Her clothes were getting soaked, but she didn't care – she had to keep searching. It was then she spotted Jack, white shirt now clinging to his back, climbing a farm gate and heading out to the fields.

Half an hour later, with all the barns and outbuildings checked, and the hosts involved in the search as well as friends and family from the party, Lucy began to feel distraught.

'She'll turn up, pet,' the farmer's wife, Pat, soothed. 'Here, why don't I make you a nice cup of tea and then we'll go look again, and catch up with the others?' They were stood out in the yard near the farmhouse's porch entrance, the rain shower now easing, but a late-evening breeze ruffled by, all too chilling against Lucy's skin. The birthday balloons were now wilting slightly.

'I'm sorry ... I need to keep going. She means everything to me.'

Memories flooded back of the two of them: Lucy still so raw from the split with Liam and hugging the tear-stained soggy-furred creature so close; Daisy digging up Lucy's newly-planted flower bed at the cottage this springtime – it had looked like a scene from some floral great escape, but she couldn't help but laugh.

Lucy found her eyes were misting. Where was she? She'd go back and re-check the Jeep. That would be Daisy's safe place. She might have trailed back, perhaps with an injury. Lucy's heart sank just thinking about it.

Then came a shout from inside the farmhouse.

'I've found her!' It was Jack's voice, jubilant.

He'd checked with Pat if it was alright to go on inside and take a look, just in case, working on a hunch that a scared and comfort-seeking sausage dog might look for a cosy sofa to curl up on, away from the party and the noisy fireworks going on outside. Jack had noticed that the farmhouse's door had been left open all evening for access to the porch-based bathroom.

Lucy was running towards the house. 'Oh, thank god. Is she alright?' She was still so scared.

Out Jack came, shirt sodden, hair all damp, bearing a still curled-up, slightly affronted-looking Daisy in his arms. 'She was snoozing on the sofa.'

'Oh, Daisy. Thank heavens you're safe ...' Lucy was so relieved. But then paused, addressing Pat and Alan who were now beside her, realising the finale of their special night had been spent hunting for a 'missing' sausage dog with a penchant for a cosy sofa. 'Oh my goodness, I'm so sorry for wasting all your time ... She's been safe inside all the while.'

'It's not a problem, lassie. All's well that ends well. I'm just glad we've found her. And we've had a lovely evening, all of us,' said Pat kindly.

'It's been a grand party, aye.' Mr Fifty Farmer stood smiling at his wife's side. 'Those pizzas were downright delicious. Went down a real treat.'

'Thank you. Oh, and thank you *all* for helping to look for her.' Lucy turned to address the gathering. 'Right, well I'd better take Daisy back to the truck, put her away safely, and finish clearing up.' She suddenly felt a little awkward after all the drama.

Relief flooded through Lucy as she walked across to Jack then, who still had the little dog in his arms. 'Oh Jack, thank you so much for finding her.' Despite her embarrassment, she felt so happy to have her precious dog back safe and sound. He passed the soft, warm creature across into Lucy's open arms, where Daisy received the biggest hug ever.

Once the dog was back safely in her pet bed, and with the boot of the vehicle *firmly* closed and checked, Lucy couldn't help but dash across to where Jack was packing away his fold-up chairs, outside of Ruby. He'd really gone the extra mile, searching high and low for the little dog. 'Thanks again,' she gushed, suddenly overcome with emotion. And as he stood tall, she couldn't help but give him a big hug too.

It felt a little surprising and yet so very natural as they became wrapped in each other's arms, holding tight for a few seconds, the rise and fall of their breath slowing together. The rest of the partygoers seemed to recede for a few moments. Just the two of them stood in the warm glow of campervan Ruby's stage-bulb lights. And even more natural was the kiss that followed, brief but tender. The little dog that had pulled them apart just two weeks ago, had very much brought them together tonight.

For a few precious moments they stayed like that, lips to lips, mouth to soft, giving mouth. Then, Lucy pulled back, as if realising what was happening. '*Oh.*' The alarm bells ringing very loudly in her head.

'Oh ...' Jack echoed, adding, 'Well, that was nice.'

'Yes, well, it was just to say thank you,' Lucy stammered awkwardly, coming back down to earth. 'I-I'd better get packed up, sorted out ... ready to head home,' she blurted out, already dashing off. Leaving Jack bemused but smiling broadly.

Chapter 26

For all her good intentions of steering clear of anything vaguely romantic with Jack, she'd only gone and bloody well kissed him! What had she been thinking? Well, she hadn't, had she? She'd just been too relieved about finding Daisy, that was it. She'd been overcome with emotion. But why, almost eight hours after that midnight kiss, was she still thinking about him ... and about how nice it had felt? To be in a man's arms again, after such a long, and yes, she had to admit it, sometimes lonely time.

He'd smelt gorgeous too, all fresh citrussy aftershave with just a hint of male end-of-a-work-night sweat. It was quite a heady combination up close, when factored with a hug that melted her to him.

Well, it wasn't going to happen again, that was for sure. Her guard was going straight back up. She'd get on with life, go visit her mum like she'd promised to today, and catch up on the family news over a bite of lunch and a good old natter. Perhaps Nonna might come along too. She could easily pick her up on her way through to the little town.

Sofia, Lucy's mum, had never remarried. She'd had a couple

of on–off relationships since Lucy's father, but nothing that had lasted. Her parents had split up when Lucy was fourteen, but she'd told Lucy several years later that she was far happier and felt much more settled on her own. She'd been there, done that and got the T-shirt with Lucy's dad, as well as having two wonderful children to show for it.

When Lucy was going through a particularly bad patch with Liam, Sofia had warned that romance wasn't all it was geared up to be. Hah, maybe Lucy was destined to go the same way. To live a simple yet contented life with her little dog, walking on the beach, running her own catering business, seeing her friends and family, with no ties. That was a good life, a purposeful life.

Yet, why did the life she was carving out for herself suddenly feel a bit empty of late? And why, last night, lying in her bed alone, had she allowed her thoughts to imagine Jack lying there beside her, tracing firm but gentle hands all over her body. Bloody hell, she really did need to buck up and back off.

She popped on her sandshoes and leapt into the Jeep with Daisy, promising herself not to dwell any longer on this crazy nonsense.

Settled outside with Nonna, Mum, and a large pot of tea in Sofia's sheltered back garden, life seemed much simpler.

Nonna was desperate to know all the details about the party with the Italian cakes, and Lucy was more than happy to chat. Neither Mum nor Nonna knew anything about Jack, and that was exactly how she intended it to stay.

'So, for the Clementine and Limoncello, you made the orange zest crème fraiche too, yes?'

'Of course, Nonna. And it went down a treat. Lots of happy customers, thanks to you.'

'Perfect, pet. Oh, I remember eating that for the first time, sat outside a little restaurant with your Papa in Sorrento. We'd gone over for a holiday. He so wanted to show me his birth-place, his family ties.' Nonna smiled nostalgically. 'Ah, I still can see that sea view. Beautiful. And the sea and sky over there. So vivid, such a deep, deep blue. And so hot, not at all like our North-East.'

'It sounds perfect.' Lucy was caught up in the description, picturing her grandparents there. The pair of them so happy. They didn't have a lavish lifestyle at home by any means, yet it was always one full of warmth and love. A holiday abroad would have been extra special.

'Oh, and the cake – summer sunshine on a plate!' Nonna continued her reminiscing. 'I loved it so much, and Papa knew the café owner's family, so they wrote the recipe down for me. I've been making it ever since.'

'Well, we're glad of that, aren't we, Lucy,' Sofia smiled.

'Absolutely.' Thinking of her grandparents, their marriage of Newcastle and Italy made Lucy smile. Two very different young lives, and yet the love they shared, and the life they had lived together, became one. Nonna and Papa's marriage had been good and solid – maybe not every relationship was doomed.

'Do you remember when we went across, Lucy? That trip to Naples and Sorrento?' Mum took a sip of tea.

223

'Yeah, course I do. It was wonderful. The food, the people, they were all so friendly. And Pompeii, how weird, yet amazing was that!' All those people's lives set in stone. Mothers, babies, schools, shops, brothels, it had totally fascinated her and her brother. With Mount Vesuvius still smoking ominously in the distance.

'Oh yes, you ghoulish pair were intrigued by all that. It was like history coming to life before our eyes. Interesting, mind.'

They'd had a five-night stay, not long before Dad had finally left. A holiday for patching up, that had apparently only showed more ripped seams. It had still been good, her parents keeping their problems under cover as they day-tripped as a family and sipped white wine and Fanta Orange in little Neapolitan cafés, and ate pasta and pizza under warm starlit skies.

They chatted some more, the three generations sat in a Northumberland garden, warmed by Mediterranean memories.

Italy had obviously crept into Lucy's heart and stayed there. Perhaps that was why, when life folded for her, when reality became all too much, her dreams took her to Papa and his pizzeria.

Chapter 27

Jack was out on the open road with Ruby, needing to clear his head. She'd kissed him. She'd only gone and kissed him. Now he knew how Lucy's kiss felt, he was having trouble getting her out of his mind.

He'd hoped she might have called that morning. Kept checking his phone, just in case. But no, not even a message. Should he call her? Just on the pretext of checking that Daisy was alright? Of course, the little dog would be – she'd been sat on a cosy sofa all evening, while they were out in the mud and rain looking for her. He sighed.

Jack soon reached the coast, taking in that first glimpse of sea view; blue-grey summer steel on the horizon. And then Bamburgh Castle, grand and dominant, all pink-beige stone and battlements. He never tired of seeing it, of how small it made him feel and his problems with it; it was always an awesome sight.

The little seaside village was bustling today, cars parked up and holiday-makers meandering with dogs and children, holding tasty ice creams, pies and goodies from the village butchers and bakery. The cricket pitch beneath the towering castle walls was a draw for picnickers and people fancying a game of kickabout.

Jack kept on going, wanting space and air. The sea-salt freshness blasting his face as he drove along with his windows wound down. The coastal road skirting the dunes now, with glimpses of the sea here and there; the Farne Islands, and their lighthouse a shadow on the horizon, way off in the distance. The beach beside him stretched for three miles, sandy bays and arcs, rocks and rolling waves. Even with day trippers and locals piling out from parked cars, it never got too busy there. But Jack kept on. He knew where he was heading now, where his soul was drawing him.

Fifteen minutes later he arrived, parking Ruby up down a seaside track. Yes, the highest dune, that was the one. It was a special place, a place that he came to when he needed time to think ... or sometimes just to be. He shoved a notepad and a pen in his rucksack, along with a can of cold beer. He intended to sit for a while and let his thoughts run free.

His pace was swift through the lower dunes, but then the climb was slower, wading in trainers up through shifting sand. It had felt like a mountain clambering up there when they were young. Every step now taking him back to those two little boys ... the joy of arriving at the summit, that king-of-the-castle moment, then hurtling down those sandy slopes, juddering bold steps and nearly tumbling over at the bottom. He could almost hear their boyish laughter.

And in winter, there was that time when Dad took the plastic sledges for them. The sand was nearly as good as snow, but not quite as fast. The exhilaration, that fear of getting tipped out. Milky hot chocolates poured out by Mum from the flask back at the car, hugged by chilly, happy hands. His family. Mum, Dad and Daniel.

Those childhood days where you believed you were invincible, that nothing bad could happen. When you believed that you'd always be together.

Sat at the top now, perched on a high sandy ridge, Jack gazed out to the deep dark-grey swell of sea, heard the peep of the white-and-black terns and the sharp cry of a pair of oyster catchers, circling above. The sun warmed him, yet inside he still felt a little cold, empty.

It had all happened such a long time ago, and yet the hurt could feel so raw. He'd tried so hard to move on, but sometimes he needed to look back too. Jack found himself trying to write, paper to hand, yet the pen dangled uselessly in his fingertips, the words were so not coming. Hmm, very like the phone call he was hoping might have landed by now from Lucy ... And still, nothing.

Love and marriage go together like a horse and carriage

Please join us in celebrating

the Wedding of

Anna and Michael

at Alnmouth Village Hall

From 7 p.m., Saturday 10th July

RSVP

Chapter 28

Should he just go ahead and ring her?

    Jack ploughed on with two more functions the following week, with neither sight nor sound of Lucy. Flashbacks to that rather gorgeous hug and the out-of-the-blue kiss at the farm party kept rising unbidden in his mind. Should he just pluck up the courage to ask her out on a date the next time they met? Just bite the bullet.

He stared at the mobile phone in his hand, then began flipping it over in his palm. It was like a game of dare he was playing with himself. Was Lucy waiting for him to call? He was so close to dialling her number. But he held back, unsure of his own motivations. His feelings were extremely sensual, he knew that. How could you not have your senses ignited by that gorgeously pretty face, the sweep of dark hair, that smile when she let it loose, her laugh? But there was something about the way he felt about her that also made him uneasy ... like he might get drawn in, beyond the physical, further than he was prepared to go. To a place where he might get hurt.

*   *   *   **

A further seven long days later, an evening wedding reception was being held at Alnmouth village hall – a picturesque coastal village with pastel-coloured houses overlooking the tranquil estuary of the River Aln. Being her first wedding booking, it was a big event for Lucy, and her nerves were already jangling. To add to that, as Lucy pulled up in her horsebox, she felt super-flustered when she saw that Ruby was there, with Jack stood in the open roof space setting up his lights and cocktail glasses, ready for action. He gave a wide grin and a wave as he spotted her. She gave a hesitant wave back, whilst looking for a space to park. Friendly was fine, she told herself, friendly she could do. But she was determined not to get drawn into Jack's charming web again – Becky would never let her hear the end of it.

A wedding ... hah, she'd never got past the engagement stage with Liam. They hadn't even got as far as booking a venue for their wedding. After five years engaged, that in itself should have set off alarm bells. Old hurts still lurked, but she rallied. They were never meant to be, and there was no point staying bitter. And as for tonight, Lucy knew that she wanted to make this event extra special for the wedding couple. She was keen to decorate the horsebox extra-prettily with a newly-purchased garland of delicate white silk flowers set above the hatch, as well as her twinkling fairy lights. She propped a rustic-looking wooden sign, that read *Mr and Mrs* in swirly white writing, on her countertop, beside a milk jug filled with fresh white carnations and fragrant freesia. An event-theming tip she'd picked up from Jack.

Jack ... don't even go there, she reminded herself, whilst

her mind wandered dangerously in his direction, and she stole a sneaky glance. Her heart gave a strange pang, catching sight of the blond scruffy-cute hair, the smart white shirt and black bow tie. He'd gone all out for this occasion too, then. She sighed and moved her gaze. The village-hall doors were flung wide open and Lucy caught a glimpse of pretty fairy lights, and beautiful white-rose and eucalyptus floral table decorations. There were tables and chairs positioned outside too, to make the most of the beautiful sea view and the summer evening, with pretty tea-light candle holders and glass jam jars filled with white rose and delicate gypsophila posies.

The guests began to gather, gravitating towards the Cocktail Campervan for a glass of bubbly. The wedding had taken place earlier that afternoon at the village church, with a lunch for close family and friends in a nearby country hotel. The newlyweds, bridesmaids and ushers had since been down to the beach for a fabulous seaside photo session. Now was the time for everybody to let their hair down and have a little fun, with the bride and groom now arriving – a dusting of sand still on their lace and linen – in an open carriage pulled by a gorgeous dappled grey horse. The couple looked so happy as they smiled and waved.

Love and marriage … go together like a horse and carriage, came to Lucy's mind. But the loud clip-clopping of the horse's hooves also sounded very much like a warning to her.

An hour later, and the lyrics from 'The Shoop Shoop Song' were booming out from the hall as part of a Golden Oldies disco mix. Lucy bobbed her head in time to the music, losing herself for a moment in the words.

Hmm, *his kiss* indeed ... Lucy's thoughts snagged once again on a certain Jack Anderson, as the romantic setting of the wedding enveloped her ... memories of that gorgeous afternoon on the beach, Jack going all out to help find Daisy. Could he really be such a heartless prat? Was Becky just caught up in the past and her own hurts? All that with Becky was eight or so years ago, after all. Did Jack actually deserve a chance? Bloody hell, no amount of pizza topping, veggie chopping, and hot-oven tending could get him out of her head.

What if ...? What if they chatted tonight as they packed up? Could she pluck up the courage, suggest a walk on the beach or meeting up to grab a coffee down at Driftwood one day? Not a date as such, just a bit of time together, see how they got on. Was it time to take a bit of a chance? Yes, Becky had warned her off, but Jack might well have changed from that arrogant young lad that Becky had known. It was many years ago, after all. People grew up, learnt from their experiences. The memories from that afternoon on the beach ... The man she'd spoken with then seemed friendly, warm, caring. Something had sparked inside her that day, she knew that.

What if ...? The thought kept tweaking in her mind, as she looked up, catching his eye just then, which lit up his cute smile. Oh my!

'A Mango Fizz and a two Raspberry Rum Smashes, please.' The tall, slim brunette at the counter gave a friendly smile as she ordered.

'Coming right up,' Jack beamed back.

Tonight's cocktails were fruity and fun. The happy couple had requested some refreshing summery punches to be served alongside the usual cocktail classics. There were lots of people in their late twenties and early thirties there, being friends of the bride and groom, as well as the usual wedding family mix-up of quirky uncles, aged aunts, flower girls and wound-up toddlers, plus a round-up of characterful village acquaintances.

'This is so cool,' the brunette continued. 'A campervan bar, it's amazing. And cocktails too ... my absolute favourite drinks, all wrapped up in a cute VW.' The young woman stopped talking then and gave a frown of concentration, focussing on Jack. 'Hey, don't I know you ... aren't you that guy from school? Yeah, Alnwick High school, back in sixth form? That's it, you were in my tutor group ... it's Jack. Jack ... Hmm ...? Help me out here.'

'Anderson, yeah. And you must be ... hang on ... it's on the tip of my tongue ... Freya.' A mousy-haired, shy seventeen-year-old came to mind. He had no idea of her surname.

'Freya Lightwater, yep, that's me. Hi, Jack.' She tilted her head, coyly.

Two of her girlfriends gathered around then. 'Have you ordered yet, Frey? It's been ages,' one asked rather loudly and impatiently.

'Of course.' She blushed pink, seeming a little downtrodden by the two bossier babes who'd just turned up.

Jack felt a little sorry for her. He also had a feeling that from her giveaway sway she might have sampled one or two of his cocktails already this evening, no doubt in addition to several glasses of the wedding reception wine.

The young woman steadied herself, holding onto Ruby's chrome counter.

'Your drinks will be ready shortly,' he addressed the annoying new arrival. 'Being hand-crafted, they do take a little while, but that's what the art of cocktail making is all about.'

Loud-Mouth had the cheek to raise her black-pencilled eyebrows impatiently.

'It's okay,' Freya added politely, 'I don't mind waiting.'

The other two women just huffed, with Loud-Mouth saying, 'You should have just ordered a bottle of bloody prosecco, Frey.'

Jack managed to hold his tongue, no use antagonising the guests.

The drinks were soon made, the Raspberry Rum Smash had been a bit of a hit tonight, and the Mango Fizz looked cool, juicy and refreshing, both drinks delightful for a summer's evening.

Freya passed the bossy babes their drinks, who then waltzed off leaving her alone again. She stayed at the counter, taking a sip of her own mango delight. 'Wow, that is *sooo* good. Thank you.'

'You're welcome, Freya.' She seemed a really sweet girl. 'Just go steady now.'

'Hah, I'm trying. It's these new shoes they're a nightmare. I wasn't designed for high heels.'

'Well watch your step, hey.'

'Will do. It's been nice chatting to you, Jack. Take care.'

'You too.'

And off she went, a teensy bit wobbly on her stilettos, to hopefully find some better friends to spend the rest of the evening with.

Later on, Lucy watched from across the way. Crikey, how many more drinks could people pack in? Despite it being well past midnight, they were still clamouring for yet another cocktail at Jack's bar, like bees round a honeypot. Lucy had been working steadily all night, but her pizza order had now been fulfilled, with lots of lovely comments coming from the wedding guests, which was brilliant. She was beginning to feel more confident with every event.

Lucy began packing up her horsebox kitchen area, cleaning every surface thoroughly. Suddenly, she heard a 'Whoa, steady on love,' from over the way. She looked up to see a young woman fall against a man who happened to be holding two drinks aloft, spilling a lurid pink one all down his smart pale-grey suit. Oops.

'Sorry, I'm so sorry!' The girl looked mortified, whilst still appearing unsteady on her feet.

'This suit cost me a bloody fortune. It's ruined now.' The chap was not at all happy.

'Okay, okay, folks. Here, take a seat.' Jack stepped down from the campervan, taking control of the situation, and helping the wobbly girl to one of the chairs that were set out beside his bar. Lucy couldn't quite make out what was said next, but it was apparent that he was trying to smooth things over. The guy wandered off, still irked, judging by the grimace creased over his face, whilst Jack crouched down and said something to the young woman.

The girl stayed there, resting her head in her hands at the little table, whilst Jack went back to serve his last few customers. It wasn't long before the disco guy announced the last track, and then there was Frank Sinatra blasting out 'New York, New York' from the hall, with some interesting high-leg kicking manoeuvres spilling over into the car park. A cluster of taxis arrived soon afterwards to collect the swaying, and occasionally singing, wedding guests as they drifted off home and to their overnight accommodation.

Finally, this might be *their* time; the end-of-night chance to chat. It could be Lucy's best opportunity to catch up with Jack, and then well, muster up the courage to ask him ... for a coffee, or something? She felt a bit nervous, and seeing there was a couple stood beside the campervan, ducked out for now, taking Daisy out for a quick stroll around the field edge instead, whilst finding her nerve.

After making a brief circuit, Lucy wandered back. She could see Jack bustling about, tidying up inside the campervan. Should she just walk right on up? All she had to do was start with 'Hello.' But damn, the tipsy girl was still there on her chair, possibly dozing, judging by her slumped-looking pose.

Jack cleared glasses into crates, emptied and wiped down Ruby's counter area and was making final preparations to shut up shop. Lucy knew his routine as well as her own by now – her time was running out. She heaved the pizza oven back inside the horsebox, was steeling herself to go across, when she saw Jack spot the young woman and go on out to her. Lucy watched as he nudged the girl awake, asking her something. The young woman just shook her head, then remained seated, looking a little lost, whilst Jack went off into the hall. Coming back again a few minutes later, he said a few words, then helped her up, hooking his arm around her shoulders. She giggled and moved in close to him, seeming to be muttering something into this ear.

Lucy suddenly felt very uneasy, scrubbing her counter top extra hard, unable to peel her eyes away from the pair of them. Jack then bundled the brunette into Ruby's passenger seat. And, were they ... kissing? Lucy craned her neck to try and get a better look, her heart hammering and sweat forming near her temples. Jack was certainly very close, helping to secure the seat belt across the girl's rather revealing chest area. Their heads close together – too close.

Lucy felt sick to the pit of her stomach. What *was* she actually witnessing? Was this the Jack she'd been warned about? The player. The charmer. The take-a-girl-home even if she is tipsy, kind of guy?

He hadn't even stopped to take the time to chat with Lucy tonight as they'd cleared up. Spotting some easier prey, no doubt, someone else to lure home to his den. Oh, and she'd been so bloody naïve, hadn't she, willing herself to give him the benefit of the doubt. Thinking they might even spend some time together, get to know each other a little more. Hah, bloody hah.

She stood and watched, with a thick lump forming in her throat, as Ruby set off into the night, with her cosy cargo of two, leaving Lucy feeling saddened and confused. But then, she reminded herself, steeling her heart once more, perhaps it was better to know what he was like. To see the real Jack in action. Whatever had just happened, perhaps she had just had a lucky escape.

Chapter 29

An eventful Saturday night – for all the wrong reasons – turned into a wet, drizzly Sunday morning. Lucy lay in bed with Daisy curled up beside her, absently stroking the dog's smooth black fur, wondering if she should bother to get up yet. It wouldn't be much fun on the beach in the mizzle, after all. Her mind flicked back to Jack and that girl at the wedding party. Had she stayed over with him last night? It was like a riddle she didn't want to solve. Why on earth was she even bothering to dwell on it? He was just some sad, playboy loser, just like Becky had warned. Lucy slumped back on the pillows, finding herself feeling wrung out.

Right, this is no good, Lucy thought, rallying. She needed a caffeine fix, something sweet and sugary, and a bit of friendly banter, and she knew just where to head. She picked up her mobile from the bedside table and texted Becky on the off-chance she might be free.

Fancy meeting for cake and coffee at Driftwood? Say 11 a.m.? X

A reply soon bounced back:

Yeah, okay then. That'll get me nicely out of some DIY

tasks Darren has decided we need to do this morning! I'll promise to help him this aft, and hopefully most of them will be done by then! X

Shall we ask Katie too? Lucy typed. Haven't seen her in ages.

Yes, of course, that'd be great. X

And so, at five to eleven, Lucy was wandering along the coastal village street in her red, cheer-you-up rain mac, heading for the comforting aromas of rich, warm coffee and just-baked goodies.

It was cosy in the café, and Lucy and Becky managed to bag the last table; the one by the front window with a glimpse of sea view, though it was a little misty today.

Abby was working today, and soon arrived to take their order.

'Hi, ladies. So, what can I get for you?' The young girl was her usual smiley self.

'Hi, Abby, miserable day isn't it, we thought we'd best cheer ourselves up with a slice of cake! So, what do you have to tempt us with today?' Lucy asked, feeling in need of a sugar fix.

'Okay, there's Driftwood's ever-popular Sea-salted Caramel Cake, a Victoria Sponge, and yes, Louise has been trying a new recipe out, a Coconut and Lime Cake, which is to die for. I sampled it earlier.'

'Yum, that's me sold,' Lucy grinned. 'Coconut and Lime with a pot of your Northumberland Tea, please.'

'I'm gonna have to have the Sea-salted Caramel. Sounds delish,' added Becky. 'Tea for me too.'

In dashed Katie, just in time to order. 'Hi folks, sorry I'm late, toddler tantrums and husband hold-ups. I'll have one of those delicious-looking cheese scones,' she said, turning to Abby, 'with a flat white please. Thanks, love!'

The girls chatted away in catch-up mode, and Abby was soon on her way back over, with the order balanced on a large tray.

'So, how was your party last night then?' Lucy asked Becky as she reached the table. Her friend had been telling her about her cousin's up-and-coming thirtieth.

'Yeah, it was great, thanks. A meal out with lots of fun, family, friends, and plenty of booze. Head wasn't too good this morning, mind. But I made it here in time, *just*, and I've rallied. The sugar hit of the Caramel Cake is what I need.' She smiled at Abby. 'What about you, Luce? How was the wedding pizza event?'

Lucy nearly choked on her tea. She fiddled with a napkin and then answered, 'Ah, good thanks, yeah ... all fine.' There was a bitter taste in her mouth, as the image of Jack heading off with that girl in his campervan filled her mind once more. A quick deflection was needed. 'Oh, and last week, what happened? I've been meaning to ask you, Abby. You seemed to be getting on pretty well with that lad at the party at the farm ... you know, the bottom half of the cow.'

'*What?*' Becky screwed up her nose, looking bemused.

'That sounds one crazy party,' added Katie with a grin.

'Hah, well, the pizza horsebox gets to go to all kind of places, I can tell you. It was good fun actually, and a really nice crowd.'

'Hah, yes ...' Abby suddenly seemed coy.

'Well, did he call?' Lucy quizzed.

The last Lucy had seen was him tapping in her assistant's number on his phone.

'Yeah, he did actually.' Abby had flushed a perfect shade of pink.

'Whoop, whoop. Aw, I'm pleased for you, hun.'

'We're going to meet up next week, actually,' the young girl added shyly.

'Aw, that's brilliant. Good for you, Abby.' Lucy was delighted for her.

'Anyway, what about *you* ...?' asked Abby.

Lucy felt the heat rise from her neck up to her cheeks. She had a dreadful feeling she knew where this was going. 'What about me?' she blustered.

'Well, the last I saw of you ... was you up close and kissing Cocktail Campervan Guy. Can't blame you, mind; he is pretty cute.'

Becky's mouth dropped open, and a chunk of salted caramel sponge plopped out onto her plate. 'You are kidding me?! Luce, how the hell could you? After everything I told you. That's a disaster waiting to happen, that is.'

It already has, mused Lucy, sadly. And so sodding soon too.

'What am I missing here?' Katie queried, trying to play catch-up with the drama.

'I warned you, Luce, that guy is toxic. Are you nuts?' Becky's cheeks had gone bright pink.

'It's okay. It wasn't what it looked like, Becks.' *Okay, so it was, but there is never going to be a repeat performance, not after watching last night's spectacle with the damsel in distress.* 'I'd lost Daisy, and well, Jack had been the one to find her. I was just so relieved and I did give him a hug to thank him. But that was it. It might have just looked like something more,' she rambled with a blush.

Abby gave a frown and looked rather sceptical, but she didn't want to argue with her new boss.

With that, Louise called over from the counter, 'Got an order to go out here, Abby.'

'Okay, I'm coming,' she replied, and then dashed away to help, leaving Lucy red in the face and feeling sore in the heart.

Oh, yes. Lesson well and truly learned.

With Becky still sat shaking her head, she and Katie slipped once again into easy chat. It seemed, Lucy hoped, they'd fallen for the little white lie.

Well done Joshua on your Graduation

and well done to Helen for putting up with me
for Fifty Years!

Join us Golden Oldies on Saturday 17th July

at home

7 p.m. onwards for food, fun and festivities.

Best wishes, David x

Chapter 30

Why did he get the feeling that Lucy was trying to avoid him?

Jack had been serving drinks for an hour already and, other than a brief reply to his 'Hello' on arrival, she'd hardly looked his way. Jeez, he never seemed to know where he stood with this exasperating, but bloody gorgeous, woman. She blew hotter and colder than anyone he'd ever met.

Ruby was positioned in the beautiful garden of a modestly grand country home. There was a marquee set up – he'd peeked in earlier – with circular tables, white tablecloths, and pretty floral displays of dark-green ivy with delicate white and yellow flowers edged with gold spray; the greenery was even intertwined down the marquee poles. Helen and David, whose home it was, had organised the party as a big family get-together for their grandson's graduation and their Golden Wedding Anniversary. There was a buffet laid out within the marquee, as well as the fabulous All Fired Up horsebox parked alongside.

Helen had mentioned wanting 'something more fun' food-wise as an alternative for the youngsters; and Jack had known just where to send her. Though from the gathering at the counter, it wasn't just the youngsters who were keen to try Papa's pizzas; all ages were being drawn by the tantalising smells of hot, baked dough, tomatoes and cheese. Even Jack's mouth was watering, and he knew exactly what to expect. At least the food was a lot more predictable than the owner, Jack mused wryly.

Back to his own clients, and this evening's bar theme was classic, with G&T's and Gin Fizzes, and chilled champagne on arrival. He'd also done a bit of research and found a gorgeous-looking shimmering Golden Champagne Cocktail to serve to those guests who fancied trying something a little different – which was elderflower liqueur fizz, stirred with edible gold-leaf flakes – just perfect for the occasion.

The marquee was buzzing from eight o'clock when a live band came on, giving a great show with plenty of toe-tapping tunes, both old and new. There was much dancing and merriment; the gathering really getting into the swing of it. It was such a lovely atmosphere, and Jack couldn't help but wish to share some of those happy vibes with Lucy. He stole the odd glance her way, but when she did finally catch sight of him, she seemed to immediately refocus, head down. And then again twenty minutes later, as their eyes met, she quickly turned and began talking to one of her customers. There was definitely something up with her – she'd been acting strangely ever since that kiss at the farm.

People were milling in and out of the marquee throughout the evening. They enjoyed Jack's bar service and were drinking steadily, but not in any crazy can't-get-them-down-quick-enough way, unlike a few of the guests at last week's wedding. Oh yes, at the end of the night, he'd made sure that Tipsy Girl had got back safely, dropping her off at home. There was a great ambience here tonight, with little kids happily dancing along with parents and older family members. Good times, making memories, at least three generations of a family enjoying themselves with close friends – these were the events that Jack enjoyed working the most. He felt a part of their special celebration; chatting with the guests whilst making their favourite drinks.

A couple, who must have been in their late seventies, strolled up to Jack's bar. The gentleman, who was white-haired and dressed in a beige linen suit, stood back, evidently admiring Ruby, and then moved in to pat her shiny paintwork with a smile.

'My, she's a real beauty, isn't she? Someone's done a grand job of the conversion, I must say.'

Jack stood proudly at his gleaming countertop. 'Well, I did much of it myself, with a few technical tweaks here and there.'

'You've done well, son.'

'Thanks, so what can I get you both?' Jack grinned.

'Oh, I think we'll stick with the G&T's, shall we, Clive?' the floral-dressed lady said.

'Perfect,' he agreed.

'Coming right up.'

Whilst Jack fetched glasses and the Hepple Gin bottle, Clive continued, 'I do love a Classic, that's why I married my good lady here, Betty.' He chuckled, whilst Betty gave a smile that crinkled around her kind blue eyes, well used to his chatter after all their years together. 'Yes, we had some damned good times, didn't we, Betty? Remember that summer we headed off to the continent? Top down in our vintage MX5 Mazda. Ah, those were the days.' Clive's eyes were a-sparkle as he reminisced.

Betty was nodding happily.

'Oh, it sounds fabulous,' Jack was genuinely interested.

'Zipping through all those rustic French villages,' Clive took up. 'Oh, and those hairpin bends in the Pyrenees. Do you remember those, my love, and the sheer drops beside us? Now, that was exciting.'

His wife pulled a dramatic face at that, as though the hairpin bends had been particularly hair-raising, and perhaps not quite such fun from the passenger seat.

Jack had to laugh as he filled their gin globes. It was lovely to hear their tale, and they seemed such a sweet couple.

As he passed over their drinks, Clive ended with the story of them breaking down on a Tuscan hillside, which turned out to be rather a blessing in disguise, as the locals were so friendly, coming to their aid and hosting them royally for two days whilst the local garage waited for parts and then helped Clive to fix up the vehicle. Jack could just picture the pair of them, in their youth and their retirement enjoying the open road, and he couldn't help but admire such a relationship – one that could stand the test of time yet still be filled with adventures.

The evening rolled on, and when he finally got a quiet moment, he decided to bite the bullet and call across to Lucy. 'Hey, everything okay? Do you need a break at all? I can come across there and keep an eye on the oven if need be?' He'd spotted that she was working on her own.

'Ah, it's okay, I'm fine, thanks.' Lucy gave the coolest flicker of a smile, then set back to shaping her dough bases behind the counter.

'Alright, well just shout if you need a hand at any point. It's no problem,' he persisted.

'Thanks.' Her eyes barely lifted.

Those gorgeous dark-brown eyes that had looked right into his on the night of that kiss. *Refocus, Jack, refocus.* He pushed on with his own tasks, slicing lemons and curling twists of lime peel. A few people strolled up, and an order came in for two Mojitos and a Sidecar, and he soon found himself chatting with a middle-aged guy at the counter, lost in his mixology moments once again.

The party continued in full swing with lots of fun, singing and dancing. Partygoers were spilling out of the marquee in search of a cool drink and a cool-down, whilst others were drifting back in. A young couple were sat at the little table beside his campervan, sipping their gin fizzes. Pizza aromas wafted enticingly on the evening breeze, whilst the pizza van owner carried on working, head down, rather aloofly. Suddenly, a sharp cry rang out from the front of the marquee. Jack looked up to see that someone was on the ground, their leg stuck out at a really awkward angle.

'Oh my, oh my!' A woman's voice rang out in a sob.

Jack recognised her as the elderly lady from the vintage-car couple earlier. Betty, that was it. He dashed out of Ruby like a shot, rushing over to see if he could help, and was soon crouching beside her. A small gathering began to cluster around them, as Jack carefully assessed the injury. He didn't want to yank at Betty's leg, as it looked slightly displaced around the ankle. He'd done a First Aid course as part of some voluntary mountaineering work he'd undertaken with a youth group a few years back. There was no blood or bone showing, which was good, but the ankle seemed to be swelling already.

'Okay, Betty, now just take a few deep breaths. Are you in much pain?' Jack's voice was soothing, calm. 'Do you think you can move that leg at all? Just test it *real* slow to start, and stop straight away if it hurts.'

Betty, bless her, had tears in her eyes as she tried to move it, gasping in anguish. It wasn't shifting easily, so she'd need to sit tight.

'Right then, you just keep still there now, Betty. We'll try and make you more comfortable.' Jack figured that an ambulance would be in order; it might well be a break or a bad sprain, but she was stuck in a really tricky place where someone else could well trip over her themselves; they couldn't just leave her splayed out like that at the entrance to the tent.

'Mate, can you give me a hand here?' he said, addressing a sturdy-looking bloke who was looking on. 'And if someone could fetch a seat from inside and pop it somewhere close by, we'll lift her carefully onto it.'

'No problem.' The burly chap replied.

'Someone's likely to trip over you here, Betty,' Jack explained, 'so we'll just get you carefully moved.' Jack had taken control of the situation. 'Oh, and can one of you call an ambulance, please?'

'I'll do it,' said the young woman who'd been sipping a Gin Fizz at Jack's bar.

'Right, arms tight around our shoulders, Betty,' said Jack. 'And, on the count of three ...'

The two men made a seat from their joined hands, wrist to wrist, and hoisted her up, just as her husband Clive appeared looking flustered. 'Oh Betty, I've just heard! What on earth have you done, my darling?'

'A little trip, that was all. So silly of me.' Betty was pale with shock and no doubt in pain, but she was trying to make light of it.

'We'll get you sorted, my love.' He took one of her hands in his own.

'The ambulance is on its way,' said the young woman with her mobile pressed to her ear. 'Might just be a little while. They're doing the best they can, but it's a busy night, apparently. Oh, and they say to keep the foot up, if at all possible.'

Jack went to fetch an ice bucket from the campervan, emptied it and upturned it. It'd make a good foot rest. He also wrapped some ice tightly in a clean tea towel, to apply to try and ease the swelling. Bless her, Betty looked a little shivery now that the shock was settling in.

'I'll get your coat, Betty, love.' Clive bustled off, leaving Jack sitting with the poor woman for a while, gently pressing the ice pack against her ankle.

'I've got a fleece rug in the truck,' Lucy called out, having seen the episode unfold. 'Hang on, I'll fetch it.' She got it and ran across to them straight away, before Betty's overcoat had a chance to arrive. 'There you go. That'll warm you up.'

Lucy had left her pizza post unattended for a brief while, but she couldn't look on and not help Betty. She had to admire the way Jack was handling the situation, but it also left her feeling confused. His actions, his instincts to help others, were often kind, yet when it came to the way he treated younger women – with his playboy-style antics – well, he seemed to be a different guy altogether. Why did everything – everyone – have to be so bloody complicated?

With the anniversary party coming to an end, Lucy listened in to the many touching words of thanks from the guests and glimpsed heartfelt hugs amongst them, as taxis and lifts turned up.

'Hey ...' Jack approached the horsebox, as Lucy was giving her work surfaces a final wipe-down.

'Hi ... you did well back there,' she said, looking down at her feet. 'With the old lady, I mean.'

'Thanks, the poor thing. Took quite a fall, didn't she?'

'Yeah, bless her.'

Lucy looked up and found herself staring at Jack's slate-blue eyes and his slightly unkempt sandy-blond hair. Her heart started to beat double-time and she felt a dryness in her throat. Why did her body have to betray her? Every time they met, whenever they were near each other, it was like he cast some kind of weird spell over her. But she knew better than that, she'd witnessed his kind of Jack the Lad antics before, and she wouldn't allow herself to sink. It would be like drowning.

It was just the two of them at the horsebox. They stood like that for a few moments, in silence, a strange awkwardness rippling through the air.

'Luce, what is it?' Jack whispered tentatively. He paused for a few seconds. 'What's going on with us?'

'*Us?* There is no us, Jack,' she blasted back, frowning.

'Oh …' He felt deflated, but persisted, 'Luce, I really don't know where I stand with you,' he continued. 'One minute you're giving me a hug … a kiss … which I have to say was rather lovely … but then, like tonight, well, you can hardly manage to speak to me.'

'You don't know where *you* stand? Hah, well, that's rich coming from you, Jack …'

Lucy took a breath. Was it time to be honest? Tell him what she knew about Becky, about his past? There was no-one around in hearing distance.

'It's like you're two different people. There's this Mr Nice Guy helping little old ladies and finding lost dogs, but then … well, with women … young women who you might date, for example,' she took a deep breath, 'then you don't seem to care much at all.'

Jack frowned at her. 'What's this about, Luce?'

'My friend, Becky …'

He didn't show any sign of recognition at the name.

'Rebecca Smith,' she clarified.

Jack merely looked vacant, which wound Lucy up even more.

'Well, she's one of your exes. One of the *many*, by the sounds of it,' she couldn't help but add the dig. 'Well, she told me *all* about your "treat 'em mean, keep 'em keen" antics. How you were seeing someone else at the exact same time as dating her ...'

'Ri-ight ... And when was this?' Jack looked bemused, but perhaps not totally surprised.

'Umm ... about nine years ago.'

'Wow, we really are keeping score.' His tone was sarcastic.

'Look, she warned me off you. Told me all about how you messed with her ... how you were seeing someone else at the same bloody time. She's a close friend, Jack.'

Jack looked chastened, as though something in this was ringing true. 'Okay, look, why not come across a minute, and have a glass of something with me? We can chat a bit more privately, and I'll tell you more about my "misspent youth" ... if you really want to hear about that.'

'I'm not sure that I do want to ...' Lucy was still indignant.

'Come on, Luce. If you're casting accusations, then at least give me a chance to explain. I'll make you up the most delicious mocktail. I know you have to drive.' His tone was conciliatory.

Should she give him the chance to tell his side of the story? Then, at least, they could move on, keep their distance, but remain polite. 'Umm, alright then.'

So, sat at the little table and chairs set beside Ruby, on a night filled with stars, Jack's truth unfolded:

'Right then, so I had a bit of a hard time around my late teens ... I wasn't a good lad, Luce, and I didn't treat women

258

with the respect they deserve. Hands up to that. I was selfish ... and I was hurting.'

So, it was true. Becky's warning was so damned right.

'And I know it's no excuse,' Jack continued, 'but, well,' he took a slow breath, 'it was after my brother died ... that time was a bit of a blur. Everything with Daniel ... it was so out of the blue. It just tore my world apart.'

'Oh Jack, I'm so sorry,' Lucy said with wide eyes, feeling slightly winded. '... about your brother.' *God, that must have been tough.*

He looked up towards the night sky for a few moments, before starting again. 'But yes, back then, these girls ... well, I didn't always keep track very well and I suppose you'd call me a player, but ... I never promised them anything. I was young, Luce ... immature. Was only thinking of myself back then. I'm not proud of it, but I'll not lie to you, it happened.'

'Oh ...' She could perhaps forgive Jack for his misdemeanours in the past; he must have been experiencing a whole world of hurt. She couldn't even imagine the pain he must have been going through back then. But then, what about the drunk girl the other night? Oh yes, she'd seen that with her own eyes ... seen him bundling her off into his campervan. That hadn't looked innocent at all.

Jack was staring at her earnestly, waiting for her to respond.

Should she go ahead and ask about the girl at the wedding? But did she really want to know? Was it worth raking up yet more of Jack's messy behaviour? It wasn't as though it'd make a difference now. It was time to back away, keep things simple between them. Time to protect herself. She didn't need any more complications in her life.

'Well, like I said, thanks for the drink.' Lucy stood to go.

She was hiding something, Jack knew it. He recognised that guarded look. Yes, his behaviour back then had been disappointing, but it was so long ago. He couldn't leave it like this. Her words didn't match the look in her eyes ... nor the way she'd hugged him, held him, kissed him that other night.

He took a deep breath.

'Lucy, stop. I like you!' There – it was said.

Lucy stopped in her tracks, her head snapping round to face Jack, her skin prickling at his words.

Jack looked at her, waiting. His heart was on the bloody line and she'd still not answered.

The silence stretched between them.

'Good night, Jack,' she whispered softly. And she started to walk away.

Jack could only watch her retreating footsteps, his heart sinking like a stone. How could he change the way she felt? His smile was sad, like he knew he couldn't put right the past, the things he'd done.

'Night, Luce,' he whispered back into the night.

HOLY ISLAND MUSIC AND FOOD FESTIVAL

SATURDAY 24TH JULY

LINE UP FEATURING: ALNWICK ACOUSTICS,
SEAGLASS, DJ DR FIZZ, ISLAND FOLK,
THE DUNELM DRUMMERS

SUMMER STARTS HERE!

Chapter 31

The beat of the music was pounding through Lucy. The bounce of the crowd, a thousand strong, pulsing through the very earth under her feet, as they sang along at the tops of their voices. Flags swayed in rainbow colours against a summer-blue sky as dry ice smoked and drifted from the stage. It was moving and rather magical. The music festival at Holy Island was in full and fabulous swing.

Lucy had only ever been to one festival before today: Leeds Fest, along with Becky, when they were just seventeen. That had been crazy but fun; a weekend of dancing, drinking, wellies stuck in the mud, sunshine and rain, laughter, and very little sleep, chatting with complete strangers (one, she remembered, dressed as a Smurf with a blue-painted face, yet no-one batted an eyelid), taking Lucy way out of her steady comfort zone. The two girls had laughed about it so much, since. But festivals became a thing of the past when she met Liam. His idea of camping was much more civilised; not spending a weekend in some cramped field with music pounding and a load of sweaty revellers.

The bands today had been fantastic so far – a great mix

of music. And though some weren't to Lucy's usual taste – being more of a Coldplay, The 1975, and nostalgic soft-rock fan herself – she'd understood that every performer had given it their all, and the local folk music was surprisingly fabulous. From her catering spot at the rear of the main stage field, along with several other eateries, she'd been able to take in the whole scene.

Lucy knew that Jack was there – she'd spotted the familiar gleam of red paintwork as he'd arrived, which had sent her stomach into an odd lurch. It was Jack who'd told her to try for a pitch, giving her and All Fired Up a leg-up again. He'd messaged her on Facebook about it and, although she knew it was cowardly, taking advantage of his generous business advice whilst staying silent, Lucy couldn't quite bring herself to reply after their last interaction.

She stepped down from the horsebox and shaded her eyes from the fierce sun, peering towards Ruby who was parked on the lower field. She sighed and just took in the vista of the festival for a moment; feeling the pulse of the music vibrating through her, the energy of the crowds and the bright sun casting everything in a golden glow.

Once the July evening kicked in – the summer sun still high in the sky, piercing through the pewter-blue expanse – the colourful stage lights came into their own. With yet more flags and huge banners swaying amongst the crowd, the sing-along chant of their responses ringing in the air, the atmosphere was electric, charged with a warm, fun, festival vibe. The weather had stayed fair, thankfully, for the participants, though the forecast for later that evening looked pretty horrendous, with warnings of a summer storm heading their way. Hopefully, Lucy mused, she'd be packed up and well away by then.

The food was smelling *so* good all around her. Lucy had been on the go, along with her brilliant side-kick, Abby, ever since they'd got there at 10 a.m., quickly setting up, and then delivering a constant supply of freshly-cooked pizzas for the ever-hungry crowd. It was now past 7 p.m. and she found herself craving one of Bob's gourmet burgers, having been parked beside his van with the smell of cooked beef and fried onions tantalising her tastebuds for hours. She might well have to nip over there, and buy her and Abby a burger. Which flavour to go for, was the magic question? Chilli burger, blue cheese and caramelised onion, bacon double decker? Honestly, his chalkboard menu was mouth-wateringly good.

Lucy was aware that Abby needed to get away sharpish, as she had a friend's 21st birthday party to head to. Abby's apologetic call had come a week ago: 'Sorry Luce, I can definitely work the festival day, but I've got a close friend's birthday party the same night. Don't panic. I won't let you down. And I love working with you.'

Lucy was cheered by that part, at least.

'And, it's a great chance to get into the festival for free,' Abby had confessed. 'Look, the real fun won't start at the party 'til ten-ish anyhow, so how about I work the festival 'til around nine thirty? Would that work?'

Lucy didn't have a lot of options, but imagined the bulk of the food orders would have happened before the girl's planned departure, as they were booked to start serving from midday. Extremely grateful for Abby's help, Lucy was pretty sure she could manage fine for the last couple of hours by herself. Yes, it would be busy, but hey ho, busy was good. Busy meant lots of paying customers and money rolling in.

Abby stayed firmly by her side until twenty to ten, when there was a lull with the crowd as the main act was coming on. The young girl then slipped away, leaving Lucy to tend to her toppings and stoke her oven single-handedly with her feet tapping away to the music all the while. The crowd were now swaying en masse and singing at the tops of their voices. Lucy found herself joining in, humming away, feeling work-tired but happy. With more bookings on the horizon, and a festival under her belt, her pizza venture was finally finding its feet – foot-tappingly so – and she was sure her Papa would be very proud of her.

Of course, after the concert wrapped up, there was another run of hungry customers getting the midnight munchies! Most were staying over in an array of tents and campervans that were positioned in the next field along, so there was no real rush for the revellers to be getting away. *Make hay while the sun shines and all that,* Lucy thought to herself as she kept up with the throng. She served out her last pizza to a chap in a now-wonky horned Viking helmet at 12:30 a.m. Wow, what a day!

It wasn't long before Jack wandered over, having finished serving himself. Lucy felt her heart rate rise rapidly, followed by a pounding in her chest. She only had to be polite, she reminded herself.

Jack looked a little awkward. Were memories of their last chat, after the anniversary do, on his mind too?

'That kept us going, didn't it,' he said, wiping his damp brow a little nervously.

'Ha, yes, it did indeed,' she replied, unable to look anywhere but at her muddy feet.

A moment's silence stretched between them, thankfully diffused by the sound of the lingering crowds.

'So, good night for you? You looked damned busy.'

'Amazing, yeah. Look, thank you for recommending this, Jack ... putting a word in for me. It's been my best event yet ... by far. Haven't managed to count all the takings yet, but boy, I've sold out of everything, and I'd brought absolutely loads with me, just in case. Phew.' Lucy suddenly found herself feeling shattered, the adrenaline buzz of the festival leaving her veins.

'You look knackered, Lucy.'

'Ah, thanks!' *Whatever happened to Jack the charmer, hey?*

'No, really, you look tired out.' He looked genuinely concerned.

'Look, I'm fine,' she said, brushing it off, not wanting to admit to Jack she did actually feel a bit light-headed now.

'Here, have a seat a mo,' he continued. 'I'll go grab you a Coke or something from the campervan, to pep you up.'

'Fine,' she said a little grumpily, stifling a yawn. She gripped the counter to steady herself.

As Jack whizzed off, she stepped down out of the horsebox gingerly, and settled on the grass beside it, leaning her back against one of its wheel arches. She'd have a five-minute break, and then it was definitely time to get packed away and get her and Daisy on home as soon as she could.

As she sat there, with Jack approaching with a can of drink, she felt a few spit-spots of rain on her face and her hands, which were now blissfully free from those damned hot and itchy protective oven gloves.

'Here.' He passed the Coca-Cola over with a tentative smile.

'Cheers, Jack.'

He settled beside her with a can of Iron Bru for himself. 'Think my energy levels are a bit depleted too. Been one hell of an event. At least I'm all set up with my tent.'

'Oh, so you're staying then?'

In half an hour, she'd be packed up and gone, ready for her cosy bed and a damned good night's sleep, followed by a well-deserved lie in.

'Yep, not much choice really. Well, not at this time, anyhow.' His tone was matter-of-fact, as his glance slid towards the causeway.

'What do you mean ...?' Little alarm bells started sounding off in Lucy's head.

Chapter 32

How could she have been so bloody stupid? Lucy had been so focussed on preparing for this festival event, planning the volumes and varieties of toppings she'd need, making homemade tomato sauce and dough-ball portions by the tonne, she'd somehow forgotten all about the fact that they were working on an island. An *island*. And yes, it did happen to be one with a causeway and a road to it, but it also had the *sea* around it.

And that sea would be rushing in around eleven o'clock tonight, as Jack cockily reminded her. Well, he could have bloody well reminded her a bit earlier, like a week ago or something. Of course, Jack who knew everything, was prepared, wasn't he, his tent all organised.

Oh yes, he had it all set up earlier, apparently on a patch of grass set back from his Cocktail Campervan, so he could keep an eye on Ruby too. He was prattling on that all he had to do was just unroll his sleeping bag. Well, good for him.

A shattered Lucy was still trying to absorb this news.

'You can come and join me if you like?' Jack couldn't help but give a cheeky quirk of his eyebrow.

After his rebuff last week, surely the lad would have given up by now, but hey, maybe he was just trying to make her smile.

Anyway, there was *no way* she'd be getting inside a tent with Jack-the-Lad Anderson. Even if it did mean a cold and uncomfortable night sleeping in the back of her truck alongside Daisy. The little dog would certainly be a safer companion.

'I've got a comfy roll mat and everything ...' he persisted.

Maybe he was just being kind, but Lucy wasn't falling for any of his hanky-panky traps. 'I'm sure you have, but I'll be fine here. It'll be dry in the Jeep. And I've got Daisy to keep me company.'

'Okay, but it'll get cold in the early hours, you know. And there's a rainstorm coming. If you change your mind, you know where I am ...'

But Lucy was resolute. Yes, it might be slightly uncomfortable and a bit chilly trying to get to sleep in the Jeep, but she'd be safe and fine, and there'd be absolutely *no* misunderstandings. 'I'm alright.'

'Okay, well why don't you at least move your truck down nearer to Ruby for the night? It's more sheltered down there, and you'll have me nearby, just in case.'

Hmm, it did sound like he genuinely just wanted to look out for her, and that did actually sound a good idea. Better the devil you know, and all that. There were lots of festival-goers about, and yes, they'd all seemed pretty easy-going and pleasant tonight, but she was a young woman on her own. She didn't have a lot of options left to her in the dark, in the early hours of the morning, with the causeway cut off for several more hours yet.

The two of them finished their cans of drink, sat side by side on the rain-spotted grass. Lucy began to feel a little more refreshed, at least. She said she'd finish packing up the horsebox, and would then drive her Jeep down nearer to Jack's campervan. It would feel a little more reassuring to have company that she knew nearby, considering the pickle she was in. Letting Daisy out for a pee, the raindrops were plopping more steadily now, and there was a whirring wind starting to build. Having checked her horsebox was padlocked and secure for the night, she moved the Jeep.

Parked up near to Ruby and Jack's two-man tent, Lucy shifted into the back-seat area, grabbing a spare – if slightly whiffy – dog rug, that Daisy had definitely been sitting on over time. The little dog was soon on her lap, determinedly snuggling in. Bloody hell, they should be going home to her nice, warm bed and getting cosy, not making do all hunched up in the back of a truck.

The odd light beamed out from around the stage area. Some security guys were there overnight, keeping an eye on things before it was all to be dismantled the next day. Lucy peeked out of her vehicle, and could make out Jack at his little tent, about ten metres away from where she was parked, pushing a rolled sleeping bag into the unzipped front of his tent.

She gave a little wave, trying to convince herself that all was well.

He shouted something out, but she couldn't quite hear,

so wound down her window, to catch: 'Night then. Hope you sleep okay ... but remember, my offer still stands. Room for two and all that. No strings attached. I'll be the perfect gent.'

'I'm fine, Jack. Goodnight.' She was resolute as she drew up the truck window. Still cursing herself for not checking the tide times, she watched as Jack crawled inside his home for the night and zipped up the tent front.

It was a weird high summer, not quite dark sky, even at almost 2 a.m., with black bulbous clouds mounting and an eerie pinky-orange glow low on the horizon. She lay down on the back seat, and hugged the little dog to her, both of them tucked under the car rug. It wasn't so bad. She'd be able to drive off again in a few hours, and catch up with some more sleep back at her little cottage on the mainland. If only she'd had a bloody boat ... Home probably wasn't even twelve miles away as the crow flew. She thought of her comfy double bed, in her low-ceilinged cosy bedroom. Oh well, she'd get back there soon. All she had to do was let herself relax.

At 3 a.m., Lucy still hadn't slept *one* wink. Her hunched position lying on the rear seat was cricking her back, and her feet felt ... well, did they actually have any feeling right now? Her toes appeared to be the only things that had gone to sleep. They didn't feel like they belonged to her anymore. Daisy was shivering in her lap, bless her. Hmm, perhaps she could run the engine to keep them warm for a while, but then she might doze and be left with no fuel left to get back home with. And, it might gas poor old Jack with exhaust fumes. *Poor old Jack*, who was probably snoozing soundly in his lovely warm sleeping bag ...

And then plink, plink, pling, pling, PLINK, PLINK, PLINK. A thousand pins were clanging on the metal roof above her. She'd never heard rain like it. Mind you, she hadn't ever been out in a rainstorm sat in a truck at bloody 3 a.m.

BOOM! A huge and unexpected clap of thunder vibrated through the vehicle, followed, within seconds, by a zig-zag of lightning that seemed awfully close. *Too close.* Wasn't lightning attracted to metal? And ... wasn't she just sat, basically, in a metal box with little Daisy, who was now quaking on her lap, bless her. Oh, shit.

The next quake of thunder made Lucy start so much, she nearly jumped out of her skin. It sounded like it was right above them. With that, the tent's zip came down, and Jack's head popped out, lit silver by the next sheet of dramatic lightning. She spotted his arm poking out of the tent, beckoning her in. He was shouting something, but there was no way she could hear a thing in this. The arm still beckoned. If she went out now, she and Daisy would be soaked to the skin in seconds. She sat still as more thunder rumbled through the air and shook the vehicle. What was the worst eventuality? Getting frazzled by lightning or having to share a tent with Jack?

And then there he was, stood by her car door in, hah, just his boxers and a fleece top, rattling her door handle. 'Come on. You can have the sleeping bag. Bring Daisy. Run!'

Rivulets of rain were already streaming down his face.

'Come on,' he repeated, 'what are you waiting for? I'm getting piss wet out here!' He sounded frustrated now.

Another boom of angry thunder.

'Okay, okay.' She hugged Daisy to her and more or less fell out of the truck. Gloopy mud sucked her feet into the dank field, as a wild wind whooshed at her and rain spat wildly, stinging her face. In seconds, she was soaked through, and then she, with Daisy in her arms, was clambering into the tent, with Jack piling in after them, zipping it up in one swift motion, the wind and rain pummelling at the tent sides.

'Wow,' was all Lucy could manage.

In the light of the torch on Jack's phone, taking in the dripping hair and ends of noses, wet eyebrows and sodden clothes, the pair of them looked like they'd been stranded at sea. Even the furry black-and-tan coat of the little dachshund was drenched. Daisy gave herself a good shake, followed by a shiver.

'Hey, it's going to be colder staying in those wet things than getting out of them,' Jack declared, as he stripped off his fleece and T-shirt in one swift motion.

Was he expecting her to follow suit? She glared at him as much as she could in the half-light of the tent.

'You can't climb into the sleeping bag like that, you'll get it soaking,' he continued, firmly.

Ah yes, she knew his game, alright. 'I'm fine. You can have the sleeping bag.'

'You are *not* fine. In about five minutes you and Daisy'll be freezing and suffering the effects of hypothermia. Get out of those wet clothes and climb into the bag; it's still dry. And, it'll still be a bit warm from me, right now.'

She wasn't sure if that was a good thing or a bad thing. But then, weirdly, that thought made her feel a bit wobbly inside. The warmth of a man's body was a distant memory these days.

'Wet stuff off, then hop on in.'

She gave a sigh … it made sense but …

'Jeez,' he tutted, then turned purposefully away, 'it's not as though I can even see in this light. I'll turn off the torch.'

Stripped down to her undies, damp clothes now left in a pile near the tent entrance on top of his, she clambered into the sleeping bag with Daisy tucked under her arm. It was warm and cosy. *Ahhh.*

'What about you?' she whispered, feeling slightly guilty now, but certainly not guilty enough to give up her quilted cocoon.

'I'll be fine. There's more meat on my bones than yours, and I do have a blanket in here too.'

'Thank you.'

'You're welcome.'

Jack left a respectful few centimetres between them, as he shifted, trying to get himself comfortable beside her. There wasn't a lot of room to distance in a two-man tent. He rolled up his damp fleece and put it under his head as a makeshift pillow.

'Night, Luce.'

'Night.'

It took a while for Lucy to doze off with all the booms and

cracks still going off like elemental fireworks around them, and the odd silver flash illuminating the inside of the tent, but then the storm began to ease. The sound of the slowing rain became rhythmic, almost comforting.

It took Jack somewhat longer to get settled. He found his heart was hammering away in his chest. Being so close to Lucy was doing strange things to him. He began to worry that she might be able to actually hear it. Or, in fact, *feel* it.

Stop. Stop it! But his body wasn't bloody listening, was it? He managed to create an extra couple of centimetres of space by backing up as near as he could to the tent lining. If she got wind of any of this *response* that was going on, she might well be out of there like a shot, and he really didn't want to think of her sat in a lightning storm in her truck like a sitting duck.

He lay there with his thoughts and, rather awkwardly, his nether regions buzzing for a while. He could hear her breathing slow, and the little sausage dog's snores begin. It was comforting and unnerving at the same time. He hadn't been this close to anyone in a long while.

It was calm and still inside the dark-blue vinyl of the tent. Morning light filtered through the material. Jack could smell perfume and skin ... feel the warmth of another human beside him. Tendrils of Lucy's dark wavy hair were tickling his cheek. *What?* Those curls shouldn't be anywhere near his face ...

Jack jerked his head upwards as he came to, just as she turned to face him. Phew, the sleeping bag was reassuringly still between them, as was the small sleek body of a dachs-hund, who was contentedly snoring, Jack realised. And what he *also* realised, was that he'd actually been spooning Lucy ... and even now, they were still that bloody close that he was actually looking into her dark-brown, rather beautiful eyes, and if he moved just one inch towards her, they might as well be kissing.

Lucy jolted back with an, 'Oh.'

'Oh,' Jack echoed. 'Awkward ...'

'Yes.'

'Sorry.'

'Hmm.'

'Yeah, I was asleep, before,' he muttered. 'Just woken up.'

'Right, well ... I suppose the causeway must be open by now. The storm's definitely blown through,' Lucy blurted out as she sat bolt upright, waking Daisy as she moved.

It looked like Lucy couldn't get out of there quick enough. She'd already managed to wriggle out of the sleeping bag and was scrambling into her still-damp clothes, Daisy giving a *humph* at being disturbed from her cosy nest in between them.

'Umm, hey look, do you fancy a coffee?' Jack said tentatively. 'Might warm you up a little. I've got my little camping stove and a cafetière?'

'Hah, you do?'

'The cafetière comes in handy for the espresso martinis. And the stove, well that's always left in Ruby.'

'Ah,' Lucy paused, her tone softening, 'yeah, alright then.' She managed a small smile, seeming to relax somewhat.

As Jack poked his head outside of the tent, he'd never have

guessed they'd just slept through a summer storm. Apart from the odd puddle and patches of mud, everything looked calm. It was *really* early, only 5:30 a.m., and the crimson-gold of a new dawn was already melting away. Jack slipped on his T-shirt, shorts and trainers, and nipped over to Ruby to fetch what he needed, soon setting up outside the tent, lighting his little stove and putting a small pan of water on to boil. He loved to have real coffee. Those warm, rich flavours – the instant stuff just didn't hit the mark.

Lucy pulled on the rest of her damp clothes, the denim shorts clinging to her hips, and came out to join him, bringing Jack's blanket from the tent, to give them a little protection from the sodden ground.

He passed her a blue enamel tin mug. 'No milk, I'm afraid.'

'That's fine.' The coffee aroma was gorgeous as it was.

The view out across the sea was glorious. Shades of azure and pewter, catching golden beams. A sky that was patchy with light cloud above them. A brand-new day. It made Jack feel hopeful.

Sat together, knees hunched, coffee hugged in mugs, with a view that was serenely beautiful, they were silent for a few moments, each caught up in their own thoughts. The world would soon be waking, joining them, the stage hands packing down all the gear, litter pickers clearing debris from the night before, and the revellers who'd camped in the field behind them slowly coming to. They'd all too soon have to head back to their vehicles, head back home. And despite Lucy's instinct to bolt, she found herself a little reluctant to break this early morning spell. Just a few more minutes, sipping good strong coffee, watching that calm and hopeful horizon. A few more minutes.

'Come on then, the sea looks gorgeous.'

Jack was standing up, suddenly swooping off his T-shirt, his shorts. 'Dare you!' He was laughing as he ran off down the field towards the water in merely his boxer shorts.

Lucy wasn't a sea swimmer by any means. But the surrounding water looked calm and cool, and after a night cooped up in the tent ... it was calling her. Despite herself, she was also drawn by this handsome male; his muscles sleek as he charged down the hill.

'Come on, Luce!' His call came loud and clear.

'What are you doing?!' she shouted after him, shaking her head.

She stood up and watched as Jack pelted towards the water, revelling in the beauty and energy of a delightful seaside morning.

'Going for a dip, of course. It's glorious!'

Lucy looked around. Nobody was watching, and even if they were, what did she really care? *Come on Luce, no more playing it safe.*

Oh, sod it! Up she stood, and ripped off her shorts, pulled up her top, now down to her undies too, with Daisy looking on bemusedly. The morning air cool and freeing around her as she ran, the dew wet under her bare feet. She was laughing too, and then ran right in to where Jack waited in the shallows. The chill of the sea suddenly took her breath away.

He splashed her, gently at first, and then more, Lucy

scooping back great handfuls of salty water at him. Both of them dripping from their eyes and faces. She then kicked up a huge arc, which totally drenched him. He pulled a grimace and lurched towards her, grabbing her up in his arms, both of them giggling, as he pretended to dunk her upside down, until she begged for mercy.

It was fun and fabulous and carefree, and Lucy hadn't laughed so much or felt so alive in an age.

Jack held her close, gazed into her eyes as he gave a smile … but then released her, diving off under a wave and beginning to swim out to the open sea. She followed him out of the shallows, swimming by his side, bobbing over the swell. Soon, they were lying on their backs like a pair of sea otters, watching the world start to wake back onshore.

Lucy turned her head towards Jack, watching the waves gently lift and lower him in the gorgeously cool water. She didn't want to think about the current fight between her head and heart, the line in the sand that had to be drawn: *friendship*, that's all it had to be. For now, for just a few more magical moments, she'd let the sea and sun nurture her on this beautiful summer's morning.

7 p.m.

On the beach

Jack x

Chapter 33

Back at her cottage, Lucy found that she couldn't drown out her thoughts of the night before. How it had felt to lie down beside Jack. To hear his breath, feel his warmth. And, as they fell asleep, so close, the inevitable touch, however brief and inadvertent. Was he so unreliable that she'd always need to keep her distance? And why, oh why, was her skin tingling just remembering being near him?

His words as they parted, ready to leave the magic of the island, still lingering in her mind:

'Luce ... take care of yourself, now.'

He'd looked her right in the eyes, and her head was swimming. This was what she wanted after all, wasn't it, a bit of distance. But now it felt far too much like a goodbye.

So many feelings crushing her inside, so many words left unsaid.

And then, after a pause, a chink in that wall re-opened, just as he was about to step inside Ruby's cab. 'Hey, and if there's ever anything you need ... or I can help with ... well, you know where I am.'

'Thanks, Jack.'

By evening, her fingers were itching to send Jack a message, but she wasn't sure what to say. That she'd had a good time, enjoyed their morning swim (she'd loved it, in fact) ... and, her mind was drifting here, enjoyed the feel of his warm body by her side? Hah, *that*, she would never admit to. But why? She was meant to be steering clear, moving on, of course. Stepping out of the danger zone.

Jack saved her the trouble, as a ping on her phone announced he'd texted her first. Her hand shook as she clicked on the message.

Look Lucy, I know things have been a bit weird between us, and I know you've reasons not to trust me. But well, I can't stop thinking about you. And it's okay to tell me to get lost, but a guy's got to try.

The text stopped there. Three glowing dots teasing her while he wrote on.

Well, I think we have a bloody good time together. I'm sure you feel that too. So, here goes. Would you like to meet up tomorrow? X

She was both delighted and seized by indecision.

Would she? Should she?
What if Papa hadn't run after Nonna with the umbrella that night? It had worked out for them, hadn't it?
What if she kept herself so walled up, she never gave

herself the chance to love again? What kind of a life would that be?

Lucy's trembling fingertips paused over her phone's keyboard, and she took a slow breath before replying, **Okay, yeah why not** – before she had a chance to change her mind.

Where are you thinking? she quickly added.

She waited for a tense second or two …

I'll come over your way to Embleton. Meet me on the beach, 7 p.m. X

Okay, let's do it. X

Lucy's heart gave a little anxious lift. Tomorrow … She'd see him again tomorrow.

Meet me on the beach, 7 p.m. X, she repeated out loud. It had a nice ring to it, she had to admit.

The next day seemed to drag. Lucy had a mound of paperwork to tackle, health and hygiene reports to keep track of, monthly accounts and her income and expenditure to update, as well as some essential ordering to do.

In fact, she had plenty to keep her occupied, but it was a damp drizzly morning, and she was finding it hard to focus. Her thoughts kept drifting to Jack and their arranged meet-up in the evening.

After lunch, the mists lifted, and she ventured out for a walk with Daisy along the back lane from the village, past the farm. Meandering as they went and passing time watching the cows and sheep graze, with Daisy barking at a chicken that was clucking and pecking her way around the farmyard. It was still only two o'clock when they got back.

Things got more intriguing when a message popped up on her phone:

BTW, don't eat much before you come out. X

She wanted to ask why, but had a feeling Jack wanted to surprise her. Maybe he was planning a picnic supper, that'd be nice. Or was the beach just a ploy, and he'd be whisking her away to some pub or restaurant? Her mind was full of all sorts of scenarios, but she told herself not to get carried away, she still felt unsure as to how they stood.

Can I bring Daisy along? she asked.

Yeah, sure. X came back.

Hmm. Still a mystery then. But she found the suspense rather thrilling.

With the countdown on, Lucy dressed casually in pale-blue cropped jeans and a Breton-style striped top. She also tied a fleece cardigan around her waist. The beach was often breezy, with the wind straight off the North Sea, and it would soon cool down there of an evening.

Ten to seven, *at last*.

'Come on then, Daisy. Let's go,' Lucy said aloud, fetching Daisy's lead.

It was thankfully now dry outside, and the little dog was more than happy to head out for another walk. In contrast, with each step nearer the bay, Lucy was feeling a strange mix of excitement and trepidation. The beach was a big expanse, especially when the tide was out. Should she text him and ask where to meet? But he'd probably wait for her somewhere near the main track from the dunes ... wouldn't he?

Oh, there was Ruby, parked up down the lane. So, Jack was already here. Oh damn, skip-a-dee-do-dah went her heart.

She went over the dunes now, following the well-trodden sand track. Passing a couple walking with a spaniel. A quick 'hello', and dog-sniff by Daisy. On again, thump-a-dee-thump went her heart.

She caught a glimpse of the blue-grey sea, appearing between the spiky fronds of beachgrass. The path opened out and she took a slow breath before scanning the bay. Oh, he wasn't waiting here on the sands as she'd imagined. There was a dog walker with a slow-ambling Labrador down near the shoreline. But otherwise, the beach was pretty empty.

Apart from ... a table covered in what looked to be a white cloth, set out halfway down to the water's edge. A man dressed in a dinner suit stood beside it. Not any man either ... it was Jack ... and he was grinning from ear to ear.

'Over here!' he called. 'Cocktails are served.'

What on earth ...!

As she approached, Lucy recognised the fold-up chairs and table which he kept in the campervan, *and* the table really was covered with a crisp white tablecloth. A cocktail shaker was set out, along with an ice bucket containing what looked to be a bottle of something bubbly, along with two flutes. There was also a platter of delicious-looking bite-sized canapés – bruschetta and cheeses, mini sausages, figs, olives, grapes.

'Jack, this is ... *crazy.*' She was smiling whilst creasing her brow, trying to take it all in. And there he was on the beach, in a black-tie-style dinner suit. 'Hah, I didn't realise I was meant to dress up for the part. Full cocktail dress might have worked better than my jeans and T.'

'Hey, you look beautiful just as you are, madam. Please take a seat.'

She didn't have an answer to that, feeling slightly stunned, so positioned herself on one of the wooden chairs as instructed, with Daisy soon settling down beside her.

'A glass of chilled champagne to start?'

'Wow, well that'll do nicely, Jeeves. Oh, I mean, Jack.' She put on a posh voice and then started giggling.

He popped the cork with a flourish, and it was indeed the real thing – someone was pushing the boat out here. And you know what, it was rather lovely to be spoilt for a change.

'Here you go.' He passed her a flute of fragrant champagne, which was popping away deliciously. His feet were bare in the sand, with the bottom inch or two of his smart black trousers rolled up.

'Cheers.' Lucy raised her glass, with a broad smile.

'Cheers.' He grinned back.

He'd gone all out with an Italian theme on the canapés too – tomato bruschetta, the cheeses were mozzarella balls and gorgonzola on crispy bites of toast. There were Parma ham and cantaloupe melon chunks on sticks; sweet, refreshing and salty bacon-flavoured all at once. Everything was so tasty, and evidently thought through.

'This is lovely, thank you.' The champagne was slipping down nicely, and Lucy found herself starting to relax. Jack really had gone to a huge effort on her behalf.

'Is this for anything special?' she quizzed, coyly.

'Nope, just the chance to enjoy good food, good drinks, the best table in the house ... and good company, of course.'

'Aw, well it's just fab.'

Being sat mid-beach on a summer's evening with full table and chairs, they did get a couple of odd looks from passers-by, as the two of them sat chatting and eating. A spaniel arrived excitedly at the scenario, having spied the dachshund there too, stopping to cock its leg for a quick pee against the table; its owner arriving seconds later red-faced and very apologetic. Lucy and Jack laughed it off, no harm done. Lucy was just relieved that it wasn't Daisy up to mischief for a change.

The last beach visitor was an old lady who paused to say good evening, adding that it was a wonderful sight to see such a handsome young couple enjoying themselves. Lucy felt herself blush a little. After all, they weren't a couple at all. Then the last of the walkers went home, the beach was theirs alone – give or take a couple of seagulls – and the sky began to soften into pastel watercolour shades of gold, peach and grey.

They chatted about the music festival, and the storm that night, neither of them mentioning the fact that they'd ended up sleeping only inches away from each other.

Then Jack created a gorgeous champagne cocktail for her. Lucy watched as he mixed the sparkling wine with Amaretto and fresh orange juice, decorating it with a stylish curl of orange peel.

'Sunset amaretto fizz,' Jack announced. 'Perfect for watching the sun go down with.'

'Oh, thank you. And that is delicious,' declared Lucy after

taking her first sip. It tasted like a warm summer's evening, and was golden-orange like the sun that was starting to set. 'You really are spoiling me.'

'I just wanted to make this evening special, that's all.' His smile was tender.

Lucy looked at him, her heart beating nervously. 'Thank you.'

Liam had never done anything like this for her, not even on the night he'd proposed. That had been a formal affair in a very nice, traditional restaurant, with a very nice traditional ring. Typical of Liam, in fact; measured, all done with quality in mind, and she had to confess to feeling happy at the time, but there was nothing that was very magical or even personal about it, nothing that had strayed outside of the well-presented box.

Tonight, even Daisy had been catered for with her own portion of mini sausages, as well as Jack having brought a water bowl for her. He'd definitely softened towards the little dog lately. Towards them both, if this evening was anything to go by.

This seemed very much like a date, like she was being wooed. And Lucy still felt that familiar conflict between heart and head rising up.

'Jack, this is all very lovely, but ... what are you wanting from me?' Her tone was blunt; she didn't want to get caught up in any of Jack's charming playboy act.

'Well, I wanted to give you an evening to remember. And yeah,' he paused, looking her in the eye, 'I have to admit I would like to get to know you more. Not just when we are working.'

Lucy wasn't sure what to say.

'Hey, let's just roll with it and see,' Jack continued. 'That is, if you want to meet up again, outside of work ...' He suddenly sounded less sure of himself than usual; the mask of cocky, confident Jack sliding as his feelings were put on the line.

Did she want to meet up again? Becky would bloody well kill her, but all that was years ago. For Jack to go to this much effort ... The way she'd felt lying next to him in that two-man tent ... How much she'd been thinking about him ever since. It was time to give him a second chance.

Lucy took a slow breath, and found herself saying, 'Yes.'

'That's cool.' He smiled, with warmth and tenderness. 'And now I have dessert – well, cake. I made it myself.'

'You've made me cake?' This man, dressed in a tuxedo on a beach, needed a medal, or perhaps a kiss at least.

'Yep, gin and tonic cake, in fact. Well, the recipe looked good, and more importantly, *easy* ... to be honest, my baking repertoire doesn't stretch to much! It's either that or rock cakes – and mine did actually turn out like rocks at school.'

'Hah, well thanks.'

He served her a slice. The cake was gorgeous; a loaf cake, drizzled with gin, tonic and zingy lime juice.

The sun was setting and night began to draw in gently around them. Lucy popped on her fleece and settled to watch the sea and sky soften with an infusion of peach and gold, deepening into a cornflower dusk.

With the cake and the remaining champagne shared between them, plus a few sneaky crumbs finding their way in Daisy's direction, it seemed the perfect finale for the evening. Lucy felt slightly tipsy, but in a pleasantly relaxed way. It also seemed to relax her tongue a bit. There was something she was curious about. He was guarded when he'd talked about his brother before, but perhaps him opening up would help to solve the mystery that was Jack.

'Jack, a while ago, you mentioned losing your brother. What happened to him?'

Jack looked out to sea, and then took a slow breath. 'He was away at uni, playing football, some inter-college match.' He stopped, Lucy saw him bite at his lip. 'He was playing football, and ... that was it, he just dropped down dead.'

'Oh god.'

'He was twenty ... just twenty years old. He had his whole life ahead of him, Luce.'

'Oh no, that's so awful. What caused it? Did he have a medical condition or something?'

'Not that we *knew* of. He was Mr Sporty Kid, well, we both were ... But yes, he did. A heart condition, one that can go undetected for years, Hypertrophic Cardiomyopathy. None of us had a clue. It was so sudden that day ... There was nothing anyone could do ...'

Lucy reached out her hand to gently cover his. She couldn't imagine losing her own brother in such a tragic way, and at such a young age. She had tears in her eyes, feeling Jack's pain too.

Jack continued, 'He'd just gone back off to uni for the start of his third year. He was doing Medicine at Leeds. He was always the bright spark, my brother.' Jack sounded proud rather than envious. 'I waved him off, got on with life back here at home; Sixth Form, parties, the usual. Then, we got that call ... It was crazy, unbelievable. That I'd never see him again ... only stone cold in a fucking coffin.'

'Oh, Jack ...' Words failed Lucy. Her heart felt so much for this man beside her in his grief. She wished she hadn't brought it up now, spoilt the magic of this evening and all of Jack's efforts, by reminding him of past tragedies. But also, somehow, she sensed that Jack might in a way be relieved to share that sad, sad history, and that she might now be able to understand him a little more.

They sat for a few quiet moments, watching the glistening pewter waves roll to shore, when it suddenly dawned on Lucy that the shore was actually *very close indeed*. Water pooled in a little rush around her feet, soaking her deck shoes.

'Oh, bugger,' Jack cursed, as the water splashed up his bare ankles, wetting his suit trouser legs.

'Damn,' Lucy jumped up. Daisy was already straining on her lead, ready to head up the beach. The little dog hated water at the best of times.

'We need to move ... and *fast*.' Jack sprang into action.

They went from grief to giggles in that moment, and started dashing up the sands with chairs, table, dachshund, glasses and plates, up to the safety of the top beach area by the dunes. Reassembling their drinks and nibbles scenario, a little more slap-dash than in the first instance, they sat back down, with legs soaked through, and a soggy dachshund, still laughing.

'Whose bloody idea was it to do cocktails and canapés by the sea?' Jack asked, ironically.

'Well, I thought it was a marvellous idea.' Her voice then softened, 'I really did love it, Jack. No-one's ever done anything like that for me before.'

'So, your ex never came up with any romantic dates?'

'Liam? Hah, no, nothing like this. He was much more traditional, a red roses on Valentine's Day, occasional meal out, kind of guy.'

Come to think of it, he wasn't very spontaneous at all. She was suddenly hit by an uncomfortable flash of memory. One time, he'd ventured to have sex – wait for it – in the bathroom of their home. A highly unusual and wild suggestion from him. And as they stood up in the bathtub (there wasn't a lot of space in their niche bathroom), he'd caught sight of the mirror, and tutted that it hadn't been cleaned properly, that there were smear marks. It would have been funny, if it wasn't so damned sad. Liam was far too bloody sensible. Thinking about it, she should have got right out and run for her life, right then! She didn't care to share that particular memory with Jack.

'You okay?'

'Oh yeah, fine.' She brought herself back to the here and now. 'Just feels like I wasted seven years of my life on that man.'

'Tell me?' Jack prompted gently.

'Oh … I spent five years waiting for a wedding that was never going to happen. Not that I knew that. We were engaged, he managed to ask the question a couple of years in, but … then it was never the right time, we needed to save more, needed the bigger house, new car, better job … And fool that

I bloody was, I went along with it. Not that I'm in any rush for any of that now though,' she was sure to clarify. 'Life's not always straightforward, is it?'

'We can all make mistakes, Luce.'

'Yep, and Liam was one bloody massive mistake. I've come to realise it was a lucky escape now.'

'Yeah, live and learn, that's what life's all about, Luce.'

'It is, isn't it?' She smiled, feeling a bit warm and fuzzy as Jack smiled back at her.

Tiny beads of stars began to glimmer in the fading sky. It would soon get dark out here. Time to pack up, to go home, back to the cottage.

As if reading her mind, Jack said, 'I thought I'd pitch my tent out here in the dunes overnight.'

Ah yes, they'd shared champagne and cocktails. He'd not be able to drive Ruby away. The memories of sleeping in that tent on Holy Island with him right beside her filled her mind, adding even more to that warm, fuzzy feeling. Was it time? Time to take that plunge? Time to live life to the full?

'Ahm ... You can come back to mine ... if you like.' The words were instinctive, and now out. Lucy really didn't want this night to end, not yet.

Their eyes met. Jack's gaze was intense, as an understanding passed between them. 'You sure?' he asked gently.

'Yes,' her voice was clear, and warm, and sensual.

Both took a deep breath, and then after finishing their drinks, they packed up the remnants of the food, the glasses, plates, folding up the chairs and the picnic table.

Walking somewhat awkwardly with all that gear back up

and into the dunes, Lucy managed to steal a shy, yet hungry, look at him. Oh my goodness, she'd be seeing, *touching*, his bare flesh very soon! Oh, blimey. Oh, wow. Oh, bloody scary. And bloody hell, no-one had seen hers in an age ...

Jack glanced back over his shoulder at her with a rakish grin.

A late-night dog walker passed by, with a brief 'hello' cast their way. Lucy felt like the middle-aged guy might be able to read her mind or something. She blushed as she recognised him and his Labrador from her regular beach walks, answering with a polite, yet slightly husky, 'Hi.'

As dusk fell deeper, they loaded all the gear into Ruby. And then, as they headed up the lane that led back to the village, Jack took her hand in his, threading his fingers through hers – like a real couple. Everything around and within her felt alive, hyper-sensitive.

A small bird tweeted, darting in and out of the hedgerow beside them, ready to settle for the night. The seagulls had already gone to roost. The world began to hush. Just the distant whisper of the waves rolling to shore.

Soon they were walking by the first row of cottages, and next, they'd turned into her little street. The horsebox was parked up there beside her cottage. Her cottage ... where they were about to go in, together. She fumbled clumsily for her house keys in her jeans pocket. Managed to get the front door open, and ushered Daisy swiftly through to the kitchen where she had her bed and her water, closing the door on her with a soothing, 'Night, Daisy.' Coming back to the hallway where Jack was waiting, leaning against the wall and looking so bloody gorgeous. Yet, he seemed a little anxious too, giving a cautious smile.

Lucy moved in towards him, so very close. *So, this was it.*

Jack tenderly brushed away a lock of her hair that had tumbled down across her eye. He grazed a fingertip slowly along the side of her chin, which he then pulled ever so gently towards him. Placing his lips on hers. And that was it, the match ignited. A passionate kiss, that warmed her from her fingertips all the way to her toes, and lit those sensual parts which had been pretty damned dormant for almost two years now, making her whole body tingle with anticipation. A gasp escaped her lips, as their kiss ended. *Oh my.*

Would they have sex right here in the hallway? *Did she want that?*

She began unbuttoning his shirt, greedily reaching inside to touch his warm, toned chest. Jack kissed her again, moving closer to press his thighs against hers. She pushed back, crushing him against the wall, feeling the hard heat of his erection through their clothes. Bloody hell, this was really happening. She'd never had sex with Liam like this. Like they couldn't wait. Like it needed to happen right here, right now.

'Oh god, Lucy.' Jack was pulling off her T-shirt over her head.

Suddenly, she realised she didn't want this to be fast and furious and over in a minute in a hallway. She wanted to make it last, to relish every damned gorgeous second. She grabbed Jack's hand and led him up the stairs. He didn't need asking or explaining. Once in her bedroom, the door left ajar, she stopped to undo the buckle on his belt, pulling down the waistband of his smart black trousers with a sense of delicious anticipation.

Again they kissed, mouth on tender mouth, not rushing now, taking it deliriously slowly in fact, both knowing what was to come, but not quite how it would happen ... yet.

A new burst of sensual energy and a tangle of jeans and underwear coming off. Jack reached around her, to unclasp her bra, her small breasts bared.

'Oh, Luce. You're beautiful.' He was gazing at her, smiling. His words melted her.

As they lay on the bed, both naked, she traced the contours of his chest, trailing her fingers over his butterfly-trembling stomach, down to his slim hips. His low groan, as she touched him, oh so lightly there, was such a damned turn-on.

His turn now, trailing kisses from her neck down to her breasts where he lingered, teasing a nipple into his warm mouth. Sucking and licking, as he moved a hand to touch her gently below, in a rhythmic rub – deliciously all at the same time. He was an accomplished lover, considerate and evidently *well-practised*, that thought slid into her mind but she pushed it straight out again. No place for those concerns here. This was about them, her and Jack, and *this* moment.

Oh – my – god, he *so* wanted her. Her touch just before, had sent him over the edge. He wanted to know her, inch by yielding inch, to make love with her. It was heady and he had to admit a little scary too, but there was no going back now. Jack could hardly wait, but he needed to know that she was absolutely okay with this. It seemed like she was *very* okay, from her eager responses. But he couldn't get this wrong; needed to show her that respect, that care.

'Luce, is this okay?'

In all honesty he hadn't expected this. Tonight, the set-up on the beach, that really had all been about getting to know Lucy more, seeing how things went. That maybe it could be the start of something ... Well, it seemed like it had got off to a flying start.

'Yes.'

That one word igniting him even more.

Her lightly tanned body laid out before him. The yearning so strong within him. He was ready, had a condom beside the bed, but took the time to kiss her once more, to elevate them both back to that same sexy plateau they were at, before the necessary precautions were in place. Fingertips tracing her breasts, her stomach, back to base until her low oh-so-sexy moan was impossible to ignore.

'Now?'

She nodded, with a smile and a clear soulful whisper, 'Yes.'

Jeez, this was it. He felt on a beautiful knife-edge as he moved above her gorgeous body, the tight pressure of resistance, and the glorious give. That warm internal embrace. The rhythmic push and pull. Her back now arching towards him, and he wanted so much to be part of her. To give, again and again. Deeper. Harder. Her soft moans driving them on. Then, that moment of teasingly-wonderful tension and exquisite release.

'Lucy. Oh, Luce.' He was lost to her. He wasn't even sure if

he'd said her name aloud or merely heard it echoing beautifully in his mind.

'Aahhhh.' Him.

'Ooooooh.' Her.

And they lay in each other's arms, with a tenderly sated
sleepiness taking them over. Curled up together, Lucy leaning
against Jack's chest, his arm angled gently around her, legs
entwined. Wow.

Chapter 34

In bed the next morning, with Lucy's head nestled sleepily against his bare chest, Jack lay thinking.

In the soft-golden rays of July morning light, he knew absolutely that he was falling for her ... big time. That this was different, *so* different from all those fun and flirty but rather meaningless dates, the one-night stands, the no-strings flings. So far, he'd managed to avoid getting in too deep, never letting anyone loose with his heart; well, not since his high-school first love way back at the tender age of seventeen.

And *then*, with the sledgehammer loss of his brother, grief pummelled his emotions, smashing up his soul. After that, he'd tried to keep his distance emotionally, keep himself contained ... never get too involved. But last night, this morning, he could feel himself unravelling. Lucy was taking him to places within himself that he'd never experienced before. Making love with her last night was soulful, beautiful ... and it totally bloody scared him.

Jack shifted carefully so as not to wake her. He got up and made his way down to the galley kitchen, dressed in boxer shorts and his white dress shirt from the day before. He realised he was going to have to get dressed back into his tuxedo trousers shortly, ready to walk back down the lane to Ruby – hah, an unusual beachside morning combo.

He found his way around Lucy's small kitchen, making coffee in the Tassimo machine. Daisy, after a few playful barks in his direction, was now snuffling around his feet, considering who the imposter was, and no doubt looking for her boss – and her breakfast, of course.

He could hear movement upstairs now, and then running water; perhaps Lucy was showering whilst he made coffee. It suddenly struck him as a strangely cosy, domestic set-up.

'Sorry, Dais, don't know where she keeps your grub. Or how much a mutt like you can eat. You'll have to wait.'

The dog looked up at him with her dark, intense eyes. The pair of them actually seemed to have come to some kind of a truce after the night in the tent – well, needs must. And if he was going to get to know Lucy more, then he and the little dog would need to rub along okay. He suddenly stopped stirring, the teaspoon poised mid-air.

Was he ... going to allow himself to get to know her more? Last night had certainly been amazing, but Jack felt that familiar tug of the past, the overwhelming weight of hurt and loss, all the little cracks in his heart suddenly heavy in his chest.

He shook it off, concentrating on stirring the coffee, one small motion at a time. *Just breathe, Jack.*

He set a second mug in place on the coffee machine, letting out a small sigh. He tiptoed once more around the downstairs area, curiosity about Lucy's abode pulling him in the direction of the lounge. A couple of paperbacks were left out on the side: *One Day* and *Pride and Prejudice*. Romance novels. Was that what Lucy hoped for, he wondered, happy ever afters and a prince charming? Could he really step up to the mark? Be that kind of guy? Last night everything had seemed magical and perfect, and all he could wish for. But today, in the cold light of day, a million questions and fears were surfacing in his mind.

His stomach suddenly felt a little queasy, a gnawing anxiety in his gut. He took a steadying sip of his coffee. Why couldn't it just be simple? Couldn't he just go with the flow? He managed it in the rest of his life. But he was no romantic hero. And the last thing Jack wanted to do was hurt Lucy. If he couldn't do this thing right, then maybe he shouldn't do it at all.

And then suddenly there she was, walking into the kitchen, hair washed, with damp dark waves curling below her shoulders, dressed in a casual but pretty floral T-shirt and her trademark cropped jeans. She was like a ray of sunshine, breezing in with a 'Morning, Daisy,' a radiant smile for Jack, and the promise of croissants to warm in the oven, as she hunted for them in the freezer.

They were soon sat at the breakfast bar, with glasses of orange juice and crisp buttery croissants spread thickly with butter and local strawberry jam. Daisy now fed, but still loitering at their feet, eager for any stray crumbs. Lucy was chatting away as they sat there together, like a real couple. And Jack couldn't help but feel a rising uneasiness.

'So,' asked Lucy, chirpily, 'what's on today, then? Do you want to do something, go somewhere ... a walk maybe?'

So, she was hoping they'd spend the day together. Head off for a romantic walk, come back home, maybe cook lunch together ... make love again ...

'Ah, I'm sorry Luce,' he stuttered. 'I promised Matt, that's the guy I lodge with, that we'd go out cycling today. Gotta be getting back soon, I'm afraid.' The white lie spilled from his lips before he even knew what he was saying. And as he markedly glanced at his wristwatch, he hated himself for it. 'And I do only have a tuxedo with me to wear,' he laughed nervously. He did in fact have shorts and a T-shirt back at the campervan. He'd intended rough camping last night, after all.

'Oh ... I see. Well, no worries. We can catch up again soon.' Lucy looked down quickly as she bit into her croissant, trying to hide her disappointment.

'Yeah, of course we can. It's been great ... last night ...' He couldn't even begin to express his feelings for this girl. But he also couldn't begin to express the rising sense of panic clouding in, a clenching in his chest.

'Yeah, it was really lovely,' she finished the sentence for him, as her soulful dark eyes held his. 'Thanks again ... for the cocktails on the beach, for everything.'

'You're very welcome.' Jack gave a smile but his fears and vulnerabilities were crowding in. He found himself feeling prickly, and far too raw with emotion.

Lucy stood at the doorway to her cottage watching Jack walk away, off through the village on a sunny Tuesday morning, dressed in a dinner suit, his dark-blond hair ruffled, as if he was doing a very smart walk of shame. She couldn't help but smile at that, but then ... a thought struck her. Was he in fact feeling a sense of guilt or shame, trying to make his escape with that quick getaway? Or was she just feeling a bit vulnerable, paranoid?

Ugh, why did relationships do this to you, over and over? Get you all excited, make you feel blissfully happy for a few magical hours, and then screw your heart up like a paper ball?

They'd shared a brief, tender kiss in the hallway as he was about to go. And then that was it. No plans made to see each other through the week. No, 'I'll call you later.' And that kiss had weirdly felt more like a goodbye than the start of a lovely new adventure for them both. Jack had seemed strangely sad as he left. Surely, the pair of them should be bouncing with excitement; they'd had such a brilliant night, after all. They should be all loved up and planning the next date. Argh, she needed to calm down, she was acting like Tigger, and it was no good for her mental state.

Lucy headed back in, closing the cottage door which she then leant back against with a sigh, wondering what really had just happened between them. Her heart was telling her one thing, but her head something else entirely.

Damn it, she couldn't even get on the phone to friend Becky for some girlie advice. Her best mate would bloomin' well kill her if she knew what she'd been up to last night, and more particularly, *who with*. It was the first sex she'd had in two whole years. And boy, how good had that making love with

Jack been. It was the first time in a very long time that Lucy had opened up her heart and her home, and let someone in. She hoped to god she wasn't going to regret it.

She gave Daisy a pat on her way back to the kitchen. 'Well, Dais, what do you make of all that, then?' She figured that the dog had about as much chance of working out what was going on with Jack Anderson, as she did.

With the day now stretching emptily ahead, and her heart feeling a little wobbly, Lucy knew she'd be better keeping busy. She made another coffee, then gave her mum a quick call, snapping up her offer of supper with her in Rothbury that evening. She also decided to call in at her brother's house en route, and catch up with them all this afternoon; she definitely felt in need of a big hug with Freddie. That emotional conversation about Jack's tragic brother was still fresh in her mind. She couldn't imagine life without her sibling, and her gorgeous little nephew. In fact, yes, she'd bake a cake this morning to take along with her, they'd love that. The Italian Chocolate Cake came to mind. She'd check out the ingredients and see what she had in her pantry cupboard, then whizz to the village shop for anything else she might need.

Back in her kitchen a half-hour later, baking helped to take her mind off what had happened in the past twenty-four hours ... though not quite enough. She could still almost feel Jack's touch; her body a little achy from the night before in a tantalisingly sensual way. Once the cake was in the oven, and putting her misgivings aside, she fired off a text to Jack, thanking him again and saying what a lovely night that had been.

She headed off to her brother's mid-afternoon, enjoying a pot of tea and slices of her home-made cake with the family. She sat outside with Olly and Alice, watching as toddler Freddie and Daisy the dog made laps of their grassy back garden; Freddie giggling all the while. For all Daisy's diva antics, she was extremely tolerant with the little boy. It was like she knew he was small, different from the big humans somehow. It was a delight to see them ambling about, and it made them all smile.

Olly got up to join in the fun, taking out a small football for a gentle kickabout. Daisy barked at it first of all, then managed to nudge it with her nose, with Freddie giggling alongside. Lucy was so thankful for her brother, and for the wonderful relationship they had.

'So, how's it all going then, Lucy? Tell me all about the pizza van.' The girls were sat together on a low wall, Alice turning to her with a smile. 'Olly seemed to have had a great night when you went off to do the birthday bash. He said your pizzas were amazing and that you did brilliantly. I even heard him telling your dad about it on the phone.'

'Ah, that's good.'

Her dad had in fact phoned her since then and asked all about the business and how things were going. He was at least showing some interest in her new venture, though still not totally enamoured with her decision to leave a steady job. She did try and visit him and his partner, Jo, every few weeks, and once in a while they'd come up to see her at the cottage too. She still loved her dad dearly, and wanted to keep in touch, but everything had changed so much when he left her mum. That security, their family unit, broken. Yes, it was all many years ago now, and Lucy got along fine with his new partner and had tried to make the best of things. But in all honesty, life had never quite felt the same. Life seemed that little bit harsher since that fragile teenager had learnt about love and the breaking down of relationships the hard way.

'And how are you all doing?' Lucy pulled herself from her thoughts. 'I bet little Freddie is keeping you busy as always.'

'Definitely. He's a bundle of energy right now ... into everything. I have to admit I quite enjoy my two work days, when he goes off to nursery.' She gave a grin. 'Thank heavens he sleeps okay. Bed at 7 p.m. for him, and a large glass of wine for me.'

'Hah, I don't blame you.'

'Aw, but look at him with Daisy there, sharing the ball. He's a joy really,' Alice conceded. 'Wouldn't be without him ... both of them.' She looked across the garden to where her boys were playing with a look of pride, of love.

It was lovely to see. It seemed very much that Olly and Alice had a good sound relationship, and that warmed Lucy's soul.

She gave a silent sigh. Would she ever be able look at someone like that?

Chapter 35

Lucy checked her phone as she pulled up outside her mum's just after 4 p.m., having gone straight on from her brother's place. *Oh*, Jack had replied to her message this morning. Her hand trembled a little, and how daft was that, she told herself, as she read:

Yeah, I had a good time too. X

Well, it wasn't the most romantic response, but ... he'd obviously enjoyed himself. For all his charm and chat behind the bar, in real life he was obviously far more reserved. But maybe that was just the way he was, and maybe Lucy was just learning to see the man behind the mask. She sat for a few moments, clutching her mobile, but nothing else came through and she held back from pinging back a reply. She didn't want to be the one left waiting again.

She stepped on out of the Jeep. It was good to be having a bit of family time this afternoon; Lucy found it grounded her. She'd made a second, smaller cake for her mum, and she'd stopped off at the local Co-op to pick up a bunch of cheerful pink roses. Flowers always brightened up a house, and sometimes, even though Sofia had several close friends in the village, and had lived on her own for many years now, Lucy sensed that her mum needed a bit of a pick-me-up now and again.

Sofia's face beamed as she opened the door to her daughter. 'Oh, how pretty! And cake too. Have you made that? My, I am being spoilt today. Thank you, pet.'

'Well, it sounds like I'm getting spoilt too. Roast chicken for dinner, did I hear?'

'Yes, well it's always a bit of a faff to do a roast just for one, but now you're here, it'll be a joy to make it for us.' Sofia grinned. 'I'll put the kettle on, shall I? And we can go and sit out the back a while.'

'Now that sounds perfect.'

Her mother's house was small, tidy and semi-detached, set halfway up the hill in the rural market town of Rothbury. The moorland landscape surrounding them was high and dramatic, rising nearby to the Simonside peaks, with the river below running through the valley at the centre of the town. Sofia's little garden had a neat patio and a grassed area, with a few well-tended shrub borders. On a day like today, it was a little suntrap too.

Sat with tea and shortbread biscuits (they were keeping the cake for dessert, so as not to spoil their appetites), with a buzz of bees from the fragrant white-petalled rose bushes and tall hollyhocks beside them, Sofia was keen to find out how everything was going with the pizza horsebox business.

'Well, it's been going from strength to strength these past weeks,' Lucy was delighted to announce.

Yes, her reputation was building, her online presence growing, and bookings were starting to come in more regularly.

So, as well as her weekly Alnwick market slot, she generally had two other bookings to attend as well. All Fired Up was finally turning a profit, and she had received some great reviews. She was feeling much more confident in her own abilities. Seeing Jack at these events had been a bonus too, but ... after last night, she wondered how that would now be. She'd just have to wait and see ... and well, she felt her cheeks flush, Mum certainly didn't need to know about that side of things.

'That's brilliant, love. I'm delighted for you. You deserve it. I know you've put in an awful lot of hard work to get this far. I'll have to come and see you in action sometime soon, when you've got the horsebox all set up.'

'Yes, that'd be great. Though it might be a bit tricky turning up to someone's birthday party or wedding! Hmm, the market could be a good one to come and visit. The one in Alnwick on a Thursday.' Lucy took a bite of buttery biscuit.

'Oh yes, I'll do that. I can have a look around the other stalls there too, and have a mooch about the town. That sounds a lovely idea.'

'Good.'

'Might even suggest it to Julia. We could make an afternoon of it.'

Sofia seemed happy with her plan. And for Lucy, it was lovely to have her mother's support too.

'You know what Lucy, love?'

'What?' Lucy turned to face her mum.

'I've seen a difference in you lately. Yes, there's a definite spring in your step, these past few weeks.'

'Yeah,' Lucy smiled, nodding. She'd felt it too. Like finally her life was turning around, that things were looking up. And … it may just have had something to do with a rather gorgeous barman being in her life too.

But then she thought about this morning, and the way he had left so suddenly. She just hoped that Jack Anderson wasn't going to be the one to trip her up.

Two hours later, with a tummy fit to burst, Lucy was sitting cosily on her mum's sofa with Daisy tucked beside her. The forecasted showers had come, but it didn't matter too much. They'd had a nice couple of hours outside, and as Mum had commented, it'd helped water the gardens.

'That was a gorgeous dinner. Thanks, Mum. It's been so nice to catch up. I suppose I'd better be heading back soon.'

'You could always stay over, pet. The spare room's always ready,' her mum offered with a hopeful smile.

'Oh, that's kind, Mum. But I've all sorts to organise and prepare for tomorrow. I've an event booked late afternoon for a kids' birthday party, so I need to get to the cash and carry too.'

She was busy, but in truth she also loved getting back to her little seaside cottage, which really did feel like home to her.

'No worries, pet. Whatever suits you best.' Sofia was pretty easy-going about these things.

Lucy sensed her mum would like to see more of her, even though they saw each other every week. 'I'll be back and visit again soon. Or, why don't you come across to me and we can go and have a treat at the little café in the village. And if you get to the market on Thursday too, that'd be great ...'

'Ooh, yes, that sounds nice. And I'll definitely pop across to see you at the market.'

'Brilliant.'

Plans were in place. And Lucy left after warm hugs with an extra plate of chicken dinner for her and Daisy to share.

The journey back to the cottage was a wet one, with large puddles on the lanes to negotiate. Summer rain. The roads were fairly quiet though, with the tourists and locals mostly nestled down for the evening.

Back home, with Daisy settled, Lucy was suddenly overcome with a huge wave of tiredness. It had been a busy day, following a rather full on and unexpected night, after all. It was soon time enough for Lucy to head off to bed. Rain pattered on the windows of the little coastal cottage, and the wind rushed in from the sea. The cottage seemed to echo with a lonely melody.

As Lucy lay down in her bed, crumpling the duvet over her, her sheets, the pillows, still smelled of *him* ... of *them*.

No more messages had come through since that *one* in reply, and he hadn't called her.

A tear crowded her eye, even though she told herself to be patient, that it was early days yet; he'd only left her bed this morning. Still, she knew instinctively that something was wrong in all this. She couldn't help but feel disappointed and so very confused.

Haltingham Village Fete

Saturday 7th August

12 noon to 6 p.m.

Local Crafts, Plant and Cake Stalls,

Tombola, Raffle

Bouncy Castle, Face Painting and Fun for the Kids!

Free Entry!

Chapter 36

It was a blue-sky Saturday in early August, and the day of the Haltingham village fete. Lucy had driven through the winding country lanes of the Tyne Valley, passing several hikers and a scenic section of the historic Hadrian's Wall en route. The Wall, built hundreds of years ago, stretched from coast to coast – ancient armies had marched there, Romans set up camp, built fortresses, lived, loved and battled there, and now ramblers trailed. The Northumberland hills rolled, and the horsebox meandered; Lucy had given herself plenty of time.

She was soon pulling into the pretty rural village of honey-coloured stone-built houses and cottages, where All Fired Up was booked in at the Summer Festival.

Troughs and baskets were filled with bold summer blooms; pinks, purples, and vivid yellows in abundance. Each cottage and house taking pride in adding their own floral tribute to the event. The village was strung with colourful bunting, which flapped gently and prettily on the breeze. There were at least twenty stalls and eateries there setting up – cakes, bakes, an ice cream van, tombola and more.

Oh blimey, Lucy's heart gave a lurch when she looked up

and spotted who was also about to park on the village green. Yep, the vintage red colours of campervan Ruby glinted in the summer sunshine. At least Jack wasn't able to pull up next to her, as those spaces had already been taken by Kate's Coffee and a fish and chip van. Lucy let out a small sigh, realising she'd been holding her breath for a few seconds – it was inevitable that she and Jack would meet at the same event sooner or later.

It had been twelve days now, and all her fears after that seemingly special night had proved to be right. Jack had never bothered to answer the next three messages Lucy had since sent, nor the two phone calls she'd tried to make. Jack Anderson had well and truly ducked out. Used her for a one-night stand. He must have set up all that so-called romantic cocktails and canapés stuff on the beach just to get his leg over. And Lucy had gone and fallen for it, hook line and sinker. She felt so bloody annoyed with herself for being such a pushover. Her blood was boiling again at the thought of it. Well, no more.

An hour later, and the pizza horsebox was ready, with the oven lit, the counter top all set up and a strand of Lucy's colourful Italian-flag bunting stretched out along the hatch. It should, hopefully, be a busy and profitable day, being a pay-as-you-go event. She was on her own today and just had to focus and keep herself occupied; with head down and sense of pride up.

Thankfully, there was a steady queue for her pizzas as soon

as the festival kicked into gear at noon. The margherita and new topping flavour, spicy nduja – a gorgeous Italian spicy sausage – were going down really well. It was a hot summer's day, and Lucy had a bit of a sweat on, bustling about multi-tasking and making up orders, then standing by the oven turning pizzas with her paddle. But that wasn't the only reason she was feeling uncomfortable. Every now and again, she'd take a sidelong glance across at Jack, who was over the other side of the green, shaking cocktails, serving and chatting to many a girl, with his trademark cocky smile in place. God, how she'd like to slam a hot tomato-sauced pizza right into that charming face of his. That would wipe the grin off of it for once.

'A pesto chicken pizza please, love, when you're ready.'

'Oh right, yes, of course.' She hadn't noticed the chap in the baseball cap arrive at the counter. 'Coming right up.' She forced a smile.

Jack glanced over to the pizza horsebox. His heart still felt raw. He'd half thought of ducking out of today's event, but that was no good, that was the coward's way, and he knew they'd have to face each other at some point.

Every message from her had twisted his gut. The beach night ... he'd loved surprising her, thinking of things to make her evening special, to make her smile, but he hadn't expected it all to move so quickly. And he certainly hadn't planned that it would all feel so damn intense. The morning after, his instinct had been to run, call a halt to it all.

But now, looking at Lucy, instead of that making him feel

better, he felt downright rotten. The guilt had been gnawing at him ever since he'd left her cottage. He'd told himself over and over, since then, that keeping his distance was best for the both of them. If he couldn't commit, then he could at least try not to hurt her anymore. He just had to see it through, then things might get easier ... in time.

Much to his relief, Jack's work was cut out for him throughout the afternoon, with him mixing summer cocktails galore: gin fizzes, Pimm's, chilled prosecco; along with draught lagers and bottled ales. He was also making fancy fresh juices, and his elderflower fizz and 'No-jito' mocktails aplenty to cool the thirsty gathering.

Concentrating on the job in hand, it was a bolt from the blue when, at around 2 p.m., he looked up to see that the next people in the queue were *his parents*. He was astounded. They'd never been to *any* of his events before. To be fair, most bookings were at private houses or party venues, but today's fête, well, he'd mentioned it to them in passing, but hadn't ever imagined they'd turn up. They'd never seemed overly keen to see him in action with Ruby, his Cocktail Campervan, in the past.

'Hey, hi, Mum, Dad. What are you doing here?' He still wondered if they were there by chance, or perhaps and most likely en route to some other occasion or outing.

'We've come to see you.' His mum smiled.

'Yeah,' his dad Simon took up, 'we wanted to see Ruby up and running. See how this cocktail thing works when you are out and about.'

It had been years he'd been working with Ruby ... they

could easily have come before, but he didn't want to mess up this historic moment with a cheeky remark. 'Well, great. Good! Can I get you anything while you're here? Mix you a summery cocktail, Mum? A cold beer for you, Dad?'

'A beer would be fantastic.'

'Mum?'

'Oh, I'm not sure. I don't want to risk a headache, drinking in the day.'

'No worries, I do mocktails and juices. What about a refreshing pineapple and lime soda?'

'Go on then, yes, that sounds delightful.'

While he was fixing their drinks, unable to suppress his surprised smile, his dad was checking out Ruby. 'She looks good son, the campervan, all very professional.'

'It's so pretty, Jack, I never imagined it all set out like this.'

Jack felt a surge of joy. His parents were actually here ... and praising his business.

He passed their drinks across with a grin. 'Thanks. And enjoy!'

'Thank you, son.' Dad was fumbling in his pocket for his wallet.

'Don't be so daft, I'll not take any money from you. I'm just chuffed you're here.'

There seemed to be a lot still unsaid between them, yet actions spoke louder than words. They were here in support, and that meant so much to Jack. He might not be a lawyer or a doctor, but he had a business that was doing well, and that he loved. Perhaps his parents might start to see that for themselves from now on.

A couple came forward asking for two Lemon Gin Fizzes. Jack's parents stood back and watched him chat with the customers whilst mixing, shaking and garnishing their cocktails. They couple soon left, happily sipping their drinks, with the bloke turning to say, 'This is amazing, mate. Cheers.'

'You're welcome, and have a great afternoon.'

A few more customers came and went. Mum went off to browse a couple of stalls, mocktail in hand. Dad stood enjoying his beer, watching his son at work, whilst soaking up a few rays of sunshine.

There was another lull, and his parents again approached the counter, Mum passing back her empty glass and Dad his bottle.

'That was just the ticket, thanks son.'

'The pineapple drink was delicious. Thank you. I'll have to get the recipe from you and make it for Mary when she next calls round.'

'Right, well I suppose we'd better be off then. Let you get on here,' Dad took up.

They said their goodbyes, ready to leave. Jack was still stunned yet delighted by their arrival. It was then his dad looked up ... at Jack, framed by Ruby and his cocktail bar. He stopped, gave a small cough, and said, 'Well done. We are proud of you, son.'

And that meant the world to Jack.

Meanwhile back at the horsebox, the time had thankfully passed quickly for Lucy, with a steady stream of hungry customers lured in by the mouth-watering aromas of Papa's pizza recipe. It was early evening already, and the festival was coming to a close with a charity raffle in aid of the local hospice. Lucy had bought some tickets earlier. Local families, tourists, young and old, were gathered on the village green. Children stood clutching some treasured new toy, bought or won at one of the many stalls, or frantically licked at drippingly-delicious ice-cream cornets (a last treat for the day). Most of the visitors looked like they'd had a lovely afternoon, with just one or two sets of parents appearing a little frazzled by this point. The raffle winners were announced and various organisers thanked, and the remaining crowd gave a round of cheerful applause. The church bells rang out thereafter, announcing 6 p.m., and it was time to head home, or indeed pack up, for the stall-holders. Lucy was delighted that she'd sold almost all of almost all her pizza bases; her cash tin was happily full.

And right then, the person she'd been trying to avoid all afternoon was heading her way. Her stomach took a dive. Lucy tried to keep her cool, determined not to say a word about the unanswered texts and calls, about the poor way he had acted in all this, but it had been brewing inside her all day. In fact, for the past twelve days, ever since the night he'd stayed over. Why in fact, *should* he get away with treating her like this? Why give her the impression that their friendship, that night, had meant something special, and then do the disappearing act?

'Hey,' Jack said softly, giving a cautious smile, having decided to bite the bullet and come across. If this was going no further between them, he had to at least speak with Lucy.

He had to show her that respect. He knew that he'd ducked out for long enough.

'Hi, stranger.' Her tone was loaded with a sarcasm that couldn't disguise her hurt.

'Busy afternoon?' he continued, ignoring the dig.

So, this is it, Lucy fumed. The first time they had seen each other in person since *that* day, and they were back to small talk. No acknowledgment that they'd spent a night together, that anything significant had happened between them at all.

Lucy had had enough ... She didn't care if anyone overheard, that people were still there on the green. 'What's going on, Jack?' she hissed. 'I've had no texts at all from you. You don't bother to answer my calls ... All that effort you made with that picnic on the beach ... and then afterwards ...' The words hung sharply, forcing memories between them. 'I-I thought what we had was good. Like we were *really* getting on. Like it was more than just that one night of casual sex.' Lucy's frustrations and disappointment spilled out.

A couple who were walking past looked across, intrigued, then proceeded on slowly, no doubt still trying to listen in.

'Yeah, it *was* good ... of course,' Jack answered flatly, giving away no emotion. 'We had fun Luce, no doubt about that but ... But I just think we could cool it, no need to jump into anything, you know?' He looked sheepish, busy staring at something near his shoe.

Cool it. Oh, yes, worm your way into my bed and my heart, and then just go and bugger off. Typical!

So, classic 'player' Jack was back, then. The proof was standing there right in front of her. She'd just been another notch on his bedpost. Arrrgh, why, oh why, had she not listened to the voice of reason that had been knocking away in her mind, *or* to close friend Becky's advice?

The village green was emptying out; this might be Lucy's last chance to air all this. Frustration and anger were stirring up her emotional outpouring: 'So, that's it? I was just like the rest of them, eh? Someone for you to pick up and drop just as quickly?'

'No, it wasn't like that ...' Jack frowned.

'So, what was it like? It doesn't look any different from where I'm standing. Dammit, I should have known better. I've seen it with my own eyes. It's the way you always are with women, Jack. One night, maybe two if they're really lucky, and then bumph, you disappear.'

Jack was on the defensive now, 'Well, at least I never made any false promises to those girls, Luce. Never pulled out engagement rings, didn't talk of getting married. Nothing like that.'

Liam was dragged to mind with that comment. Her private confession to Jack now spilling out. It was a cheap hit.

'Well, let's face it, you'd never be able to commit to such a thing,' Lucy blasted back. She certainly was *all fired up* now.

'Okay,' Jack said fiercely, 'so some of my past relationships might have been fly-by-night things. Others, maybe a month or so.'

'God, you actually managed a whole month, did you? *She* must have been special,' Lucy couldn't resist the dig.

Jack just gave her a look, raising one eyebrow. 'But I never promised anything, that's not my way. Anyway, all that was years ago ...'

'Hah, you could have fooled me.'

'Like I already told you, I was young, Luce. And yes, back then, I probably did act like a dick.'

'Or was ruled by one,' she fired back.

He gave a wry smile, at that. *God, she looked bloody gorgeous when she was angry.*

'Okay, okay.' He put his hands up, as though giving in. 'I was hurting,' his tone changed, 'and yes, I was selfish back then. But you know, women do that too. There are lots of women happy with the one-night stand thing.'

'Well, Becky certainly wasn't ...' And, *she* certainly hadn't been, Lucy admitted to herself.

A moment or two of silence hung between them.

He was so bloody exasperating. But in some ways, Lucy had to begrudgingly concede that he was right. Was it *their* expectations in the way – Becky's, hers – not anything he'd in fact promised?

But then Lucy remembered that girl, the tipsy one, the one who Jack shovelled into his campervan at the end of the village wedding do. What *had* she witnessed that night? She'd been trying to give him the benefit of the doubt. But now, given the way he'd treated her, that really didn't seem innocent at all.

She launched back in, unable to quell the burning anger in her veins. 'Okay, so what about that girl who fell over tipsy that night of the wedding event? How did you treat her, eh Jack?'

'What are you talking about?' he shot back, angrily.

'The one you scooped up, bundled into the campervan and took home. That poor girl had had far too much to drink.'

'Well, that's just what I did ...' He frowned as he spoke, '*I took her home.*'

Jeez, he was so bloody blasé about it, too. 'Well, that says it all, doesn't it? Bet that didn't last more than one night either.'

'Luce, what are you banging on about? I just said I took her home. To *her* home.' He spelled it out.

'Oh.' His tone and the look on his face made her stop her rant.

'She was an old school friend, Freya. So, what ... you thought? You are joking me, Luce. You think I'd take her back to mine in a state like that, to take advantage of her or something? I can't believe you think that badly of me.' It was Jack's turn to feel affronted, and rightly so. 'Her so-called friends had buggered off, and I just made sure she got home safely. Not that I have to justify myself to you.'

'Oh ... Jack, I'm sorry. It just looked like ...' Lucy's voice trailed. She had got this so wrong.

'Well, if you believe I'm that much of a low-life, that just confirms that there's not much hope for you and me at all.'

And with that, he stormed off, back to Ruby, slamming the camper van's door.

Leaving Lucy with an even more battered heart than she'd started with.

Chapter 37

But Jack didn't go home, not for long anyhow. He parked up on Matt's driveway, gave Ruby a thorough post-event clean, grabbed a few camping items, and set off again, stopping at the local mini-mart for a few essential food purchases. He headed off for the hills of the Scottish borders, which were just over half an hour's drive away. Remote moorland valleys, where you could easily find yourself alone. Where you could stroll, letting the mountain air fill your lungs, clear your head, and watch the late-night sun go down in a blaze of gold, dipping down over the magenta crags of the horizon. Well, that was the plan. It certainly had to be better than sitting in his room watching TV or scrolling through Instagram ... or dwelling on the bloody row he'd just had with Lucy.

He parked the campervan up at a remote beauty spot in a valley, then walked the hillside with his tent and camping gear on his back. The climb was invigorating, but now he'd stopped and set up camp, his plan not to think about Lucy was failing miserably. She seemed to creep back into the spaces in his head at every opportunity; when he was working, when he was lying in bed trying to sleep, when he was driving, sat here on a hillside in the middle of nowhere. There was no way he was going to forget her, and he really needed to.

He opened a can of ale, set his little stove up to cook the bacon and eggs he'd brought with him, buttered some soft white sourdough bread, and looked out at the sheep grazing in the valley below. He focussed on this simple task, turning the bacon over in the pan; the smell tantalising as the fat crisped golden-brown. At least he hadn't lost his appetite. He added the egg to the frying pan a minute or so later, listening to it sizzle beside the bacon, waited for it to cook, then turned it all out onto a plastic plate, and ate.

Supper with a view. And what a view it was – rolling hills, deep valleys, rugged moorland with sheep grazing, and the sky, a fading blue turning to gold with wisps of high feathery peach-tinged cloud zigzagging across it, as the sun began to dip.

Did Lucy really think he was such a tosser that he'd take some drunken girl home to sleep with her? Jeez. Or, was she just riled up about everything, much like he still was? The night they'd spent together was special, but he still had to admit it totally scared him too. Being with someone. Giving so much of yourself to them. That ache of vulnerability. When you loved, you lost ... He'd been there, and he *never* wanted to feel that depth of pain ever again. If he took this step back from Lucy now, then at least his head and heart wouldn't be all over the place like some kind of emotional roadkill.

He took out his notepad and a biro from his backpack, and looked out across the rocky crags, moorland grass, prickly gorse bushes. The words were there in his mind, ready, flowing through to his fingertips:

Your faces haunt me.
The one I lost.
The one I could yet lose.
In these hills, as dusk begins to settle, shadows deepening
*   in the valley.*
The sky lifting to a blaze of sunset gold, brushed with
*   magenta, burnished copper.*
Will I ever find you again?
Should I dare?

Jack put down his pen. He suddenly didn't know which way to turn, or what the endgame was anymore. He'd been protecting himself for so long. Keeping going, moving forward, as much as he could. Keeping the blinkers firmly on. Stopping himself getting involved. But had he been missing what really mattered? He'd not let anyone in for such a long, long time. Was that the only way?

Not being loved, meant not getting hurt. But hurting Lucy was hurting him too. He could see that now.

His head was spinning.

He'd watch this glorious sunset fade and then sleep on it, he decided. He had a small hipflask of single malt whisky in the pocket of his rucksack. He found it, and sipped it slowly as the light faded. It warmed him through.

Yes, he'd stay here and watch the stars come out one by one, like vibrant white pin-pricks above him. It was a mild enough night. He laid out the roll mat and sleeping bag in the open air, and just lay there looking up, trying to sort through this crazy kaleidoscope of thoughts and emotions, feeling like a dot in the universe, a dot full of hurt and confusion.

Chapter 38

'Girlfriend, you are kidding me, right?'

Sat at a corner table in the Driftwood Café, with a latte and a very large slice of Victoria sponge in front of her, Lucy was finally spilling the truth to Becky about what had been going on with Jack.

Becky's mouth dropped open as she was about to load it with a cream and jam scone.

Lucy felt herself go pink as the heat of shame rose within her. 'Oh, I wish I was joking, Becks.'

'So, you ... you willingly let Jack, waste-of-space, all-time player, dickhead, into your home *and your bed*. Are you crazy? Do you have some kind of masochistic wish to get hurt again? Just put yourself in line, Luce. Wow, I didn't think you were *that* stupid.'

'Nor did I,' Lucy conceded sheepishly, her latte cooling untouched before her. 'I just got caught up in it all. He went to such an effort with that picnic and the cocktails on the beach, and we'd been getting on great as friends before that.'

'Tactics. That's all it was.'

'I've been a bloody idiot, haven't I?' Lucy felt her shoulders slump.

'Yup.' Becky took a huge bite of her scone. 'Hey ...' she softened, 'we can all get things wrong sometimes. Oh, god, you did take precautions, I hope?'

'Of course.'

'Phew. So, it's nothing you can't move past. Live and learn, Luce. Live and learn. You'll be fine. And next time listen to your old mate, Becks.' Her friend gave her a little dig in the ribs.

'I bloody well will.'

'Oh, on that note, there is someone interested in a date.'

'With you?'

'Don't be so daft, I'm all shacked up with Darren. No, *you*.'

'Huh, how's that? Becks, no,' Lucy didn't really like where the conversation was suddenly heading, 'Nope, I *really* don't feel ready for dating just now. After this disaster, I'm going to hole up back at the cottage with Daisy for the rest of the year, maybe the decade.'

'Ah-oh, no. You've got to get back out there, Luce. Show dickhead barman you're living your best life. That someone else is keen. Show him what he's missing.'

'I really don't think so, Becks.'

'It's just a mate of Darren's, and I'm not asking you to get married, just go on one date. Loosen up a bit.'

'I loosened up far too much, and look where that got me.'

'It was just with the wrong guy, Luce. This bloke is lovely. Darren knows him from his uni days. He's just moved back up this way. Got a job in Morpeth, something to do with computers I think, and well, he's just finding his feet, trying to make some new friends. Just say you'll give it a try, just once. Nothing heavy, just a drink out or something.'

Lucy could tell Becky wasn't going to let this rest. And, she did kind of feel she owed her one, after not taking her friend's advice over Jack.

'Alright, alright. Just for a drink, and for a couple of hours tops. No cosy meals out or anything. Nothing too datey.'

'Datey? Is that even a real word?' Becky gave a wry smile. 'Okay, yes, granted.' She clapped her hands. 'I'll get it sorted.'

Lucy sat and sipped her now-cool latte, feeling a little queasy. *Frying pan into the fire* came to mind.

Chapter 39

Four days after her chat with Becky, and it had all been arranged – that girl was nothing but keen. There was no going back now.

Lucy checked her look in the mirror. She'd gone for a red floral-patterned summer dress with black ankle-tie espadrille sandals. Being summer, her skin was olive-tanned with a healthy Mediterranean glow, inherited from Papa's side of the family. She wore her dark hair loose, and it fell in its natural wave, to just below her shoulders. Well, she'd do.

She was feeling a bit nervous. Other than meeting up with Jack, and god knows what classification that would fall into, she hadn't 'dated' since Liam left her almost two years ago. What would they talk about? What if there was no chemistry? And, what if she did actually like this new guy? Okay, she reasoned with herself, it was just for a couple of drinks and a couple of hours. He, *Angus*, had suggested they go to a pub in a village not far from Alnwick, about six miles from Lucy's home. He was going to pick her up at the cottage, but then she had organised a taxi home for herself at ten o'clock, not too early and not too late. But that still meant a full two and a half hours together – which could prove tricky if they didn't get on. Still, Becky had assured her that he was a nice guy; her friend having met him a couple of times as a mate of Darren's.

A dark-grey, shiny-clean Lexus saloon pulled up outside the cottage window, dimming the light inside her living room. Oh, this was him. He'd mentioned having a Lexus.

'Well, here goes, Daisy. Wish me luck.' Lucy popped the little dog into her kitchen crate, then took a slow, steadying breath. 'Be a good girl, now. I won't be too long.' She tossed a couple of dog biscuits in with her canine pal, and left Daisy munching contentedly.

Lucy stepped outside, and took a steadying breath as she turned to lock the cottage door. As she approached the car, the guy in the driving seat gave a small wave, and leaned across to open the passenger door from the inside. 'Hi, Lucy.'

'Hi,' she replied with a nervous smile.

He had dark-brown hair, cut short, green eyes, good teeth. All in all, not bad-looking. But, in that second, the face in her mind was Jack's. She pushed the image away, as she took up the passenger seat.

'Angus.' He offered his hand formally across the gear stick. 'Nice to meet you.'

'Pretty little cottage.'

'Yeah, it's lovely, and I really like the village here too. So handy for the beach.'

Beach walks, beach canapés, cocktails … Jack was lurking dangerously inside her head once more. Would that fly-by-night barman just butt out of her thoughts!

'So, where is it you live?' she asked.

'Ah, I'm renting just now. On a new estate in Morpeth. Modern, easy to look after. Handy for the A1, and getting to work.'

'Right.' Wow, this felt very like old territory; in fact, like the kind of life she'd just escaped from. The conversation was feeling stilted already. But they'd only just met, she conceded. She needed to give him a chance.

He was a steady driver, and the journey passed in polite chit-chat. Angus worked in IT – she knew that much as Becky had filled her in a bit – explaining that he did contract work for small and medium businesses who didn't have their own in-house IT technicians. He'd studied computer science at Newcastle University, gone to work for BT for a while, and then went into partnership with an acquaintance who was keen on setting up an IT solutions company in North Northumberland. He told her that several IT companies were based Newcastle way, but there weren't many options here on their doorstep. They'd secured some good contracts already, including one for the Alnwick Gardens working for the Duchess of Northumberland, no less, setting up a new computer network for the office and shop facilities. He sounded very proud about that. And apparently the business was prospering, going from strength to strength.

'Hence the new Lexus,' he beamed. It was like he was trying to convince her how good a prospect he was too.

'Well, that all sounds impressive. Well done you.'

'And what about you, Lucy? What's your line of work?'

'Oh, I have a pizza horsebox.'

Angus quirked an eyebrow.

'I travel to events,' Lucy explained, 'set it all up, and cook my own hand-crafted pizzas.'

'Right, well that sounds ... fun. Different.'

'Yeah, I'm just getting established, but it's going well so far.'

'Good. Though I have to say I'm not much of a pizza fan really. Prefer healthier food.'

'Oh.'

Well, that halted the conversation.

'Ah ... I'm sure yours will be good though,' he then mumbled on feebly, trying to dig himself back out of the conversational black hole he'd just dropped them in.

Lucy gazed out of the window at the passing fields, wondering what on earth she could say next. This was so different from her drive out in Ruby after that first beach afternoon, with the windows wound down and she and Jack singing like loons.

Ten minutes later, they arrived at The Black Swan Inn, pulling up into one of the few spaces left in the rear car park.

'Well, here we are,' Angus announced, stating the obvious.

'Lovely.'

It was a relief to arrive. She certainly felt in need of a drink. Perhaps a glass or two of wine would loosen up the chat a bit. Angus insisted on buying the first round, and they found a table tucked cosily in a corner. He talked some more about various IT projects he'd undertaken; filling her in on his love for what went on behind the scenes in a computer. Asking had she heard about the benefits of business intelligence, data mining (she was visualising men with spades digging up words and numbers at that point) and enterprise architecture, blah-blah? By the end of this rather long-winded conversation, she was more bamboozled than when they'd started. This was exactly why people paid good money to get someone like Angus to deal with their computer problems. Because they didn't want to have to learn about all the complex (and boring) background stuff themselves, they just wanted to be able to use the damn things. She didn't actually share those thoughts with Angus however, sensing they wouldn't go down too well.

Lucy was ready for another drink soon enough, and headed off to the bar to buy the next round. She didn't want Angus to feel he had to pay for her all night. She leaned against the smooth, lacquered wooden bar top, waiting her turn.

The main door of the pub swung open, catching her eye, and, *oh shit*. What were the bloody chances? Of course the person walking through the door had to be Jack Anderson. Lucy's skin went all prickly and a strong impulse to hide rose up inside her.

He quickly spotted her too; looked across, his brow furrowing for an instant with surprise.

Jack approached cautiously, no sign of the cocktail-man bravado in his step. 'Hey, good to see you,' he said awkwardly. 'Didn't expect to see you here,' he added, with just a hint of his gorgeous smile.

'No, nor me you.' Lucy's heart was hammering away in her chest.

'So, who are you with?'

'Oh, um, just a friend. He's over there.' Lucy pointed across to the corner, where Angus was finishing his pint.

Jack's eyebrow quirked as he glanced in Angus's direction, who in turn gave them a brief nod. 'Ah, right, I see.' Jack's smile soon turned to a frown.

What did it matter to him who she was with anyway, Lucy mused. He was the one who'd given her the cold shoulder. The one who'd told her they should 'cool it'. Thankfully, the barman turned to her to take her order at that point. 'Yes, a white wine and a pint of Diet Coke, please.'

Jack shifted slightly, ready to place his own order. One of the friends he'd arrived with, the tall one, moved nearer, seeming to look her up and down, before saying, 'Hi.'

'Oh, hi ...' Lucy answered politely.

'Ah, this is my mate, Matt ...'

She really didn't feel comfortable standing around making conversation in the circumstances, and guessed Jack was feeling awkward too. The barman placed her drinks on the bar top and she quickly paid. 'Well, I'll see you around, Jack.'

'Yeah.'

She couldn't figure out the look that Jack was giving her at all.

With that, she picked up the two glasses and headed back over to their table, her heart still thumping. Back to making small talk with nice-guy Angus, whilst trying to avoid more mind-numbing in-depth IT conversations.

Jeez, he'd come here to try and chill out a bit with his mates, and take his mind off stuff. Matt had noticed he'd been a bit 'off' lately, and had suggested coming out for a few beers along with another pal, James. It had sounded a good idea at the time to Jack. Right now, though, it seemed like the good idea had well and truly backfired. In fact, Jack felt like he'd just landed in front of the firing squad.

'Is that her?' Matt gave him a nudge.

'Who?' Jack was pretending to play it cool.

'The girl that you've just been talking to at the bar. Is it *her*? Whoever's been messing with your heart and your head lately?'

Jack just shrugged non-committally. He really didn't want to get into any of that here, especially not with *her* sat a mere five metres away from him, looking cosy with some other bloke, chatting away and laughing as she flicked back her dark hair. Jack was relieved when the barman turned to him soon afterwards.

'Yes, mate? What can I get you?'

'Ah, great. Three pints of Morretti, thanks.'

The lads found a spot nearby, standing at a tall barrel-shaped table. Unfortunately, it had a direct view over to Lucy's corner of the bar. Jack found himself feeling suddenly hot and uncomfortable. He shifted, so at least his back was to her now.

'Nice pint,' he commented. The lager was cool and refreshing.

'Yeah, hits the spot, doesn't it,' James answered.

'So, what's the crack, lads? Any unusual animal antics at the vets, Mattie?' Jack needed to lose himself in everyday conversation, wind down a bit. That was what he was here for, after all. But every now and again – despite the story of the Labrador who arrived at the vets wobbly and foaming at the mouth, with its owner getting redder and redder at the questioning as to whether the dog could have eaten anything poisonous, and finally confessing that Bertie had eaten his owner's supply of homemade cannabis cookies – Jack couldn't help but twist his neck to take a peek at the pair of *them* sat in the corner. It was like some kind of masochistic game Jack was playing with himself. Even though it was weirdly painful to watch, he found himself unable to ignore Lucy.

'You okay, Jack?' Matt asked, after finishing his waggy tale.

'Yeah, yeah, fine.'

'You just don't quite seem yourself, mate.'

'I'm alright. Might just nip to the bathroom, though.'

The bar area was feeling awfully claustrophobic right now. Jack got up to take a bit of a breather, intending to give himself a bit of a talking-to, as well. What was wrong with him? If he didn't want things to go any further with Lucy, as he'd made quite clear to her at the village festival recently, then why the hell was he feeling so goddamned shitty right now? Was it mere jealousy? He didn't want her, but no-one else could have her, kind of thing? And didn't that make him the biggest, most selfish coward in the world?

To top it all, just as he was stood at the urinal taking aim, in walked Lover Boy! That was all he bloody well needed. Jack turned slightly at the sight of the guy. Jealousy rose within him. Well, he hoped this guy had a small, in fact, a *teeny-weeny* penis; Jack was well aware how immature his thoughts were right now but he couldn't seem to stop them.

He washed his hands, stealing a backward glance in the mirror at Lover Boy. Dark, neat hair. Smart, designer-label clothes. Jack couldn't help but wonder which of the posh cars outside he might own? But at least, he thought proudly, there was no smart car out there which could possibly match his gorgeous Ruby for style and character.

Move on out, Jack, he told himself. *Exit to the bar, immediately, and have a nice evening with your mates.*

'Alright Jack? Ready for another?' James lifted his empty pint glass, about to head off to the bar for refills.

'Absolutely.' He'd never felt bloody readier.

An excruciatingly slow half-hour later, Jack had to watch as Lover Boy guided Lucy with his hand gently (or was it possessively?) past their table to the exit. Jack gave a polite nod. 'See you then, Luce.'

'Bye, Jack.'

She didn't bother introducing her other half, and Jack was mightily relieved at that. The situation was excruciating enough, as it was.

He watched her leave, with the other guy's arm still pitched at the small of her back. Jack felt a lump in his throat, remembering that particular curve of her naked body so very well. He'd let her go, and that was the end of it, he told himself, as he watched the bar door close. It was for the best.

But why did it still feel like this was only the start of something ... what was all this crazy stuff going on inside of him? It was like Lucy had set off some seismic wave, shaking everything up. He found himself dreading the fallout of this earthquake.

Chapter 40

'So, hun, how did it go?' Becky was on the line, bright and early the next morning.

'Ah, well ... it didn't really, Becks.'

'Oh, how come?' her friend sounded disappointed.

'No, to be fair to Angus, it was fine. There just weren't any sparks flying.'

'Ah well, it can't have been all bad. He's got a good job and a nice car, so I hear.'

'Yeah, the car was very nice. Leather seats and everything.'

'Well, there you go.'

'We just didn't seem to have an awful lot in common. And then, he ground me down with talk of megabytes and pixels.'

'Oh, I see. Not the most riveting chat then!'

'And when we got onto the spyware, malware and viruses, well honestly, I'm now afraid to turn my computer back on again. In case it's already got the equivalent of computer venereal disease ... I have very basic protection, apparently.' Lucy giggled.

'Aw, he'd have just been trying to help you out, Luce.'

'Maybe, but he just wasn't my type and I have to confess, it wasn't very scintillating conversation for a night out.'

'No, perhaps not. Not exactly a turn-on, I suppose.'

They both chuckled.

'Oh well, I'll put it down to experience.'

'You do that, girlfriend. And, hey, there are plenty more fish in the sea.'

And Lucy had a feeling her friend would be trying her hardest to hook her up with more of those fish very soon. She daren't mention the *other* guy who was at the pub last night, who despite it all, was still in fact very much on her mind. The one she'd already told he ought to sling his hook.

Two days later, and Lucy was flicking through her phone trying to get some good images for promotional posts on the All Fired Up Instagram and Facebook pages, when she scrolled across a photo of Jack stood beside Ruby from months ago. It was the first night they'd ever met. She'd taken a few snaps of the venue, and there he was, caught in the frame.

She couldn't help but smile. He looked so handsome, confident and happy ... and yes, a little cocky too. Yet she'd seen that there was a gentler, more vulnerable side to him, despite it all.

What had it all been about between them? Had he won her over just to leave her? Had that been the plan all along? And if so, if he was such a twat, then why couldn't she shake thoughts of this guy off?

Memories. Magical moments on the beach. Laughter.

Holding hands and oh, so much more. It still didn't make sense. And boy, it still hurt.

A dachshund's damp nose edged up against her leg.

'Hey, Daisy. Do you want a cuddle?'

She lifted her pet's solid little body up to her lap, giving her an affectionate stroke.

'Me too, baby. Me too.'

At least dogs didn't have game plans or commitment issues. If a dog wanted affection, it just came right up and asked you for it. They were straight down the line with you. Hmm, Lucy mused, humans could learn a lot from their four-legged friends.

Chapter 41

Jack couldn't shake off this horrid feeling of negativity. He tried cracking on with work, throwing himself into events with his usual aplomb, polishing Ruby to the nth degree, spending time with his mates, with his Xbox, heading off cycling, taking long hikes ... but whatever he did, there was this sinking feeling inside, like a shadow was creeping around after him.

Seeing Lucy with another guy like that. Well, it had hit hard. But it bloody well served him right. He should already have apologised for the way he'd behaved after that night they'd spent together. He hadn't wanted to say it in a message, but the next time he'd seen her he should at least have spoken up. But then they'd had that silly row at the fête. And it was hardly ideal in the pub, with a new man in tow, was it?

He pictured how it might have panned out. 'Oh, hi there. And hey, Luce, sorry about giving you the cold shoulder since our night together.'

Well, that was either a punch-up in the making with new guy Lover Boy, or a pint of cold beer tipped over his head from Lucy. Either way, he probably deserved it.

He was due to visit his parents; he liked to call in on them regularly. It was all down to him now, after all. It had been nearly a week since the village fête and he was still cheered by the fact they'd turned up in support like that. That was a glimmer of light in the gloom.

He was soon there, after just a fifteen-minute journey, pulling Ruby up in the driveway. He rang the bell, and walked right on in.

'Hi, Mum, Dad,' he called out.

'Oh, hello love.' Mum came out from the kitchen with a warm smile. 'It's just me. Your dad's on a course.'

'Ahh, golf course?'

'You've got it!'

They both grinned. It was dad's favourite place to escape these days.

'Shall I put the kettle on?'

It was half past ten. Ideal tea and biscuits time in the Anderson household.

'Yeah, go on then, thanks. Oh, I brought you these.' He'd picked up a box of hand-made chocolates, from a fabulous-looking stall at an event he'd been working at in the harbour village of Warkton. He handed over the pretty gold box; the label read *The Chocolate Shop by the Sea*.

'Oh, they look lovely. Thank you, Jack.' It was nice to brighten Mum's day. Goodness knows they all needed a little light in their lives.

'I'm sure your dad will enjoy helping me out with them later,' her smile widened. 'Yes, he's right into his golf now the weather's turned for the better. I don't mind really, keeps him occupied, and gives me time to potter about in the house and garden unencumbered.'

'Hah, yes.'

Mum started filling the kettle, then took down a teapot from the kitchen cupboard.

Jack had a sudden flash of memory. He and Daniel as younger teens deciding to practise their golf swing and chipping. Only this was taking place *inside*, in Dan's bedroom. It had been a rainy day, and well, they hadn't fancied getting wet. Dad had gone ballistic when he'd walked into the room, alerted by the unusual knocking sound, to find the pair of them in action. There were still circular dent marks on Dan's ceiling to this day.

'You okay, Jack?'

'Yeah, just thinking about Dan and the bedroom golf practice ...' Jack said, sharing his thoughts. Sometimes he needed to talk about those memories. In fact, they all did. It helped keep Daniel alive in their hearts.

'Oh goodness, yes. Your dad went mad at the pair of you, didn't he? Mind you, I don't know what possessed you to start practising in the house.'

'I know. It was a bit crazy. But it seemed a good idea at the time. I think it must have been raining outside or something.'

'Gosh, the capers you two got up to ...' Mum's eyes looked a little watery, whilst she held onto her smile.

Jack wished so much they could get up to some capers now. And, he wished he could share some of this recent weird emotional stuff with his brother too. Dan was always more settled with his girlfriends; he somehow had seemed ready for 'grown-up' relationships from the get-go. Jack's mind drifted to Dan's last steady girlfriend and the life his brother might have had. The 'if onlys' and 'what might have beens' were still painful.

The tea was poured, and Mum pulled out a chair at the dining table. Jack followed suit. There was a second or two of silence between them. Just the tweeting of birdsong drifting in from the open French doors that led out to the back garden.

'Jack, are you really alright, son?' Mum's tone had changed, softened.

Should he open up, share some of his confused feelings about Lucy with his mum? But it just seemed too big a step. He could hardly make sense of it himself, never mind be capable of explaining it to someone else. 'Yeah, I'm fine.' Jack's front remained firmly in place. Not many people got to break down those walls, not even his parents. He'd spent too long trying to protect them from his grief when they had their own to deal with; his current problems didn't seem much compared to what they had all been through.

'Okay. Well, you know where we are if you ever need us.' An olive branch of love and support.

'Thanks, Mum.'

Jack took a gulp of tea, and dived into the old metal biscuit tin, a Christmas family tin Mum had saved one year that they'd been using ever since. He eventually found a jammy dodger. He felt safe here in this house, loved and comfortable, even though it was filled with a myriad of memories ... but he certainly didn't feel able to prise open his soul.

We're Getting Hitched!

Happily Ever After Begins for

Robert Thompson and Jennifer Wade

On Saturday 21st August

At Bamburgh Castle.

Service 1 p.m., followed by a Wedding Breakfast.

Cocktails, canapes and pizzas to follow from 7 p.m. in the Castle Courtyard.

Carriages at Midnight

Chapter 42

The castle's honey-blush stone walls and crenelated towers rose majestically at the far end of the coastal village of Bamburgh, looking like something out of a fairytale. A beautiful seascape filled the horizon behind it. The happy couple getting married, Jen and Rob, were going to be lucky with the weather today, by the looks of it. A little blowy, perhaps, but with a gorgeous blue sky and a mere hint of confetti cloud as the backdrop. Lucy approached the stunning venue of her next event with a sense of nervous anticipation, not least as she knew that a certain someone would be there too.

Today's special couple seemed really lovely when they'd chatted on the phone with her, several weeks ago now, to organise her gourmet pizza catering for the evening do. Jack, true to his word in supporting her business-wise at least, had mentioned her pizza horsebox to them, when they'd told him they were looking for some additional evening catering. The traditional wedding breakfast was due to take place mid-afternoon within the castle, after the marriage ceremony in the King's Hall.

So, Lucy already knew that Jack would be here. As the castle towered before her, and she indicated, ready to turn off from the village road, a twist of anxiety about seeing him once more started to put her insides through the wringer.

The last time she had seen him, she was on a date with another guy. And what a disastrous night that had been. There'd been no more personal texts, nor calls between her and Jack for a few weeks now. She'd merely allowed herself a quick peek at the couple of photos she had of him saved on her phone. That one of him stood by Ruby on the first night they had met, and the other from their spontaneous cocktail-in-the-dunes afternoon. It made her smile to look at them. A third image, one that was never taken but was in fact safely stowed in her head and her heart, was of him sat beside her at dawn, the morning after the storm, looking out to sea, talking whilst they drank coffee from tin mugs. His golden hair lit by the morning sunlight. His smile gentle, just for her.

Enough! What she needed to do was to focus on the job in hand, she told herself. Remain professional, stay calm. The more times they met like this, surely the easier it would become, and they could get back to being catering acquaintances. Why did that thought make her heart dip? Anyway, she had Abby with her to help today, as she anticipated a really busy spell from 8 p.m., when they were booked to start serving. There would be plenty for them to do in the meanwhile, setting up and getting organised.

Lucy drove the horsebox up the curving driveway to the

castle gates, where a friendly sixty-something man with thick white hair, after confirming their booking, let them in through an amazing cast-iron portcullis entrance. A warden would be there on hand at the top of the inner driveway, he advised, to show them where to park.

There was a large cream-coloured tipi positioned on the grass of the inner courtyard, evidently the setting for the evening celebrations. An area of white-painted table and chairs was set up outside of it, with flower posies in ivories and cream with deep-green foliage on each.

'Aw, that is *sooo* pretty,' gushed Abby. 'This is amazing.'

'It is pretty awesome, isn't it. A wedding in a castle by the sea. They'll need a supper to remember too.'

'No pressure then, Luce.'

'We'll do them proud with Papa's pizzas, I'm sure.' She had a few tricks up her sleeve to make tonight extra special for the couple too. She was determined to make her pizza experience the best it could possibly be for her customers.

Oh, Jack was already there, with a gleaming Ruby positioned at one side of the tipi. Vintage Ruby had been decorated in keeping with the wedding theme, with pretty white flowers and foliage in an arch-like canopy over the lifted rooftop, which Jack must have created especially for this event. The campervan looked fabulous, she had to credit him with that. Lucy too had taken on board that tip, to theme differently for each booking and give that personal touch. So, for today, she had splashed out on a gorgeous *Mr and Mrs* banner and grey-and-white bunting, with a couple of pearly-white helium balloons to tie to the horsebox, and two pretty jugs of white carnations and delicate gypsophila ready to set out on her counter top.

Guests soon came spilling out from the castle building, all in their smart suits and posh frocks. There was a natural lull in the proceedings, as they'd now finished the wedding breakfast and were building up for round two. Some made the most of Jack's services; topping up the late-lunchtime champagne and wine levels with fabulous cocktails and bottled beers. Several couples and groups of friends took a stroll around the grounds, some climbing the battlement walls for a better view of the long sweeping bay and the sea.

There was more hubbub and excitement as they re-grouped at the tipi area just before 7 p.m. Soon afterwards, the bride and groom appeared, Jen in a stunning fitted ivory lace dress and Rob smartly suited in navy, coming out from the castle hand in hand. A big 'hoorah' broke out, with lots of clapping from the gathering. The newlyweds looked so happy, as Rob swept Jen literally off her feet and carried her into the tipi, for the first dance. With the tipi sides flapped open by the entrance, Lucy couldn't resist stopping her work and watching for a little while. The groom whispered something to his new wife, and she smiled broadly, then planted a joyful kiss on his lips. Oh, to be so sure of each other, to promise a lifetime together. That strength of emotion was held so magically in the way the pair of them looked at each other.

As the music came to a close, Lucy couldn't help but glance Ruby's way and in the direction of a certain barman, who just happened to be looking her way too. For a second or two their eyes met ... and held. Lucy felt the glimmer of a smile cross her lips, but she quickly pulled it back, closed her heart, focussing once more on the safe image of the happy couple on the dance floor.

The evening rolled on. With the wedding guests growing hungry, a queue started to build for Lucy's Papa-style pizzas. Her assistant, Abby, was all go taking orders, and hand-stretching the dough bases. She was a natural, and could pull the dough to exactly the right shape and thinness with a deft hand and light touch, just how Lucy had shown her. Lucy was in charge of loading the toppings, then baking each pizza with a quick turn halfway through, and keeping the pizza fires burning. They worked as a slick and contented team.

After the mad 8–9 p.m. rush, things eased a little at the horsebox, and Lucy could take in the party surroundings and activities once more. With many of the guests now dancing, drinking, or sitting out on the wooden chairs chatting as the summer sun began to set, Lucy couldn't help her gaze moving across to the campervan. Three adult bridesmaids, wearing gorgeous floor-length dresses in a pretty pale-lilac shade, were gathered around Ruby, chatting, gesticulating and giggling. Jack was his usual charming barman self. She could hear him commenting about a violet gin cocktail he'd make for them all to try: 'the perfect drink to match your gowns'. Then he went into mixology mode, crushing ice, using his shaker theatrically, blending perfect lilac shades of alcohol with a dash of tonic and a splash of personality.

'There you go, ladies. Enjoy!'

It was all just an act, she realised, a part he played whilst working. An act that was required for him to be the fun, charming barman everybody wanted. But the *real* Jack was the one she witnessed before and after these events. The one who'd made her cocktails and canapés on the beach, the one who'd shared his summer storm tent, the one who was shyer, a more thoughtful soul. A soul, she now had to admit, she had fallen for, if only for a while.

It had been a hectic day, running the outdoor bar for this wedding function, but Jack liked the buzz, and the guests seemed a good bunch, easy-going and fun.

Jack spotted the wedding couple strolling his way. Jen's arm linked with Rob's, and both had smiles like Cheshire cats. Getting married obviously suited some people.

He hadn't had a chance to catch up with them since the ceremony earlier and called out, 'Hey guys, huge congratulations!'

'Aw, thank you.'

'Cheers, mate.'

'Hey, let me fix you a Wedding Day Cocktail. And this one's on me.'

'Ah, thanks.'

'Sounds great.'

'It'll just take me two minutes to make. It's called a French 75.'

'Sounds intriguing.'

'It's a champagne-based cocktail with gin and lemon.'

'Perfect,' Jen replied, adding, 'can I have a glass of water first, though? This'll go straight to my head, I'm sure, and I need to keep going. Don't want to miss a second of this amazing day. It's been brilliant, hasn't it, Rob?'

'Just the best.' Her new husband gave a broad grin.

Jack smiled too. It was great to see this couple, and in fact everyone he'd met today, enjoying themselves. When events like this worked out so well, Jack took a pride and a pleasure in being a part of that.

'Yeah, I've been getting good vibes here all day. Your guests are certainly having a great time.' As he spoke, a conga was winding its way past the campervan and around the castle's courtyard. Young and old snaking past with much hilarity. 'Here you go.' He passed across a large glass of water to Jen with a garnish of ice and lemon.

'Delightful.' Jen gulped it down. 'Just what I needed.'

'And now for the *pièce de resistance*.'

The newlyweds watched as Jack measured out gin, squeezed fresh lemon juice, added a splash of his homemade sugar syrup, shaking it over ice, and then pouring it all into two sugar-dusted flutes which he topped with chilled champagne.

'Enjoy!'

Carefully, flutes in hand, they looped their arms through each other's, and took a synchronised sip. 'Oh wow, that is divine,' said Jen with a beam of a smile.

'Brilliant, mate. Cheers.'

'Cheers to you both! Enjoy the rest of your special day.'

'Oh, we will!'

It really was a magical setting. And even commitment-phobe Jack had to admit that the happy couple seemed good

together. Relationships could sometimes work out. Love ...
marriage ... committing yourself for life. Some people could
get away with it. His mum and dad, despite the worst
happening and them losing a son, were still strong together.

To have that conviction, that faith in each other ... it still
stunned him. How you could ever know ... did you ever know?
Or was it just that it was worth bloody trying, at least? Would
he ever, one day, regret not trying?

Jack didn't get time to dwell on the answer to that, with
one of the bridesmaids dashing over. 'Hi-i,' she gave Jack a
cute wave. 'Jen, over here!' she called out. 'Mum wants a photo
with Auntie Eleanor.' With that, the bride was whisked away
and her new hubby Rob was left at the bar.

'You two seem great together. Congrats again,' Jack said.

'Yeah, well it took him long enough to get round to it.'
One of the ushers had strolled up, listening in.

'Right?' Jack was curious.

'Thought it'd never happen, me.' The chap was tall, tie
loosened off, with a sheen of sweat from all the dancing
shining across his brow.

'Don't mind him, it's Jen's brother,' said Rob with a chuckle,
giving the guy a friendly pat on the arm.

'Ah, can I have a bottle of Peroni please, mate?' the brother
asked Jack. 'And a glass of that gorgeous champagne for the
missus.'

Jack made the order up, and then the guy moved on.

'Back to practise my killer dance moves,' he joked with a
wiggle of his hips.

They couldn't help but smile.

'So ... a bit of a slow burn, was it? You and Jen?' Jack found himself intrigued about how this perfect-looking wedding came to be.

Rob took another gulp of his cocktail. 'Yeah, bit of a story that. More of a near-miss, mate. Between you and me, I nearly wrecked it all. Was a total idiot.'

'Oh, right. How come, if you don't mind me asking?' Jack instinctively opened and placed a bottle of chilled beer beside the groom.

It wasn't unusual for personal revelations to spill out at the bar, it often seemed to be a part of Jack's job – lending an impartial ear.

Maybe the layers of daytime drinking loosened the groom's tongue, or perhaps he was just punch-drunk on love, but he began to open up.

'Cheers. Ah, well it was no secret, so I don't mind talking about it.' He took a swig of the cool beer. 'Yeah, Jen kept hinting about settling down, getting engaged, and well ... I couldn't get my head around it. We were fine as we were, or so I thought. Then, I had a bit of a panic ... about being tied down and all that ... Told Jen we needed a break.'

Rob looked across at his new wife then, now dancing and holding hands with both a little girl and an elderly lady, smiling and laughing. 'Worst thing I ever did, mate. Yeah, I moved out, late nights drinking with my mates. Seemed fun for a week or two. Even headed off for a couple of lads' holidays. Well, we hit the clubs. The girls out and about looked about twelve ... and well, we'd all changed, hadn't we? Some of us had kids back home, so we ended up playing golf and having a few quiet bevvies. The rock and rollers that we were!'

Jack chuckled empathetically.

'I suppose we'd all grown up a bit,' Rob continued, shaking his head. 'It didn't feel like freedom at all. I felt bloody miserable the whole while, and I missed her. I nearly lost her, mate. It took a long while after that to bring her round, to make her realise that she meant the world to me.'

Rob took another sip of beer, shaking his head, yet smiling as he looked over at his bride once more. 'She's the best thing that ever happened to me. I just didn't see it at the time.'

'Ah, all's well that ends well, hey mate,' Jack added reassuringly.

'Absolutely. She's made me the happiest man today.' A beaming grin broke across his face.

'Well, cheers to that.' Jack lifted the glass of water he'd got for himself behind the bar.

'Yeah, cheers. Thanks, mate,' Rob raised his beer bottle. 'On that note, I'd better get back to the party and my lovely wife, I suppose.' He gave a happy wink.

'Yes indeed. Enjoy the rest of your night, you two.'

'We will ... and all the years to come. Hey, thanks for listening.' The groom grinned and gave a huge thumbs up.

Jack felt his heart fill, Rob's words resounding in his ears. *She's the best thing that ever happened to me.*

He suddenly had a feeling that he was the one who should be thankful.

Chapter 43

It was the Cinderella hour. 'Carriages at midnight' for the wedding guests, with a hum of taxis waiting in the car-park area outside the portcullis gates. A few close family and friends were fortunate to be able to stay in rooms at the castle overnight, but most were on their merry way.

It was time to pack up and clear up for Lucy and Abby, who were now preparing the horsebox for its exit home too. It had been a gorgeous wedding event, and Lucy had enjoyed the privilege of working in such an amazing setting, and for such lovely people. They really were a special couple and evidently made for each other.

She was just getting the last bits in the horsebox when she saw a familiar figure wandering across in her direction: Jack.

'Hey,' he said.

'Hi.' Lucy paused, her damn heart lodging up near her throat. How did he still do that to her?

'Busy?'

'Yeah, but it was good, wasn't it?' she stammered. 'What a lovely atmosphere.'

'Yeah ...'

Jack then stood silent for a moment, looking slightly awkward.

There was so much they both needed to say, and yet ... It just seemed so damned hard.

Abby moved behind Lucy, thoughtfully heading out of the horsebox, a black bin bag to hand, ready to clear paper plates and debris from around their pitch.

'Lucy, can we talk for a minute?' Jack finally said, looking serious.

'You go ahead,' Abby offered with an understanding smile. 'I'll keep an eye on the oven and things. It's no problem.'

'Okay ... thanks, Abby.' Lucy removed her apron and her protective gloves. She stepped down out of the horsebox and made her way across the grass to Jack, experiencing an unsettling whirr of mixed emotions.

'Let's walk.' Jack led her towards the battlements, and they made their way up the stone steps to a wide rampart that overlooked the inky-dark sea. You could hear the rush of the waves breaking on the shore from up there. It was soothing, elemental.

They stood with a polite space between them, looking out across the shadowy swell of sea, feeling the cool breeze ruffling their hair.

Jack then turned to her. 'Luce, are you seeing someone?'

What was he on about now? Ah ... of course, the night at the pub. IT Angus.

'Ah ... the other night, you mean?'

Jack nodded, looking grave.

'Hah no, that was just some weird set-up date thing.'

'Oh ...?' He was still frowning.

'Didn't work out that well, to be honest.'

'Oh, well, good ... I mean ...'

'It's okay, it was good ... to see the back of him.'

They both gave a relieved smile; a glimpse of a shared grin in the half light.

They then leant side-by-side against the battlement wall, looking out over to the indigo horizon. The moon was waxing, but bright enough to light ripples on the sea's surface with silver tips.

Jack released a slow steady breath. 'Lucy, what I really want to say is that I'm sorry. And it's a long-overdue apology. I treated you badly. I shouldn't have stayed over that night.'

'Oh.' Did he mean he regretted it altogether? That it was a mistake? She didn't know how to answer. What she'd felt that day, that wonderful night, with Jack ... it wasn't just sex for her. It had meant so much more than that. And all those other days ... when they were getting to know each other. The end-of-function late-night chats, that crazy night of the storm ... It was like they knew each other, in those heartfelt moments, and whilst she'd told herself it was all futile, she had to admit she bloody well missed him so much.

Even when Liam had left her, weirdly it hadn't left this gut-wrenching feeling that *she* ... no, *they* had to try and find a way back to each other somehow. Yes, it hurt with Liam – a hell of a lot – but the pain was more about wasted years, wrong turns, being let down.

And then, of course, she'd gone and accused Jack of taking advantage of some tipsy girl. Argh, she'd got that all so wrong.

No wonder he was bloody annoyed with her. Regretted spending the night with her.

'Jack, I'm sorry too. I should never have accused you of taking that girl home, of taking advantage, when I didn't know any of the facts.'

Jack nodded. 'Thank you, I appreciate that. So, truce?'

'Yeah, truce,' she replied with a gentle grin.

It felt like a weight had been lifted.

Lucy felt Jack's arm wind gently around her shoulders; it was welcome, with a chill wind now blowing in off the North Sea.

A surge of happiness washed over her, feeling his touch, his warmth there beside her. It was still damned confusing – who knew if they were they friends or something more? But for tonight ... it was a big step forward.

Lucy took a deep breath. The words were on the tip of her tongue, but she was afraid to speak them, to spoil the moment.

I've missed you, stayed in her mind, and reeled in her heart.

The feeling of having her in his arms again was overwhelming, disconcerting. Jack couldn't let this moment go, not yet. She gave a little shiver and he held her close. Listening to the sea. Watching moonlight glint on the crest of distant waves.

But was he afraid to let her go, or let her stay?

'Tomorrow,' he blurted out, 'can we go for a walk or something? Talk things over some more?'

Lucy looked up at him and gave a tentative smile. 'Yes ... okay.'

'Can I pick you up? At yours? Ah ... there's somewhere I'd like to take you.'

'Okay, sure. Just say a time.'

So, they arranged that he'd come to the cottage for ten o'clock.

Jack knew he couldn't mess this up. Not anymore.

Chapter 44

Jack arrived outside Lucy's cottage at ten on the dot. His heart beating like a drum in his chest, as he gave the door a firm rap. Finally, he felt like he was doing the right thing ... the *only* thing he could.

'Hi,' he greeted her.

'Hi there.' Lucy opened the cottage door; looking gorgeous in pale denim shorts teamed with a yellow spotted T-shirt. Her hair was loose, with dark curls bouncing beneath her shoulders. Her deep-brown eyes held his as she gave a nervous smile.

Ruby, who'd been given an extra polish this morning, was parked up outside, gleaming in the sunlight.

'Your carriage awaits.' Jack gestured towards the campervan and gave a silly bow.

'And what a beautiful carriage she is too,' Lucy answered sincerely. She'd grown so fond of the characterful vintage campervan. 'Morning, Ruby.'

'Right then ...' Jack couldn't help but feel anxious.

'Oh, hang on, can Daisy come too?'

Lucy didn't yet know where they were heading.

'Yeah, of course. I've grown to quite like the little mutt now. But don't let on to the Devil Dog, mind, or she'll be taking all kinds of liberties.'

They both laughed; the tension dissolving a little.

'Hah, come on then, Dais. You're coming too,' Lucy called out, and the dog soon appeared eagerly at her feet. Lucy swept her up in her arms, locked the door, and walked over to Ruby, where she climbed in, placing Daisy in the footwell. And, off they set.

'So, where are we off to?' Lucy asked, intrigued. 'This is all very mysterious.'

'Ah, now that would be telling ... It's not far. Just somewhere that means a lot to me.' Jack needed to show her the place before he told her about it.

'Ah, okay.'

Lucy was curious, but didn't push for any more information, sensing that Jack needed to do things his way today. Last night, the two of them together, talking up on the battlements, had held a hint of magic, of new possibilities, but she was also afraid. Afraid of assuming *anything*, afraid of letting herself get hurt again, and afraid of getting this new second chance all wrong. She needed to tread carefully.

The journey passed in a pleasant meander through the coastal country lanes. They made light conversation en route, about how lovely the function had been last night, the good spell of weather they'd been having, Daisy's latest antics and so on. Finally, they turned into the small beachside car park at Morwick Sands.

So, this was it, Lucy mused.

It was a pretty sandy beach that Lucy knew well; she'd often come here for a stroll or a picnic with a friend or her parents, before she lived in her own seaside cottage. It was very scenic, but Lucy didn't think there was anything particularly unusual or surprising about it. But you never quite knew what was going to happen next with Jack. And Lucy suddenly realised that was one of the things she loved about him. Oh, bloody hell ... Was this love or friendship? Perhaps an olive branch, or something more from Jack?

They left Ruby, and wandered along a track in the dunes that ran parallel with the beach. The dunes then rose to a steep mound far higher than any of the others, with several sandy tracks winding up to it, that made it look like a mini volcano, or perhaps an ice cream, dribbling as it began to melt. Though her mind was whizzing, Lucy tried hard just to focus on the moment. The feel of the warm sun on her back. The spiky fronds of marram grass catching her bare calves. The sense of relief that at least she and Jack had found some level ground.

There were several people strolling down on the beach, but no-one else was in this part of the dunes. And, just a step ahead of her, Jack had gone awfully quiet.

'Are we going up?' Lucy asked, breaking the silence and bracing herself for the climb.

'That's right, come on.'

Daisy found this part tricky, her little dachshund legs soon beginning to slip in the steep and shifting sands of the path that meandered to the top. Lucy scooped her up, helping the short-limbed dog on her way, bless her.

Lucy's own muscles burned as they climbed the last rise to the summit. And then, they made it to the top, where Jack stood for a moment looking pensively out to sea.

'Wow, gorgeous view,' Lucy commented, gazing out across the azure and gold tints of the bay, watching a flock of terns reeling in the summer breeze, all the while wondering what this walk was all about.

'Yeah ... we used to come here as children. Me and Daniel ...'

'Oh, I see.' It was beginning to make sense. And Lucy knew she needed to stay quiet a while and listen.

'Used to seem massive, this dune,' Jack started. 'It's just small really. Took us ages to climb it back then. Hah, then we'd run down as fast as we could. Race to the bottom. Mum and Dad waiting there on the beach. Hurtling down, the two of us ... The number of times I nearly tripped up! Somehow, I stayed on my feet.' He was smiling softly as he remembered, though there was a trace of tears in his eyes. He was still staring out to sea, when he spoke again. 'This is the place where we scattered his ashes.'

'Oh, Jack.' Lucy felt so sad for him. Just then, she wasn't sure what else to say.

'It's okay ... it's alright,' Jack continued. 'It's a special place. I feel close to him here. Sometimes I come here just to think. Came here last night, after the wedding ... and I thought ... long and hard.' He turned to face Lucy, taking a deep lungful of air. 'I thought ... about life ... about you. And I realised I've been hiding ... from life, and from love. Thinking I was protecting myself ... but I wasn't. I was hurting myself ... by not letting anyone in.' He let out a slow breath.

Lucy found she was holding hers.

'By not letting *you* in,' he repeated, looking right at her, hopeful, yet still hurting. 'I bolted after that night together, Luce. And I'm so sorry I hurt you. It wasn't because I didn't care about you ... I-I cared too much ... and it scared the hell out of me. And I know I went about it all wrong. But the way I felt about you ... it was like nothing else I've ever experienced.'

This moment felt pivotal – a time of memories, and of moving on.

Lucy felt all her fears, all the uncertainty, dissolve. 'We've got everything at our fingertips, Jack. All we have to do is reach out and touch it.'

She held out her hand towards him.

He grasped her fingertips, and then drew her towards him. They stayed like that for a few heartfelt seconds, looking into each other's eyes, seeing so many layers of emotion captured there, nervousness as well as desire, caring, vulnerability. Lucy tilted her head towards him ... The kiss that followed was tender, meaningful, sensual, and tasted of salt, of honey, of hope.

He took Lucy in his arms and lifted her, giving her a happy, giddy swirl, right there at the top of the sand dune. 'I love you, Lucy. Have done from the first time I bloody saw you!'

'Hah, even with a naughty dachshund peeing on your sign?'

'I think that's what did it, to be honest,' he grinned.

Lucy beamed as he popped her back down to the sandy ground. She was silent for a moment, drinking him in with his gorgeous sandy hair and his warm, kind eyes. 'I love you too, Jack.'

Daisy swirled around their legs, tail wagging happily.

'Race you down the hill!' Jack shouted out, as he began to set off.

'Hey, that's cheating,' Lucy giggled, about to take up the challenge.

But they didn't race, they ran together, holding hands over the bumpy bits ... laughing and smiling as they went.

Recipes from the Seaside Cocktail Campervan

Morpeth Mule
(Serves 1)

Ingredients
50ml vodka
Ice
½ lime
2 thin slices of fresh ginger (optional)
Fentiman's ginger beer (or other brand)
Fresh mint leaves

Equipment
Copper cup, or tumbler
Stirrer

Method
Pour vodka into your cup or tumbler, add crushed ice. Squeeze in your half lime and add the spent lime portion plus a couple of sliced shards of fresh ginger. Top with ginger beer, stir and add a few sprigs of fresh mint. *Deliciously refreshing!*

Raspberry Rum Smash
(Serves 1)

Ingredients
Ice
50ml dark rum
30ml raspberry liqueur
25ml raspberry syrup
40ml raspberry purée
25ml lemon juice
Raspberries and mint for garnish

Equipment
Cocktail shaker and strainer
Tumbler glass
50ml and 25ml measurer (jigger)

Method
Fill shaker with ice. Add all ingredients to shaker. Shake for 30 seconds.
Fill tumbler glass with ice. Strain contents into tumbler glass.
Add garnish.
Enjoy!

Sunset Amaretto Fizz
(Serves 2)

Ingredients
50ml Disaronno
75ml fresh orange juice
20cl sparkling wine or champagne
Strips of orange zest to garnish

Equipment
2 flutes
Jug and stirrer

Method
Mix Disaronno, juice and sparkling wine in a small jug. Stir gently.
Pour into two flutes. Garnish with orange zest.
Sip as the sun goes down!

Sea Breeze
(Serves 1)

Ingredients
50ml vodka
100ml cranberry juice
50ml grapefruit juice
Ice
Thin slice of lime

Equipment
Highball glass
Stirrer

Method
Half-fill a tall glass with ice, then pour in the vodka, cranberry and grapefruit juice. Stir gently, then garnish with a lime slice. *The perfect seaside cocktail!*

Virgin Mojito
(Serves 1)

Ingredients
25ml sugar syrup
3 limes, juiced
A small bunch of mint leaves
Ice
Soda water
Lime wedge and mint leaves for garnish

Equipment
Highball glass
Muddler (*or* small bowl and rolling pin)
25ml measurer (jigger)
Stirrer
Fruit juicer

Method

Muddle together the sugar syrup and leaves in a highball (tall) glass using a muddler (or a small bowl and the end of a rolling pin). If using a bowl, transfer the muddled sugar syrup and mint leaves to a highball glass. Add the lime juice and some ice to the glass. Top up with soda water. Stir. Add garnish.

Enjoy!

Jack's Gin and Tonic Cake

A moist and zingy loaf cake. The perfect treat.
(Serves 8)

Ingredients
200g (7oz) unsalted butter, softened, plus extra for greasing
200g (7oz) caster sugar
4 medium eggs
200g self-raising flour, sifted
½tsp baking powder
Finely grated zest of 1 large or 2 small limes
1tbsp gin

Syrup
60g (2oz) caster sugar
4tbsp gin
4tbsp tonic

Icing
200g icing sugar
2tbsp lime juice
2tbsp gin

Decoration
1 lime zested and 1 lime sliced thinly, cut in half-moon shapes

Method
Preheat oven to 180C (350F/Gas 4). Butter and line a 900g loaf tin.

Cream together the butter and caster sugar; an electric whisk is ideal for this. Add the beaten eggs, bit by bit, whisking all the time. Gently whisk in the sifted flour, baking powder, lime zest and gin.

Spoon into your tin. Bake for 45 mins. Check with a cake skewer; if it comes out clean, take cake out of oven; if not, give it another 5 mins. Remove from oven and leave to cool slightly whilst making the syrup drizzle.

Put the sugar, gin and tonic water into a small pan over a low heat. Stir until sugar dissolves. Turn off heat.

Poke your cake lightly, at least 10 times with a cake skewer/fork, then drizzle over the syrup. Leave to cool in the tin.

Once cooled, remove from tin and place on wire rack (removing the liner).

In a small bowl, add your icing sugar and gradually mix in the gin and lime juice till you get a *thick* pouring consistency – too thin, and it'll just slide off the cake. Pour icing over cake and sprinkle over some lime zest. Wait for 5 mins, then add some lime slices down the middle of the cake to decorate. Leave to set.

Serve with a cup of tea, or indeed, a glass of G&T alongside!

Nonna's Clementine and Limoncello No-flour Cake

*Can also be made as gluten-free.
A syrupy, zesty, summertime cake.
(Serves 8–10)

Ingredients
375g of clementines (approx. 4)
1tbsp limoncello *(please check this is gluten-free or use lemon juice instead)
6 large eggs
225g caster sugar
250g ground almonds
1tsp baking powder *(use gluten-free baking powder, or omit this item)

Method
Put whole clementines in a pan with enough cold water to cover the fruit, bring to the boil. Simmer with lid partially on for 2 hours. Drain, and set aside to cool. Then cut each clementine in half and remove any pips. Put clementines, skin and all, into a food processor, and blitz to a pulp (or do by hand). Add the limoncello or lemon juice.

Pre-heat oven to 190C/170C Fan/Gas5/375F.

Butter and line a 20cm/8in springform pan with baking parchment.

Add all other ingredients to the food processor and mix. Or beat eggs with an electric whisk or by hand. Add sugar, almonds, baking powder. Beat well, then finally add the pulped orange and limoncello (or lemon juice) and mix through.

Spoon into your prepared tin and bake for an hour (checking at around 35–40 mins and cover with foil, if need be, to prevent any burning), or until a skewer comes out clean.

Leave to cool in the tin, on a rack. When cold, take out of tin.

Delicious served with crème fraiche stirred through with a sprinkle of clementine zest.

This cake keeps well and is even scrummier a day after baking, but hey-ho, you may not want to wait that long!!

Lucy's Chocolate Mousse Cake
(Serves 8–10)

Ingredients for the Chocolate Cake
25g (1oz) cocoa powder, plus extra for dusting
2tbsp boiling water
175g (6oz) caster sugar
175g (6oz) self-raising flour
1tsp baking powder
2 medium eggs, beaten
175g (6oz) margarine
½tsp vanilla essence

Method
Preheat oven to 180C/160C Fan/Gas 4.

Grease and line a deep 8in/20cm round springform cake tin with baking parchment.

Put cocoa powder in a large bowl and mix to a smooth paste with the boiling water. Add all other cake ingredients and beat together, ideally using a hand-held mixer.

Spoon into your prepared tin and level with a palette knife. Bake for 30–35 mins, or until a skewer comes out clean. Allow to cool in the tin.

Meanwhile make the chocolate mousse:

Ingredients for the Chocolate Mousse
25g cocoa powder (sifted)
2tbsp boiling water

225g (8oz) dark chocolate (ideally 70% cocoa solids)
350ml whipping cream (or double)

Ingredients for the garnish
Any of: raspberries, strawberries, chocolate curls

Method
Mix cocoa powder to a paste with boiling water. Put aside.

Place the chocolate in a bowl and melt over a pan of simmering water, stirring continuously. Allow to cool a little. Mix with your cocoa paste, stirring well.

Beat cream until soft peaks form, taking care not to overbeat. Gently fold the melted chocolate and cocoa mix into the whipped cream and combine.

Pour onto the now-cool baked cake whilst it's still in the tin. Level with a palette knife and refrigerate for 3–4 hrs or overnight.

Top with a dusting of cocoa powder, and some delicately placed fresh fruit (raspberries or strawberries are ideal).

*This cake needs to be kept in a fridge.

Deliciously decadent!

Easy Pizza

This is Caroline's recipe, not Lucy's – as she'd be making her own Papa's pizza dough and using the San Marzano tomatoes! But this one is quick, easy and very tasty indeed! Makes one large pizza – enough for 2 people with a side salad.

Ingredients
1 x 385g (or similar) pack of ready-made fresh pizza dough
25g garlic butter (or crush a clove of garlic; add with salt and pepper to some softened butter)
150g tomato passata, approx. 12 fresh basil leaves torn (or ½tsp dried basil) and ½tsp dried oregano, all stirred together
150g grated mozzarella and 75g grated cheddar
Toppings: cooked chicken fillet (approx. 150g), chorizo, red onions, ham, sliced mushrooms, peppers, pineapple, goat's cheese, chillies, chargrilled veg – any combo you like, really!
Garnish: fresh rocket and a drizzle of balsamic glaze (optional)

Method
Pre-heat oven to 220C/200C Fan/Gas Mark 7.

Roll out your ready-made dough to a large circle or oval. Lay on a pizza baking tray (ideally) or a large flat baking tray. Spread with your garlic butter and cook for 6 mins, to start crisping the pizza sides.

Spoon over your tomato sauce evenly, taking almost to the sides.

Add half the cheese, then your choice of toppings. My

favourites are chicken, thinly sliced chorizo, red onion and red pepper; or try chopped ham and mushrooms; or red pepper, onion and goat's cheese.

Sprinkle with the rest of the cheese.

Bake for a further 10–12 mins until golden crispy and the cheese is all oozy and melted.

Garnish with a handful of rocket and a drizzle of balsamic glaze.

Delicious! Even better served with a glass of wine or a prosecco.

A Letter from Caroline

Thank you so much for choosing to read *The Seaside Cocktail Campervan*. I hope you've been delighted to spend time with Lucy and Jack and Daisy Dachshund, whilst touring Northumberland with the fabulous classic campervan, Ruby. Hopefully, you've been curled up with this novel with cocktails and cake, or a slice of scrumptious pizza to hand!

If you've enjoyed this book, please don't hesitate to get in touch or leave a review. I always love hearing my readers' reactions, and a comment or review makes my day and also can make a real difference in helping new readers to discover my books for the first time. You'd make this author very happy.

You are welcome to pop along to my Facebook, Instagram, and Twitter pages. Please feel free to share your news, views and recipe tips, or why not drop by to read all about my favourite cocktails, latest bakes, see Jarvis (my crazy-lovely spaniel) on one of our gorgeous Northumberland walks, and find out more about the inspirations behind my writing.

It's lovely to make new friends, so keep in touch. Thanks again. Take care, and see you soon!

Caroline x

Facebook: /CarolineRobertsAuthor
Instagram: @carolinerobertsauthor
Twitter: @_caroroberts
Website: http://carolinerobertswriter.blogspot.co.uk

Acknowledgements

This book was written during the COVID-19 pandemic lockdowns of 2020. Amidst such strange and unprecedented times, it was a joy to be able to head off (in my imagination) with Jack's Cocktail Campervan and Lucy's pizza horsebox to join in all these celebrations.

Most of my research had to be done over the phone and online, and big thanks go to Minnie of *Minnie's Mobiles Bars and Pizza*, Graeme of *Fizz on the Tyne* and Richard of *Crusts and Castles* for all their insights into the mobile catering world and for giving up their time to answer my many questions. Thanks, especially, to Minnie for providing several of the cocktail recipes! I wish you all the very best with your business ventures.

Also, to Mary (next door) thanks for the inspirational touch of adding limoncello to the Clementine Cake recipe, and to my daughter, Amie, for delighting my tastebuds and inspiring me with her Gin and Tonic Cake. (Cakes and cocktails do work together, I promise you!) Thanks to Marie for her easy pizza tips. And to John Eyre for his insights into vintage VW Campervans that came just at the right time for the edits.

Big thanks, as always, to my fabulous editor Charlotte Brabbin and to the whole team at One More Chapter, HarperCollins. And to my lovely agent Hannah Ferguson and the team at Hardman & Swainson.

To the Northumberland Chapter of the Romantic Novelists' Association, thank you. We will all meet again soon! Tea, cake and chat are long overdue. And to all the libraries, bookshops and their staff who support my books, here and across the world, many thanks.

A big hug and thank you to all my family and friends. Prosecco and parties are on the way!

My readers, last but never least, thank you for all your wonderful support, reviews, comments and for taking the time to chat on Facebook, Instagram and Twitter. You make it all worthwhile, sitting for hours writing away in my little room. Thank you to all the fabulous book bloggers out there too! I hope my books bring you a little escape and happiness.

I do hope you enjoyed *The Seaside Cocktail Campervan* and your adventures with Lucy and Jack.

Cheers!

Caroline x

**Don't miss these other gorgeous cosy romances in
the Pudding Pantry series**

All available to buy now!